MAGE ERRANT

BOOK I

JOHN BIERCE

To my cat, because why not.

To my favorite family member,
because an apple made of actual gold
is way out of my current budget.

MAGE ERRANT

BOOK I

MAGE ERRANT, BOOK 1
Published by AETHON: Vault
In association with Aethon Books

ISBN 978-1-63849-408-9 (hardcover)

First AETHON: Vault Edition: September 2026

Printed in the United States of America.
1st Printing.

Aethon Books
www.aethonbooks.com

Vault Storyworks
www.vaultstoryworks.com

Cover design by Steve Beaulieu | Cover art by Fernando Granea | Supplementary book art by Adam Cahoon
Print formatting by Kevin G. Summers, Adam Cahoon, and Rikki Midnight.

Cover and interior art by Fernando Granea. Cover design by Steve Beaulieu.
Print design by Kevin G. Summers.

JOHN BIERCE
PART 1
INTO THE LABYRINTH

CHAPTER ONE
HUGH OF EMBLIN

HUGH of Emblin wasn't good at much, but he was very, very good at hiding. Which was good, because he really needed to be.

"Where are you hiding, sheepherder? The longer it takes us to find you, the worse it will be for you!"

Hugh slid farther back into the space behind the bookshelf. Rhodes and his friends might have chosen him as their favorite victim, but their attention span usually wasn't too long. If he stayed hidden long enough, they'd eventually get bored and find something else to amuse themselves.

Hugh waited until the noise had faded, then slowly let himself relax-too soon, unfortunately. A hand reached in and grabbed his arm, then hauled him out into the library aisle. Hugh stumbled to his knees on the polished granite floor.

"Now, what are you doing in the library, sheepherder?" a voice asked.

Hugh took a deep breath and looked up. Rhodes Charax was smiling down at him, two of his lackeys grinning at his shoulders. Rhodes was everything Hugh wasn't— tall where Hugh was short, muscular where Hugh was skinny, handsome where Hugh was forgettable, nobility where Hugh was the son of merchants, blue-eyed to Hugh's brown eyes, blonde to Hugh's dark hair, and a far, far better mage than Hugh had any hope of being. Even Rhodes' white uniform was clearly custom tailored to him, unlike Hugh's poorly fitting, off-white uniform from the academy's supplies.

"Everyone knows sheepherders can't read, so that can't be why you're here. Why are you here, sheepherder?"

"I'm not a sheepherder," Hugh said quietly. He could feel his face going red.

"What's that?" Rhodes said.

Hugh glared at him. "I'm not a sheepherder."

Rhodes kicked Hugh in the ribs, sending him sprawling.

"Didn't anyone ever tell you not to lie to your betters, sheepherder?" Rhodes said. "Though maybe if you were about to claim that you were one of the sheep I might believe you."

Rhodes' goons snickered at that. Hugh clenched his fists as he clambered to his knees again.

"You should stay on the ground where you belong, sheepherder." Rhodes lifted back his leg to kick Hugh again, but a voice intervened.

"I imagine that where he belongs is in class— the same as you three."

Rhodes and his friends spun around in alarm, and Hugh used that as an opportunity to scramble to his feet.

"It's our free period." Rhodes didn't even seem worried. Not that he had any reason to be concerned. He'd done worse in class without getting in trouble. It wasn't any surprise- Rhodes' family had immense political influence even hundreds of leagues outside their borders.

"Well, spend it somewhere else." The mysterious voice sounded unamused. Hugh couldn't get a look at the man yet past the bullies. "You're not exactly using the library for its intended purpose."

Rhodes shot Hugh a look that promised this wasn't over yet, but strode off with the others. They all burst into laughter while still in earshot. Hugh winced. Rhodes was always worse for days after the rare occasions a teacher or other mage interfered.

The librarian that the mysterious voice belonged to studied him. He was tall and wiry, with a scruffy head of brown hair that looked like it hadn't seen a comb in days. He couldn't be much more than twice Hugh's fifteen years.

After a few moments of silence, the librarian sighed. "What's your name?"

"Hugh." Hugh looked away from the librarian, hoping that he would move on so that Hugh could find somewhere to be alone.

"Just Hugh?"

"People call me Hugh of Emblin, sir. To distinguish me from the other Hughs here."

The librarian gave him a curious glance. Hugh could already feel the usual questions coming. Mages weren't ever born in Emblin, and yet Hugh had been. Not that he'd ever amount to much of a mage. But, to his surprise, the librarian didn't ask him about being from Emblin.

"Would you like me to report those other students to your instructors?" the librarian said.

Hugh gaped at him in surprise for a moment. The librarian waited patiently. After a few moments, Hugh collected himself.

"Wouldn't do any good, sir," Hugh said.

The librarian cocked an eyebrow at him. "Wouldn't do any good?"

Hugh just stared at the ground, waiting until he could leave. Eventually, however, he realized the librarian was ready to wait all day for an answer.

"That was Rhodes Charax, sir."

The librarian just gave him the same level gaze.

"Rhodes' uncle is the king of Highvale, sir. Not to mention he's the most promising mage in our year. All the teachers just stand to gain by staying on his good side. I'm just a nobody, though. None of them are going to stick their heads out for me."

The librarian seemed to consider that for a while, then sighed. "Very well." He started to walk away, then turned back towards Hugh. "Next time, try hiding in the stacks instead of the main law section. Much better hiding spots, plus the reading material is much more interesting." He looked like he wanted to say more, but turned and left.

Hugh sighed. He'd gotten off easy this time, at least. And the tip about the stacks wasn't a bad one.

Hugh, thankfully enough, didn't run into Rhodes and his lackeys on the way to his next class. That didn't make him feel much better, however. His next class was Basics of Unattuned Spellcasting- or, as everyone called it, Cantrips. It was supposed to be one of the easiest classes for first years like himself who hadn't attuned yet, but was yet another reason why life at Skyhold had been such a nightmare for him. For anyone else, it should have been a dream come true- being sent to study at the

Academy at Skyhold, one of the most prestigious mage schools on the entire continent at Ithos.

Anyone else wasn't Hugh.

Hugh slipped into a desk at the back of the class, where he was less likely to draw attention. The students that didn't participate in Rhodes' harassment of Hugh didn't care about his presence, so he really just wanted to avoid the teacher's attention. Unfortunately, the eager young woman teaching today almost immediately noticed him.

There hadn't been enough full mages that wanted to teach first year classes this year, so Hugh's class had been stuck with a rotating population of journeyman mages. He didn't know this one's name, but it didn't matter. Every new journeyman thought they could be the one to solve the infamous Hugh of Emblin's problems, and in the end they were all proved wrong.

Today they were supposed to be learning a spell to set a stick on fire-about as basic as it came. Hugh paid careful attention to the teacher's description of how they should channel their mana, even though he already knew what she was going to say. He'd been in the library to read about this spell ahead of class, desperately hoping he could get a spell right for once. It had been on his way back that Rhodes had found him.

Hugh took a deep breath and focused on the stick he held. Some of the other students were having a little trouble, but most already had their sticks at least smoking. He visualized the forms perfectly, and channeled his mana just so. He could tell that the teacher, as well as a number of his classmates, were already watching him to see how he would mess things up this time.

"Once you all have figured out setting the sticks on fire, we'll move onto controlling the intensity of the flame, and maybe even to changing their colors."

Hugh's stick exploded with magical light, then abruptly went dark again. He tried to shut his eyes in time, but his vision remained filled with spots.

The stick wasn't even charred.

"You're a menace, sheepherder," someone nearby whispered. Several other students were muttering and complaining as well.

"I'm not a sheepherder," Hugh muttered.

"Everyone's bound to mess up sometimes. Give it another try, Hugh," the teacher said.

Hugh blinked away the last of the spots from his eyes and looked around. Everyone was staring at him now.

"How's he going to screw it up this time?" someone else whispered.

Hugh swallowed angrily and focused on the stick again. First, visualize the spellforms- the invisible geometric diagrams you were supposed to envision to cast a spell. He'd spent a solid hour memorizing them. He knew them inside and out. Next, channel the mana. You couldn't push your mana into the forms- mana flowed like water, and pushing it would do about as much good as pushing on a stream. The geometric designs you were supposed to envision helped you guide mana's flow.

The mana flowed perfectly into the forms, at exactly the right speed. It flowed precisely where it should. And nothing happened. No- something was happening.

A small handful of dim sparks fell from the stick and vanished before hitting the desk.

"Come now, Hugh, you can do it. Let's try again," the teacher said. The whole class was still whispering to themselves and watching him with amusement. He couldn't blame them- he had to be the most incompetent mage to ever arrive at Skyhold.

Hugh took a shaky breath, then focused on the stick again. Visualize your forms. Channel your mana. Visualize your forms. Channel your mana. Visualize your forms. Channel your…

The stick jerked out of his hand and smacked him in the forehead. The whole class burst into laughter.

The teacher made Hugh try six more times in front of the class before she finally gave up. She hadn't done it to be cruel to Hugh- she was genuinely trying to help him. That didn't make Hugh feel any better disposed towards her, or to the classmates who found him a topic of pity at best, amusement or even scorn far more often.

Eventually she'd had to move on. Hugh just sat in the back of the class staring at his desk, not even trying to pay attention. When class got out, he trudged out of class near the back of the pack. Everyone else was chattering excitedly on their way to dinner, but he barely looked up past his feet. The teacher called out to him, but he pretended not to hear her over the sound of his classmates.

He arrived to dinner late, and had quite a wait in line before he managed to get his food. It was fish and potatoes again tonight. Some of the other students complained, but Hugh didn't mind- the meal reminded him of home. Potatoes and fish were two of the things that Emblin had plenty of- the others being timber and sheep.

Hugh sat at a bench by himself, hoping desperately that no one would try to sit near him or talk to him. Thankfully, no one did. He spotted Rhodes across the dining hall sitting with his lackeys and a couple of girls. Rhodes noticed him back and said something to his table that made them all laugh, but didn't do anything else.

Most of the meal went by in a sullen funk, Hugh slowly picking at his food. Towards the end of the meal, though, he overheard something made him pay attention.

"...Dragonslayer is going to be there!" one of the students at the table behind him said.

Hugh perked up. Could they mean...

"No way," a second student said. "Aedan Dragonslayer hasn't taken an apprentice in years."

"I overheard two teachers talking about it," the first student said. "He's picking a new apprentice this year."

Hugh turned around to listen at this point.

"Who do you think he'll pick?" another student said.

One of the students, a hanger-on of Rhodes', noting Hugh watching, grinned maliciously. "Maybe he's planning to pick Hugh." The table burst into laughter. Hugh flushed, and turned back to his food.

"He might have slain dragons, but teaching Hugh might be a task too challenging for even him." The table burst out laughing again, and Hugh stood up abruptly. He grabbed his plate and brought it to the scullery window, then stalked out the door. Rhodes, thankfully, had already left dinner.

As Hugh trudged back to his room, he sank even deeper into his funk. They had just a few short weeks before the Choosing. Every year, hundreds of mages looked over the students, choosing one or two as apprentices. Every student got picked by someone, but not all mages were equal. Most students were picked by a fairly average, run of the mill mage- one whose contributions to Skyhold weren't great enough that they could get away with not taking on apprentices. The more prestigious a mage was, the earlier they got to choose their apprentices- Aedan

Dragonslayer, as one of the most famous mages alive, had likely already chosen his apprentice weeks ago, though it wouldn't be announced until the Choosing ceremony. A great many of the students were taken on by various working mage groups within Skyhold- the cleaning staff always needed mages to help take care of things like alchemical reagent spills, for instance.

Hugh doubted anyone was going to Choose him. He'd just keep waiting and waiting, until he was all by himself in the Great Hall. Maybe, if he was lucky, he'd get picked by the cleaning mages.

Lost in his own thoughts, he didn't notice that his door was open until he reached out to open it. Inside, his room was a complete disaster area. His uniforms had been trampled, his blankets ripped. Someone had pissed on his mattress. His books were lying on the ground, pages bent, and his sling- one of his only mementos of Emblin- had been cut to pieces.

Hugh stood in shock. Rhodes and his friends had been relentless before, but they'd always left his room alone. His room had been locked, and just about the only magics that Hugh was actually capable of were wards- his room had been well defended, for a first year student. Rhodes and his friends shouldn't have been able to break through them- wardbreaking wasn't even taught until second year. Rhodes must have convinced a teacher to privately tutor him on the topic.

If he didn't even have the privacy of his own room, Hugh felt like he'd go insane. He had nothing else. He didn't have any friends. No one from Emblin ever wrote him, ashamed that a family of good Emblin stock should have a mage in it. He'd been rushed off to Skyhold almost the instant his mage gifts became apparent. It was worth it to his family to hide their shame. Not that they'd ever had any pride in him in the first place.

Hugh slammed his door shut, slid down to the floor, and then buried his head between his knees to cry.

CHAPTER TWO

THE CHOOSING

AFTER he stopped crying, Hugh wandered the halls in a daze for hours. Whenever he heard or saw someone, he turned down a different hallway. He even avoided the guards. Eventually, though, he found himself somewhere familiar- the library.

The glowing crystals that lit the halls and library gave off light constantly, so he had no trouble seeing. He avoided the main sections of the library, since there would likely still be people there even at this hour, and headed into the stacks.

The librarian had definitely been right about the number of hiding spots. The rest of the library levels accessible to first year students were all built into neatly laid out tunnels. The stacks, however, looked like they'd been an afterthought, crammed into a jumbled mess of disorganized rooms and tunnels, with overcrowded shelves and even study desks piled with books. He found an aisle that had been blocked off by another shelf, forming a hidden hallway. He found another room filled with wooden crates of old textbooks, where he could easily hide.

Best of all, however, he found an almost entirely empty room forgotten behind a row of shelves whose books hadn't been touched for so long they were covered in dust. It even had a door that opened inwards into the room- which was for the best, as otherwise the shelf wouldn't have let the door open. There were a few empty shelves, a pile of old textbooks, and a desk in the room. Most amazing of all- there was a window.

The glass of the window was old and discolored, the frame warped and old, but Hugh still managed to force it open. He found himself looking westwards into the night, out over the immense sea of sand known as the Endless Erg. He'd sailed over the Endless Erg on the last leg of his voyage to Skyhold on one of the great sandships. While it wasn't actually endless, it was immense, and far too dangerous to cross on foot. If the blistering heat during the day didn't get you, the icy nights would, or the lack of water, or the horrifying monsters. The wind was blowing particularly coldly tonight, given how close it was to midwinter.

When Hugh looked down, he could see the sandship port far below him. As he looked around, he could see more of Skyhold itself. Skyhold was carved into the sides of a massive mountain that split into two peaks near the top. The mountain was riddled with tunnels and towers. Keeps, balconies, and other structures rose from the sides, built into the mountain itself. Tens of thousands of people lived in Skyhold, though no one had an exact count. There were nearly three thousand students at the academy alone- nearly a third of which were in their first year.

Hugh must have spent hours just gazing out of the window. He'd seen very little of the outside over the last few months- none of the classrooms or student rooms had windows, and many days he'd been too busy to find a window or balcony. Hugh couldn't remember the last time he'd actually gone outside. When he finally pulled himself away from the window and shut it, a plan had already taken shape in his mind.

Over the next few hours, Hugh carefully smuggled his possessions into the hidden library room. He salvaged the clothes and blankets he could- Rhodes and his friends had clearly been in a hurry when they ransacked his room, because the damage was much less bad than he'd originally thought. There was no way Hugh could sneak his mattress into the little room even if he wanted to, but he'd be fine sleeping in a nest of blankets for now. His books and other personal items easily fit on the desk and shelf. There wasn't a chair for the desk, but he managed to- with considerable difficulty- drag one from the stacks into the little room. The very last thing he did was craft new wards for his room.

It was well into the early hours of the morning when Hugh finished, and he fell asleep the instant he curled up into his blankets. He didn't dream at all.

Hugh missed his morning classes, but he wasn't overly broken up about it. There was a field trip outside to some of Skyhold's magic defenses today in Mana Theory class, so he wouldn't be missed. By the afternoon, he felt ready to head to class. Thankfully, he managed to pass the day without incident- even the new Cantrips teacher decided to leave him alone after yesterday's failures.

Over the next few days, Hugh fell into a new pattern. He scrounged the stacks for old sacks, discarded papers, and the like, eventually managing to construct a crude but comfortable mattress. The ruined school uniforms were surprisingly easy to get replacements for- students were expected to ruin quite a few uniforms while learning magic.

The stacks had their own bathrooms. They weren't as nice as the restrooms in the student halls, but they still had the same running water (a luxury that Hugh hadn't known back in Emblin), and even if there weren't showers, he could still get clean enough using rags and the sinks.

Even with how well hidden his new lair was, Hugh wasn't completely comfortable with his current wards. His old wards had proven insufficient to protect his old room, but living in a library had its perks. He managed to find an old book on wards that had been misshelved in the stacks- only the most basic introductory spellbooks and magic theory texts were supposed to be shelved in the public access areas of the library, but this book looked to have been misplaced for decades. It was at least a century old, and even though its wards were archaic and old fashioned, they were a lot more effective than anything he'd had access to so far.

Hugh didn't dare bring lamps into the library, and the room didn't have glow crystals of its own- but basic light spells were the only other type of magic he felt comfortable with other than warding. It had still taken him much longer to learn them than normal- his early light spells kept shining far too brightly and blinding him- but he'd eventually mastered them, much to his (and his teacher's) surprise.

Hugh had never been much of a huge reader back in Emblin- they'd only ever had a few books. Even then, Hugh did his absolute best to stay out of his family's way, so he really hadn't had the chance to read much, preferring to wander around the woods instead.

Here at Skyhold, he'd taken to reading with a vengeance. It had been his only real escape from his misery. Now that he was living in the library, he found himself reading far more than ever. He devoured books on history, botany, and astronomy. He read through countless bestiaries describing magical beasts- finding, to his amusement, that it was extremely common for any two bestiaries to radically disagree on the basic details of monsters.

Hugh also spent quite a lot of time watching the librarians' origami golems. Many of the librarians were paper mages, and crafted folded paper golems to accomplish a wide array of tasks. Paper cranes and miniature paper dragons were folded up messages that would unfold themselves upon reaching the receiver of the message. Knee high paper monkeys were regularly sent down into the stacks to retrieve books. Hugh helped more than a few of them retrieve a difficult book from the stack shelves.

Surprisingly, none of the faculty seemed to notice his disappearance from his dormitory room. Or maybe it wasn't surprising, given how little they expected from him.

While his teachers didn't seem to notice or care, Hugh constantly worried about the librarians. He was very careful to plan out his routes and move very cautiously through the stacks during the day, to make sure he ran into as few librarians as possible. None of them seemed to pay him much attention- the library was immense, and the publicly accessible stacks alone would have been the size of a small fortress if they had been built outside the mountain. Hugh was hardly the first student to evade bullies by hiding in the stacks- though he doubted that actually living in them was particularly common.

He ran into the librarian who had rescued him from Rhodes several times over the next few weeks. The librarian never approached him, but he often gave Hugh odd looks. Hugh hadn't noticed it before, but the librarian's uniform was very different than most librarians- instead of the short, light grey coats that most librarians wore, his coat reached down to his knees and had red trim. Hughes had no idea what that meant. The librarian also always seemed to have a satchel overstuffed with books and scrolls at his side.

Rhodes definitely did notice Hugh's absence from the student dormitories, on the other hand. Hugh frequently found himself having to spend long periods evading Rhodes to keep him from following into the library. He even started eating in another cafeteria- one out of favor with the students for its distance from the dorms and the large number of journeyman mages and librarians who ate there. Hugh didn't mind any of that.

Rhodes, spoiled of much of his fun, began stepping up his harassment campaign even more when he had the chance. Hugh rarely had a day where he wasn't tripped in the hall or zapped with whatever new cantrip Rhodes and his lackeys had learned in class.

Still, life was much better than it had been for a while. Hugh couldn't say he was happy, but it was bearable.

The day of the Choosing came at Midwinter, just under a month after Hugh had moved into his little library room. His classmates had talked about nothing else for weeks- even Rhodes stopped paying much attention to Hughes as the day drew closer. People gossiped constantly about what master they'd pick if they got to choose (Aedan Dragonslayer was the current favorite) and what sort of mage they'd like to become.

Mages wandered up and down the halls constantly, talking to various students, watching classes, and otherwise making a nuisance of themselves. With all the chaos, most teachers largely gave up on trying to get much teaching done.

The actual process of the Choosing was considerably less chaotic than it seemed, however. Mages didn't have to wade through the entire listings of potential first year candidates to find an apprentice- they only needed to look through the list of candidates with appropriate affinities.

Everyone had their own affinities- types of magic that it was easier to perform. The mana that everyone channeled from the Aether around them was identical, but it got converted in the body to different types. A mage with an affinity for fire could more easily convert aetheric mana to fire mana, a mage with an affinity for plants could more easily convert aetheric mana to plant mana, and so on and so forth. There were hundreds of known affinities, and many of them overlapped considerably with one another. To make it even more confusing, many mages had overlapping affinities- a mage with affinities for fire and earth, for instance, could probably train a mage with a magma affinity.

You didn't necessarily have to train in a style of magic that matches your affinity, but it was much, much harder to train a different affinity. Many mages, in fact, couldn't accomplish it at all. And, once you'd trained enough with a type of mana, you became attuned to it, and it became much harder to attune to other styles of magic. Few mages successfully attuned to more than two types of mana, and many stuck to just one. There were a few unusual mages out there with three or more natural affinities, but they were very, very rare. Rhodes, unfortunately, was one of them.

That was Hugh's second big problem. He didn't seem to have an affinity. If he'd been a competent enough mage to start with, maybe that could have been a plus for him- any full mage could have probably taken him on as an apprentice. It would have been much more work to attune, and Hugh doubted he could have acquired more than a single attunement, but it would likely have been doable. Combined with his complete failure to be able to work magic, however? Hugh honestly doubted whether any mages would want to take him on. Maybe the janitorial mages- you just needed to be able to channel mana into devices to work with them.

So as the date of the Choosing had approached, nearly everyone but Hugh got more and more excited, while he grew more and more anxious. And now it was here, and Hugh had seldom been so miserable.

Hugh could barely make himself listen to Headmaster Tarik's speech. Normally he would have been riveted to every word she said- Tarik had been one of the mightiest stone mages on the continent in her prime, and was said to have singlehandedly raised a fortress in a week during one of the Havath Dominion's wars of expansion, stopping them in their tracks. Today, though, Hugh could only miserably imagine everyone else getting chosen, then being left unwanted by himself in the cavernous Great Hall.

Tarik eventually stepped away from the raised dais onstage, which was enchanted to project the speaker's words across the Great Hall. As she stepped off, the first mage to take an apprentice stepped onto the dais- Aedan Dragonslayer.

Mages got to choose their apprentices in order of prestige, and there was no-one more prestigious at all of Skyhold than Aedan Dragonslayer. He'd earned his name while still a journeyman, single-handedly slaying a rampaging ancient frost wyrm in his homeland of Tsarnassus. Since then he'd slain at least a dozen full grown dragons, two more ancient wyrms, and countless drakes, wyverns, and other draconic relatives. While draconic foes were his specialty, he had fought more than his share of other monsters as well- most notably an enormous hydra lurking in a ruined Ithonian city in the heart of an impassible jungle. Stories of his deeds were even told by the magic-hating people of Emblin.

The key to Aedan's success? He had no less than five attunements. The students weren't exactly sure what they all were, but it was known that he could fly and hurl lighting at the very least, and there were countless other rumors. One of the more ridiculous but tenacious rumors claimed that he could turn into a dragon himself.

Hugh would be lying if he claimed he had never dreamt about apprenticing to Aedan Dragonslayer. His mana reservoirs were considerable in size for his age, even if he didn't have anything else going for him. Realistically, though, Hugh had never imagined them to be more than just dreams- his inability to cast most spells, mixed with his lack of an affinity? He'd never be able to be a combat mage.

Aedan spent at least a minute staring out over the crowd sternly. Any other wizard would be expected to immediately announce their new apprentice, but the grey-haired, battlescarred mage could likely get away with standing there however long he wanted. The entire audience was silent and tensely awaiting Aedan to speak- even the other full mages. Finally he opened his mouth.

"Rhodes Charax of Highvale," he said, then simply stepped off the dais.

Hugh's heart plummeted into his stomach. He'd never seriously expected to be chosen by Aedan, but for Rhodes to be chosen instead? Hugh was ready to slink out of the Great Hall then and there.

The rest of the students didn't agree, however. Rhodes' many friends, admirers, and lackeys all applauded fiercely. Rhodes himself looked absolutely triumphant as he got up to meet Aedan by the side of the stage to begin his apprenticeship.

Hugh could barely make himself pay attention for the rest of the Choosing. He did note a few of the more interesting selections, however. Sulassa Tidecaller, a water mage who had once redirected an entire river to put out a forest fire, chose a pair of twins- a boy and a girl- who had blue eyes and hair that changed shades like the surface of the sea. Artur Wallbreaker, a seven foot tall, muscle-bound metal and stone attuned mage that carried a hammer that must have weighed more than Hugh, chose a youth that was clearly his son, and looked like he'd end up even bigger than his father.

For the most part, Hugh just sunk further and further into his own misery. The Choosing took most of the day to finish, and Hugh just stayed seated as more and more students left. Soon enough a quarter of the hall had emptied, then half, then three quarters. There weren't a lot of mages left to pick apprentices before the various work groups started picking theirs. At this point, all Hugh hoped for was to not be picked by the janitorial mages.

Hugh was feeling almost ready to burst into tears at this point. Not, of course, that many of the other mage students left looked too happy-there was no glory in getting chosen by a work group. Everyone dreamed about being apprenticed to a master, not just sitting in more large classes for several more years. There were just a few individual masters left, and…

"Hugh of Emblin."

CHAPTER THREE
MASTER

HUGH whipped his eyes back to the dais, convinced he'd misheard. On the dais was standing the last person Hugh would have expected- the librarian who had saved him from Rhodes and told him about the stacks. He felt a brief moment of hope, then saw two other students walking towards the stage, and his heart sank. Masters almost never took more than two apprentices.

Then the librarian looked right at him, and repeated himself clearly.

"Hugh of Emblin."

In a daze, Hugh got off the bench and stumbled towards the stage. Hugh had been chosen! He hadn't been abandoned in the Hall on his own after all. He didn't even know his new master's name or affinities, but he felt more relief than he'd ever felt since his magic first manifested.

As he walked closer, however, doubts had already started to flood his brain. His new master must just be representing the library work group… except Hugh could see the head librarians and his assistants still waiting to announce their selections. It must just be pity, then- the librarian had seen Hugh bullied, and then he must have looked at Hugh's records and seen how incompetent Hugh was. By the time he reached the stage, he was absolutely convinced of it.

Hugh was, to his own shame, absolutely fine with getting a master out of pity.

His new master looked at Hugh and his other two new apprentices as he stepped off stage, then simply gestured for them to follow him. The tall, slender mage walked at a pace that Hugh had to struggle to keep up with. As they strode out of the Great Hall, Hugh took the opportunity to study the other two apprentices, whose names he hadn't caught. It was no surprise that he hadn't met them before, given that there were over a thousand first year mages.

The first girl was taller than Hugh by several inches. She had the dark skin and long pale hair- closer to white than blonde- of one of the residents of the southwestern coast cities. The girl also had what looked like thin, treebranch shaped burn scars on her hands and one cheek. She had absolutely no expression on her face, and kept her eyes straight ahead.

The other apprentice was even shorter than Hugh. She was pale, with a brilliant shock of long red hair. She also had more tattoos than anyone he'd ever met before. The tattoos were interlocking geometric designs done in a brilliant blue- it almost looked like someone had tattooed spellforms all over her. They ran down her arms to her fingers, up her neck, and even onto her forehead and cheeks, though not onto the rest of her face. Hugh had never seen anyone like her, and hadn't the slightest clue where she was from. As he eyed her, she noticed him looking and gave him a furious glare in response. Hugh looked away quickly rather than maintain eye contact.

After a minute or two, Hugh finally worked up the nerve to speak to his new master, albeit barely above a whisper. "Sir… I'm, uh… I'm afraid I didn't catch your name."

The red-haired girl spoke up scornfully. "You didn't even catch your own name the first time, so no wonder."

Hugh winced.

The librarian turned around to face them, but didn't slow down at all. If Hugh had tried to walk backwards at even half that speed he would have immediately fallen down. The gangly mage gestured at himself. "My apologies- this is my first time taking apprentices, so I'm quite new to all this myself."

That hardly inspired Hugh's confidence.

"I am Alustin Haber, Librarian Errant," he said. Alustin- while still walking backwards and seemingly without looking- stepped to his left to avoid running into an incredibly overweight mage and his two new apprentices. "In case you didn't catch each other's names, this young gentleman here is Hugh of Emblin, the tall young woman here is Sabae Kaen Das, and our heavily tattooed friend is Talia of Clan Castis. Without waiting for a response, Alustin whirled back around.

The short redhead- Talia- glared at him. "I'm not your friend," she whispered.

Hugh looked away from her. Sabae was still just staring forwards, her face set in stone.

They group walked in silence for a few more minutes. Hugh had just realized that they were heading for the library when Sabae finally spoke up, loud and clear.

"Master Alustin, what's a Librarian Errant?"

Without slowing down, Alustin whirled around to face them again. "Excellent question, Sabae! A Librarian Errant is a mage who is sent out of Skyhold to retrieve books- grimoires stolen from our collection, tomes hidden away in the trapped and cursed lairs of long dead magicians, badly overdue textbooks, that sort of thing." Alustin turned back around and continued walking.

Hugh blinked in surprise, then lowered his gaze back to his feet. That… that actually sounded somewhat exciting. Much more so than he'd expected. He hadn't expected Alustin to be a battle mage. But… why would a mage like that want an apprentice like Hugh?

No one spoke again until they had reached the library, and even then it was just Alustin greeting other librarians, all of whom seemed quite pleased to see him, and gave the new apprentices plenty of curious looks.

Alustin's office was far into the librarian-only portions of the library. Alustin stopped at an unlabeled door that looked like it opened onto a broom closet, but when he unlocked it, revealed a shockingly spacious office- mages could likely hold combat practice in here, except for the low ceiling. Alustin didn't hit his head against it, but it certainly wouldn't be safe for him to jump.

"Come in, come in, don't be shy!" Alustin said.

The walls were lined with overloaded shelves and huge chalkboards inscribed with cramped handwriting, complex diagrams and spellforms, and a number of surprisingly good drawings. After a moment, Hugh realized that the floor was a huge chalkboard as well.

In the back was a massive desk that looked like it had belonged to an old headmaster or even a king, but was at least a century past its prime, covered in chips, gouges, and even a few splinters. Hugh was sure there was absolutely no way the desk could fit through the door, and definitely not down the narrow wrought-iron spiral staircase leading upwards in one corner of the room. The desk was piled with countless books, scrolls, and sheafs of paper. Hugh wasn't even sure there was room to work. Instead of the normal wooden chairs you'd expect, there was an absolutely immense leather armchair behind the desk. Even the tall Librarian Errant would be dwarfed in it. Like the desk, it was well on its way to the garbage heap. In front of the desk were three equally battered but comfy-looking armchairs.

Alustin strode over to his desk. The apprentices moved to follow, but Talia abruptly came to a halt halfway across the room. Hugh and Sabae drifted to a halt behind her, confused.

"What in the all the thousand hells do you want with an absolutely useless mage?" Talia said. She seemed even angrier than before.

Hugh felt his face heat up. That's why she'd been so angry. She knew Hugh's reputation, and was insulted that he was tagging along with them. He snuck a glance at Sabae, and saw that she was staring off to the side, and looked more stone faced than ever. She couldn't even look at him, she was so embarrassed to be lumped in with him. He...

"You're not useless, Talia," Alustin said.

...What?

"Don't you go telling me it's snowing at midsummer, librarian. Not a one of my clan could make anything of me, or any of the tutors they found," Talia said. "I should have been a proper warmage like my parents and brothers, and instead I'm just a useless mess. I should warn you, though- I might not have any future as a battle mage, but I'm not letting you turn me into some paper shuffler who never sees the light of day. I won't let you pity me, either."

Hugh didn't have the slightest clue what was going on. Talia was... talking about herself? Then why was Sabae...?

Alustin watched Talia calmly throughout her outburst.

"You're not useless, Talia." Alustin looked at Sabae, then at Hugh. "None of you are useless. None of you have failed as mages. The Academy has failed all of you. You were expected to simply conform to the same curriculum as everyone else, but magic isn't that rigid."

"What sort of nonse...", Talia said.

Alustin talked right over her. "I didn't pick you out of pity, or because I wanted extra hands to sort through papers. I picked the three of you because I think you have potential, because I think you could become great mages."

Talia looked nearly as dumbstruck as Hugh felt. Even Sabae finally had an expression on her face as she gave Alustin a sharp look. Alustin was… he was…

Alustin was crazy.

Hugh couldn't keep his mouth shut anymore. "Every single teacher that's tried to teach me has given me up as a failure. I'm no real mage, I'm… I'm just some sort of freak."

Alustin gave him a flat look. "It's best not to trust what everyone knows, Hugh." Alustin shuffled a pile of papers on his desk. "Everyone said I'd never succeed as a battle mage, and I proved them all wrong."

Hugh shut his mouth.

Alustin actually looked a little angry now. "Skyhold has begun to treat students as though they were interchangeable, as though there was only a single way to teach magic. They keep increasing class sizes and expecting everyone to learn identical spells from a book." He leaned forwards. "Magic doesn't work like that. There are countless paths of magic, and when the Academy runs across one that deviates too far from their norm? They've become entirely unable to handle it."

Alustin took a deep breath and seemed to calm down. "I meant to wait until later to discuss this with each of you individually, but it seems that we should get this over with now. Each of you has falsely been led to believe themselves useless as a mage. I intend to prove otherwise."

Alustin sat behind his desk, then gestured to the chairs in front of his desk. "Sit."

No one moved for a second. Sabae, interestingly, was the first to move. Hugh quickly followed her, and Talia hesitated for a moment, then claimed the third armchair. As Hugh settled in, he found that the armchair might be hideous, but was absurdly comfortable.

"It's not my place to tell your stories to each other," Alustin said, "and, in fact, I only know bits and pieces of them, despite extensive research. I highly encourage you to share your stories with each other, but I won't require it. I will, however, be telling you about each others' magical problems."

Hugh felt himself start to redden. He'd thought that…

"I don't do this to shame or embarrass any of you. In order to work together, mages must understand one another. Over the next few years the three of you will be working together constantly. Understand?"

Sabae nodded curtly. Hugh hesitantly nodded himself, and even Talia eventually grunted.

Alustin took a deep breath. "Talia here was born to a line of powerful fire mages. Her family was so confident she'd be another that they gave her flame-enhancing spellform tattoos before her affinities had even manifested. Unfortunately, Talia isn't a fire mage. Her affinities lie incredibly strongly in bone and dream- both rare and powerful affinities. Her tattoos, however, have inhibited her abilities to control her gifts- they force her into trying to control her affinities as though they were both fire, which has resulted in at least one destroyed classroom."

Hugh glanced at Talia, who promptly shot him back a challenging glare, as if daring him to say something. He looked away quickly. Her problem sounded awful, but at least she had affinities. Maybe there was some way to remove her tattoos?

"Sabae was also born into a powerful lineage of mages- storm mages each possessed of triple lightning, wind, and water affinities. Sabae, however, seems to completely lack the ability to control her powers more than a few inches away from her body. For many mages, that might not be a problem, but storm mages don't do anything up close. Sabae, unusually, was also born with a fourth affinit…"

At this point Sabae gave Alustin a direct glare. "No."

"I wasn't going to share your story, Sabae, merely your…."

"That is part of my story, Master Alustin."

Alustin stared at her for a moment, then sighed. "Very well. The two of us will speak of this later."

Hugh was a bit shocked. Double affinities were quite common. Many mages who lacked a second affinity still developed a second attunement- it was much more work without a natural affinity, but still worthwhile. Triple affinities, however, were extremely rare. And Sabae apparently had four affinities. Even with her apparent personal setbacks, that was absurd. The only mage he'd heard of with more was Aedan Dragonslayer, with five.

That, of course, reminded him of Rhodes. How many affinities must Rhodes have in order for Aedan to have chosen him as a student? There's no way that even being royalty would have impressed Aedan enough on its own.

"Last, but not least, we have Hugh."

Hugh jumped a little in his seat, then reddened. The other two both had fixable problems. Whatever Alustin claimed, Hugh was just…

"Hugh's problems managed to go undiagnosed by any of his teachers for some time. I only figured them out myself after several weeks of research. I was curious about him after the first time we met. Hugh here, as you might have heard earlier, is from Emblin."

At this point Talia interrupted. "Everyone knows that no mages come from Emblin. It's just a bunch of sheepherders."

Hugh looked away from the others. "I'm not a sheepherder," he muttered.

"I believe I said something about things that everyone knows, Talia."

There was a pause, then Talia made a grunting noise. Alustin apparently decided that was enough of an apology for interrupting and moved on.

"It is true that very few mages come from Emblin, but it's not due to any particular trait of the people that live there. Emblin is, in fact, one of the deepest mana deserts on the entire continent of Ithos."

Hugh looked back at Alustin. "Emblin's not a desert, sir. It's mostly forests and mountains." Alustin gave him an odd look, and Hugh quickly looked away.

"A mana desert, Hugh, not a regular desert."

"What is it, Master Alustin?" Sabae asked.

"A mana desert… did they teach you nothing of the flow of the Aether in your classes yet?"

No one said anything. Alustin sighed. "That's an entire lecture all of its own. For now, let's just say that Emblin has very, very little mana available to use. Even fully trained mages must struggle to channel any mana from the Aether there, which is why they visit there so seldom. A new, untrained mage in Emblin would essentially be unable to channel any mana at all. Emblin likely has as many potential mages as any other nation, they merely never learn to use their abilities."

Hugh hadn't ever heard anything like this about Emblin before. Everyone back home said that the reason there were no mages there was because they'd driven them all out in the centuries after the fall of the Ithonian Empire.

"Hugh, if he'd been any weaker, never would have manifested any abilities at all. He was, however, born with an astonishingly powerful talent- at only fifteen, his mana reserves are as large as those of many fully trained mages. As he gets older and farther along in his training, they will only grow even further."

Hugh had what now?

"And, in order to begin manifesting any magic whatsoever, his system was forced to strain much, much harder to channel mana. This is why you have so much trouble with cantrips, Hugh- your body is trying to flood every spell you perform with far too much mana."

Hugh blinked. "Too much mana, sir? All this time, it's just been a matter of too much mana?" His mouth worked silently for a moment, then he started laughing. It wasn't a happy laugh at all. It was either laugh or scream.

After a couple minutes, Hugh finally calmed down a little bit. Talia and Sabae were both staring at him oddly, while Alustin just looked patient.

"Not just that, no. If that had been it I would have just alerted your teachers and left it at that. You have two other oddities with magic. First of all is your apparent lack of any affinities. It's extremely rare for someone to lack any affinities. Not unknown, but very, very rare. It's not especially good or bad- on the one hand, someone without affinities could attune to any type of mana they chose, unlike most mages… but on the other hand, it would be immensely more difficult than normal."

Talia snorted. "Getting to pick your attunement sounds like a blessing to me, so long as you're not afraid of a little work."

Alustin ignored her.

"Then there's Hugh's unusual skill with wards."

Hugh just stared at him. Unusual skill with wards? They were nearly the only spells he could do right, and they clearly weren't that effective, considering how easily Rhodes had gotten through. Also…

"How do you know about my wards, sir?"

Alustin gave him a wry look. "I investigated all three of you extensively before I chose you. Your wards are better than those of many full mages. Most first year wards can't do more than merely make a loud noise when someone crosses over them. Your wards, on the other hand, actively dissuade them from wanting to cross them in the first place. On top of that, they can differentiate between targets- they don't affect you at all. The wards of other first years just affect everyone."

"Is it just a matter of him being able to push more mana into them?" Sabae asked.

Alustin shook his head. "Hardly. Wards are complex, difficult beasts to wrangle. Just pushing more mana in would collapse them. No, Hugh is doing something much more unusual. He's imbuing them with his own will."

"I'm what?" Hugh said.

"You're actively pushing your willforce into your ward spellforms, allowing you far greater control."

"I..." Hugh said, then went quiet. He really had no idea what that meant.

"Will imbuing can be learned, but there's only one type of mage that has no natural affinities alongside a naturally occurring will imbuing talent."

Hugh could feel the other two apprentices staring at him.

"You, Hugh, are what is known as a warlock."

CHAPTER FOUR
APPRENTICE

HUGH looked around frantically. "I've never made any deals with demons!" he said. He could feel his heart pounding in his chest. Talia and Sabae were both edging away from him in their chairs, looking like they couldn't decide whether to fight or run.

"No one here thinks you've made any…" Alustin said, then sighed. "You haven't been taught what a warlock is, either, have you?"

Hugh had edged back as far in his chair away from Alustin as he could, terrified. "I'm not a warlock!" he squeaked.

Alustin sighed again. "Calm down, Hugh. No one here thinks you've made a contract with a demon." Noticing the expressions on the faces of the other two, he sighed yet again. "Talia, Sabae, he hasn't made any deals with demons. Everything's fine."

Sabae gave Alustin a suspicious look, but seemed to calm down a bit. Talia, on the other hand, looked like she was about to fight Hugh if he even twitched.

"A warlock is a specific type of mage who develops abilities by forming magical pacts with various powerful entities," Alustin said. "Yes, a few warlocks sign contracts with demons for power, but they're very rare. If I even suspected Hugh had made a deal with one, I'd take drastic measures."

Hugh wasn't particularly comforted by that.

"Warlock contracts can be made with all sorts of beings. Elementals, dragons, spirits… even sufficiently powerful magical items. The only requirements are that the being be magical, powerful, and sentient, or at least capable of developing sentience." Alustin pushed his glasses back up his nose. "The gryphon riders of Tsarnassus? They're technically warlocks who have formed magical bonds with their gryphons. Likewise, the Sacred Swordsmen of Havath are warlocks who have formed magical pacts with their weapons." Alustin frowned after mentioning Havath.

"How the hell can you sign a contract with a sword?" Talia asked.

"The answer is long and involved, so let's leave it for another time," Alustin said. "For now, you just need to know that warlocks get to choose the being they contract with. They should choose very, very carefully- their choice determines the attunements and abilities they get, and if they don't negotiate carefully, the terms can be very, very bad. And I wouldn't go around telling people Hugh's a warlock, either- their bad reputation might not be entirely earned, but that won't matter to a lot of people."

The other two finally seemed to have stopped giving Hugh suspicious looks.

"Of course, Hugh wouldn't be nearly so interesting if he were an ordinary warlock."

Hugh didn't like the sound of that very much.

"Most warlocks have minuscule mana reservoirs. They don't need them- they get power through their contracts. Hugh, however, with his massive mana reservoir, offers some… interesting possibilities."

The three apprentices sat silently for a moment. Alustin watched them, then smiled.

"So! Time to discuss your classes!"

Alustin was having all three of them drop all of their magic related classes- they'd only be taking History and Mathematics normally, and he was transferring them all to morning classes. Afternoons, apparently, were all his- something he said with a rather sinister smile.

Before they left, Alustin handed each of his apprentices a book. Talia received a thin little volume entitled simply "Dreamfire." Sabae received a slightly larger manual of mana channeling techniques- albeit one that looked much older than even Hugh's books of wards. Hugh, however, received a truly massive tome that required both hands to hold. The book was entirely bound in leather- though not, Hugh suspected, from anything as common as a cow- and embossed with intricate spellform diagrams.

"Galvachren's Bestiary?" Hugh said. "Sir, I've read lots of bestiaries. They're all mutually contradictory nonsense."

Alustin smiled. "Most of them have at least a few grains of truth, but yes, they're mostly nonsense. Galvachren, however, produces the finest bestiary on the continent. He's also somehow managed to enchant all of the copies so that he can update them whenever he needs to. When I got my first copy, I was your age, and the book was only half that size."

Hugh stared at the book in astonishment. It would still be the biggest book Hugh had ever read even if it were half its current size. It must weigh at least twenty pounds.

"Why do I need a bestiary, sir?"

"To start researching for potential contracts, of course. You'll want to jump to the section on individual entities powerful enough to deserve their own entries, it's near the back."

It was Hugh's turn to sigh as he lifted the book.

"You can all go for now, though I expect to see you all here tomorrow," Alustin said. "One thing before you leave, however: Please stop calling me Master or Sir. Alustin will be fine."

As they left the office, Hugh immediately strode off back towards his hidden lair, carrying his new book in both hands. He didn't even notice that Sabae looked like she wanted to speak to Talia and him. Hugh took his usual circuitous route through the stacks to get home, dodging origami golems on the way, then sidled behind the bookshelf to get into his lair. It was much, much harder than usual, considering the sheer size of Galvachren's Bestiary.

When he got inside, he stopped in shock. His room was completely different. His makeshift bed had been replaced by an actual mattress with a bed frame. His rickety furniture had been replaced by much sturdier furniture, and the shelves lined with books on warlocks, grimoires of wards, and even, he noticed, a few novels. There was a clock atop one of the shelves. Glow crystals had even been installed in his walls. Even his window was different- there were curtains now, and the warped frame with the discolored glass had been replaced by a brand new, well-made window.

There was a note lying on his new bed. It read: "I can't be having any student of mine sleeping on a bed of trash." It was signed *Alustin Haber, Librarian Errant.*

Hugh stared at the note in surprise for a while, then dropped the bestiary on his desk to examine his wards. As best as he could tell, the wards were completely untouched. Surprised, he sat down on his bed.

Hugh started trying to figure out how Alustin had gotten through the wards- or, for that matter, gotten an entire bed into his lair- just since he'd last been in the room that morning. It was at that point that the events of the day caught up to him.

Hugh burst into tears.

> ***Phragmos Mast-Biter:*** *Phragmos is a foul-tempered Kraken off the northern Ithonian coast. He dwells in a massive sea cave underneath one of the cliffs coming off the northern Skyreach mountains. Quite a few fleets and powerful mages have challenged Phragmos, but none have ever returned. He doesn't always attack passing ships, but sailors are well advised to stay far from his cave.*

What kind of powers would forming a pact with a kraken give him? The ability to breathe underwater, maybe? Supernatural strength? A water attunement? And what kind of price would a kraken demand in return?

> ***Asterion:*** *Asterion is a truly unique creature. He resembles a minotaur in form, if a minotaur were twenty feet tall and made entirely of a piece of the starry night sky hauled to earth, with eyes like suns. Asterion roams up and down the Skyreach Mountains, and is rarely to be found in the same place twice. He's only been seen visiting the same place a few times- an ancient, ruined city that predates the Ithonian Empire. He seldom pays attention to humans and avoids settlements. When irritated, however, he is an implacable foe. Asterion has never been seen to eat or sleep.*

It had taken hours for Hugh to finally relax. He'd worked himself near to hysteria the last few days with worry over the Choosing, but it had gone better than he'd ever truly anticipated. The revelation that he wasn't worthless as a mage had been an even bigger shock yet.

> ***Zzthkxz:*** *Zzthkxz is an elephant sized spider found in the depths of the Labyrinth below Skyhold. This huge arachnid enjoys asking riddles of and toying with her prey before carrying back to her web to become part of her larder.*

Hugh was a little startled to find mention of a monster below Skyhold. He'd heard of the Labyrinth before, of course- it was mentioned in most of the stories about Skyhold, and first year students were frequently warned never to enter it. It was filled with traps and roaming monsters, to say nothing of the simple threat of getting lost in its passages. It far predated Skyhold, and was thought by many to be one of the main reasons Skyhold was built where it was- for all its dangers, adventurers and mages willing to brave its depths often returned with powerful magical items and rare magical substances.

> ***Heliothrax:*** *Heliothrax is an ancient sun wyrm, a dragon of immense size and power. She's quite friendly towards mankind, and has been known to aid mankind against various magical beasts. There are tales of her dating back to the early days of the Ithonian Empire.*

Heliothrax sounded far more interesting to Hugh than any entry he'd encountered so far. An ancient sun dragon and defender of mankind? What powers would she grant him? Flight? Light and flame attunements? Heliothrax was going straight to the top of his list. A part of Hugh couldn't help but think that forming a pact with Heliothrax would overshadow even apprenticing to Aedan Dragonslayer.

> ***Jaskolskus, the Living Pyroclasm:*** *Jaskolskus is an ash elemental of immense age and power. He seldom leaves the volcanic caldera he resides in, but when stirred to anger is capable of wiping out entire cities.*

Hugh wanted to contract with something powerful, but approaching Jaskolskus seemed… well, entirely insane. Elementals were difficult to communicate with or understand at the best of times, not to mention easy to anger. And an elemental as powerful as Jaskolskus… Nope.

> ***Karna Scythe:*** *Karna Scythe is the newest queen of the gorgons, only having held power for about a century and a half. Unlike most gorgon queens of the past, she's proven willing to tolerate human visits to the labyrinth her people guard, and even engage in trade with some humans.*

Dawn was closer than dusk by the time Hugh finally left the bestiary on his desk (open to the entry of Ephyrus, the Fallen Moon, an immense jellyfish that floated through stormclouds above the jungles of southeast Ithos) to go to sleep.

CHAPTER FIVE
LESSONS

THE next morning, Alustin's apprentices met at his office. Hugh was the last to arrive- living in the library didn't do much to prevent oversleeping after staying up too late.

Talia opened her mouth to say something- a complaint about Hugh being late, he wagered- but before she could say it the door popped open and Alustin poked his head out.

"Excellent, you're all here! Come in!"

Hugh hurried in after Alustin to avoid a confrontation with Talia. He headed for the chairs in front of Alustin's desk, only to have Alustin snag him by the shoulder and turn him towards one wall, where one of the chalkboards had been erased.

"Second lesson!" Alustin said.

"Second lesson?" Hugh said.

"I'm not actually keeping track," Alustin said.

Hugh thought better of responding to that.

Talia and Sabae caught up with them as Alustin began drawing on the chalkboard.

"So you wanted to know about the Aether," Alustin said.

"Not really," Talia said.

"The Aether is like the ocean," Alustin said, rapidly drawing a crude picture of the sea. Hugh noted that it looked nothing like the beautiful drawings on the other walls.

"What's the Aether, and why do we care if it's like the ocean?" Talia said.

Alustin turned to look at them. "The Aether is where mages get all of their power. It is pure mana that permeates every corner of the world. And, like I said, it is like the sea."

"Are there fish?" Talia asked. Hugh was fairly confident she was being sarcastic.

Alustin opened his mouth to answer, but Sabae spoke first. "Will you quit interrupting? You might not have any interest in learning, but we do." Talia glared back at Sabae- and, to his discomfort, Hugh as well. He looked away quickly.

Before Talia could interject again, Alustin spoke up. "I certainly hope there's no fish in the Aether. That's… something of a terrifying thought." He shook his head. "Anyhow, it's like the ocean in that the Aether ebbs and flows like water. It has currents and depths, and prefers to take the path of least resistance. Unlike water, however, it cares not for what lies in its way or the pull of gravity. It flows freely, unless…"

Alustin turned back to the chalkboard and resumed adding details to the seascape. He said nothing for a moment, until Hugh realized that he was waiting on someone to answer.

"Unless it's forced into moving!" Talia said. Sabae glared at her.

"I highly, highly recommend against trying to force the Aether currents to do anything. Have you ever tried forcing the ocean to do anything?" Alustin said, not even turning away from his drawing.

That actually seemed to give Talia pause.

"You can't force the Aether to move, but you may forge channels for it to flow through. Your body does this naturally, absorbing and storing mana from the Aether. Spellforms may then be used to take your stored mana and utilize it. As your body absorbs mana from the Aether, it drains the mana around you. Then, at a speed that depends on the density of the Aether nearby, it fills back up, like a pond filling in the hole left by a bucket."

"Is it possible to channel mana directly from the Aether, instead of letting it refill your mana reservoirs?" Hugh asked.

Alustin hesitated in his drawing. "Hypothetically, but it's so dangerous and of so little benefit that few try it. The mana of the Aether is pure and unattuned, and has few uses. It only becomes attuned within your body. It's better to wait for your body to refill your mana reservoirs naturally. Those that have tried it generally only do so for the sake of saying they have." He looked contemplative for a moment.

"Back to the topic of our lecture. The natural ebb and flow of the Aether results in huge differences in the available mana. Some places, like Emblin," nodding at Hugh as he mentioned Emblin, "have Aether with such low density that a few paltry cantrips can leave it dry for hours. Other places, like Skyhold, have such rich and dense mana fields that thousands of mages casting spells daily can't even make a noticeable dent. Of course, you can still exhaust yourself casting spells- the Aether around here refills much more quickly than your mana reservoirs will."

Alustin turned back towards them. Somehow, he'd turned the crude drawing into a gorgeously detailed landscape. Hugh had genuinely never thought chalk capable of portraying that level of detail.

"So, what's the next question I want you to ask?" Alustin said.

The apprentices were silent for a moment, and then Sabae spoke up. "Where does the mana come from?"

Alustin smiled. "Exactly."

Talia spoke up. "Everyone knows that one. It comes from life itself."

Alustin's smile vanished, and he wagged his finger. "What did I say about things that everyone knows, Talia?"

He whirled back around to face the chalkboard again and drew a circle. "That was the leading theory for many centuries, but there's one huge, gaping hole in the idea. Namely, that mana deserts and mana rich regions don't seem to correspond to what's living there. The Endless Erg, for instance, is quite desolate, aside from a few monsters, and yet has incredibly rich mana. Emblin, on the other hand, is largely covered in pine forests, and yet has next to no mana. Scholars came up with thousands of explanations for this seeming paradox, each more intricate than the last. Eventually, the whole house of cards came tumbling down around half a century ago. We don't need to go into all the details, but what we now believe to be the source of the Aether?"

By now Alustin had fleshed out the circle into a detailed map of Anastis, with the continent of Ithos front and center. He'd marked Emblin and the Endless Erg on the map as he mentioned them.

"It's the death of the universe itself."

The apprentices were silent at Alustin's proclamation. The first thing that popped in Hugh's head was that Alustin really, really enjoyed dramatic pauses.

"The what of the what now?" Talia said. She looked as startled as Hugh felt. Sabae, of course, hadn't shown a reaction other than narrowing her eyes a little.

"The universe," Alustin continued, apparently pleased at their reactions, "is slowly wearing down over the countless eons. On some far distant day in the future- likely long after the last human has withered to dust and the last star has been extinguished- it will grind to a halt. This slow weathering of the fabric of the universe itself is what generates the Aether- it's a waste product of the dying of the universe."

Hugh took a few moments to process this. He opened his mouth to ask another question, but Alustin seems to have already moved on. "We're off to the library. As my apprentices, you'll all be permitted into the uppermost restricted level, but don't attempt to go any deeper- not only is it forbidden, it's dangerous. Magical libraries tend to have a life of their own." Before any of his apprentices could react, he was already striding towards the door.

As they followed him out of the office, he once more whirled to walk backwards facing them. "So, Sabae: Tell me what you thought of that book of mana channeling techniques."

Sabae sighed. "They're all useless. They require you to channel mana at such high densities that any spells cast with them would be incredibly hard to control even without my… difficulties." She unconsciously rubbed at some of the branching scars on her hands as she said this. "If I tried to cast a spell channeled like that, it'd turn out even worse than usual."

Alustin smiled. "That was, in fact, exactly why those techniques haven't seen use in centuries. There was a brief fashion of casting overpowered, uncontrolled spells in the decades after the fall of the Ithonian Empire- it was supposed to display your primal nature, or some such ridiculousness. I'm going to need you to start practicing those techniques immediately."

Sabae actually showed emotion at this. She started to splutter, but Alustin had already addressed Hugh as he led them down a staircase- still walking backwards- into a section of the library that first year students weren't allowed into. This was the first section to contain more advanced grimoires, as well as some actually enchanted books.

"So, has our resident warlock chosen any potential contractees?" Hugh had, in fact, brought a long list of potentials, starting with Heliothrax.

"Warlocks have tried to contract with Heliothrax for centuries, she has no interest. A small number of warlocks have made pacts with Asterion, but you have to find him first, which is an immense challenge of its own. Darsammeth would potentially work, but he's one of the most popular entities to sign pacts with- anyone familiar with warlocks would be prepared to face one of his contractors. Ephyrus… bold choice, but we've already got a storm mage," he said, waving at Sabae. In the end, Alustin left only Asterion as an acceptable option. "You're on the right track, though. Keep looking."

Hugh started to ask what, exactly, the right track was, but Alustin had once again moved on. "Talia, how did you enjoy your read last night?"

Talia glared at Alustin. "It was a children's story. A children's story about a mage that made children sleep better by burning away their nightmares with a flame that only existed inside their dreams."

"I admit, it's not the most rigorous scholarly work ever, but it's a start, isn't it?"

Talia glared even harder. "A start to what, helping little children sleep well?"

Alustin laughed at this. "No, to being a battle mage. You'd be wasted as anything else."

"How is a children's tale supposed to help me…"

Alustin, however, had swiveled around to walk forwards again, dodging an origami messenger crane flapping through the air. Hugh was now absolutely convinced that Alustin lived for being dramatic.

"This, my apprentices, is the Great Index."

So far as Hugh could tell, the Great Index was just a dictionary sized volume lying open on a pedestal at the end of a row of shelves. Its pages were blank, and there was a quill pen and an inkwell lying next to it.

Talia pointed down the rows. "That looks like another Great Index fifty feet that way, Al."

Alustin winced. "While I prefer that you not address me as master, I'll have to decline being called Al. And I might have exaggerated a little bit. This book is merely an access node to the Great Index. The Great Index is a semisentient magical construct with the ability to keep track of every volume in this library. At least, every registered volume- there are more than a few that have slipped through the cracks. You can use the Index to search for volumes by their title, subject matter, or even their contents. So let's give it a try, shall we?"

"Crazy librarians?" Talia suggested.

"Dreamfire it is! Excellent suggestion, Talia," Alustin said.

He dipped the pen in the inkwell, then wrote "Dreamfire" on the top of the page. Nothing happened for a few moments, then, in a neat, easily read script, the titles and locations of books began to appear. Alustin waited for it to stop, then with a wink to his apprentices, tore the page out of the book.

Hugh was convinced that another librarian must have heard, and that they were all about to get in trouble, but Alustin merely wrote on two more pages- "Dream attunements" and "Dream manifestations."

He dragged them across the library hunting the titles on the list. As he led them, he began to tell them of dreamfire.

"While it is an amusing tale, that book on dreamfire I had you read was far from a useful one for your needs, Talia. Dreamfire itself is a much, much stranger phenomena. This has to do with the unusual nature of dream attunements, which are among the most versatile attunements out there. They can first be used to alter and manipulate the dreams of a sleeping person. As in the story-book, the most common form of dreamfire is one such technique that can be used to do so." Alustin examined a title on dreamfire for a moment, then reshelved it. "Meddling with the dreams of others, unfortunately, likely won't be possible for you, except for the dreamfire technique. Your tattoos prevent you from channeling dream mana to actually affect the dreams of others otherwise- unless, of course, you wish to make your target dream of fire. So yes, I suppose, I will be training you to purge nightmares from children."

"The second use of dream attunements," Alustin said, handing a title to Talia, "is for illusion. It's much harder to craft illusions with dream attunements than light attunements, but it is quite possible. Sabae, why are you not practicing those mana channeling techniques?"

Sabae jumped. She, like Hugh, had gotten quite absorbed in Alustin's lecture. She mumbled an apology, then her eyes seemed to unfocus as she began concentrating on channeling her mana properly.

"Dream illusions often seem… less solid than light based illusions, but they're far, far more powerful- they can actually hold an element of solidity to them." He handed Talia another book and a scroll. "Which leads to the third use of dream mana- manifesting fragments of dreams physically into the world. It's a powerful, dangerous technique, and one only usable by the most powerful and focused dream mages. Normally it would be at least a decade before you could even attempt it."

"So why are you having me attempt it now?" Talia said.

"Your tattoos, of course," Alustin said, handing her yet another book.

"Shouldn't they make it harder for me to, uh, summon dreams?" Talia said.

"Manifest dreams. And yes, yes they will. With a single exception." He smiled broadly. "Fire."

Talia stared at him wide-eyed for a moment, then smiled broadly. "You're finally talking my language, Al."

Alustin sighed. "Alustin, please. I should note that manifest dreamfire is going to behave very, very differently than normal fire, and I have no idea how your tattoos will alter that, other than significantly. So no experimenting and trying to manifest dreamfire unsupervised, if you please." He added a couple more books to Talia's now huge stack.

"That should about do it for now. Don't forget, however, that dream is only one of your attunements." Alustin glanced at the three pages he'd torn out of the Index, then threw them behind him. Before they hit the ground, however, they folded themselves into origami golems- a dragonfly, a crow, and a winged serpent- and zoomed right back in the direction of the Index access node they came from. Alustin saw Hugh watching them. "The pages will reattach themselves to the access node when you're done with them. It's part of the Index's enchantment."

Alustin led the three of them to another Index access node, where he proceeded to write a series of search terms across pages. Hugh caught "basic spellform theory", "spellform architecture", "formless casting", "warlock contracts", and "mana layering", among others.

"For Hugh," Alustin said, "we're going to be grabbing two types of books. The first type," handing a book to Hugh, "are merely various theoretical guides to warlock contracts. Essential, but a bit bland. I will not, of course, be teaching you to craft an actual warlock contract anytime soon. More excitingly, Hugh, you're going to be reading a number of books on the basic theory behind spellform construction."

This didn't sound particularly exciting to Hugh.

"Unfortunately, I doubt you'll be able to simply start putting less mana into most of your spells, Hugh. You spent the earliest, most critical part of your magical development having to pump entirely too much mana into every effect, even if they were purely subconscious. So we'll need to instead give you different spellforms that can handle the larger mana flow."

That did sound a bit more exciting to Hugh.

"I could give you a simple list of spells to memorize, but that would, in the end, leave you a much, much less flexible mage. Rather like most of the other mages Skyhold produces these days, honestly."

"I'd be happy just being normal, sir." Fantasies about making a pact with a legendary dragon aside, not standing out of the crowd sounded pretty nice to Hugh.

"Alustin, please, not sir," Alustin said, dropping a weighty tome into Hugh's arms, "and merely being normal is hardly something to be happy about. Instead, we're going to make sure that you can improvise spellforms on the fly, so you can have a spell for any occasion."

By the time Alustin was done picking out books for Hugh, he felt like he was going to topple over from the weight of the stack. He glanced over at Talia, who appeared to be trying very, very hard to pretend that the weight of her equally large stack of books wasn't bothering her.

Alustin threw away several more Index pages, which folded themselves up and flew away. "I haven't forgotten you, Sabae. For you, we'll be gathering up more practical manuals on two topics- formless casting and mana layering."

Neither term meant anything to Hugh, but a look of shock came onto Sabae's face. "Formless casting is supposed to be incredibly dangerous! Students are strictly forbidden from attempting it until at least their fourth year."

Alustin chuckled. "Unless your master declares otherwise, that is. Do you know why formless casting is forbidden?"

Sabae started to open her mouth, then hesitated.

"What's this formless casting nonsense?" Talia said.

"Formless casting," Alustin said, "is the practice of casting spells without a spellform. It's faster, more powerful, and has a nasty tendency to result in spells that go horribly, horribly wrong, especially once they've gone more than a few feet away from the caster. Sound familiar?"

Sabae gave him a flat look. "So you're telling me that we're going to solve my inability to cast spells at a distance by learning a way of casting spells that makes it even harder to cast spells at a distance?"

Alustin smiled. "Nope. We're not going to have you cast spells at a distance at all."

Sabae looked like she was about to explode at him when he raised his hand in a placating gesture. "Unfortunately, thanks to your..." Alustin paused, "personal story which you don't want shared, there likely isn't much hope of you ever learning to use spells at any significant range. We are, instead, going to teach you to become an effective close quarters combat mage."

Sabae raised her hands up in the air, showing off her thin, branching scars. "I've tried that, sir. Lightning was never meant to be a close quarters magic."

Alustin smiled. "You've never tried it under my instruction."

Sabae started to look hopeful for a moment, then her face sank. "Even if you can teach me how to do it, close quarters magic just doesn't work, sir. By the time I close the distance between me and my foe, they'll have had plenty of time to pelt me with spells from afar. That's the reason there aren't any close quarters combat mages."

"Alustin, please, not sir," Alustin said with a sigh. "And as for there not being any close quarters combat mages, I believe Artur Wallbreaker would be surprised to hear it."

Sabae started to say something, then closed her mouth, looking pensive.

"Artur Wallbreaker," Alustin said "has dual iron and stone attunements. He channels them together to create a nigh-unbreakable suit of armor around him during battle, as well as massively empowering that over-sized enchanted hammer he carries everywhere. While he can use his attunements at a distance, he very, very rarely does so, as it drastically reduces the effectiveness of his armor and his hammer. To use his mana the way he does, he uses the second technique I'll be having you read about- mana layering."

Alustin handed Sabae a couple more books. He also spotted a book on the shelf that apparently interested him, and tucked it into his pocket. "Mana layering involves making your mana revolve in extremely tight flows all around your body. It reduces your ability to cast spells at a distance while you're doing it, but that's not a concern with you. It will, eventually, allow you to construct your own magical armor, like Artur does. It'll also likely make several powerful movement techniques available to you, allowing you to close the distance to your foes faster."

Alustin considered another book, started to hand it to Sabae, then changed his mind and reshelved it. "And, by the way, those high density mana channeling exercises I was having you read about? Those will massively enhance the effectiveness of both your mana layering and your formless casting."

Alustin threw aside the last few index pages, which promptly folded themselves into a tiny flock of geese and flew away. "Oh, and Artur Wallbreaker's third secret? Lots and lots of physical and combat training. You'll all, by the way, be learning that."

Hugh was pretty sure that the amount of books they were each carrying already counted as physical training.

CHAPTER SIX

SILENCE IN THE LIBRARY

ALUSTIN escorted them over to a nearby table, where he simply told them to get reading, and that he'd be back in a few hours.

Hugh couldn't set down his pile of books fast enough. He spent a few moments rubbing his sore muscles before he opened any of the books.

Even though he wanted to dive right into the books on warlock contracts, he made himself pick up one of the books on basic spellform construction instead.

The three had sat there reading silently for around an hour when Sabae slammed her book shut. "So is this how things are going to be for the next few years?" she said, giving them each a flat look. "We're just going to silently pretend the others don't exist?"

"That might be nice," said Talia, glaring at Sabae.

Hugh tucked another book inside the one he was reading as a book mark, then glanced up at the two of them briefly before turning his gaze back to the table.

"We're stuck with each other, so we might as well make the best of the situation," Sabae said.

Talia glared at her for a moment, then sighed. "Fine. What did you have in mind?" She didn't sound especially curious.

Sabae paused for a moment. "Well… why don't we tell each other about ourselves?"

Talia snorted. "You've made it pretty clear that you don't want to tell us about your story already." She glanced at Hugh. "You want to tell us your story, sheepherder?"

Hugh's cheeks heated up. "Not a sheepherder," he said, then opened his book back up.

No one spoke for a few minutes. Hugh noticed, however, that none of them seemed to be turning any pages in their books.

Finally, Sabae spoke again. "My fourth affinity is in healing."

Hugh and Talia looked up in surprise.

"What?" Talia said.

"My fourth affinity is healing," Sabae said.

No one said anything for a moment, then Talia spoke up. "Why would you not want people to find out that you had a healing affinity? They're damn useful."

Hugh didn't have the slightest clue why she wouldn't want people to know, either. Emblin was the only place he'd ever heard of that distrusted healers, and they distrusted all magic.

Sabae hesitated before speaking. "My family has defended the port city of Ras Andis for centuries. Each generation has produced powerful storm mages to shelter the city from storm or invasion. My mother, Andia Kaen Das, is powerful even by the standards of our family. Our family arranged my mother's marriage when she was very young, to the heir of a family of powerful sea mages. They expected her to go along with it quietly, but…" she gave a wry smile, "my mother might be the single most headstrong woman alive."

"Instead of marrying the sea mage, she eloped with my father, a simple healer. My family refused to recognize the relationship for years, and exiled my mother from their estate after she bore me. Even so, they were good years. My father was a kind man, and our family was happy. He ran a small clinic in the city that we lived above. He let people pay what they could, when they could, and earned us many friends among the poor. My mother, rather than compete with the storm mages of her family for work, instead worked as a mere water mage, purifying and tending to wells that were otherwise ignored by the city. The neighborhood councils couldn't pay her much, but they spared what they could. We weren't well off, but we never went wanting."

Sabae paused again. "Then the Blue Death arrived in Ras Andis. A freighter sailed into the city with its crew already sick, but the city failed to quarantine it in time. Within weeks, it had spread through the entire city- especially the poorer neighborhoods."

"What's the Blue Death?" Talia asked.

Sabae was silent for a moment. "Vomiting. High fever. Aches. Then the body temperature begins to plummet. They die almost like they'd walked out into a blizzard, even in the middle of the summer in one of the southernmost cities of Ithos."

Sabae idly played with one of her books. "My father died tending to the poor. He might have staved off the disease himself, but for how much energy he expended healing others. Many in my family died as well, and they finally reached out to my mother once more. For a time my mother resisted, thinking that they only wanted her back because my father had died, but something had broken in her with my father's death. We were welcomed back with open arms. I was eight."

"Those years were not bad ones. My family was kind and considerate of me, a bastard child they'd hardly met before. They treated me as though I'd always been there. I often felt out of place and uncomfortable with our family's wealth, but they were always patient and kind. I think that they truly regretted their rejection of my mother over the years, and had wanted to take her back long before, but could not bring themselves to until the tragedy of the plague.

"My mother, however, began to chafe at living at the family estates. She soon began accepting shipboard contracts, shepherding merchant fleets safely through stormy waters. She rarely came home, and seldom for more than a couple of weeks."

"A few years later, my affinities manifested. My family was excited at first- they had expected me to have perhaps one or two of the family affinities, likely alongside healing. Children rarely inherit all of their parents' affinities. Instead, I had all three and healing. Then, of course, my curse manifested instead. They genuinely tried to teach me to control my magic farther than a few inches from my body, but all attempts failed in the end. Even my mother, on one of her rare visits back, proved unable to help."

"They never blamed me, and never treated me badly, but I could tell that they all considered it the fault of my parents, that they blamed my father for polluting the Kaen Das line. What made it worse is that they were right. Many healers, like my father, completely lack the ability to do magic at a distance, in exchange for greater control up close. They seldom feel the lack, but it ruined me as a storm mage."

"My family sent me to Skyhold in hopes of a solution, and the school readily offered their help- no school had ever had the patronage of our clan before, and I hope you understand that I do not mean to be arrogant when I say that it is of considerable worth. I am the first Kaen Das ever sent for schooling in the magical arts outside of our family, and likely the last as well. Not, in truth, that I am much of a Kaen Das. Since I arrived, however, the teachers, unable to come up with a simple solution, have distanced themselves from me, not wanting my failure associated with them. Some students have tried to befriend me, but only for my family's reputation and wealth. A few teachers have tried to teach me healing, but healing is what ruined me as a storm mage, and I will not deepen my family's shame by learning it."

There was silence for a moment. Then Talia finally spoke up. "I bet it's going to feel good rubbing your powers in their face in a few years." She grinned at Sabae. Sabae blinked for a moment, then a faint smile crossed her face as well. Hugh grinned a little himself, but ducked his head when the other two looked at him.

"I'd never let myself hope before I met Alustin," Sabae said. "If he can teach us what he promised…"

"Unless he's just completely insane," Talia said, smiling.

Hugh somehow found the nerve to crack a joke. "Can't it be both?"

Talia snorted with amusement, and Sabae chuckled quietly. Hugh found himself smiling a little.

They were all silent for a moment until Talia spoke up. "I suppose it's my turn to tell a story."

"Clan Castis," said Talia, "is not the biggest of the clans of the Northern Skyreach Mountains. In fact, it's one of the smallest. It isn't the richest, nor the oldest, nor the best positioned. It is, however, one of the most feared. We've stood a thousand battles and won a thousand battles." She grinned. "Well, most of a thousand battles."

Hugh doubted this was much of an exaggeration. The northern mountain clans were famous for their belligerence and territorial behavior.

They constantly raided each other and many neighboring countries, most of which eventually just decided it was cheaper to pay them tribute each year than to try and root them out. Not that it wasn't tried repeatedly, but even the Ithonian Empire had never fully conquered the clans.

"The secret to our success is twofold. The first is our command of fire. Over half the tribe are fire mages. Many of them are quite weak, but quite a few each generation are extremely powerful. In large numbers, though, even the weak fire mages are a force to be reckoned with. We're not versatile in our magic, but with fire, you don't have to be."

"In each generation, one of the most powerful fire mages is chosen as warleader. Not necessarily the most powerful fire mage is chosen- the elders also judge candidates by their wisdom, courage, and other qualities. The warleader only leads the tribe in battle, but we have a great many battles." She smiled at that.

"My father, like his mother before him and her father before that, was chosen as warleader. He was the second most powerful fire mage in his generation."

"My mother was his chiefest rival for warleader in his generation. She was even more powerful than my father. In the end, what cost her the position was two things- her tiny stature and her unquenchable temper." She smiled to herself. "She hated my father for years after that. Only after he'd proven himself in battle time and time again did she allow him to court her."

"I am the youngest of seven children. Each and every one of my brothers is a powerful fire mage. Several of them are, in fact, even more powerful than either of our parents. Our territory has already expanded greatly since they began joining our battles. One will assuredly be the next warleader. And then I was born."

"My parents had long wanted a daughter. My parents would gladly have spoiled me, but I never had the patience for ribbons or toys. I was wandering into the mountains and fighting other children from the day I could walk." She looked particularly proud of that fact. "My parents, expecting me to be a fire mage as powerful as any of my brothers, went to the elders of my tribe early for my tattoos."

She pulled back her sleeves, revealing more of her tattoos. They were clearly spellforms, but of incredible complexity. "These tattoos are the second half of our success. My tribe has spent countless generations experimenting and learning. We tried countless patterns, inks, and other variables. We sought out enchanters, other fire mages, other clans that enchanted tattoos. Several generations ago, one of my mother's ancestors even traveled to another continent to learn from a tribe there who used tattoos to improve their mastery over wind."

"Our tattoos increase our attunement to fire to an unparalleled degree, beyond even our techniques and training passed down through countless generations. They also make us highly resistant to heat and fire. We are the mightiest fire mages on the planet. Even our non-mages are tattooed with different spellforms that provide fire resistance beyond that of our mages."

"Why…?" Sabae began.

Talia lowered her hands and shook her head. "Too much of the fire resistance spellforms can begin to interfere with a mages offensive power."

Talia grew pensive. "There's a side effect to the tattoos, however. They interfere with other attunements. Not that there are many other attunements present in our tribe, but we do intermarry with other tribes. Normally, that's not a problem. You can't use the other attunements, but you can still use fire."

"My parents, however, had me tattooed even before my gifts began to manifest. The earlier you can catch the gifts manifesting, the deeper the attunement to flame can be. Tattooing before one's gifts even begin manifesting results in the deepest attunement of all, but it's a risk seldom taken, for if one isn't a mage, their tattoos are a waste, and their fire resistance cannot further be improved. With six brothers and two parents who all number among our tribe's greatest mages, however? No one thought it was a risk. If that weren't enough, my parents had the elders design me the most elaborate, powerful tattoos our tribe had ever attempted up to that point- a design that wouldn't even work unless it was tattooed before one's gifts begin to manifest."

Talia's frown grew deeper. "And then my gifts did manifest. Bone and dream. My gifts were useless, and my father was furious. He thought my mother must have slept with a man of a different tribe. They burnt down several acres of alpine forest in their arguing. Eventually, seers confirmed I was truly his daughter, but…" she grinned briefly, "my mother made him sleep with the dogs and goats for weeks before she let him come back inside. Clan Castis rode out on raids many times during those weeks."

"My parents and the elders of my tribe journeyed far and wide for answers. My brothers each traveled to a different nation, to consult their wisest sages. Each failed, one by one, until only my eldest brother had not returned. On Midwinter, months after he had left, he returned to Clan Castis with word from Skyhold that they would take me. They made no promises, but they offered hope. Clan Castis has never sent its children to learn from the great academies before. We would bind ourselves to no nation, but Skyhold, of all the great schools of magic, has no allegiance to any nation."

Talia frowned. "Upon arriving here, though, I found myself ignored and dismissed by teachers and students alike as a useless barbarian. Many even thought of me as illiterate, even when I showed them I could read." Talia gave the other two a brief challenging look. "After all, there is little else to do but read and tell stories when winter traps us in our cabins and lodges."

"It seems that the faculty here thought my brother had exaggerated, that my problems were easily solved by anyone not a foolish barbarian. When it proved otherwise, they turned away rather than face their own shortcomings. Alustin is the first one to offer anything but dismissal in months. Truly, I had planned to simply walk away from Skyhold before Alustin chose me."

They were all silent for a moment, then the girls turned to face Hugh. He realized that they intended him to tell his story. He felt his cheeks start to grow red, and looked back and forth between the two.

Sabae seemed to take pity on him. "Take your time, Hugh. We're not going to bite you." She gave a pointed glance at Talia, who didn't notice.

Talia, who had been staring intently at Hugh, spoke up. "I… need to apologize to you, Hugh. I've been acting an ass towards you- both of you, really. You haven't done anything to deserve it." She said this, of course, with a fierce glare, as if daring either of them to reject her apology.

"Don't worry about it," Sabae said. "Your story makes your anger entirely understandable."

Hugh, in a quiet voice, simply said "Thank you." He looked Talia directly in the eyes as he did so, though he looked away immediately afterwards.

Talia seemed to relax a bit. Hugh, on the other hand, tensed up as the other two looked back at him and he realized that they actually wanted to hear his story.

Talia and Sabae's stories were like something out of a story. They had the kind of pasts that heroes out of tales did. Hugh… Hugh had the story of a nobody. No-one could possibly… Hugh stopped that line of thinking and a few deep, calming breaths. Then a few more. Then one last, long breath.

"I… I don't have any mages in my family. No grand history, no prized family name. We were just simple village folk. We lived in Cedarvale, a little village high up in the alpine forests of Emblin. My father ran Cedarvale's lumber mill, my mother was a lumber merchant's daughter. Simple folk. Not wealthy, except by the standards of Cedarvale." He looked up and grinned nervously. "There were only about four hundred people living in and around Cedarvale, so the standards weren't particularly impressive."

Hugh stopped talking for a few moments. He stared at the table, trying to sort through his thoughts. Out of the corner of his eye, he say Talia open her mouth to say something, but Sabae shook her head.

"When I was ten, our house burned down. My father carried me out, but when he went back for my mother and baby sister, the roof collapsed."

He went silent for a few more moments.

"My father's brother and his wife took me in. They were sheepherders, and had eight children already. My uncle sold my father's mill, so they should have been able to afford to care for me easily, but always complained of the cost and the difficulty."

Hugh 's voice took a bitter turn. "They hardly spent anything on me. They dressed me in hand-me-downs from my cousins and made sure they were all fed first. They put me to work with the sheep, and I was willing- but they never bothered to teach me anything or help me, and I've always been small for my age. They soon made it very, very clear I was useless as a sheepherder. Whenever my cousins and I argued, my aunt and uncle would never take my side. We lived far out of town, so there weren't other children to play with. I ended up spending most days out wandering the woods."

"They never meant to be cruel or neglectful. They were just too busy to spare much thought to me. Having me out of their hair most of the time was a blessing. The instant my powers started manifesting, they shipped me right off to Skyhold. Emblin is suspicious of magic, and prides themselves of their lack of mages. My aunt and uncle made it clear I wasn't welcome back, and they haven't written since."

"Since I got here… it's… I…". He took a deep breath. "No one wants to be friends with a country bumpkin who can't do the smallest piece of magic right. The only thing I'm good for is as the butt of jokes. A few teachers tried to help me, but until Alustin came along they all gave me up as a waste of time."

Hugh felt out of breath- it'd been quite literally years since he'd talked so much. He hadn't looked up once since he started the story- he was sure the other two would be scornful of how… bucolic and back-woodsy his story was.

As the silence stretched on, he felt his face start to heat up and turn red, but he didn't look up. Finally, Talia spoke up. "Hugh."

Despite himself, Hugh looked up. Sabae looked sympathetic, but Talia looked absolutely furious. He felt his cheeks grow even redder, and he wanted to sink into his chair.

"Your family isn't worth the water they drink. Anyone who would treat their own blood like that in need are honorless snakes, and they deserve to get sheared with their own sheep. Though I reckon it's probably hard to tell the difference."

Hugh just stared at her, mouth open. Then he looked at Sabae, whose expression looked slightly startled. Sabae's expression quickly grew resolute, however, and she nodded at him. Hugh looked back and forth for a few more moments.

Then he burst out laughing. It really wasn't that funny, but he'd been so wound up and stressed while telling his story that he couldn't help it. Any reaction other than scorn was completely unexpected, and actually getting angry for him?

The other two stared at him for a few seconds as he just kept laughing. He tried to stop laughing to explain, then started laughing even harder. After a few more seconds, Sabae's normally reserved facade broke fully, and she started chuckling as well.

Talia glared furiously at both of them. This just made Hugh and Sabae laugh even harder. She looked like she was about to start yelling at them, but when she opened her mouth a laugh popped out as well.

When Alustin arrived a few moments later, he found all of them laughing hysterically. Talia had actually fallen on the floor. It might have been the first time they'd ever seen Alustin look surprised.

That just made them laugh even harder.

CHAPTER SEVEN
TRAINING

HUGH's life began settling into a routine after that. He started each day very, very early with a quick breakfast. After that, it was time to exercise. Alustin hadn't even remotely been joking about the physical training. He had them doing strength training exercises and running laps around one of the larger training rooms. What made it even worse is that Alustin would run alongside them, actually giving them lectures as he did so- on the nature of the Aether, on common attunements, on their own attunements, on the utility of cantrips (and their sore under-use by most mages), and countless other topics. He'd expect them to listen, and to answer questions, even while completely out of breath.

Then it was time to clean up for their history and mathematics classes. Hugh normally didn't have any trouble with math- he'd always been decent, if not great, at it. Being exhausted every day he had it, however, didn't help him much. He fell asleep more than a few times in both classes. Where before he would have remained asleep until the teacher noticed, Sabae or Talia would wake him up now- Sabae generally a bit gentler than Talia. When he needed to, he returned the favor.

After that, it was time for lunch. They were usually too tired to talk much, but Hugh still valued the time with others. Hugh wasn't sure the other two counted him as a friend, but they didn't seem to dislike his company.

Their magical training each day began after that. Hugh was drilled on the basic construction principles of spellforms until he began seeing their geometric shapes in his dreams. He wasn't learning any actual spells yet, unfortunately. Even with Alustin's promises, it didn't feel like he'd improved that much as a mage.

Except, of course, when it came to wards. Alustin had thrown book after book of ward design and theory at him, giving him lecture after lecture. The book throwing wasn't always metaphorical, either- once Hugh had begun crafting wards meant to guard him against physical attacks, Alustin started throwing books, pens, and any other objects he had to hand at Hugh.

He also demanded that Hugh grow faster and faster at crafting the wards, often giving Hugh just a few moments to prepare a basic ward circle before beginning to throw things. Hugh began carrying several sticks of chalk with him in the pockets of his trousers so that he could always be ready to craft a ward.

Hugh also continued to work his way through the immense bestiary. Incredibly few of the entities he chose met with Alustin's approval. Thus far, his list was still only three entries long- Asterion, the starry minotaur spirit, Uolos, an immense frost serpent dwelling in the far north, and Dagan Spireborn, the ghost of a warrior who died centuries ago keeping a narrow mountain pass clear of monsters, and who still maintained his vigil.

Alustin hadn't given Hugh a lot of clues about his upcoming plans, but he had let slip that he intended to take the three of them out of Skyhold next summer in order to gain Hugh a contract, as well as to test the abilities of all three of the apprentices.

Sabae and Talia had personalized training programs of their own, as well as being taught more cantrips- Alustin was obsessed with cantrips, apparently. Sabae spent hours every day practicing her high density mana channeling and mana layering. When she got to the point where she could carry out either one effectively, Alustin started her on practicing both at once. Hugh got used to seeing breezes blow in a narrow circle around her, and to the occasional loud bang as her mana got loose from her control. The tall girl hadn't been started on formless casting yet, but Alustin had her learning the theory and doing mental exercises to prepare her for it.

She also spent an hour each day doing physical combat training, separately from Talia and Hugh. She spent many of those days with Artur Wallbreaker, who was apparently pleased to have a regular sparring partner for his son. Sabae also met regularly with a succession of guards, traveling adventurers passing through to delve into the Labyrinth, and other warriors to teach her various lessons. She focused primarily upon unarmed combat techniques, but was introduced to a great many weapons and weapon styles, so that she could be familiar with them in case she came up against them.

Alustin had tried to convince Sabae a number of times that she should start developing her healing affinity into a full attunement, but had been entirely unsuccessful. Sabae had absolutely no interest in doing so. Even now that she was being taught battle magic, she still seemed to blame her healing gift for her inability to follow her family's traditions and training.

Talia's training consisted of hours and hours sitting unmoving, trying to manifest dreamfire. Hugh hadn't realized how rare dream attunements were and how difficult to control they were, even without Talia's disadvantages. There were, apparently, few enough dream attuned at Skyhold that they could be counted on the fingers of one hand. Many with dream affinities were actively discouraged from pursuing attunement with them if they had any other affinities to focus on. Of those that did pursue dream attunement, many died during training. Manifest dreams were as chaotic and protean as actual dreams, and a manifested dream sword could easily transform into a serpent and bite its wielder. It took singular force of will to control the form of manifest dreams.

She had only managed it a handful of times so far. Once the candle-flame of dreamfire she'd successfully manifested transformed into a cloud of stinging bugs that vanished after leaving welts on the three of them. (Alustin, of course, was untouched.) A second time the flames had frozen solid, fallen to the floor, and shattered into nothing. The few times she managed to manifest stable dreamfire, it had an unearthly appearance- it burned an unstable purple-green color, and the light it cast made objects seem to warp and twist.

Her work with dream-based illusions was progressing a little more swiftly, but not in a particularly useful way. Her illusions only showed up in the shape of flames, albeit flames made of horses, trees, castles, dragons, and other fragmentary dream shapes. Talia would never make for much of an illusionist.

Unfortunately, Alustin hadn't yet figured out a way for her to use her bone attunement. He claimed he had a couple of promising leads, but nothing more. Dream's versatility was easier to use with Talia's spellform tattoos than the relatively more focused nature of bone attunements.

At the end of the day, Hugh would head off to eat dinner by himself in the smaller dining hall. He usually spent a little bit of time reading his assigned texts and browsing the Bestiary once he got back to his hidden lair, but as often as not he just passed out in bed the instant he got back.

> ***Kleteletet, the Cloud Serpent:*** *Kleteletet is a forty foot long serpent made entirely of venomous mists made solid. It only appears on moonless nights in the jungles of southeast Ithos, and its victims take hours to die inside its stomach, unable to escape, although their screams make it out just fine.*

Hugh definitely wasn't adding Kleteletet to his list.

Every Fifthday, the students were all given the day off. With the grueling training schedule Alustin ran them through, Hugh needed it-and assumed the others did too. Hugh generally stayed in his secret room in the stacks reading. He was still looking for a entity to contract with.

> ***Tetragnath:*** *Tetragnath is a hive mind spanning millions of spiders. Their webs completely cover huge portions of the Aito forest in Tsarnassus. In the depths of Tetragnath's web are supposedly found a number of incredibly rare plants in high demand by alchemists. Few make it out alive from its forest, but burning down the woods to clear out Tetragnath would also burn the valued plants, and Tetragnath shows little interest in expanding its territory, so it's tolerated more than most similar threats.*

There were a surprising number of spiders listed in Galvachren's Bestiary. Apparently magical spiders became intelligent and powerful enough to be listed in it quite often. Or, possibly, Hugh just kept reading the sections with more spiders in them. It was hard to tell, given how often the book changed. Galvachren apparently added entries to the book on almost a daily basis, as well as regularly moving entries around within it. There didn't seem to be any sense to the orders of the entries, either.

> ***Chelys Mot, the Earthshaker:*** *Chelys Mot is a turtle of immense size, with a shell almost a hundred feet across. He has the ability to control earth and stone, and is even capable of generating localized earthquakes. He is short-tempered and*

dislikes being disturbed, but can be reasoned or bargained with if one is polite. He generally moves around on the northern edge of the Endless Erg.

Hugh whistled. Chelys Mot seemed like an excellent option. Powerful, approachable, and relatively close by. He quickly wrote him down on the list of entities to show Alustin.

Intet Slew, the Blood Boiler: *This half dragon, half demon creature has a habit of...*

Hugh paled a bit. Nope. Definitely not Intet Slew. Not a chance.

Lasnabourne, the Seaflame: *Lasnabourne is an ancient phoenix who nests atop one of the volcanic jungle islands to the southwest of the Ithonian continent. This phoenix isn't hostile towards humans, often engaging in conversations to hear the news from the continent. He eats mostly whales and sharks caught in the sea nearby. Interestingly, unlike other phoenixes, his flames don't seem to be dimmed at all by water, and he can sometimes be seen deep below the surface, still burning brightly as he dives for his prey.*

Hugh added Lasnabourne to the list. Talia would be interested in hearing about Lasnabourne's underwater flames, as well.

It'd been about three weeks since the Choosing, and Hugh was happier than he'd been in years. Aedan was apparently a demanding master, as Rhodes hadn't had the time to harass him at all during that time. The privacy his secret library room afforded him was genuinely soothing- especially now that he'd been able to apply his progressively improving skill at wards to his room. And even if Talia and Sabae didn't consider him a friend, they were at least friendly towards him.

Keayda, the Merchant of Truths: *This ancient naga lich's library is one of the greatest in the world, and to any who bring Keayda knowledge, books, or scrolls he doesn't yet possess, he is willing to grant answers of equivalent value. Keayda is known to have an especial interest in historical texts. Those who cross Keayda or try to steal from him, however, get their skin turned into parchment for his journals.*

Huh. What sorts of affinities would a naga lich bequeath on him? Naga, beings with the torsos of humans, but with long snake tails instead of legs, could have as many different affinities as humans, though poison affinities were far more common among them than among humans. Since he was a lich, a form of sentient undead, maybe he'd grant Hugh a bone affinity? The turning skin to parchment thing was a bit ominous, but Hugh didn't have any intention of stealing from Keayda. He thought for a moment, then wrote Keayda's name on the list.

> ***Andas Thune:*** *This relatively young dragon has already carved out a surprisingly large territory for himself from those of his older, larger draconic neighbors. This lightning dragon is also an incredibly capable illusionist, and…*

Hugh's stomach rumbled. It was about time for lunch, so he dragged himself away from his desk and put his shoes on. Before he left, he opened his window to look out. Even this early in the spring, the days were brutally hot. Skyhold stayed a fairly consistent temperature year round, thanks partially to powerful enchantments, but mostly because it was largely underground.

Hugh watched a sandship pull into Skyhold's port. A flock of lesser desert drakes, no bigger than geese, playfully weaved in and out of its masts and sails. To either side of him, he could see people bustling around the balconies, walkways, and courtyards of Skyhold. He smiled and turned to go.

Hugh's smile lasted him all the way out the library and well on his way to the dining hall.

Then he heard a voice that made his smile drop away like it had never been there at all.

"Sheepherder!" Rhodes called.

Hugh winced. This was just what he needed. This is what he got for not paying better attention to his surroundings. He turned around slowly to face Rhodes, who was standing in the middle of the hallway intersection that Hugh had just passed.

Rhodes had a huge smile plastered on his face. "I've missed you, sheepherder! My master has kept me so busy that I'm sure you've forgotten your place by now."

Rhodes was accompanied by the blue haired and eyed twins that Sulassa Tidecaller had picked at the Choosing. Both the boy and the girl were giving Hugh amused looks. Hugh scowled and looked down at the ground, preparing to run.

"Nothing to say to me, sheepherder? That's too bad. I was hoping to hear a little bit about your new master. You know, the librarian."

"I'm not a sheepherder," Hugh muttered.

The twins laughed, and Hugh clenched his fists.

"What's he teaching you? How to shelve books? No, he'd have to teach you to read first. Was he really that desperate that he'd need an illiterate sheepherder for an apprentice?" Rhodes laughed, and the twins laughed along with him.

"Maybe he's teaching you a little paper magic? Now there's an affinity useless enough that you might have a chance with it."

Hugh's fists clenched even tighter. Though in truth, he actually didn't know what Alustin's attunements were- the few times one of his apprentices asked, he always managed to change the subject in such a way that you didn't notice until afterwards.

Hugh didn't stand a chance in a fight against Rhodes- he hadn't even when all Rhodes knew was a few basic cantrips. His new master should already be guiding him through attuning, so Rhodes likely had much more powerful magic available to him now, while Hugh had really only gotten better at wards. If he'd had a few seconds he could have drawn a ward, but without any time to prepare...

"Don't just stand there like one of your sheep, sheepherder. Tell us about your new affinity," said Rhodes.

The twins had spread out to either side of Hugh. He could tell that things were going to progress to a beating here in a moment. He could hear his heart pounding in his ears as it started beating faster.

"Don't just stand there like a lump, sheepherder," Rhodes said. He reached out towards Hugh, and then just... stopped. His face turned pale, and then he grabbed his crotch with both hands and dropped to the ground. Behind him, pulling back her foot, was Talia. Sabae stood just behind her.

"Hugh's no sheepherder," Talia said.

Hugh felt his mouth drop open in shock.

"You bitch!" growled Rhodes, slowly picking himself up from the ground and holding himself. "Do you know who I am?"

"You're the spoiled brat who's messing with our friend," Talia said. "Do you know who I am?"

One of the twins- the boy- finally spoke up.

"You're that barbarian bitch who can't control her magic at all," he said.

"And you're the useless storm mage whose family didn't want her anymore," said the girl.

Sabae's normally impassive face broke out in a scowl. She opened her mouth to say something, but Talia spoke first.

"I do know who you are, Charax," she said to Rhodes. "I am Talia of Clan Castis."

Rhodes' face grew red. Talia chuckled.

"I remember the story of when Highvale decided they'd had enough of our raids, and sent an army to try and punish us a century or so ago. Five thousand warriors and two hundred battle mages, and we caught them in a valley and incinerated them. It only took a hundred of us, and not a single Highvale soldier survived. We didn't lose a single warrior." Talia smiled even more broadly. "And they were lead by the then Crown Prince of Highvale. Your ancestor, I believe."

Rhodes bellowed wordlessly, pain forgotten. He brought his hand forward in a classic battlecasting pose, and sparks of lightning began to crackle around his fingers. Hugh flinched, ready to throw himself to the ground.

And then Sabae punched Rhodes so hard he went flying. A gust of wind blasted out of her closed fist as it struck his chest, and he was launched into the boy twin. Both of them were sent sliding a good twenty-five feet down the smooth stone floor, and Rhodes' lightning dissolved into harmless sparks. Hugh and the girl twin were knocked down to the ground by the wind as well.

Talia ran over to Hugh and hauled him up by his hand. Sabae was staring at her fist in shock. Talia dragged Hugh past Sabae, and yelled "Don't stick around after tweaking a dragon's tail, Sabae!" Sabae blinked, and turned to follow Hugh and Talia.

Hugh glanced back, and saw Rhodes glaring at them. Hugh had just been a petty amusement for the nobleman before, but the look he was giving them now? It was pure hate.

They ran through the hallways for several minutes before stopping to rest. Alustin's training programs were already showing their worth- before, Hugh doubted he could have run half as far.

After she'd caught her breath, Talia burst out laughing. "The looks on their faces! The look on your face, Sabae! That was amazing."

Hugh nodded in agreement. His heart was still racing, but not just from the run.

Sabae looked at them for a moment, then laughed. "I suppose Alustin's training programs actually are working, aren't they?"

"I thought you couldn't do magic at a distance?" Talia said.

"I wasn't. I just built up the wind around my fist and released it when I struck, and it just… naturally flowed in the direction of the strike. Before, it would have dispersed wildly in all directions," Sabae said. "This time, it just… followed the strike."

Talia and Sabae chuckled for a few moments, and then Sabae frowned and turned towards Hugh. Hugh still felt sick to the stomach from the encounter.

"This isn't the first time, is it?" Sabae said.

Hugh looked down at his feet. His cheeks flushed and his stomach began to twist itself back up again. They'd seen how much of a coward he was, and they'd want nothing to do with him now.

"No," he said in a quiet voice.

No one said anything for a moment, then Talia spoke up. "That pampered little bastard. Why didn't you tell us, Hugh? We'd have had your back in a heartbeat."

Hugh didn't say anything for a moment, then finally worked up the nerve to speak, though even quieter than before. "I didn't want you to see how much of a coward I am," he said.

He didn't want to look up, but all of a sudden Sabae stepped up to him and grabbed his shoulders.

"Rhodes Charax is half again your size, has probably had combat training from the time he could walk, has multiple attunements, none of your disadvantages, is being trained by Aedan Dragonslayer himself, and had two friends at his back. If I know his type, he probably had friends when he did this before, too. Fighting him on your own would have been foolishness, not courage."

Hugh stared at her in the eyes for a moment. She seemed absolutely serious. He grew uncomfortable at her unblinking stare and turned his gaze towards Talia. Talia had an angry look on her face.

"If anything, Rhodes is the coward," Talia said. "With all the advantages he has, he still only faced you with backup."

Sabae nodded, and seeing that Hugh looked uncomfortable, let go of his shoulders. "We were walking to lunch when we ran across you, would you care to join us?"

Hugh just nodded, not trusting himself to speak. They set off towards the dining hall- the larger, student dining hall that Hugh had avoided for weeks. Talia and Sabae talked about the blow she'd struck as they walked, Hugh walking behind them. Talia wanted to call it a gust punch, while Sabae wanted to call it a wind strike.

After a couple of minutes, Hugh worked up the nerve to speak again. "Talia, did… did you mean it when you called me your friend?"

Both of the girls turned their heads back to look at him.

"Of course you're our friend, Hugh," said Sabae. "Why would you think otherwise?"

Talia's face had resumed its customary furious look. "Because he's an idiot, that's why! How dumb do you have to be to not realize you're friends with someone! If I…"

As Talia ranted at him, Hugh felt a small smile creeping across his face. It wasn't as big as his earlier smile, but it felt much, much better.

CHAPTER EIGHT

LUNCH

Talia, Sabae, and Hugh had just gotten their food when someone called Sabae's name. Hugh looked over to see a huge, muscular teen with curly black hair and skin darker than Sabae's waving at them. It took him a second, but then he recognized him as Artur Wallbreaker's son and apprentice. Sabae waved back, then headed over to the burly teen's table. Hugh paused uncertainly, but followed after Talia walked that way as well.

"Hugh, Talia, this is Godrick, son of Artur Wallbreaker. Godrick, this is Hugh of Emblin and Talia of Clan Castis." Sabae sat next to Godrick, while Hugh and Talia sat across the table from them.

"It's great ta meet yeh," said Godrick in a slightly too loud voice and a thick accent that Hugh couldn't place, and reached across the table to shake Talia's hand. Hugh, not wanting to be rude, followed suit, and regretted it immediately. It was like shaking hands with a bear. His hand *hurt* after that squeeze. He didn't think Godrick had squeezed so hard on purpose, though- he was immediately obvious as one of those people who didn't have a mean bone in his body, or even a less than joyously friendly bone.

Hugh thought people that friendly were exhausting.

"Sabae's told me a bit about the two a' yeh, but she won't tell me what yer affinities are. She told me ah've got to ask you if I want ta know," Godrick said. "Mine are pretty close ta me da's- Ah've got stone just like him, but with steel instead a' iron."

"What's the difference?" Talia asked.

"Iron mages can affect any iron an' iron alloys they want, steel mages can only affect steel with any real strength," Godrick said.

"So a steel attunement is just weaker than an iron attunement?" Talia said.

Godrick didn't seem at all offended. "Not at all- it's quite stronger, in fact. It's the way things work with similar attunements- the more specific the attunement is, the more powerful it tends ta be, at the cost of versatility. Ah might not be able to affect regular iron more than a tiny bit, and my da's iron not at all, but he can hardly touch my steel directly with his power, and he's miles ahead a' me. Doesn't matter too much, since ah'm mostly just usin' it to make mah hammer hit harder."

He leaned forwards. "It's a bit a' a secret, but since we're all friends here, I'll tell you something else, too."

Wait, friends? Hugh had just met the guy.

"We just met you," Talia said. She'd apparently been thinking along the same lines as Hugh.

Godrick waved his hand dismissively. "Any friend a' Sabae is a friend a' mine. 'sides, if ah wanted to hear your secrets, gotta offer something of mah own, right?"

Hugh wasn't sure what to say to that, so he kept to his usual strategy of not saying anything.

Godrick leaned forwards towards Hugh and Talia and dropped his voice to a whisper. "Ah've got a third affinity as well. Just a weak one, but it's a good 'un." He smiled broadly. "Scent."

Hugh blinked. Scent? How was that…

Talia whistled. "You're a stink mage? Remind me never to kick you in the britches."

Hugh shot Talia a confused look.

She caught it and explained. "There are only a couple Clans that Clan Castis avoids fighting. One of them, Clan Derem, specializes in scent mages. Their villages are the most wonderful smelling places on the planet, but get into a fight with Clan Derem? A stink mage can have a whole raiding party vomiting in seconds, and making skunks smell sweet compared to them for weeks."

Godrick chuckled. "Ah doubt ah'll ever be that powerful, but ah can sure give someone a bad day or two. And against monsters with powerful noses? Ah can give them a really bad day." He grinned even wider. "And ah can do this."

Hugh sensed a brief surge of mana coming from Godrick, and all of a sudden his relatively bland smelling soup smelled absolutely heavenly, and he was reminded how hungry he was. He tucked into the soup with a vengeance. The flavor didn't quite match the scent, but it was definitely improved from normal.

Maybe Godrick was alright after all.

"Ah also get a much better sense a' smell out a' the deal, which is nice. Can track by scent a bit," Godrick said, before tucking into his soup as well.

Talia gave him a considering look, then gave Godrick an abbreviated explanation of her affinities, tattoos, and training. When she mentioned manifesting dreamfire, his eyes widened.

"That's a crazy difficult skill ta' master! From what ah hear, most dream mages can't even attempt manifesting dreams before they're journeymen."

Talia grinned. "I've already done it."

It was Godrick's turn to whistle.

Hugh heard a faint sound and looked to Sabae. She was pursing her lips as though she were trying to whistle, but she was failing miserably. Sabae saw Hugh looking and quickly put her normal reserved look back on her face, but he could see her blushing a little.

"What about yerself, Hugh?" Godrick said.

Hugh jumped a little.

"Hugh's situation is… a little sensitive," Sabae said.

Godrick looked curiously between Hugh and Sabae. "Can't he tell me on his own?" He didn't sound offended, just curious.

"Good luck with that," Talia said. "We're his friends, and we can barely pry two words out of his mouth. Shyest kid I've ever met."

Hugh, feeling surprisingly ornery at that, spoke up. "Two words."

Everyone stared at him for a second, then Godrick burst out laughing. His laugh was as huge as the rest of him. Sabae quickly followed suit, while Talia just glared at Hugh. Hugh just looked down at his food and smiled.

"Nah worries if yeh don't feel like talking, Hugh. No debt, mah story was freely given ta yeh."

Godrick smiled broadly at Hugh, and turned to talk to Sabae about their combat training under his father.

Hugh sat quietly for a couple minutes eating his soup. When a lull in the conversation finally occurred, he spoke up. "I don't have any affinities."

Godrick blinked, and for the first time in the conversation, looked like he didn't know what to say.

"Not yet," Hugh said, and looked back to his food.

Godrick finally got his mouth working. "That's a cryptic statement if ah ever heard one." When it became apparent that Hugh didn't intend to say any more, he grinned. "Ah like a good puzzle."

Talia elbowed Hugh in the side. He looked at her, startled and a little offended.

"Look who's in line," she said.

Hugh looked up and spotted Rhodes in line glaring at them. The twins were there as well, but their glares paled besides the hate in Rhodes' eyes.

Godrick whistled again. "There's an angry fella. What did yeh three do ta make him mad like that?"

Sabae quit trying- and failing- to copy Godrick's whistle again. "Talia kicked him in the fork," she said.

Almost at the same time, Talia said "Sabae hit him with a gust punch so hard he and his goons there went flying."

Sabae gave Talia a dirty look. "Wind strike."

"Gust punch."

"Wind stri…"

"Gust strike," Hugh interrupted.

Godrick stared at the three of them in shock, then burst out laughing, this time so loud that a number of students around the dining hall looked at them. Rhodes turned bright red.

"Ah don't know tha Winter twins too well, but that Rhodes is a' prideful fella. He wasn't real happy when ah turned down his invitation ta join his labyrinth team. Didn't want to join someone who seemed ta take it fer granted ah'd do so."

Hugh looked at Godrick in confusion.

"The team yer supposed ta assemble fer tha first year final?" Godrick said, catching Hugh's look.

Hugh just shrugged.

"First years delve into the Labyrinth below Skyhold for their final at the summer solstice," Sabae said. "They're only permitted to explore the first level, which is fairly safe. Most students come back. You need to do it in teams of four, though, just in case."

This did not especially comfort Hugh. The Labyrinth was hellishly dangerous, everyone knew that. Even ignoring the monsters and traps, the maze itself changed its shape regularly.

Godrick had a thoughtful look on his face. "Ye know, there are four a' us…"

Talia gave him a glare. "You've been planning to ask us that since we got here, haven't you?"

"Guilty," Godrick said with a grin.

"Sounds good to me," Sabae said.

Talia gave Godrick an appraising look, then snorted. "You look like you can handle yourself in a fight, and failing that you can carry us if we get tired. Fine by me."

Everyone looked at Hugh expectantly. He hunched down a little at the attention, but then sighed. "That'd be fine, I guess."

Godrick seemed to take that as words of the highest praise, and clapped Hugh on the shoulder while smiling broader than ever. "Ah knew ye'd come around, bud. We still need ta ask me da and yer master, but ah reckon they'll be fine with it."

Hugh rubbed his shoulder ruefully. He was fairly sure he was going to bruise.

CHAPTER NINE
SPELLFORM

Hugh's routine changed quite a bit after that. Godrick started joining them for many of their morning exercise sessions, as did his father. Artur Wallbreaker was even bigger up close than Hugh had expected, both in sheer physical size and personality. He made Godrick seem quiet and demure at times. His hair and beard- both immense in size- were shot through with strands of white, and he had more scars over his bulging muscles than Hugh could count. He was, if anything, even friendlier than Godrick.

Most of the rest of the day went the same until lunch. Alustin's three apprentices (though not Godrick, who ate lunch at a different time) talked much more than they used to. Even Hugh started talking a bit more often as he grew comfortable with the others.

During the later part of the afternoon, as they trained in magic, Talia and Sabae showed immense progress.

Talia could now consistently manifest dreamfire, and even hurl fist-sized bursts of it at targets with a fair degree of accuracy. Dreamfire, disturbingly, didn't always burn its target, but always damaged it somehow. Sometimes the target would be frozen solid, other times aged until it crumpled to dust, or on one memorable occasion, diced into hundreds of perfect half inch cubes. Still, three out of every four times, dreamfire behaved mostly like real fire. Alustin still hadn't figured a way to develop Talia's bone affinity yet, unfortunately.

Sabae had shown massive improvement, at least with her wind attunement. She could regularly release gust strikes with her blows now. She had begun the rudiments of developing it into wind armor- she could now manifest bracers of swirling wind around her forearms that resembled faint tornadoes. They couldn't deflect a lot, and Sabae could only maintain them a few seconds at a time with the current size of her mana reservoirs, but they were enough to significantly cushion most blows. Alustin still cautioned her against using her water or lightning affinities, and Sabae still refused to use her healing affinity.

Hugh's list of potential contract partners had grown- Chelys Mot the earthquake tortoise, Lasnabourne the phoenix, and a sentient, plant controlling tree in the same archipelago as Lasnabourne were all new additions approved by Alustin.

Hugh, however, hadn't cast a single spell other than his wards and his basic light spell. He'd learned why the light spell worked- unlike most other cantrips, it was built to accept a highly variable amount of mana, so that its relative brightness could be adjusted easily enough. It had been much more capable of accepting the huge amounts of mana he couldn't help but dump into every spell.

All Hugh did was just keep learning more and more about spellform construction. He learned what the various basic shapes did, how they relate to one another, and how the speed and turbulence of mana flows were affected as they went through turns and intersections at different angles. But Alustin still didn't teach him to cast any spells.

He often found himself extremely frustrated by the end of magic training, but he still always found himself looking forwards to dinner. He always ate with Talia and Sabae, and Godrick managed to make it most nights as well. He always enjoyed himself, and found himself contributing more and more often to the conversation- though no one would be quick to accuse him of being talkative.

Rhodes never did anything, but Hugh noticed that very few students were willing to sit near the four of them. Hugh guessed Rhodes had made his dislike of them known to their peers.

It was his lack of progress at magic, however, that really began to grate at him.

Finally, about three weeks after the confrontation with Rhodes and meeting Godrick, he reached a breaking point in Alustin's office. Sabae was off doing combat training, while Talia had been sent to the library to retrieve a number of books, including a rare biography of an Ithonian Empire dream mage.

"Why haven't you taught me any spells yet?" Hugh demanded of Alustin.

Alustin quirked his eyebrow at Hugh. "I thought that's what I've been doing."

"You haven't yet, though!" Hugh said. "I don't know any new spells outside of my wards."

Alustin seemed to consider for a moment, then nodded. "I definitely have been teaching you new spells, you just haven't been listening."

Hugh spluttered for a moment, but Alustin cut him off.

"What did I tell you I'd be teaching you at the very beginning, Hugh?"

"How to adjust spells to work for me, and how to improvise my own spells" Hugh said.

"Exactly. I don't believe I ever told you I'd be teaching you spells on their own. The whole point of learning spellform construction is that so you can craft your own." Alustin grabbed a sheet of paper and a quill, handing them to Hugh.

"You're going to craft a levitation spell to lift this book."

Hugh glared at Alustin, then at the book he'd set in front of Hugh. "How am I supposed to do that?"

"Draw a foundation for your spellform."

Hugh paused for a moment, then started sketching. The foundation was the most critical part of any spellform- it was what channeled the caster's mana into the rest of it. Hugh chose to go with a high capacity, octagonal foundation line.

"Now draw your definitive lines." These lines were what guided the mana into the form it needed to be- in this case, the skewed diagonals he drew were what told the spell that it was supposed to bestow kinetic energy onto its target.

"Now draw your aiming lines." These short, branching lines coming off the definitive lines told the spell what direction the kinetic energy should be applied towards.

Alustin leaned back in his chair. "Now use it."

Hugh carefully memorized the diagram he'd drawn, then focused on the book. He drew the octagon in his mind's eye, followed by the skewed diagonals, followed by the branching aiming lines. Targeting the spell was done by application of the caster's will- everyone, apparently, invested at least a little bit of willforce into all their spells, though few could invest as much as Hugh could into his wards. Finally, he carefully let his mana flow into the spellform.

The book launched itself upwards from the desk at high speeds, slamming into the ceiling. Hugh stopped channeling mana into the spellform at the loud bang, and the book promptly crashed back onto the desk, bending a few of the pages.

Hugh felt himself turn red. "It still didn't work right! This has all been a waste of time!"

Alustin picked up the book and smoothed out the pages. "It levitated, didn't it?"

"Sure, but it didn't stop when it was supposed to!" Hugh said.

Alustin grabbed another sheet of paper, and swiftly drew out another spellform- it had the same definitive lines and similar aiming lines, but a very different foundation line.

"This is the standard basic levitation spellform," Alustin said. "All it has is the foundation line, the definitive lines, and the aiming lines. What happens when you try to use it?"

Hugh glared sullenly. "It explodes, or releases a flash of light, or it smokes a bunch."

"And what's the difference between the two spellforms?" Alustin held them up side by side.

"The foundation line on the standard spellform is built to only handle a little bit of mana- considerably less than I put into it," Hugh said.

"Which is why it reacts so badly- the mana you channel into the spellform is too much for it, and it shatters the spellform," Alustin said. "Your new spellform, however, did not shatter, since you gave it the capacity to handle your mana."

"So why did it fail?" Hugh said.

"It didn't. Try it again."

Hugh gave Alustin a skeptical look, but recreated the spellform. Once again the book launched itself to the ceiling, startling Hugh into releasing the spell.

"Again, but this time don't lose concentration when it hits the ceiling."

Hugh tried a third time. He carefully recreated the spellform in his mind, took a deep breath, and then channeled his mana into it. The book shot upwards, but this time, Hugh managed to avoid losing the spell. After the book hit, it just… stayed there, stuck to the ceiling.

"Unlike the standard spells, you're not getting random, chaotic results, because you're not shattering the spellform," Alustin said. "The standard levitation spell only lifts small objects a couple of feet because that's all the mana the foundation line channels into the effect. Your spellform, however, can channel enough mana to lift this book… around twenty or thirty feet, I'd wager."

The book, which had remained pinned against the ceiling, abruptly shot off along the ceiling to one side, slamming against the office door. Hugh lost concentration in surprise.

"Your aiming lines weren't the best, unfortunately- the aiming lines in the standard levitation spell horizontally stabilize the levitated object, whereas your spell allows it to transfer its vertical force into horizontal force. It likely would have launched the book off to the side as well if it had managed to actually lift the book all the way to the top of your spell."

Hugh stared at the book for a moment.

"If you'd wanted to reduce the height the book rose to, there are a couple of ways to do that," Alustin said. "What is known as a restrictor line can be applied to the aiming line to limit the top of the effect. A venting line can be added to the foundation line to release any mana over a certain amount before it becomes part of the spell. Additional definitive lines could be added to the spell- say, light lines to make the book glow- in order to use up more of the mana so the book wouldn't have launched itself so high."

Alustin paused and looked at Hugh straight in the eye.

"You're going to learn about all of these and more, and they'll all give you much, much greater versatility with your spells. You could have been creating spellforms of your own for a few weeks, now, though. You should have figured that out by now, Hugh. You can't expect your teachers- even me- to just hand you everything. You need to learn to find your own answers as well. But…" Alustin smiled broadly, "I'm happy to congratulate you for creating your first original spell. You've already achieved something that many mages never even attempt in their entire careers."

Hugh blinked, then smiled.

Just then, however, Talia entered the office and promptly tripped over the book Hugh had been levitating, sending her armful of books tumbling across the floor.

"What idiot just left a book right in the entryway? Were you trying to break someone's neck?" Talia sounded like she was prepared to rant for quite a long time. Hugh's smile turned a little sheepish, and he got out of his chair to go help Talia pick up her books.

Hugh spent the next few days levitating things constantly. He found out a few things pretty quickly.

First off, while his friends were excited for Hugh, they were less appreciative of having their stuff launched across a room.

Second, that spellform crafting was far, far more daunting of a task than he'd appreciated. His first attempt to alter the aiming lines so that the target of his spell wasn't launched off to one side resulted in the spell trying to crumple the levitated object. He'd tried to simply use the aiming lines from the standard levitation spell, but it was far from that simple- it turned out that the different foundation line changed the requirements for the aiming line. So he had to figure out how to adjust the aiming lines appropriately.

When he tried it again, it didn't try to crumple the levitated object, but it did spin it at a high speed. It seemed that the changes to the aiming lines necessitated that they be moved slightly farther down the definitive lines, which in turn…

Hugh quickly started realizing why so few mages tried to learn spellform construction, and he started to seriously question the sanity of trying to master the skill of doing it on the fly.

He did a little research, and found that the average mage generally memorized a dozen or fewer spells- there was a reason most mages carried spellbooks filled with different spellforms and their descriptions. In order to cast a spell they didn't have memorized, they had to sort through their spellbooks to find the spellform. Not very useful in battle, though most mages weren't battlemages.

So being able to construct spells on the fly had some pretty clear advantages in versatility. Still, the sheer difficulty of doing the task was daunting- most spellform crafters didn't even try, instead creating new spells in shielded labs in case they went wrong, carefully testing and preparing them before selling them.

Alustin apparently expected far, far more from Hugh than he'd ever realized.

Hugh also looked a bit into enchanting- there was definitely quite a bit of overlap between the two. Enchanting, however, was a whole different kind of complication, because the runes and glyphs used in enchanting were a specialized type of spellform designed to work on a physical object, rather than via a mage- glyph and rune spellforms had to be drawn very, very differently. Not to mention the mana conducting tolerances of the materials being crafted had to be factored into their crafting, and…

Enchanting looked fascinating, but Hugh wanted to stick to trying to master just one discipline absurdly beyond his skill level for now.

Still, these experiments with his levitation spell alone showed Hugh exactly how far he had to go, and he redoubled his efforts at his studies. One major concern, however, was that he was learning spellform crafting at the cantrip stage, rather than as a fully attuned mage- he wasn't sure if there would be any important differences between the two.

Alustin, when asked, laughed. "I was wondering when you'd ask that! The answer is no- even most high level spells involve quite a bit of unattuned mana, and cantrips aren't actually entirely unattuned. Your basic levitation spell uses mana tinged with gravity and force attunements, and your basic fire starting spell uses fire tinged mana."

"So what's the point of attunements, then?" Hugh said.

"The simplest answer is that without attunements," Alustin said, "you can only provide slightly attuned mana to a spell, not the deeply attuned mana that spellforms for deep attunements need. You can use unattuned mana to light tinder for a campfire, but you can't throw a fireball with it."

"So developing my spellcrafting now…"

"Will most certainly apply after you contract with a magical entity and attune, yes. Speaking of which, do you have any more candidates for us to look at?"

CHAPTER TEN

THE LAIR REVEALED

HUGH carefully added the last restriction line to the spellform in his mind's eye, and oh so carefully channeled the mana into it, and... He held his breath as the head sized stone sphere, covered in chalk markings, hovered up into the air about three feet.

"Yes!" he said.

Talia rolled her eyes. "You levitated another rock. We've seen you do it a thousand times at this point."

Hugh grinned. "Throw some dreamfire at it."

Talia gave him a skeptical look. They were in one of the student practice chambers. Talia was taking a break from her training to refill her mana reservoirs, while Godrick and Sabae sparred on the other side of the room.

"Why would I do that?" Talia asked.

"Just try it," Hugh insisted with a grin.

Talia rolled her eyes at him, but stood up. Almost leisurely, she lobbed a fist size ball of dreamfire at the sphere.

The sphere dodged upwards, letting the fireball pass below it. The dreamfire slammed against the stone walls of the room, which were enchanted to prevent damage from spells- at least any spells students could cast.

Talia narrowed her eyes, then glared at Hugh.

"So you made a spell that lets you personally control the height of the sphere? You could have practiced that without bugging me."

Hugh grinned. "Nope. Try again."

Talia launched another fireball, and the sphere dodged to the left, narrowly avoiding being hit. Talia glared at it, then launched a pair of fist sized fireballs- one straight at it, one above it.

The sphere dodged downwards.

Talia growled, then let loose a veritable storm of projectiles.

The sphere dodged every single one, never moving more than a foot from its original location.

At this point, Godrick and Sabae had stopped sparring to watch. Talia was actually working up a sweat, and her rate of fire had dropped significantly. Finally she stopped and whirled on Hugh.

"What did you do to that thing? It's jumping like a man who just fell in a snowmelt stream."

Hugh grinned even wider, then hurled an acorn sized pebble at the sphere. It hit the sphere without the sphere trying to dodge at all. "I warded it. Whenever the ward detects dream mana approaching it, it sends out a directional mana pulse. Then I created a levitation spell set to react to those pulses, so that the sphere dodges dreamfire accordingly. The spell then brings the sphere back to the midpoint."

Talia stared at him again, then turned to face the sphere again. She launched a single dreamfire bolt at the sphere. Hugh watched smugly, convinced that there was no way she'd hit.

The dreamfire bolt headed straight for the sphere. It swiftly dodged out of the way, only for the dreamfire bolt to simply… stop. It hung in midair, right at the centerpoint where the sphere usually hung. The sphere, having completed its outward movement, simply swung back into the center. Right into the hanging dreamfire.

Hugh's jaw dropped as he watched a chunk of the stone sphere seem to sprout into vines and then wither away, leaving a fist sized hole in the sphere. Talia grinned, then launched several more dreamfire bolts at the sphere.

All of them hit. The ward spellform Hugh had drawn on it in had been broken by the first bolt, so it was no longer sending out the directional pulses. With a slightly embarrassed look, Hugh stopped channeling mana into the spell, and the broken remains of the sphere dropped to the ground.

"Nice try, Hugh," Talia said, grinning.

Hugh sighed, then went back to his assigned practice. He was supposed to be combining multiple basic cantrip effects into a single spellform. Thus far he'd topped out at three- he could levitate an item, make it glow, and make it emit a noise. He hadn't managed any other combination of cantrip effects, however.

It'd been weeks since he'd successfully cast his first levitation spell. At this point, he could replicate all of the basic cantrips students were expected to know at will, as well as doing a lot of basic modifications of them on the fly.

Which, given the limited power of cantrips, left him functionally months behind most of the other students. Until he got a warlock contract with a decently powerful magical entity, he wouldn't be able to really start catching up with the other students. Everyone else at this point was already well on their way into learning to attune.

Hugh was getting more and more stressed out as the labyrinth test approached. Admittedly, everyone else was stressing out about it as well, but at least everyone else on the team had real magic to contribute.

Still, even with that stress hanging over his head, Hugh was happier than he could ever remember being since his parents had died.

He'd shared the full details of his mage situation and being a warlock with Godrick eventually, and much to his surprise, Godrick found the whole thing extremely exciting. He'd actually started helping Hugh find possible contract partners. He hadn't told Godrick much about the rest of his past, but Godrick seemed to respect his privacy. He wasn't sure how much the others had told Godrick about their stories.

Hugh found himself spending less and less time in his hidden lair, which he still hadn't told anyone about, and more and more time with Talia, Sabae, and Godrick. The four trained together for the labyrinth daily now, and many of their reading assignments were now on the nature of the labyrinth, accounts of the inside, and dangers commonly found there.

Rhodes hadn't tried anything in weeks, which was a lovely change as well. Of course, Hugh was seldom alone and vulnerable anymore.

It was on a Fourthday evening after dinner that Hugh's lair was discovered. He'd split ways with the others after dinner and doubled back into the library, declining Godrick's invitation to the group to spend the evening out on one of the balconies watching sandships dock.

Hugh had taken his usual convoluted route back to his lair, dodging past origami golems and librarians, but to his later chagrin, wasn't paying that much attention to his surroundings. He ducked behind the bookshelf his door lay behind- the contents of which he'd replaced with dull accounts of tax law and defunct trade agreements, to further disinterest passerby in looking at his shelf- and through his heavily warded door.

He'd sat down at his desk to start working on his newest projects when his alarm wards went off, making his glow crystals start flashing off and on. There was a loud banging noise as some of the more active wards went off, and someone started cursing.

Hugh realized that someone had followed him back to his room and panicked. His wards were set to go off if someone tried to open his door. It must have been Rhodes. He'd just been biding his time, waiting for Hugh to be alone and inattentive.

Hugh scrambled for the window, considering trying to climb outside. He hadn't even opened it more than partway when he remembered that his window opened onto a sheer rock face. He panicked, frantically looking around his room for some way to escape, when he recognized the cursing outside.

Hugh sighed. He was still shaking a bit, but walked open to the door and opened it. "Talia."

Talia glared at him. She was lying on top of the bookshelf that had hidden his door, which had been knocked over by his wards going off. She was bleeding pretty badly from a cut over her eye, and it looked like she'd have quite a few nasty bruises soon.

He reached down to help her up, and she smacked his hand away.

"This is how you greet a friend, is it?" she demanded.

"I… I didn't know you were coming," Hugh said.

"No, because you never trusted us enough to tell us where you live," Talia snapped. Her face was growing red with anger.

She'd risen up onto her feet, and looked like she wanted to punch him. Hugh's stomach curdled a little bit. It wasn't that he didn't trust his friends, he'd just somehow never gotten around to telling them about his room. It was a little paranoid, maybe, but it wasn't about them, he knew they would never…

"What are you just standing there like a great lump for? Not even going to apologize for almost killing me?"

Hugh tried to say something, but nothing came out of his mouth. Talia growled and shoved him. Hugh went toppling down to the ground.

"I thought we were friends," Talia said.

By the time he'd stood up, she was gone.

It took Hugh several hours to finish picking the bookshelf back up and re-shelve the books.

He spent a while trying to work on his new project, but couldn't keep focused. He switched over to trying to browse the Bestiary more, but eventually just gave up and went to bed after spending hours reading and rereading the entry on Kraggoth Claw-Mane, some sort of insane chimera imprisoned below the capital of the Havath Dominion.

He didn't even bother to take off his clothes when he got in bed, and barely slept that night. He kept having nightmares about forming his pact with some sort of shadowy monster who demanded Hugh's friends as the price for his power.

Fifthday was even worse. A few times he tried to make himself leave his lair, but he never made it farther than a few dozen feet away before his heart would start racing and he felt like he needed to throw up. He didn't even go to the dining hall to get food- not, that is, that he felt hungry. He spent most of the day in bed, drifting in and out of shallow dozes. He only left to go to the restroom and drink water from the bathroom in the stacks- and even with how few people used it, he was still especially careful not to run into anyone.

The only thing that Hugh accomplished that day was rebuilding his wards. This time he made sure to build in exemptions for his friends.

If Talia even wanted to be his friend anymore.

He'd finally made his first friends and now he'd ruined it. Talia wouldn't want to see him anymore and everyone else would take her side and…

Part of Hugh knew that his anxieties were completely unjustified. Talia dealt with her problems head on, she didn't scheme or gossip. She'd most likely just tell everyone else she got in a fight.

Most of Hugh, however, was more than ready to believe the worst, no matter how ridiculous.

Hugh didn't dream that night.

On Sixthday morning, Hugh sat on his floor under the window, knees under his chin, staring at the door. He'd turned down his glowcrystals and closed his curtain, so his room was dark as night. He knew he should get out of bed and go to morning training, but the thought of leaving his room was entirely too much for him. He just kept replaying the conversation with Talia in his head, cursing himself for being so incompetent with other people. Classtime eventually came and went, as did lunch.

Hugh had just slipped back into a light sleep, still sitting under the window, when someone knocked on his door. His eyes shot open, and his heart started pounding a mile a minute. He didn't move. Nothing else happened for a moment, and Hugh started to try and convince himself that it had just been a dream.

"I know you're in there, Hugh."

It was Talia.

Hugh opened his mouth to say something, but nothing came out.

"Hugh…"

He heard a light thunk on the door, like someone hitting their forehead against the wood.

"I'm sure you've upgraded your wards even more, and they'll blast me across the library this time, but I'm coming in."

Hugh's heart was hammering even harder.

The door opened. Talia was standing on the other side, arm shielding her face in preparation for a blast that never came. She had a bandage on her forehead, and several bruises on her arms. She slowly lowered her arm, and Hugh quickly looked at the floor so he wouldn't meet her gaze.

Talia stood in the doorway for a few moments, her eyes adjusting to the dim light that made it in past the bookshelf. After a few moments, she took a couple steps into the room.

"I built exemptions into the ward for you three this time," Hugh whispered.

He heard Talia sigh, then she turned up the glowcrystals in his room. He curled up a little more.

Talia shut the door, then slowly walked over to Hugh. She stood there silently for a minute, then lowered herself to a sitting position on the floor in front of him.

Neither said anything for a few minutes. Finally, Talia spoke up.

"I'm sorry, Hugh."

Hugh didn't say anything.

"It might have bugged me that you hid where you lived from us, but I should have talked to you instead of following you. I violated your privacy. I tried to open your door even though I knew how private you were and how good you were with wards. Then, rather than own up to my own idiocy, I got mad at you instead."

She didn't say anything for a moment.

"I calmed down and felt like an ass within the hour, but I was too embarrassed to come back here. I was completely convinced that you were probably furious at me, so I spent all of yesterday training and avoiding everyone. This morning, I had to drag myself to training, and when you weren't there… I felt awful. The others asked if I knew where you were, since they hadn't heard from you since Fourthday dinner."

Talia paused again.

"I was a coward and told them you hadn't been feeling well. They all bought it, except maybe Alustin, but he didn't say anything." She sighed. "I couldn't focus at all today. I slipped away after training was done to come talk to you, but I must have stood out there for an hour before I found the nerve to knock."

She didn't say anything for a few minutes, just sat there.

"Please say something, Hugh."

Hugh wanted to say something, but couldn't even manage to lift his head from behind his knees.

"You… you probably want me to leave. I'll… I'm sorry, I shouldn't have come." Talia stood up to leave. As she turned to go out the door, Hugh finally worked up the nerve to lift up his head and speak.

"Wait."

Talia stopped, and slowly turned around. Hugh stared at her for a moment, tears running down his cheeks, then looked back down at the ground.

"Don't go."

Talia stood there for a moment looking at him, then slowly walked over and slid down the wall to sit next to him. She wrapped her arm around him, and didn't say anything as he cried.

Hugh and Talia must have sat there quietly for at least an hour before he finally managed to get his thoughts in some form of order.

"I thought you didn't want to be friends anymore," he said weakly.

Talia glared at him. "Don't be an idiot, of course I…". She stopped midsentence and grinned, though there wasn't any real humor to it. "I came here to apologize, and end up yelling again. I'm really not the best at apologizing."

She squeezed him tight around the shoulders. "I was just angry and being a huge pile of goat droppings towards you. Of course I still want to be friends. If, that is, you still want to…"

Hugh nodded firmly, and Talia sighed in relief. Neither of them spoke for a moment.

"Something in me's broken, Talia," he said. "I… can't stand up to Rhodes when he bullies me. I'm in constant terror that you three will stop wanting to be friends with me. We have one argument and I go almost catatonic for two days."

Talia started to say something, then paused. "Hugh, you don't have to answer if you don't want to, but… when you told us your story that day in the library, you left out Rhodes' bullying. Was there… was there more you were leaving out too?"

Hugh didn't move or say anything for a moment, and then nodded his head.

Talia's forehead wrinkled in concern. "Hugh, your aunt and uncle… no one… did anything… to you, you know…" She sounded extremely uncomfortable.

"Nothing like that," Hugh said. "No one ever… nothing like that." He took a deep, raggedy breath. "But it was a lot worse than I let on that day, yeah. And… I've never really had any friends before. I was always pretty shy and bad with people, even before…"

"Do you want to talk about it?" Talia said.

Hugh shook his head. "Not… not right now."

Hugh was happy when Talia pretended not to notice that he was crying again, but he was grateful when she squeezed him even harder in a hug.

Once Hugh had collected himself again, and wiped his face on his sleeve, he sat up a bit. He gave Talia a weak smile. "Would you like the tour?"

Talia grinned. "Sure."

Hugh pushed himself to his feet. "This over here is my bed. That's my desk, and over here," he said, pulling open his curtains, "is my window."

He popped the window panes open as well. Talia gasped. The sun was just going down on the horizon, and the dunes of the Endless Erg hand been painted in lurid sunset shades. A sandship was just pulling into Skyhold's port out of the Endless Erg, and a flock of drakes was playing in the air over it.

"Hugh… this is… this is…" Talia punched him in the shoulder.

"Ow! What was that for?" Hugh said.

"I'm jealous, this view is amazing! I doubt Rhodes even has a room with a window, let alone a view like this. How'd you find this place?"

Hugh told her the story of how he'd first met Alustin, then eventually found this room. He told her about the Choosing, and how he was sure that Alustin must have magicked in the bed somehow.

Then he showed her his new project. She grinned wickedly when she saw it. "Now that's going to come in handy during our labyrinth test." Hugh started to tell her more about it, only to be interrupted by his stomach growling.

"When's the last time you've eaten, Hugh?"

Hugh, embarrassed to say he hadn't eaten since before their fight, looked at the ground.

"The dining hall should still be open, if you want to join me," Talia said. "I haven't eaten anything since lunch, so I'm starving."

Hugh nodded.

Talia chuckled, and turned towards the door. She paused before going out, though. "You should get changed before we go. Don't take this the wrong way, but you smell really, really bad. I'll just wait outside your door for you."

She shut the door behind her.

Hugh sniffed at his shirt and winced.

CHAPTER ELEVEN

BIRTHDAY

TALIA, to Hugh's gratitude, never told anyone about how she found his lair, and as far as anyone else was concerned, he'd just been sick.

He did, however, make sure to finally invite the others to visit his lair. It quickly became one of their favorite places to hang out. They smuggled several armchairs and a coffee table into his lair so there'd be enough room for everyone to fit, and Hugh often had to boot his friends off of his desk when he needed to do homework.

Hugh had thought it would be stressful to have that much less privacy, but it was actually really nice. He was able to relax in his room in a way he wasn't everywhere else.

He did, however, make sure to upgrade the wards to help keep noise coming from inside the room muted. Neither Godrick nor Talia was the best at the whole keeping quiet thing.

It was precisely two weeks before the summer solstice when Hugh got woken up by his friends all jumping on top of his bed. Thankfully, Godrick had the good sense not to jump on him, though Talia and Sabae were heavy enough.

"Happy birthday!" shouted the three together.

"Bwuh," was the most cogent thing Hugh could muster. He eventually managed to boot the three of them out of his room long enough for him to change, but they were back in the instant he was done.

"Presents!" said Talia, hurling a cloth wrapped bundle at Hugh. It bounced off his chest before he caught it. Whatever it was, it was metal and heavy for its size. He rubbed the spot on his chest where it had struck him before unwrapping it. Inside the bundle was a dagger in a leather sheath. The pommel of the dagger, decorated with patterns that resembled flames, had been what had struck him in the chest.

"Did ye just throw a knife at him?" Godrick asked, grinning. Talia kicked him in the shin.

"It's a Clan Castis dagger," Talia said. "It's not enchanted or anything, but it's well made and sturdy. And we only give them out to friends of the clan, so be careful with it!"

"I will," Hugh said, grinning.

Talia poked him hard in the stomach.

"Seriously, take care of it. You can show this knife to anyone in Clan Castis, and they'll be honor-bound to help you. Though you can expect a lot of questions about where you got it afterwards."

Hugh looked at the dagger, then bowed a little over it. "I'll take good care of it, Talia. This is a better gift than I deserve." She nodded, looking a little embarrassed.

"My turn," Sabae said, elbowing the other two aside. She handed Hugh her present. It was a paper wrapped bundle about the size of a pillow. Hugh started to tear it open, then grinned, picked up the knife Talia had given him, and used it to cut the package open.

Inside were two books. One was a thick, leatherbound tome. Unlike Galvachren's Bestiary, however, it was still well within normal book size. There was an adjustable leather strap running from either end of the binding- the book was clearly meant to be worn over the shoulder. There was also a strap with a latch holding the book closed, which Hugh undid to reveal all blank pages. There were several quills and a couple sticks of drawing charcoal strapped inside one cover. A pocket sewn onto the shoulder strap turned out to have a compact inkpot stored in it.

"My family sent me this spellbook, but since I'm learning formless casting, it's not much use to me," Sabae said. "It's a lot bigger than normal spellbooks, so I figured it would be handy for you to take notes in and plan out spells."

Hugh grinned and flipped through its pages. A normal spellbook was small enough to fit in the pocket of a pair of trousers, and merely contained one or two spellform diagrams per page, with some details about each. It was meant to be used quickly. This book, however, would be absolutely perfect for planning out spells in detail.

He picked up the second book. This lizard-skin bound volume was small enough to fit in his trouser pockets- about the size of a more conventional spellbook. He flipped it open, expecting to see it blank, and instead was greeted with intricate and absurdly cramped handwriting and diagrams. As he browsed through it, he realized that the whole book was filled with notes about constructing wards on a massive scale- big enough to encompass a fortress or even a city.

He looked up in shock. "This is…"

Sabae was grinning. "That was my great-grandmother's notebook. She specialized in wards, and could build stormwards powerful enough to protect a ship at sea or even shield an entire city from a hurricane."

"I can't take this," Hugh said. "This sort of thing is priceless."

"My family has already made copies of it, so they were happy to send it when I asked them to. They also told me to tell you that if you ever get good enough to make wards like this, you've always got a job with them."

Hugh swallowed, not knowing what to say. Sabae grinned, and gave him a hug.

When she stepped back, Talia elbowed her in the side. "Of course you've got to go and one-up me with a better present. Now I just have to hope Godrick one-ups you."

Godrick looked a little embarrassed to hand Hugh his present. "Ah didn't even wrap mine."

Godrick's present was a hollow glass marble. The glass was clear and etched with complex spellforms.

"Ah managed ta convince one of tha enchanting instructors ta help me make it in exchange for helping him make himself one. Only worked thanks to mah scent attunment."

"What does it do?" Sabae asked. Hugh had been trying to puzzle out the spellforms etched into the marble himself, but they were fiendishly complex, and considerably different than the spellforms he was familiar with.

"It eats scents," Godrick said. "Rub it in yer armpits and it'll… eat the scent, make ye smell better."

Hugh blushed a little, but grinned. He definitely had a little bit of an issue with getting a bit ripe-smelling, so this would be incredibly handy.

Talia hugged Godrick. "Definitely my favorite present Hugh's gotten today."

Hugh grinned and made a rude gesture at Talia, but hugged Godrick as well.

Then something occurred to him. "Wait, how did you know it was my birthday today? I don't think I ever told you all about it."

"Alustin told us," Sabae said.

Of course he had.

"So we were planning to drag you to breakfast and then go spend the day watching sandships at the port, if you were interested," Sabae said.

That did sound pretty fun to Hugh. He hadn't been back down to the port since he'd arrived at Skyhold. But...

"That does sound fun, but I have a better idea."

"Are ye sure this is ah good idea?" Godrick asked again. Despite his formidable size, he was by far the most nervous of the four of them.

"Nope, but it's a fun one!" Talia said.

Hugh rolled his eyes. "It'll be fine, Godrick."

Hugh, in his explorations of the stacks, had discovered something interesting- a door leading into the deeper levels of the library, the ones far below the levels Alustin had given them permission to enter. To the levels that were forbidden to students. Though, really, the door wasn't the interesting part- there were a large number of doors in the stacks that led to those levels. What made this door interesting was that it had apparently been forgotten about by the library staff, and the wards on it allowed to slowly decay.

The fact that the door was on the lowest, most dimly lit level in the stacks, in the back of a store-room packed close to the ceiling with books, the entrance itself of which was partially hidden behind another shelf probably contributed to it being forgotten. They actually had to climb over the crates full of old textbooks and the like to get to the door. Hugh was surprised he'd found it in the first place, even given all the hours he spent exploring the stacks. He'd just trusted his gut.

With all the time Hugh had spent practicing his wards, he'd picked up a decent bit about ward-breaking as well. In retrospect, all that Rhodes had probably needed to disrupt the wards on his old room was simply a sharp knife to cut the design, along with a simple spell disruption cantrip. Wardbreaking wasn't nearly so difficult as their instructors had let on at first.

That is, at least for basic wards. This ward was a different beast entirely. If it hadn't been ignored and decaying for decades, there was no way Hugh could have attempted to break it. It was hellishly more complex than anything Hugh had ever attempted himself. Instead of the simple chalk he used for his wards, it was worked into a brass band set into the floor in front of the door. And instead of just being a one-off defense, it had multiple layers- a permanent physical shield, among others.

Hugh carefully sketched the ward patterns on the first pages of his new spellbook as the others watched. It was, Hugh thought, a pretty fitting first thing to draw in his new notebook.

The others had been surprisingly patient so far, just sitting on the piles of books filling the storeroom. Well, Sabae being patient wasn't a surprise, but Talia being patient definitely was.

Hugh grinned. The ward had looked nauseatingly complex at first, but at its base it operated the same as any of the wards Hugh had ever drawn- a sequence of spellforms bound together in a sequence, with conditions outlined in the spellforms that would detail when the ward would be activated and what effects would result. If Hugh tried to simply sever the ward, it would be set off.

On the other hand, if Hugh was careful, he could certainly modify the conditions for setting off the ward.

Hugh gave his diagrams in his new journal one last careful look and pulled a stick of chalk out of his pocket. He carefully set to work on the ward.

"Are you supposed to be drawing off of the brass, Hugh?" Talia said. "Doesn't seem like a good idea to me, wards are supposed to be in a straight line or circle."

Well, she had been patient for a while, at least.

"Wards don't have to be any shape, so long as they're continuous," Hugh said. "Drawing them in straight lines or circles is mostly just convention, along with being two of the most convenient shapes for wards."

"Mostly?" Godrick said nervously.

"There are cases where the shape matters more, but this isn't one of them," Hugh said.

Talia started to say something else, but Sabae hushed her. Talia stuck out her tongue at Sabae.

Hugh shook his head and went back to adding the additional spellforms to the ward. They'd essentially act as a bypass, redirecting the flow of mana away from the spellforms that would prevent Hugh and his friends from passing. The wards would still be operational, they just weren't worried about students passing through anymore. Of course, if the ward hadn't decayed, Hugh could never have gotten close enough to do this.

Very, very carefully, Hugh added one final connecting line, and… the chalk began to glow as the mana passed through it. It dimmed almost immediately, but Hugh could sense the mana was moving through it correctly.

"We're good to go! Be careful not to step on the chalk, that'll disrupt the bypass," Hugh said.

"It's really safe?" Godrick asked.

"Probably," Hugh said.

"Probably?" Godrick said.

"Probably," said Hugh, and opened the door.

CHAPTER TWELVE

THE TRUE LIBRARY

On the other side was… another storeroom, this one full of bookbinding supplies. Hugh shouldn't have been surprised- both sides of the door would really have to be out of the way in order for it to have been neglected. Hugh still felt his heart start beating faster as he stepped through the door, however.

Talia was so close on his heels that she almost pushed him through the door. Sabae followed soon after, with Godrick hesitantly taking the rear. Hugh pushed through the piles of bookbinding materials to the door out of the storeroom. Cautiously, he pushed it open, and then gasped in shock.

Hugh had expected the restricted section of the library to resemble the upper library. He was so, so very wrong.

The room they found themselves in was by far the largest room Hugh had ever seen in his life. The restricted section of the library was roughly cubical, and must have been at least four or five miles to a side. The room looked considerably bigger than the mountain Skyhold was built into. The walls were entirely lined with books, with a balcony winding completely around at around one story intervals. The balcony they were on was close to the top. If that had been all the books in the room, it would have been more books than Hugh had ever imagined even existed.

It wasn't even close to all the books in the room.

Immense stone bookshelves, hundreds of feet high, floated in neat, orderly rows in the huge space in the center of the room. Floating islands drifting near them had bookshelves, reading rooms, and in one case, what looked to be a thriving forest on top. Hugh spotted a couple of cubes with bookshelves on all the sides- including the bottom. There were a few paths leading out into the center room, stepping stones scattered here and there- but Hugh couldn't see a way to get to most of the floating structures.

Thousands upon thousands of origami golems were visible, tending to tasks all over the library. Books seemed to frequently decide to fly about on their own- some simply hovering through the air, others flapping their covers and pages like wings.

All of this was lit by a profusion of glowcrystals, floating wisps of light, and even a tiny sun orbiting the floating island with the trees on it, but the room was so huge the overall impression was one of general gloom and dimness.

Hugh silently walked forwards to the edge of the balcony. When he looked downwards, he couldn't even see the bottom of the library, except for a blue-white, unearthly glow coming from far below. The others silently stepped alongside him.

"How… how is this even possible?" Sabae said. "This is bigger than Skyhold. Bigger that the mountain Skyhold is built into. There can't be this many books in the entire world."

No one answered her. They all just stood there silently for ages. Hugh could see quite a few librarians, but the closest one had to be at least a half mile away.

"So much better than tha port," Godrick whispered finally.

Talia elbowed Hugh.

"What was that for?" Hugh said. "I swear, being friends with you is at least one third collecting new bruises."

"Look, an index node!" Talia said, not seeming to hear Hugh. Or choosing to ignore him.

The foursome strode over to the index node. The blank-paged volume was considerably larger than the index nodes in the upper library.

"What should we look up?" Sabae asked.

No one said anything for a moment, then Talia stepped up to the book. She picked up the quill beside it and simply wrote "dreamfire."

Nothing happened for a moment, and then in precise, bold letters, printed out a single sentence.

What about dreamfire?

Hugh stared silently at the book for a moment, then looked at Talia. She stared back at him. She slowly looked at the others, who just stared at her as well. She turned back to the book, and begin writing in it again.

What are some advanced dreamfire manifestation techniques?

What sort of techniques?

Combat techniques.

Nothing happened for a moment, then the words vanished off the page, it tore itself out of the book, and drifted up into the air. It revolved a few times, then began folding itself. Within seconds, a hummingbird origami golem fluttered in the air in front of them.

Talia slowly reached out to touch it, but the hummingbird shot away from her, coming to a halt twenty feet farther down the balcony. She turned to look at the rest of them, and then they all set out as one. Every time they approached the hummingbird it would dart off again to wait for them farther down. After about half a mile of walking, the hummingbird darted over to the shelf, where it hovered in front of a book with a fraying green cloth cover.

Talia reached out to the book. The instant her finger brushed it, the hummingbird darted off towards the nearest index node, where it unfolded itself and inserted itself into the book.

Talia pulled the book off the shelf. It looked like it would fall apart if anyone even looked at it for too long, but it was apparently much sturdier than it looked. The pages were lined with hard to read, handwritten text. Talia was slowly flipping through the book when the four noticed something. The letters were starting to glow with the purple-green light of dreamfire itself.

"Ah think ye should close tha book, Talia," Godrick said. Tiny tongues of dreamfire had actually begun to lick up from the letters at this point.

Talia slammed it shut. Hugh noticed that many of the threads that composed the cover were actually glowing, in patterns that looked suspiciously like spellforms.

No one said anything for a moment.

"How many of these books do you think also do stuff like that?" Sabae said.

"Quite ah few, ah'd guess," Godrick said. He shuffled nervously. "Ah reckon ah know why it's forbidden ta students."

A thought struck Hugh, and he strode over to the nearest index node. He picked up the quill on its stand, dipped it into the ink, and began to write.

How many books are in here?

The Index took a second to reply.

Unknown.

Then how do you keep track of all the books?

I only track the books that have been indexed.

How many books have been indexed?

Twelve million, four hundred thousand, seven hundred and sixty two.

As Hugh and the others watched, the sixty two became a sixty three, then a sixty four.

Where do all the books come from?

The Index paused for another moment.

Information restricted. Reason for query?

Hugh blinked, then quickly wrote again.

Just curious, it's not important.

The book didn't respond to that.

Hugh leaned back and looked at the others.

"Well, we know at least a few of them come from Alustin and the other librarian errants," Sabae said.

"Can ah try?" Godrick said.

Hugh passed him the quill.

Books on using scent attunements in battle. Preferably books that aren't booby trapped and are safe to handle.

How strong is said search preference?

Exceptionally strong.

The page tore itself out of the book, folded itself into a dragonfly, and shot off fifty feet down the shelves.

"I think we should split up and each meet back here in an hour," Hugh said. "There's more here than we could read in a lifetime."

Everyone nodded in agreement, eager to explore. Godrick headed off after the dragonfly.

Talia quickly stepped up to the book, and repeated her query on dreamfire- this time, however, making sure to include the bit about not being booby trapped. She then left in the same direction as Godrick, in pursuit of a tiny paper dragon.

Sabae stepped up next.

Do you have anything written by members of the Kaen Das family?

Yes. Fourteen private journals, three training manuals, a significant collection of personal correspondence, and an unknown volume that can only be opened by blood descendants of the Kaen Das family.

Sabae looked at Hugh in shock, then turned back to the book.

Take me to the unknown volume, please.

The page tore itself out of the book and folded itself into an origami fish, which promptly swam the opposite way from Godrick and Talia. Sabae turned to follow it.

Hugh stared at the index node for a time. What did he want to ask it? He was already overloaded with potential contract partners with Galvachren's Bestiary alone, so not for more potential options… Hmm.

Directions for completing a warlock pact.

Alustin had taught him a lot about warlockery, but he'd refused to share the spellforms to complete a warlock pact so far.

The page tore itself out of the book and folded itself into a tiny balloon, with a basket dangling below it. Hugh followed it for a time, until it abruptly made a left turn.

Off the edge of the balcony, into midair.

As it did so, a series of stepping stones flew from out of the depths of the room, forming a narrow footpath. The stepping stones floated independently, each about a short pace apart. Hugh gulped. He knelt down, reaching out to touch the first one. It felt absolutely stable, like it were embedded in an actual floor.

Then he reached around it and below it. There didn't appear to be anything holding it up.

Hugh stood up, and slowly rested his foot on the first stepping stone. He put more and more weight on it, but it never moved.

He pulled his foot back, turned around, and walked back to the nearest index node.

If I were to rip out pages before writing on them, could I write on them later and still get directions?

Yes, though it would only be necessary if you were going into a section of the library with few Index access nodes.

Hugh looked back out at the footpath.

He tore out four pages and tucked them into the back of his new spellbook, then latched it shut again. He carefully adjusted it to make sure it was secure over his shoulder, then walked back to the stepping stones.

Hugh took a deep breath, and carefully stepped out onto the path.

It was… a little easier than Hugh had expected. The stepping stones were decently large, and comfortably close together.

Unfortunately, Hugh still had to look down at his path to make sure he didn't fall, so he was staring down the miles tall drop the whole time. He crossed above several floating islands, wound between a massive pair of shelves filled with engraved clay tablets, and had to stop to let a flock of grimoires fly by. And the whole time, the drop loomed below him. Distantly below him he could see that blue-white glow. As he stared at it, he swore he could see something shifting and moving inside of it.

Abruptly, the path of stepping stones simply came to a halt against the side of a massive floating bookshelf. It must have extended two hundred feet above and below Hugh. At the end of the path the stepping stones had carefully organized themselves into a broad, level platform. Hugh gratefully stepped onto it, and eyed the origami balloon. It was floating in front of a rather bland, boring looking volume.

Hugh pulled it off the shelf.

The 74 Uses of Dragon Dung.

That… didn't seem quite right.

Hugh pulled the book off the shelf, but the balloon stayed right where it was. Behind where *The 74 Uses of Dragon Dung* had sat was a thin black volume. Hugh pulled it out, putting *The 74 Uses of Dragon Dung* back on the shelf. The instant he touched the black volume, the balloon flew away.

He opened the black volume to its first page.

In a well practiced, easily readable handwriting, the author had penned a short warning.

This volume is strictly forbidden from being read, except by those ranked at least Bishop or higher in the Church of The Eternal Heavenly Flame. In it are detailed some of the foulest, most pernicious pieces of magic ever devised. This volume only exists in order to offer ways to defeat these spells, in the off chance these heresies ever resurface and must be confronted again. Be warned, the spells grow progressively more deranged towards the end of the book. The original scribe was driven quite insane by recording them, and ended up having to be committed to an asylum.

The warning was followed by a table of contents. The warlock pact spell was the third in the book, between something called Blisterpox Curse and a truth spell that apparently burned any lies spoken into the skin of the victim for the rest of their life.

Hugh wondered if it was significant that he'd never heard of the Church of the Eternal Heavenly Flame before.

He flipped to the warlock pact, expecting to see some hideously convoluted spellform.

It was fairly convoluted, but it was also surprisingly familiar. It was essentially structured similarly to a ward. It had places to write out the contract, as well as two blank spaces that the signers of the contract would touch at the same time to complete the ward and seal the pact. He did note that, indeed, the scribe who'd copied this spell down was different than the one who penned the warning.

Hugh pulled out his spellbook and quickly copied the warlock pact into it, along with all the relevant details. He made sure to hide the pact far towards the back of the book, so someone casually opening the book would be less likely to see it.

He probably wouldn't need the spell before this summer, when Alustin was supposed to take him to find a contract partner, but he wanted it just in case.

He finished copying the warlock pact down, and resisted the urge to peek farther back into the book. No sense in tempting fate. He tucked the slim volume back behind *The 74 Uses of Dragon Dung.*

Hugh pulled out one of the pages he'd pulled out of the index node, and requested a book on the principles of constructing large-scale wards, like the ones in Sabae's great grandmother's journal.

The journey wasn't nearly so bad this time- most of the route took him back along the path he'd followed before, merely branching off about halfway back, then returning. The book he found was a dry volume on mana loss rates and determining factors in ward efficiency. It didn't look entertaining, but it certainly looked useful.

He continued to keep his eyes down on the stepping stones the whole way back again, trying to keep down the vertigo. When he finally reached the balcony again, he grabbed the railing and took a deep breath. It felt really, really good to be standing on ground he couldn't see through.

Someone cleared their throat. Hugh looked up.

Talia, Sabae, and Godrick all stood looking uncomfortable in front of him. Between Hugh and his friends, however, stood Alustin, who raised his eyebrow at Hugh.

"Oops," said Hugh.

CHAPTER THIRTEEN

PUNISHMENT AND PREPARATION

ALUSTIN did not look amused.

"So whose idea was this little trip?" he said.

"Entirely mine," said Hugh immediately. "They only came along because it was my birthday, and I really wanted to do this."

Alustin arched his eyebrow.

"How interesting. I have four students all trying to take credit for the same plan."

Hugh opened his mouth, then shut it again.

Alustin sighed. "Well, at least no one can claim you aren't loyal to one another. I can, however, claim that you're all idiots for coming here in the first place. There is a very, very good reason why this room, the Grand Library, is forbidden to all but full mages. The Grand Library kills an average of two hundred people a decade, the vast majority of which are fully trained mages."

Talia mouthed "two hundred?" in shock.

"This part of the library is horrendously dangerous. It's the largest known collection of enchanted books in existence. Even many of the non-enchanted volumes are highly dangerous. Some contain information that can drive you mad, others are actually constructed of poisonous plants, for whatever insane reason."

Hugh thought guiltily of the book he'd found the warlock ritual in, but didn't say anything.

"How did you even get in here?" Alustin said.

No one said anything for a moment, then Hugh spoke up. "I reworked one of the wards."

Alustin stared at him for a second, then narrowed his eyes. "Don't lie to me, Hugh. How did you get in here? Did you steal a librarian's key?"

"I'm not lying!" Hugh said. "I really reworked one of the wards."

"He did," Godrick said defensively. "He's really good with wards."

Alustin stared at Hugh for an uncomfortably long amount of time. "Show me."

Hugh led Alustin to the storeroom door they had gotten in by. Alustin spent at least fifteen minutes staring at the ward, and at Hugh's notes. Finally, he looked up at Hugh.

"How long did you spend studying the ward?" Alustin said.

"Maybe thirty minutes?" Hugh said.

"Not even that," Sabae said.

Alustin sighed. "I'm torn between wanting to yell at you for messing with a ward that could have killed you and being impressed that you managed to bypass the ward at all."

"Kill me?" Hugh said. "Those spellforms should have just hurled me back, right?"

Alustin looked at him seriously. "At normal ward power levels, yes. We haven't particularly covered how wards are affected by the materials they're moving through to any great degree yet, however. Even as degraded as this ward is, however, with the power supplied by the library, you would have been mashed to a pulp."

Hugh felt a little sick.

Alustin sighed, then gestured them all out of the storeroom and back into the immense library room. "I'll send some librarians to take a look at this and restore the ward. And to safely remove your changes. In the meantime… Let's see what you all got."

Everyone looked blankly at Alustin.

"Your book selections, let's see them."

The four sheepishly handed over their books.

He spent a few moments browsing their selections. "Hugh, excellent choice, if a bit advanced. Let me know when you run across anything you don't understand in here- which will be often. That being said, what provoked you to look into large-scale wards? They're fiendishly difficult, and there's not a lot of demand outside some specialized applications."

Hugh told him about Sabae's great-grandmother's journal, and the family's potential job offer. Alustin actually looked impressed at that.

"I'd definitely like to take a look at that journal myself, if that's alright with you."

Hugh nodded, happy to talk about anything other than them trespassing.

"Onto the topic of Sabae… what on Earth possessed you to choose a book that can't be opened?"

"I can open it," Sabae said.

Sabae held out her hand. Alustin somewhat hesitantly handed the volume back. Hugh hadn't seen the book yet- the cover looked like glass or crystal, but with an actual storm bound inside. Hugh could even see the occasional bolt of lightning.

The instant Sabae touched the book, the storm drastically increased in intensity. Sabae opened it without a problem, and flipped through a few pages. Her hair appeared to be drifting in a faint breeze coming from the book, even after the pages stopped moving.

"This volume can only be opened by myself or another blood member of my family."

Alustin held out his hand. "May I take a look?"

Sabae appeared to think for a moment, then extended the open book. "Of course."

The instant Alustin reached for it, she snapped it shut and dropped it in his hand. "If, of course, you're a blood member of the Kaen Das family."

Alustin looked frustrated for a moment, then walked with the book over to the nearest index node. He spent a few moments writing in the node, then tapped on the page three times with his knuckle, and the text erased itself.

"In that case, Sabae, as much as it pains me to give an enchanted grimoire of unknown contents away, I believe this is yours, and not the library's." Alustin reluctantly handed the grimoire back to Sabae, who tucked it under her arm, face composed.

Alustin turned to Godrick, examining his volume. As he did so, Hugh noticed a self satisfied grin briefly flash across Sabae's face. "Hmm.

A perfectly reasonable choice, though I should note that the book is enchanted as well- it magnifies any scents it encounters, so be cautious with it, and don't bring it into any dining halls or restrooms."

Talia's book on dreamfire also passed muster. This one, thankfully, was not enchanted- Hugh doubted the first book on dreamfire would have passed.

"Well, at least I can't fault your choice of book selections," Alustin muttered. "So, punishments: You're all required to memorize everyone who has died or gone missing here in the Grand Library in the past decade, as well as their cause of death if it's known. It's been a relatively safe decade, we've only lost… one hundred and forty three, last time I checked."

Hugh looked out over the colossal room and gulped.

"Should… should we head somewhere else for this talk?"

Alustin grinned. "Now you're starting to respect the library properly. You should be fine so long as you stay with me and don't touch any books without asking me first. Still, though, it might be best if we do head out."

Alustin had turned to lead them out- not, Hugh noticed, by the storeroom door they'd come in by, when Talia spoke up. "How can this place be so huge? It's bigger than the entire mountain Skyhold is built into!"

"That's because this room isn't precisely inside of the mountain."

"It's an extradimensional space?" Hugh said. He'd read about those- they increased the size of internal spaces, but were notoriously challenging enchantments to pull off, and they only increased available space a little bit.

Alustin stared off into space.

"In a sense, yes. The room started off that way, but the enchantment was only going to increase its internal size by a relatively small amount. Due to… unforeseen interactions with the magic of the labyrinth, however, it ended up much larger than expected, among other effects."

"What sort of interactions?" Hugh said.

"What was this space supposed to be originally?" Sabae said.

"What kinds a' other effects?" said Godrick.

Alustin gave them a cryptic look, then started walking.

"Let's get you all out of here."

Hugh had one more question. "What was that light down near the bottom?"

Alustin answered without looking back at him.

"It was the Great Index. Now let's go."

Alustin hadn't been joking about making them memorize everyone who had died in the Grand Library.

> ***Anna Coldspark:*** *Fell to her death by not paying attention to the footpath she was supposed to be following.*
>
> ***Unknown Mage #12:*** *Found half starved and dehydrated, as though they'd been wandering the Grand Library for years.*
>
> ***Helgrim the Corpulent:*** *Eaten by a flock of spellbooks.*
>
> ***Durham the Grim:*** *Went missing without a trace. Two years later, a biography of him with covers of human bone and pages of human skin was found in the Library.*

Hugh grimaced and looked away from the list, then turned back to their other assignment.

Alustin and Artur Wallbreaker had decided that rather than spending the last two weeks before the labyrinth trying to teach the apprentices a few new spells, that they'd instead focus on three things: Practicing the skills they already had, learning more about the labyrinth, and, of course, memorizing the list of the victims of the Grand Library. Thankfully, they made the first two a much higher priority.

They still expected at least some memorization of the list by the apprentices in the meantime, unfortunately.

The reading about the labyrinth was much, much less disturbing than the reading about the Library. While the labyrinth was extremely dangerous, the uppermost level was considerably less so. Some students died during this test, but it was pretty rare- and, of those, the overwhelming majority died by being foolish and going to a lower level. Still, deaths had been known to happen on the first floor, which is why students were required to travel in teams.

Unfortunately, they wouldn't be able to plot out a route through the labyrinth beforehand. Like the more dangerous lower levels, the top level of the labyrinth was apparently capable of altering its shape. No one had ever seen it happen, but they'd seen the results.

Still, there tended to be a few common themes. The first level was roughly circular, with multiple entrances on the outside. In the center was a large, circular room with a stairwell leading downwards to the next level. It was the main exit to the lower levels, though other stairwells down were known to occur.

In that center room would be waiting a team of full mages, who were there for three purposes- to hand out tokens to students who made it to them proving they'd been to the center, to prevent students from going farther down, and to prevent especially dangerous monsters from moving upwards onto the first floor. The students merely had to reach the center room, retrieve a token apiece from the mages, then make it back to any exit.

Of course, it wasn't that simple. Apart from being a fiendishly difficult maze, even the first floor of the labyrinth had plenty of traps and monsters. Nothing a decently trained apprentice mage couldn't handle, generally, but plenty of students failed every year.

So Hugh and the others spent hours every day reading past accounts of the first floor, guides to the various creatures and traps found there, and planning out their strategy.

The time spent mastering their abilities was where things really got brutal. Before, Alustin and Artur had merely demanded competence when teaching. Now, however, they were demanding perfection, and it was exhausting. Sabae was expected to be able to release a gust strike on demand, and she was expected to be able to manifest wind armor over her shins and calves for minutes at a time as well. Talia's targeting with her dreamfire bolts was expected to be perfect.

And Hugh? Hugh was expected to be able to cast all of his basic cantrips perfectly, without any delay. This… really wasn't that much of a challenge at this point, but that didn't relieve Hugh that much. Simply speaking, without a warlock pact, Hugh's lack of attunements made him by far the weakest member of the team. Hugh's large mana reservoirs meant he never really ran out of mana casting cantrips, but there definitely was a hard upper limit on the power of cantrips.

His special project should help a little bit, but Hugh was still extremely worried about holding his friends back. Not just in that their team would have one less effective combatant, but that they'd have to spend time actively protecting him.

When he confronted Alustin about it, Alustin merely told him that "he just needed to trust in himself and in his friends."

Hugh did trust his friends. He just didn't trust himself.

CHAPTER FOURTEEN

ENTERING THE LABYRINTH

HUGH stared at the massive stone doors to the labyrinth. They were crystalline and opaque, rather than granite like the rest of the mountain. Hugh couldn't make out any details, but they were covered in absurdly intricate spellform engravings. He hadn't the slightest idea of what they did.

"Tha doors are made a' quartzite," Godrick said nervously. The huge youth looked as nervous as Hugh felt, toying with the massive steel sledgehammer he'd be bringing with him into the labyrinth. "It's basically sandstone that's been crushed and heated over millenia. Much stronger, but much harder to manipulate with mana."

"It just looks like a big lump of dirty crystal to me," Talia snapped. She fingered the two daggers on her belt irritably. She'd been even more impatient and standoffish the closer the test got, and now that it was here, she looked like she was ready to explode at the slightest provocation. Hugh had noticed, however, that her foot hadn't stopped nervously tapping since they'd arrived at this labyrinth entrance.

"Crystals are just shinier rocks, aren't they?" Sabae asked. She looked almost as cool and collected as usual, but her shoulders were just a little bit stiffer, her movements just a little bit jerkier, and her normally calm voice sounded just a little bit forced.

Godrick opened his mouth to respond when a mage strode through the crowd of students to the door. Hugh didn't recognize her, but that wasn't surprising- there were thousands of full mages in Skyhold, and not all of them could be as well known as Aedan Dragonslayer, Sulassa Tidecaller, or Artur Wallbreaker.

"Apprentices, if I could have your attention," the middle-aged woman called. It took a moment, but eventually everyone quieted down. Amusingly, the instructors who had come to watch their students set off were among the last to quiet down. Hugh looked back to see Alustin looking straight at him. Alustin nodded, and Hugh took a deep breath and looked back at the mage in front of the doors.

"In just a few short moments I'll be opening these doors for you to enter. You will enter in three minute intervals by team in the order announced. We will be sending the teams judged most capable first, since there will be a higher risk of earlier teams encountering monsters and other threats. The other five doors to the first level of the labyrinth will be opening at the same time. In order to pass this class, you'll need to make it to the center of the first level of the labyrinth…"

Hugh couldn't help but tune out the mage a little as she repeated the rules and warnings they'd all heard a dozen times before. He rocked back and forth on the balls of his feet and stared at the massive, crystalline doors nervously. He was sure that his team would be very far down the list. Even with a magical powerhouse like Godrick on their team, the reputations of the others as useless in one way or another would surely drag them down the list. Hugh especially. Alustin might be changing things for them, but they'd have to prove themselves to have anyone believe otherwise.

The one thing Hugh was really happy about? Rhodes and his team were entering from a different door.

"…and, under no circumstances are you to take any stairway down or other downward path. Even if you see another student lying injured at the base of a short ramp heading downwards, you are not to help them. Instead, take note of the location and let the first instructor you see know."

There was silence for a moment as the mage unraveled a scroll.

"First team: Godrick son of Artur Wallbreaker. Sabae Kaen Das. Talia of Clan Castis. Hugh of Emblin."

Hugh overbalanced and fell in surprise.

Godrick caught Hugh before he fell very far and set him back on his feet. Hugh gulped nervously and looked around.

Everyone was staring at them. He could see them whispering among themselves, and even overheard someone say "Emblin." He felt his face turn red.

"If you'd start a line by the door, please," the mage with the scroll said.

Hugh gulped.

Sabae was the first to move, and the other two quickly followed her. Hugh took a second longer, then hurried to catch up to them. He could feel everyone still staring.

"Tannis Rootborn, Elia Karnath…" Hugh glanced back at the second team. They all looked incredibly intimidating. One had an arm that appeared to be made of a living treebranch, inscribed with intricate spellforms. Another was hairless, and had what looked to be glowing wires embedded in her otherwise bald scalp. The third looked to be partially covered in frost, and the final one had what looked like scarabs climbing all over them.

"Why aren't they going first?" Hugh whispered to Sabae as they came to a halt in front of the doors. "They look absolutely terrifying!"

Sabae glanced back at the second group, then back at Hugh.

"Hugh, I don't know if you've noticed, but we look somewhat terrifying ourselves. Godrick's the size of a house and has a hammer most people couldn't lift; Talia is almost entirely covered in spellform tattoos, looks like she wants to bite someone's throat out all the time, and has a reputation for destroying classrooms; and I'm covered in scars and from one of the most respected mage families on the continent."

Hugh blinked. When she put it like that he supposed his friends were fairly intimidating. But… "I'm not, though. I'm just a skinny little country bumpkin."

Sabae frowned at him. "Look at the teams that are lining up right now."

Hugh looked back. Several other teams had lined up already, and they all looked almost as intimidating as the team just behind them. Especially a short figure in a cloak whose shadow kept moving on its own.

"They're all terrifying," Hugh said.

"They're all visibly terrifying," Sabae said. "You're in the first group, and you look… utterly normal. No weird tattoos, no bonded magical weapons passed down through your family, no familiar. No costume to try and make yourself look more dangerous, either. Their imaginations must be running wild trying to figure out what kind of mage you are."

Hugh was taken aback at this. He looked back at the other apprentices in line again, and realized something.

They were all more terrified than terrifying. The student with the treebranch arm couldn't stop nervously tracing the contours of his arm. The shadow of the figure in the cloak wasn't being aggressive, but was twitching nervously.

"They're all as nervous as we are, Hugh. Most of them probably count themselves as lucky they're not going first."

Hugh took a deep breath and nodded. Sabae was probably right about that. And the other students were definitely correct to count themselves as lucky.

It was at that point that the librarian paused in reading her list. "We'll finish lining you up in a moment, but it appears to be time to send in the first team."

Hugh felt his heart rate pick up even more.

The mage strode over to the doors and rested her hand on a particular spellform pattern. It began to glow with a warm, pulsing light. She then strode over to the matching pattern on the other door and did the same. The instant she took her hand off of the door, light began to travel outwards from the glowing patterns along the lines of the spellforms. Within instants, the crystalline doors were covered in glowing lines that intersected, split, merged, and formed eye-twisting geometrical patterns. Then, the light seemed to sink downwards into the crystal.

Then the doors simply went dark.

For a single moment, Hugh felt relief at the thought that something had gone wrong, and that they wouldn't have to take the test after all.

Then the massive doors silently and slowly opened inwards onto darkness.

Hugh and the other apprentices stared into the darkness of the labyrinth. None of them made any move to step forwards.

"Well?" prompted the mage who had just opened the doors.

Hugh gulped and looked at the others. Then, as one, they stepped forwards toward the doors. Hugh compulsively checked his equipment as he strode forwards. Dagger from Talia on his belt, check. Spellbook over his shoulder, check. Waterskin, check. Secret project… check.

As they strode across the threshold of the labyrinth, the temperature dropped abruptly. Not to the point where extra clothes were needed, but enough to where Hugh felt a little uncomfortable.

The walls of the labyrinth were back to the normal granite of Skyhold, but they were intricately covered in spellform designs that made even the ones on the door look simple. They covered every inch of the walls, floor, and ceiling.

The room of the labyrinth that they'd entered was a half-moon in shape, with the door out on the flat wall. It was lit solely by the light coming through the door. There were three hallways branching off from the curved wall, each quickly fading into darkness.

"Which way should we go?" said Hugh. He crafted a basic light cantrip in his mind's eye, then summoned it in his hand.

"If this were a normal maze," Sabae said, "we should just pick a direction and take it whenever we came to a turn, but that's not an especially effective strategy in this labyrinth."

They all stood silently for a moment, and then Talia nodded to herself. "Doesn't really matter which way we go, then. We just need to figure out the curve of the circle and head inwards."

Talia strode towards the hallway on the right. No one else moved for a second, then everyone else rushed to catch up with her. Godrick summoned a light from his hand as well.

"Ah'm supposed ta be in front with Sabae, remember?" Godrick said.

Talia snorted, but let Godrick and Sabae pull in front of them. Their team had not one, but two close-range combat mages, so it made sense to put them where they would be the first to run into any threats. Most teams didn't have any, so their team might actually have an edge in case of ambushes.

They all stayed quiet as they strode down the hallway. It curved gradually, and soon the only light visible came from Hugh and Godrick's cantrips, and the only noise came from their footsteps.

"I wish we could have used yarn or chalk to mark our path," Hugh finally muttered to himself. He almost jumped at how loud it sounded in the quiet of the hallway. The others all looked at him, and he blushed. "I know why we can't, I'm just saying." The enchantments of the labyrinth seemed to have been built with the intention of, among other things, preventing people from cheating while navigating the maze. Strings would be cut, chalk would wash away, and so on and so forth.

No one spoke for another minute or so, until they came to the first fork in the path. The right-hand path continued along the same curve they were walking, but the left-hand path seemed to head inwards.

"Like Talia said, we do need to head inwards," Sabae said.

They cautiously started down the left-hand path. They were only a few hundred feet down it when Talia hissed and came to a halt.

"What is it?" Hugh said.

"Shh," hissed Talia.

Everyone remained silent. After a few seconds, Hugh heard it too-some sort of chittering, scuttling noise. He couldn't tell which direction it was coming from, though.

"Behind us!" said Talia.

Hugh whirled around, aiming his light cantrip behind them, but didn't see anything. Godrick and Sabae moved forwards in front of Hugh, and Talia stepped beside him. Godrick readied his hammer, while whirlwinds had begun to spin around Sabae's forearms and calves. Dreamfire was rising out of Talia's palms. Hugh pulled his secret project out of his belt pouch.

"Somethin' smells awful," Godrick said. Hugh sniffed, but didn't smell anything yet. It must be Godrick's scent affinity helping him smell things farther away.

Something came skittering out of the darkness on all fours and stopped, hissing at them.

It was about the size of a cat, with a batlike face and a fleshy, humanoid body and a protuberant gut. Clumps of hair stuck out of it almost at random, and Godrick was right- it stank horribly.

"It's an imp!" Hugh said.

"A what?" said Talia?

"A lesser demonspawn. About as smart as a rat, and much more vicious. They also…"

Almost a dozen more came into the light and began hissing. Hugh could hear more in the shadows, and see some of their eyes glinting in the dark.

"Run in packs," Hugh finished weakly.

The first imp launched itself into the air at Godrick. Before it could get close, Talia sent it flying with a blast of dreamfire. It crashed to the ground, melting into a pile of goo.

As if that were a signal, the other imps began launching themselves at the foursome. Godrick yelled and smashed his sledgehammer down, pulping two of them. Sabae kicked one, releasing a gust of wind that sent a whole crowd of them flying backwards. Talia launched dreamfire bolt after dreamfire bolt into the crowd, each of which exploded, crushed, froze, or aged an imp into oblivion.

"Hugh, do something!" Talia yelled.

Hugh shook off the fear that had gripped him and readied his secret project.

It was a sling. An ordinary sling, just like the one he'd used back in the woods of Emblin to hunt rabbits and pheasants. He'd crafted this one out of leather he'd found in a bookbinding supply store-room. It was well made, but nothing special. The ammunition, however...

The ammunition was special. He'd spent hours on every single little sphere of rock, painstakingly carving wards into them. He only had a dozen of them, so they'd better work.

Hugh spun up the sling, wardstone in the cup, and released it straight at the floor in the crowd of imps. The instant the wardstone struck the stone floor, the spellform was broken, and all the energy stored up inside the ward was released.

And there was a lot of energy stored in it. At least a half dozen imps were caught in the blast. They weren't just killed- they were pulped. A shower of liquefied imp splattered over the four of them, smelling even worse than when they were alive.

Talia wiped imp gore from her face and glared at Hugh. "Well, don't quit now!" She hurled another dreamfire bolt at an imp. This one, surprisingly, actually just burned.

Hugh quickly began spinning up his sling again, as Godrick impaled another imp with a spike of stone he summoned from the floor and Sabae sent a gust of wind scything across the floor with a kick, tumbling imps wildly.

The fight against the imps seemed to go on for hours, though it was probably only minutes. By the time they were done, they were drenched in bits of imp, and a solitary straggler scuttled off into the darkness the way it had came.

"Well, that's these clothes ruined," Talia said.

Everyone stared at her for a moment, then burst out laughing.

Once the hysterical laughter had stopped, Hugh began casting a new cantrip. This was one of his favorites- a cleaning cantrip. He used it to suction off the imp goo off of all of them.

"You might be my favorite person right now," Sabae said.

Talia sniffed herself.

"We still smell awful," she said. "Godrick, think you can do some scent magic?"

Godrick shuffled his feet a bit. "Ah'm not tah great with scent magic yet. Ah'd probably make things worse."

"I've got that one covered too- with a little help from Godrick," Hugh said. He rummaged through his belt pouch, finally pulling out a little glass sphere- the scent removing sphere Godrick had given him for his birthday.

"Now this is why we're the team that was sent in first," Sabae said, grinning.

They were attacked twice more by imps on their way towards the center. They won through both times, though Godrick got a nasty bite on one leg and Sabae's hands were repeatedly clawed up. Each time, Hugh happily cleaned up afterwards. They were also attacked by some sort of turtle spider that was nearly six feet across, but it was relatively slow moving, so Talia just pelted it with dreamfire as they retreated until the thing died silently.

They didn't find many traps, surprisingly. Tripwires, dart traps (usually unpoisoned), and non-fatal pitfalls were supposed to be common on this level, but they only found a single dart trap (which hit Godrick right in the backside, much to the others' amusement, especially Talia's) and a coughing gas trap.

The maze itself made a much more formidable challenge. They hit dead ends six times, found themselves going in circles twice, and frequently heard monsters or other students around a corner, only to turn it and find nothing. Hugh was sure that they were getting steadily closer to the center.

They reached the center of the first floor about two hours into the test. The center was a huge round room about two hundred feet across, with a large spiral staircase descending into the floor in the center. A good half-dozen mages maintained a magical dome-shaped barrier over it. The spellforms covering the walls, floor, and ceiling all seemed to lead out of the hole the staircase descended into. Or maybe into it.

They weren't the first team to arrive- despite being one of the first teams in, they were the eleventh team to get to the center. One other team was there when they arrived, and they mentioned encountering far, far more traps, including a snake trap, but no monsters. Hugh glanced at his bag of wardstone projectiles- he only had four left.

The mages in the center room handed out tokens to all four of them. "Remember," one of them said, "you can only pass the test if you return out the exit with a token. If you lose yours, you'll need to return here."

"Can other teams try to steal our tokens?" Talia asked.

"They can, but it won't count as a win for them- the tokens only work for the apprentice we hand them to. You'll still have to return here, though."

The mage shook all of their hands and wished them luck.

"Does anyone have any preference for which path we should take out of the center?" Sabae asked.

"Let's just go back the way we came," Talia said, and started to head back that way. Sabae grabbed her by the shoulder and stopped her.

"Odds are that won't work- the labyrinth seems to dislike backtracking. Trying to do it usually leads you farther away."

Talia shrugged. "You all paid a lot more attention to the books on it than I did."

Hugh gestured towards one of the hallways leading outwards. "Let's take that one."

"It looks like all a' tha others," Godrick said.

"My gut is giving me a good feeling about it," Hugh said.

No one had any better ideas, so they headed down that direction.

About ten minutes after leaving the center, Hugh heard a click and froze.

"Did anyone else hear that?" he asked.

"Hugh, don't move," Talia said. "If you move, it'll activate."

Hugh looked down. The spellform he'd stepped on had sunk slightly into the ground and was glowing. Hugh could hear a rumbling sound in the distance.

"That's not how spellform traps work!" Hugh yelled. "Everyone run!"

He followed his own advice and took off forwards in a dead sprint.

Everyone else followed him, and just in time, too- a massive, spherical boulder dropped out of the ceiling above the spot where they had been standing. Everyone came to a halt, staring at it. It hadn't started rolling after them, thankfully.

"I thought you had a good feeling about this path, Hugh?" Talia asked.

"I did," Hugh said. "We're all okay, so I wasn't wrong."

Spellforms began to light up on the spherical boulder.

"Nevermind, I was wrong, everyone run!"

The boulder started rolling after them. Purposefully.

"I'm never trusting your gut again, Hugh!" Talia said. They all started running again.

The boulder chased them for a solid ten minutes before its spellforms dimmed and it gave up the chase. It had followed them relentlessly until then, even turning to follow them down the various forks they'd taken. Well, probably followed Hugh, since he triggered the trap, but the others weren't likely to abandon him.

If it hadn't been for the physical training that Alustin had demanded of them, Hugh doubted they could have kept ahead of it.

The square chamber they found themselves in had three exits- the one they'd come in from and two others placed on the adjacent sides of the room. The final wall was blank. They stayed there for several minutes catching their breath before Talia spoke up.

"Hugh, which way is your gut telling us to go? Because my gut's telling me we should go the opposite way from that."

Hugh ignored her, staring at the blank wall without an exit. He narrowed his eyes staring at it, then opened his sketchbook.

"Something's weird about that wall," he said.

He quickly began sketching the spellforms on the wall, identifying the important ones.

"Shouldn't we get moving?" Sabae said.

"Hold on just a minute longer," Hugh said.

Hugh grinned, looking back and forth between the wall and his drawings. "Hah! There's a secret door hidden here!"

"Really?" Godrick asked excitedly. "Will there be treasure behind it? Me da found his enchanted hammer in the depths of the labyrinth."

Hugh pulled out his chalk. "Let's find out."

It took another ten minutes before he was done altering the spellforms with chalk. The secret door was held shut by a spellform that was incredibly close to a ward in function. It was supposed to be opened by knowing… the answer to some sort of riddle, it looked like, but Hugh was able to bypass it.

When he drew the last chalk mark, the ward and the chalk marks drawn on it all lit up. The circular segment of wall in the middle seemed to just… dissolve away.

Hugh passed through the entrance first, not bothering to wait for Sabae or Godrick to go first. He was a little consumed by dreams of treasure, to say the least. He'd strode about halfway into the room when someone came in a doorway on the other side.

Rhodes.

Rhodes and Hugh froze, staring at each other in surprise, as their respective teams filtered into the room after them.

Rhodes armed for battle looked much more intimidating than usual. He wore a fine chainmail shirt, some sort of magical headband covered in glowing jewels and spellforms, and had a spear with a long metal head hovering in the air next to him. It didn't appear to have any spellforms attached to it, so Hugh guessed Rhodes was holding it up with his attunement- or at least one of them.

The blue haired twins were with him as well, as was another boy who had lines of purple, glowing energy running up his arms. The twins were casting light generating cantrips.

No one spoke for a minute until Rhodes broke the silence.

"Well, well, well, look what we have here. A worthless sheepherder, his two whores, and a dumb brute."

Hugh flushed red. Talia stepped forwards, growling audibly, but Sabae spoke up first.

"Really? That's the best set of insults you can come up with? I'm going to have to give it a… solid D grade."

Hugh blinked at her.

"The sheepherder bit you've used often enough, and it clearly gets to Hugh, but calling us whores? That's just lazy. And calling Godrick a dumb brute? You should see his homework sometime, we go to him for help more often than not."

Rhodes blinked in confusion. Sabae was smiling cruelly at Rhodes.

"No offense to either Hugh or Talia, but angering them isn't exactly hard," Sabae said.

"Especially not Talia," Godrick muttered. Talia kicked him in the shin.

"So, if you'll excuse us, we'll be going now. We've got a test to finish." Sabae turned to leave.

"You're not going anywhere unless I say you can!" Rhodes snapped.

"Really?" Sabae said.

"Yes, really!" Rhodes snapped.

"No, I was asking if your banter could get any more boring and unoriginal. You really have depended on your position more than your wit, haven't you?"

Hugh's mouth was hanging open in shock as he stared at Sabae. He felt a grin slowly creep across his face.

"What do your cronies think? You there, with the blue hair, are you actually that impressed with Rhodes' insults?"

The twins, not sure who she was referring to, looked at each other in confusion. Rhodes, standing in front of them, didn't see that, and seemed to assume that they were being silent because they couldn't make themselves praise his insults. He turned bright red.

"You can't…" he started, then Sabae interrupted.

"Where you about to tell me that I can't talk to you like that? Which, normally, would be followed by me telling you that I just had, and then you'd demand by what right I dared do so, and so on and so forth. Let's just skip all that, shall we? We have better things to do."

Talia started laughing. Rhodes' glare snapped to her.

"You damn…"

"Where you about to call her a barbarian, Rhodes?" Hugh said. "Or maybe a ginger bitch? Sabae's right, you're really pretty predictable."

Hugh felt shocked at his own courage. He might be no match for Rhodes, but… he'd always faced Rhodes feeling like he was alone before, like he had no one to back him up.

This time, he'd be damned if he was going to let that rich asshole walk all over him.

Hugh had never seen Rhodes this angry before. The female twin reached her hand out to Rhodes.

"Let's go, they're not worth it."

Rhodes shrugged off her hand and snarled.

"You… you… you worthless…" Rhodes looked like his head was about to explode.

Rhodes' spear hurling itself through the air at them clued Hugh into the fact that maybe they had pushed things a little too far.

The spear crossed the room in the blink of an eye, but came to a dead halt inches in front of Hugh's face. Rhodes bellowed, but the spear didn't move even a fraction of an inch closer.

Hugh looked behind him to see Godrick's face straining with effort. He'd managed to use his steel affinity to catch the spear just in time. Godrick's face screwed up even tighter with effort, and Hugh was afraid for a moment that he would lose the battle of wills.

Instead, the spear crept backwards an inch.

Slowly but surely the spear crept backwards across the room. About halfway across, it flipped over, the point facing towards Rhodes.

Things happened very, very quickly all of a sudden. Rhodes ducked and surrendered control of the spear to Godrick, and it clattered against the wall behind him. At almost the same moment, Rhodes released a bolt of lightning straight towards them. Hugh was convinced he was about to be fried like an insect.

Sabae caught it.

Everyone stared at her for a moment in shock as she clutched the writhing lightning between her fingers. Hugh could see burns forming on her hands. Then, with a jerk, she hurled it away from herself, right at the floor between them.

At which point Hugh noticed something he really really should have noticed before.

There weren't any spellforms on the floor in this room.

The lightning hit, and the floor shattered apart.

Hugh fell.

CHAPTER FIFTEEN

THE DEEPS

HUGH barely thought as he fell, and just started crafting a spell as fast as he could in his mind's eye. He used the most powerful spellform foundation he knew. He added his definitive and aiming lines quickly, then added a series of modifying lines that would let him start the power off low and quickly grow higher, rather than going full power off at once.

While he was doing this, he was trying to correct his tumble so he could focus on the ground. He managed to slow his fall enough to focus his cantrip light on the ground, and then frantically activated the spell.

Hugh could feel the mana flooding out of his reservoirs like nothing he'd ever felt before, and then he felt himself slowing. He came to a near complete halt, then his feet gently touched down on the ground. He frantically looked around him, and sighed as he saw his friends touch down on the ground next to him just as softly. The spell had worked. Hugh felt utterly drained magically. Stopping four people from falling to their deaths was far, far beyond the power levels cantrips were meant to channel.

No, six people. Rhodes and the male twin were down here too.

Hugh readied himself to continue the fight when he saw Sabae crumple. Godrick managed to catch her before she hit the ground.

"I'm okay," Sabae said. "Just… that took it out of me."

"Yeh caught lightning! That's amazing!" Godrick said.

Talia advanced towards Rhodes. "She caught *his* lightning. What the hell is wrong with you, Charax?"

Rhodes was looking around frantically. "We're below the first level! We shouldn't be here. We really shouldn't be here."

Hugh blinked, then looked around. They were in a roughly cylindrical room leading upwards. He glanced up the shaft, seeing a light far above where the other two members of Rhodes' team waited above. Then, something glinting plummeted down.

Rhodes' spear.

Hugh frantically reached into his pouch for his sling and a wardstone, but Rhodes didn't have any interest in fighting them. He caught the spear in his hand, and the twin grabbed the shaft as well. With a burst of wind that pushed Hugh backwards a few steps, Rhodes launched himself and his teammate into the air, rapidly moving up the shaft.

"A real courageous dragonslayer in the making, that one," Talia said dryly.

"So he's got a wind attunement too," Hugh said, "on top of his lightning and steel attunements."

"'e doesn't 'ave a steel attunement," Godrick said. "'e's got a wood attunement. He was pushing on tha shaft of tha spear, not tha head. That's why ah could overpower him."

"He was right, though," Sabae said. "We really shouldn't be here."

Up above, the light from Rhodes' teams light cantrips had vanished.

"If we wait here, maybe they'll alert an instructor like they're supposed to?" Hugh said.

Talia looked at him and snorted.

Hugh sighed. "Right, can't count on that."

"You're right to be worried," a voice from the shadows said. Hugh whirled to face one of the entrances into the room. As he did so, a huge shape unfolded itself out of the pitch black hallway. And kept unfolding itself. And kept unfolding itself. "You seem quite wonderfully resourceful for your age. Most students would have died from that fall, but not you, young warlock. Still, these depths are far, far too dangerous for apprentices."

The figure, a full fifteen feet in height now, stepped into the light.

Hugh gasped, and he heard equally frightened reactions from the others.

It was a demon.

The demon was surprisingly similar to the imps they'd come across on the first floor. It had a batlike face, hairy protrusions all over its body, and arms that were disproportionately long, ending in razor sharp claws. In addition, however, it also had a long, hairless, prehensile tail ending in a stinger. Some sort of black ichor dripped out of the tip of it, sizzling when it hit the ground. The demon's most notable feature, however, was its gut. It protruded outward grotesquely, with transparent skin showing its intestines. They resembled nothing so much as a squirming mass of tadpoles.

"No need to be afraid, Hugh. I intend you no harm." The demon smiled in what it probably intended to be a reassuring manner, but the mouthful of fangs it revealed did quite the opposite.

"How do you know my name?" Hugh demanded.

"I watch the academy above me quite closely, Hugh," the demon said. "You may call me Bakori. It's merely a fragment of my name, but the rest would be… difficult for you to pronounce."

Hugh took a step back towards the others. "What do you want?"

"I want to help you. I bear no ill will towards the academy or its residents, despite their… antipathy towards my kind. Oh, and while we're at it, I should apologize for the behavior of my spawn. Imps aren't… the most polite or intelligent of beings."

"Help him how?" Talia demanded suspiciously.

Bakori glanced at her, then back at Hugh. "By offering him the power he needs to save his friends."

A suspicion grew in the back of Hugh's head. "You want me to sign a warlock pact with you."

"To put it simply, yes. These levels are extremely dangerous, and it's improbable that you'll make it back to the surface alive. I know how important your friends are to you, Hugh, and I'm quite willing to help you save them." Bakori smiled again.

"And what if I decline? You eat us?" Hugh said.

Bakori gave Hugh a hurt expression. "I'm offended that you'd think so low of me. Just more examples of the hate your kind holds for mine. No, if you refuse, I'll simply allow you to go your own way."

Hugh opened his mouth to reject Bakori's offer out of hand, and then paused. Bakori… wasn't wrong about their chances. Alustin and the other instructors had repeatedly drilled their warnings about the lower levels to the apprentices, noting how many students who even ended up on the second floor died. This… seemed like it was well below the second floor.

"What floor are we on?" Hugh asked, stalling for time.

"The sixth," Bakori said.

Hugh stood thinking as Bakori waited patiently. The sixth level was even deeper than Hugh had expected. Most adventurers visiting Skyhold seldom made it this far without extensive preparations. What chance did he and his friends have to escape on their own?

"Well, young warlock? What will it be?"

Hugh opened his mouth to answer, terrified that it was going to be the wrong choice, when Talia spoke up again. "He won't do it."

Sabae spoke up right on Talia's heels. "Hugh's too good of a person to make a deal with a demon."

Godrick spoke up next. "We'll find a way ta get back ta the surface on our own somehow."

Bakori looked at the three. For a brief instant, irritation swept across his face, then he turned back to Hugh.

"Do they speak for you, young warlock?"

Hugh couldn't find his voice at first. He hoped he was making the right decision here. He swallowed, then spoke up. "They do."

Bakori stared at him expressionlessly. "Very well. I'll leave the four of you to it." He turned to leave, then paused. "Though, if you change your mind, Hugh, you must only call my name three times in a row and will me to your side, and I will come to you, no matter the danger you are in. I offer not just power, but friendship as well."

With that, Bakori crouched to fit back into the tunnel and was gone.

"So what do we do now?" Sabae asked. She was standing on her own again, somewhat recovered from catching Rhodes' lightning bolt.

"We find our way back up," Talia said, not taking her eyes off of the exit Bakori had taken.

"How are we supposed to do that?" Hugh said.

"We stick together," Godrick said, "and we keep our heads clear."

"We should head out now, before that demon changes his mind about eating us," Talia said.

"He's not going to eat us," Hugh said.

"How do you know?" said Talia.

"Because he wants me to sign that contract with him. He wants something from me, and he's not going to rest until he gets it."

Everyone was silent for a time.

"Is there any way for us to get back up this way?" Sabae asked.

Godrick walked over to the wall. "Ah could try reshaping tha stone inta a ladder."

He reached out towards the stone. There was a flash, and he pulled his hand back, cursing. "Damn stone burnt me!"

Hugh walked over to look at the spellforms on the wall. They were very, very different than any spellforms he'd seen in the labyrinth so far- they were constructed to carry a truly massive amount of mana through their lines. It was all directional, as well- the mana was only moving upwards.

"I think this is some kind of mana conduit," Hugh said. "I've been wondering about whether the labyrinth absorbs or releases mana- it seems like the latter."

"Maybe we should focus less on trying to learn, more on trying to get out of here?" Talia said. "Is it safe for Godrick to reshape or not?"

"Definitely not," Hugh said. "Any more changes than he tried to make probably would have overloaded him with mana and incinerated him."

Godrick paled at that.

"Well, can you… turn off the mana conduit?" Sabae said.

Hugh shook his head vigorously. "That's way, way past my skill level."

"We should get a move on, then," Talia said.

The others nodded in agreement.

Hugh gave the exit Bakori had taken one final look, before turning to follow his friends.

The sixth level of the labyrinth was similar to the first in a few ways- the tunnels were the same size, and the spellforms still covered nearly every surface. There were plenty of differences, though. The tunnels were more rounded than square, but the biggest difference was the noise.

Where the first floor was almost deathly quiet, the sixth floor… never was. There was wind down here, for some reason, and it was never silent. Worse, the wind carried other noises on it- chittering, footsteps, growls, and grinding mechanical noises. The four of them clustered closely together as they moved slowly down the hallways of the labyrinth. No one spoke. A few times Hugh thought he saw something moving at the edge of the light their cantrips provided, but it always vanished when he looked closer.

None of them had any idea what the layout of this level was like- they'd only seriously studied the first level. Students were never sent this deep. Just to be cautious, they moved extremely slowly, though they had to fight their desire to get out of there as quickly as possible. Running across a trap this deep could be fatal.

They'd been moving through the branching corridors for about an hour when they came across something different.

The room they had stumbled into was nearly the size of the Great Hall where the Choosing had taken place. The ceiling wasn't as high as the Great Hall's, but it was still several times the height of the hallways.

And, best of all, there was a tunnel leading out of the upper story of the room.

The other notable feature of the room was the stone statues. They were everywhere- statues of knights, gargoyles, bulls, and more. Instead of the tough granite the walls were made of, the statues were carved out of marble.

Hugh pointed at the tunnels up above. "I'd bet that that tunnel is part of the fifth level, not the sixth.

Talia cursed. "How are we supposed to get up there? Stack up the statues?"

Godrick waled over to the wall. "Ah could try ta reshape a ladder out a' tha stone, but it would take a while."

Hugh checked the spellforms on the walls. "It doesn't look like these walls will react like the ones before, it should be safe for you to reshape the stone."

"I'd rather wait here and have a sure way up than wander more and potentially run into monsters," Sabae said.

Godrick nodded and walked over to the wall. He reached his hands out, and the stone started to slowly reshape itself like putty in his hands.

Unfortunately, that wasn't the only stone that started moving. The statues nearby started creaking and moving, jerkily moving their heads towards the apprentices.

"Goatshit in a picnic basket," Talia said.

"Should we run?" Hugh asked.

Godrick strode up beside them, sledgehammer at the ready, as the statues slowly closed in on them. "We can still fight our way out a' here, if we need to," he said.

Sabae shook her head. "We might not get a better chance to move up to the next level. Get back to the ladder, we'll hold them off for as long as you need."

Sabae clenched her fists, walked up to the nearest statue, an armored knight, and unleashed a gust strike at it.

It rocked backwards a little bit, but otherwise nothing happened. Sabae scrambled backwards just in time to avoid the statue swinging its stone sword at her. Hugh shuddered at the thought of what the heavy sword might have done.

"They're too heavy to knock back with wind," Sabae said.

Talia grinned. "My turn."

Talia launched a series of dreamfire bolts into the same statue. The effect this time was much more apparent. The first dreamfire bolt cracked the knight statue's chest. The second froze off one side of its face. The third shrank the knight's sword, and the fourth… the fourth set the knight on fire. The burning stone unleashed a plume of foul-smelling smoke, and the knight crumpled to the ground.

"Eat that, you faceless freak!" Talia cackled.

"So… now we've only got a few dozen left to go," Hugh said. He glanced back at Godrick. The rungs he was shaping out of the stone extended a good six feet upwards already.

Talia started pelting more statues with dreamfire bolts, but even at the slow speed they were moving, it took multiple dreamfire bolts to fell each one, and they were already surrounded by the statues. There's no way Talia would be able to hold them all off like that.

Hugh pulled out his sling and another wardstone. He took a deep breath, spun up his sling, and fired the wardstone at a statue carved in the shape of an elderly woman. The statue was actually knocked off its feet, and part of its jaw had been blasted away. None of the nearby statues had been affected, however, and Hugh only had three wardstones left. As he watched, the statue climbed back onto its feet.

"Anyone have a plan?"

"Ah can take them," Godrick called from partway up the wall.

"Not all of them, and not in time," Sabae called back. "Keep working on the ladder."

Talia paused in her barrage, panting.

"There's been something I've been wanting to try for a while now," she said.

She seemed to strain, and then a thin stream of dreamfire projected out of her finger. She used the stream to carve a half circle in front of them, and where it touched, dreamfire licked up from the stone.

Talia let the stream die and focused on the half-circle of dreamfire. The purple-green flames licked up higher, and the line widened to almost three feet thick as she did so.

"I can't hold this up forever," Talia said, "so hurry up, Godrick."

The statues continued advancing on the dreamfire barrier. Their edges seemed to blur and twist, and they seemed to gain a semblance of life in the light of the dreamfire that they'd lacked before.

The first statue, a burly wrestler in a loincloth, reached the edge of the dreamfire barrier. It paused, slowly jerking its head from side to side to examine the dreamfire. Then it ponderously stepped forwards. As it did so, the dreamfire licked upwards, and the statue began melting- though the drops began falling upwards.

It completely collapsed halfway through the barrier, and the dreamfire rapidly crackled up around it. Talia had begun sweating heavily at this point. More of the statues had reached the edge of the barrier, but most seemed content to wait for it to die down.

Then a large stone bull tried to step across. The dreamfire shattered it before it was halfway across, but more beads of sweat were popping out on Talia's face.

"Hurry up, Godrick," Hugh called.

More and more of the statues tried to cross, but each was destroyed by the dreamfire. By the sixth statue, Talia had collapsed to one knee. Her tattoos had begun to glow.

Then one statue made it across.

The stone ape was burning badly, but it hadn't collapsed yet. It turned to Talia and began to stride towards her. Hugh began to fumble for a wardstone, but Sabae got to the statue first. She punched it right in the cracked center of its chest, and this time she got a reaction. The wind from her strike forced its way deep into the cracks, fueling the dreamfire consuming the ape to much greater heights.

The ape exploded away from Sabae, sending shards of burning stone into the barrier and out into the crowd. Several more statues caught on fire from the shrapnel.

Hugh glanced back up at Godrick. He was over half-way to the tunnel mouth. Just another minute or so should be long enough, he hoped. Godrick looked eerie in the light from the dreamfire, though not as bad as the statues.

Another couple of statues stepped across the barrier. One, an immense stone turtle, collapsed immediately upon stepping out. The other, a stone gorgon (whose snake hair, to Hugh's relief, didn't move on its own), was badly burning, and was blasted to pieces by Sabae in the same way as the ape.

Quite a few statues in the crowd were burning as the dreamfire spread through the crowd now, but more were pressing forwards towards the barrier. Talia was barely holding the barrier up now, and Hugh rushed over to support her and keep her from collapsing onto the ground. Her tattoos were glowing brightly enough that they cast shadows.

"Ah'm almost to the top," Godrick called. "Ye should follow me up now."

Hugh heaved Talia to her feet. He forgot how small she was sometimes, given how much space her personality took up. He started walking her back towards the ladder.

Several more statues stepped across the dying barrier.

"Talia, climb!" Hugh basically lifted her up the ladder. As she slowly started to climb, the dreamfire barrier guttered out, then died entirely, leaving a pit nearly a foot deep in a crescent where the barrier had been. Talia's tattoos dimmed at the same time. The statues that had already been set on fire continued burning, but many of the statues that had been hesitant to cross the fire before had begun advancing on the students.

Sabae hammered apart another burning statue with a gust strike as Hugh started up the ladder after Talia.

"Sabae, let's go!" called Hugh.

Sabae sent out one more windstrike- this one ineffective- and rushed to the ladder. Godrick had already reached the tunnel above them, and was helping Talia up into it.

Hugh was about halfway up when Sabae screamed. Hugh looked down to see that one of the statues, a blindfolded judge, had seized her by the ankle. Hugh frantically reached for his remaining wardstones, but before he could grab them, Godrick's massive sledgehammer hurtled down into the statue's face. Its head crushed, the judge let go of Sabae's ankle and fell to the floor.

Hugh breathed a sigh of relief as Sabae began climbing again. His breath caught when another stone knight began to jerkily lift himself up the ladder. The beheaded judge then stood up and began climbing as well.

"Faster, Sabae!" Hugh called, then began climbing again. Godrick hauled him up into the tunnel when he got there. Hugh collapsed on the floor of the tunnel as Godrick hauled Sabae up. Talia was already lying on the tunnel floor.

"I think my ankle's broken," Sabae said. Godrick moved to look at Sabae's ankle, but Hugh shot up from the floor and grabbed Godrick's shoulder.

"Are they still climbing the ladder?" Hugh asked, walking over to the edge of the tunnel. He looked down to see the knight just a few feet below him. "Godrick, they're climbing the ladder."

Godrick walked over to the edge and smiled. "Ah thought that one out already. It's a lot easier ta destroy than ta create."

Godrick stomped, and the rungs of the ladder fell off the wall one by one from the top down, taking several statues with them. A couple of the statues smashed on hitting the ground, though most survived.

Godrick reached down and summoned his hammer with a visible effort. It started to rise, but a morbidly obese statue grasped it by the handle and tried to haul it back down. Godrick grunted with the effort of fighting it for the hammer. He looked on the verge of running out of mana when a dreamfire bolt slammed into the statue's shoulder, shattering it. The hammer abruptly flew to Godrick's grasp, nearly knocking him backwards as it did so. The statue's hand was still attached to the handle, and Godrick knocked it off with distaste.

Hugh collapsed against the tunnel wall, panting. They'd made it, somehow.

CHAPTER SIXTEEN
A FATEFUL CHOICE

No one moved for several minutes. The only light was coming from the burning statues below, so they were more in shadow than not. Eventually, Hugh hauled himself to his feet and summoned a light cantrip. He looked around their surroundings.

The tunnels of the fifth floor were radically different than the first or sixth floors. Instead of smooth polished granite, the tunnel they were in was rough-hewn sandstone, and barely tall enough for Godrick to stand upright in. Instead of being engraved onto the walls, the ever-present spellforms in the labyrinth were painted on in a flaky white paint. Hugh doubted they were as fragile as they looked, however.

The fifth floor wasn't as quiet as the first, but it was much quieter than the sixth, and most of the noise they were hearing came from the statue room.

Godrick had started tending to Sabae's ankle. They weren't sure if it was broken or just badly sprained, so Godrick chose to just encase Sabae's whole foot in a stone cast, as well as crafting her a stone crutch.

"This is going to slow me down a lot," Sabae said.

"We need ta avoid more battles," Godrick said.

No one answered. Hugh doubted any of them seriously thought that was a possibility. Talia looked like she was barely awake after the amount of mana she'd spent. Even as rich as the Aether was down here, it would take some time for her reservoirs to refill.

"There shouldn't be any sandstone down here," Godrick said. "The mountain's a solid block of granite."

"It's the labyrinth," said Sabae, as though that explained everything.

Maybe it did.

Hugh looked farther down the hallway, and almost yelled in shock. There was something down there. When it didn't move, Hugh eased forwards.

It was a human skeleton, dressed in tattered rags.

This time, Hugh did yell.

Godrick rushed down to his side, lowering his hammer when he saw what it was.

"How long has he been here, do yeh think?" Godrick said.

"A long time, I imagine," Hugh said.

Hugh began to turn away, then spotted something shining. He crouched down to see something shining inside the skeleton's ribcage. He reached in and pulled the object out, dusting it off with his hand.

It was an amulet of some sort. It was only about the width of his thumb, and about half that in length. It consisted of a simple, polished oval stone attached to a silver clasp. A narrow band of silver ran along the border of the stone from the clasp. Incredibly tiny and intricate spellforms ran up and down the clasp and the band. It looked like there had been a cord or leather band that had once held it in place, but it had long since eroded away.

The stone wasn't shiny, or particularly valuable looking. Instead, it was a dull red-orange, almost like the color of brick, with stripes of a dark red brown running across it at an angle just off the horizontal. The lines weren't totally straight, but curved slightly, with gaps between some of them. It looked almost like…

"It's a labyrinth!" Godrick said.

Hugh flipped it over. The back looked almost identical, except that the stone was flat instead of rounded. More spellforms ran down the back of the clasp, which covered the top quarter of the stone's back.

Hugh and Godrick walked back to the others to show them the stone. None of them knew what it did, but they all agreed it had to be enchanted. Hugh tucked it into his belt pouch.

It took them another ten or fifteen minutes before they were ready to move on. Talia still looked exhausted, Godrick wasn't that much better off, and Sabae winced in pain with every step she took. Hugh was the only one still in decent condition.

And even with all the strides forwards as a mage he'd taken in the past few months, Hugh was still mostly useless.

No one looked back into the statue room as they were heading out. No one wanted to.

As they set out, Hugh walked next to Talia.

"We would have died if not for you," he said.

"I'm sure you all would have figured out something," Talia said.

Hugh shook his head. "Godrick's hammer barely slowed those things down, and Sabae couldn't touch them until you'd damaged them. Your dreamfire is really, really powerful, Talia. A regular fire mage wouldn't have been able to do anything to those statues."

Talia blushed a little.

"Alustin knows what he's doing, I guess," was all she said.

No one said anything for a while after that. The increasing number of bones they came across probably had a lot to do with that.

Most of the bones were broken and shattered, and few were human. Most looked like they'd come from various monsters. Hugh began having to step carefully to avoid them. They briefly stopped to consider turning back in hushed whispers, but no one wanted to face the statue room again. They kept on the lookout for a turnoff, but so far they hadn't had any opportunities to take another path.

The four grew more and more tense as they moved down the tunnel. Godrick didn't even curse when he hit his head on the ceiling.

Hugh couldn't help but notice splashes of dried and crumbling brown here and there atop the white paint of the spellforms.

The number of bones had increased to the point where Hugh was about ready to go back and face the statues when the room opened up into a large cavern with two exits. The cavern was big enough that their light cantrips barely reached the far wall, and was absolutely littered with bones. They piled several feet into the air at some points. Stalactites and stalagmites jutted out of the ceiling and floor of the cave.

Hugh glanced at the exits. One exit looked like a continuation of the tunnel they'd been in, while the other was much, much larger.

Godrick gave the cavern a nervous look. "Stalactites an' stalagmites don't form in sandstone," he said.

"That's what you're worrying about?" Talia said irritably.

"It's wrong," Godrick said.

"It's the labyrinth," Sabae said.

"I think we should take the smaller exit," Hugh said. "The big one gives me a bad feeling."

"What did I say about us trusting your gut?" Talia said.

"Ah'm getting a bad feelin' from it too," Godrick said.

"I'm going to say we avoid the bigger exit as well," Sabae said.

"If you're all for it, it's fine by me," Talia said. She poked Hugh in the stomach with a finger. "But if it turns out badly, it's Hugh's gut's fault."

Hugh rubbed his stomach surreptitiously when Talia turned away.

They were about halfway across the cavern when they heard the noise of distant chittering. It was coming from the big exit.

"What is it?" Hugh said. "More imps?"

"Ah don't think so," Godrick said. "Ah don't smell imp. Ah smell… shellfish?"

A swarm of little flying things burst out of the big tunnel. Hugh assumed they were insects at first, but something seemed *wrong* about the way they flew.

Talia launched several dreamfire bolts at the swarm, but had to stop after only a few. Hugh reached for a wardstone, but before he had a chance, the swarm was on them.

They weren't insects, but instead were beetle-winged orange crabs. Hugh yelled as they began biting and pinching his exposed flesh, and he heard the others do the same.

"Get down!" Sabae yelled.

Hugh threw himself downwards just before a massive gust of wind hit him. It launched him across the stone floor until he crashed against a stalagmite rising out of a pile of bones. Flying crabs and more bones pelted against Hugh as the wind continued. He felt himself slipping, and grabbed onto the stalagmite desperately. He slowly felt himself slipping off it, but before his grip was dislodged, the wind died.

Hugh took a second to stand back up. He was covered in bruises and squished crab bits. Sabae was standing looking exhausted, with her palms pressed together over her head where she'd clapped them together. Godrick had managed to grab Talia and sink his sledgehammer into the stone floor. As he watched, Godrick loosened the rock with a spell and it flowed away from the hammer.

"What in the name of the Hundred Clans was that?" Talia asked. She incinerated a single flying crab that had survived the gale.

Sabae looked exhausted. "Uncontrolled release of wind," she said. "The sort of thing I'm supposed to be learning not to do."

Godrick sniffed his shirt. "Hey Hugh, think yeh could do that cleaning cantrip again?"

Hugh started cleaning off the crab guts from their clothing, and passed around the glass scent absorbing sphere. At least he was useful for *something*, he thought bitterly.

They were just getting ready to move on again when something else burst from the big exit. It was another crab, but this one was seven feet tall, and its shell was at least twice that in width. It charged straight at them through the piles of bones.

Talia launched a single dreamfire bolt, which dissolved halfway to the crab. Sabae and Godrick readied themselves- Sabae charging up wind mana in a rapidly constricting sphere around her fist, and Godrick readying his hammer.

Hugh, for once, was ready. He still had his hand in his belt pouch, putting away the glass sphere, so he was able to rapidly pull out a wardstone. He snagged the sling off his belt and spun it up. The crab looked heavily armored, so if he wanted to hurt it he needed to hit some sort of weak spot…

There. The mouth. He just had to get past the twitching crab mouthparts first.

Hugh took a deep breath, aimed, then let loose on his exhale. The wardstone flew straight and true at the crab.

And hit it on the carapace several feet from the mouth.

The blast was enough to put a few cracks in the crab's shell, but it didn't even slow down. Hugh frantically searched for one of his two remaining wardstones, but before he could pull one out of his belt, the crab crashed into Godrick and Sabae.

Sabae's wind punch barely affected the crab, and it sent her flying with the back of a claw. She somehow managed to direct another blast of wind at the floor, arresting her fall.

Godrick's hammer, however, put a massive dent in the crab. Blue ichor dripped out between the cracked shards of the carapace.

The crab, unfortunately, was far from dead. It knocked him over with another backhand from a claw, and the huge youth rolled into a pile of bones. He managed to get his hammer up in time to block another blow from the crab claw, but he wasn't able to block the crab's leg striking at him. It pierced directly into Godrick's leg, and he screamed, dropping his hammer and grabbing at the crab's offending limb.

The crab opened its claw, reaching down for Godrick.

Time seemed to slow to a stop. Hugh's grasping hand found one of the last two wardstones, and he started pulling it out of the belt pouch, feeling as though he were swimming through honey.

Beside him, Talia screamed wordlessly, and her tattoos flashed to life.

And the bones beneath the crab began to grow.

It looked like flames made of bone were rising out of the scattered bones on the floor, but at close to the speed of an arrow shot. The flame-shaped bones impacted the base of the crab's carapace. They pierced the shell in several places, and actually *lifted* the entire crab off the ground. Godrick was lifted as the crab's leg rose, until the crab's leg slipped out of his thigh. He screamed in pain as he fell back to the ground.

After a few seconds, the bones stopped growing, leaving an enraged crab trapped in a massive bone outcrop. It started flailing its claws wildly, battering at the bone outcrop.

Cracks started to form in the bone, but not from the claw's actions. They were starting at the base and growing upwards. And they were *glowing*, like the embers in a hearth.

"Get Godrick away from there," Talia said, and collapsed.

Hugh briefly stepped towards her, then turned and ran towards Godrick. He managed to get Godrick standing on his one good leg somehow, and started helping him hobble away. He could feel heat emanating from the bone outcrop, until it started to feel like standing near a furnace.

"Get out of here, Hugh," Godrick said. "Ah'll be fine."

Hugh ignored him, and kept helping Godrick forwards.

"Hugh, ah…" Godrick started.

"No," Hugh said, and kept helping. The heat had grown to the point where it was almost painful, and he could hear a loud cracking noise behind them.

Godrick looked behind them. "Get down," he yelled, and tackled Hugh onto the ground.

Just in time for the entire bone outcrop to violently explode.

Even under Godrick, Hugh felt a violent wash of heat and pressure, and he felt several shards of bone slice along the skin of his arm. He blacked out for a moment, but when he came to shards of bone and bits of crab were still pattering down onto the ground.

"You can get off me now, Godrick," Hugh said.

Godrick didn't say anything.

"Godrick?"

Scared now, Hugh managed to wriggle out from underneath Godrick's bulk. He gasped when he saw Godrick's back.

Godrick's shirt was burnt clean off his back, and a number of shards of bone jutted out of his skin, including one that had at least six inches jutting out of his back, with who knows how much inside him. The skin on Godrick's back was horribly burnt, and even charred in places.

Hugh was worried that Godrick was dead for a moment, until he saw Godrick's back shift as he took a breath.

"NO!" Sabae hobbled over to Hugh and Godrick as fast as she could in the stone cast, falling to her knees beside Godrick.

"He's still alive, but I don't know for how much longer," Hugh said worriedly.

Sabae was crying now. She reached out towards Godrick, but stopped before she touched his back.

"No," Sabae said quietly.

She reached out with both hands and planted them solidly on Godrick's back. She took a deep breath, and then her hands began to *glow.*

Hugh took a step back in shock. Lines of light spread out across Godrick's back. Godrick's burns receded as the lines passed them, and bits of bone were forced out of the wounds as they closed. Even the big shard of bone forced itself out of his back, revealing a terrifying length of bone that had been embedded in Godrick.

The lines of light shot down to Godrick's leg, clustering around the hole that went through it. It started to knit itself together.

Then the light simply went out, and Sabae fell backwards.

Godrick hadn't been completely healed, but it looked like his breath was coming much more easily now. His bleeding had lessened, but he looked stable. Sabae sat up and gave Hugh a despairing look.

"I said I'd never use my healing affinity," she said.

"You just saved your friend's life," Hugh said. "There's nothing for you to be ashamed of."

"It doesn't matter," Sabae said. "We're all going to die down here anyways."

Hugh didn't say anything. He glanced over at Talia, who was stirring on the ground.

He felt rage bubble up inside of him. Not at the crab monster, or the statues, or even Rhodes, without whom they'd never have been dropped down here. No.

The rage was targeted at himself.

Hugh was still useless. He could craft a ward or put together a cantrip, but when it really, counted, he couldn't protect himself or his friends.

Hugh turned and stomped off. He pumped more mana into the light cantrip drifting at his side, until it was so bright it almost hurt to look at.

"Hugh?" Sabae said.

Hugh ignored her, and stomped over to the big exit. He strode a few paces down it. The tunnel quickly opened into another, smaller cavern with no other exits, and no crabs that he could see alive in there. There was a shallow pool of water with what looked like egg-sacks in it, however.

Hugh stomped back out to the others.

"There's no crabs left in that side cave, and it looks more defensible than this one."

Talia had limped over to them.

"What's the point?" Sabae muttered. "We're not going to make it out of here."

"You never give up," Talia said. "You haven't failed until you do."

Sabae looked up at the two of them, then simply nodded.

Somehow, between the three of them, they managed to haul the unconscious Godrick into the side cave. The instant they had cleared the bones from a patch of ground and laid Godrick into it, Talia and Sabae passed out next to him. Hugh thought briefly about waking one of them to keep helping, but dismissed the thought.

They were the ones who'd done everything to help save them, while Hugh had done nothing. Hugh slipped his spellbook off his shoulder and got to work.

The first thing he did was anchor several light cantrips on various stalactites and stalagmites, so that the cavern was well lit.

Hugh started piling up the larger bones at the narrowest point of the entrance to the side cavern. It took him hours, but he eventually managed to construct a barricade of interlocking bones across the entrance. He doubted it would keep out any really determined creatures, but it was better than nothing.

He attended to the pond next. He tested the water with a simple cantrip. It wasn't the cleanest, but it wouldn't poison them. He refilled all of their water bottles.

His gaze turned to the crab eggs, and his eyes narrowed.

On the spot, a cantrip seemed to assemble itself in his mind's eye. It was essentially just a basic levitation cantrip, remarkably like the first one he'd ever successfully cast, but much, much more carefully targeted.

Carefully, so as not to break any, he slowly levitated all of the eggs onto the shore of the pond. He then picked up a femur, and systematically obliterated every single egg. He smashed the gelatinous spheres over and over again with the bone, splattering himself and his surroundings with their foul-smelling contents.

After a while, the femur cracked, and Hugh threw it to the ground. The others somehow hadn't woken up from the noise.

Hugh started searching the room for any treasure like the amulet he'd found on the skeleton earlier.

There wasn't much- the crabs didn't seem to be intelligent, so any treasure that ended up in here did so largely by accident. He found a few gold coins, an enchanted dagger, and a shield so badly battered Hugh doubted its enchantment worked.

Once he was done with that, he reinforced the barricade some more, and crafted some wards behind it to further shield them.

Then he cleaned all the crab ichor and bits off of himself and his friends, using the little glass sphere to remove the stench as well.

Then he just sat down by the pond. He looked around for something else to do, but there was nothing else.

So he just sat there with his thoughts.

Hugh really was worthless. He hadn't been able to help his friends at all. His wardstones had proven to just be useless trinkets, especially given that he had been dumb enough to not have a way to easily have them on hand, just putting them in his belt pouch. When the statues had attacked, he couldn't do anything, and the other three had to save him. When the crabs attacked, the same thing happened. Hugh did nothing but hold the team back.

If Hugh hadn't been with them in the first place, they never would have gotten into this mess. Rhodes wouldn't have gotten so angry and started the fight, and they never would have fallen down here.

When danger came, his friends had stood up to the challenge. Talia had used her bone affinity for the first time to save them from the crab. Godrick had literally thrown himself in front of an explosion for Hugh. Sabae had broken her vow not to use her healing for Godrick. Hugh, though? Hugh was just dead weight.

A little voice in the back of Hugh's head tried to remind him of the levitation spell he'd cast that had saved his friends, but he ignored it.

The longer Hugh sat there, the angrier and angrier he got at himself. He hated himself like he'd never hated anyone before- not his aunt, not his uncle, not his obnoxious cousins, not his uncaring teachers before Alustin, not Rhodes. The world would be better off without someone like him. Nothing good came out of a mage from Emblin.

His anger grew and grew, and Hugh felt like it was going to explode out of him, until, all of a sudden, it just… drained away.

Hugh burst into tears.

Hugh had no idea how long it had been when he finally stopped crying. He just felt empty and broken inside. His friends were going to die, and there was nothing he could do. Hugh was a worthless piece of nothing.

He looked over at them, and then narrowed his eyes.

No. There was one thing he could do.

He padded over beside their sleeping forms, but didn't wake them. Instead, he grabbed his spellbook and strode over to the pond.

He sat down on the shore of the underground pond and stared at the book in his lap for a moment, then looked up at the pond.

It was… actually kind of beautiful. Hugh had no idea how long they'd been in the labyrinth, but it felt like it must have been at least a day already. Hugh was bone tired. Every muscle in his body ached, and he had cuts and bruises everywhere. Even a burn on one hand that he had no memory of acquiring.

For all the horrors of the labyrinth, the pond was peaceful. Gentle ripples reflected the light from his cantrip onto the ceiling of the cave, and he spent quite a while just watching the patterns the light reflected on the ceiling.

Eventually, though, he took a deep breath and unlatched his spellbook. He slowly rifled through the pages, carefully inspecting the notes on the various wards he'd constructed in the short weeks since his birthday. When he got to the blank pages, he moved a little faster, but still couldn't force himself to turn them with any urgency.

Eventually, however, he reached a page near the back of the book. A page where he'd drawn a warlock contract he'd taken from a book of forbidden rituals.

There was a way he could help his friends, and all it would cost him was a deal with a demon.

"Bakori. Bakori. Ba…"

CHAPTER SEVENTEEN

THE CONTRACT

Before Hugh could finish saying Bakori's name a third time, something slipped out of the back of the spellbook and brushed his hand. His voice caught in his throat.

They were just three blank pages of paper, but Hugh suddenly felt hope rise in his heart.

They were pages he'd torn out from an Index Node in the Grand Library.

Hugh slowly pulled out the pages from the back of the spellbook, his hands shaking. He stared at them, warlock contract completely forgotten.

The index pages had the ability to lead you to any book in the library collection.

The pages could show Hugh and his friends the way out of the Labyrinth.

Hugh desperately scrambled for a quill and inkpot. He got them out and slammed the spellbook shut, using it as a writing desk.

His hands were shaking so hard he splattered ink across the page. He couldn't think of what to write for a moment, then smiled.

72 Uses of Dragon Dung.

The page did nothing for a moment, and Hugh's heart felt like it was going to stop. Abruptly, however, the page lifted up into the air and began to fold itself. It felt like it took forever, but when it was done, a simple crane hovered in the air in front of Hugh.

The crane darted out over the pond, circled back, flew over Hugh's sleeping friends, then flew back to Hugh.

Then, to Hugh's despair, the page unfolded itself and landed atop the book. On it was written two short sentences.

Current location unknown. Unable to locate requested volume.

Hugh's hopes crumpled. He angrily threw the pages to one side and stared at the warlock contract again.

He should have known there was no other way out of this. There'd be no easy solution for Hugh the Worthless.

Hugh took a deep breath and prepared to summon Bakori.

Then he stopped, and his eyes flicked back to the Index pages lying on the shore next to him.

Then his eyes flicked back to the contract.

Then back to the pages.

A tiny spark of hope appeared in Hugh's heart again.

Hugh frantically snatched up the pages from the beach again.

What was it that Alustin had said on the day of the Choosing, when he first told Hugh he was a warlock?

Warlocks could pact with any sentient being.

Or any being with the capacity to become sentient.

And Alustin had told them that the Index was already semisentient.

He wet his quill in his inkpot again, and set it to the page below.

Unable to locate selected volume.

Are you still connected to the rest of the Index?

I am the Index.

I mean, is this page still linked to the Index?

Yes, though some directional functionality remains limited.

Hugh took a deep breath before setting his quill to paper again.

I want to form a warlock pact with you.

There was no reply immediately. Hugh waited for what felt like eternity, even though it must have only been a few seconds. His heart started to sink, convinced this was a waste of time.

Then, finally, new words appeared.

You want *what?*

Hugh smiled.

I want to form a warlock pact with the Index.

One moment. Processing unique request.

Hugh waited impatiently. It took almost a minute before the page responded again. The letters this time appeared bolder, and appeared to have a little more life to them. If Hugh was going to try and describe the emotions of letters, he'd say they looked shocked.

Why would you possibly want to form a warlock pact with the Index?

I'm an apprentice who got trapped in one of the lower levels of the labyrinth by accident while taking my final test for the year. My teammates are wounded and exhausted, and me gaining affinities from a warlock pact is the only chance of us making it out of here alive.

...Who is this? Attempting to prank or confuse the Index is a serious violation of Library rules.

My name is Hugh of Emblin. My teammates are Sabae Kaen Das, Talia of Clan Castis, and Godrick, son of Artur Wallbreaker. I'm not trying to prank you. We're trapped on the fifth level of the labyrinth- if the demon who tried to get me to sign a warlock contract with him was telling the truth, that is- and though we have a temporary safe spot, who knows how long it will last.

...Demon?

It's a bit of a long story, but yes, there's a demon named Bakori wandering around down here who has offered me the power to save my friends, but I'd really rather not sign a contract with a demon.

Understandable. Contracts with demons tend to turn out very, very badly.

Hugh was starting to suspect that the Index was a little more than semi-sentient, as Alustin had called it.

This is... an exceptionally unusual request. Give me a few minutes while I verify your story.

Hugh leaned back and allowed himself to smile.

That wasn't a no.

It took quite some time for the Index to respond again. Hugh wasn't sure how long, but eventually more words scrawled across the page.

Your story checks out. The four of you were reported to have fallen, but scrying attempts for you over the last day have all failed- a normal result when attempting to scry the labyrinth. Your status as a warlock is by no means common knowledge, so it seems improbable that it could be anyone other than you.

So you'll sign a contract with me?

Normally I would simply say no, but in this case, I feel circumstances might demand it. I must ask one question first, however.

Hugh's heart felt like it was going to stop when the Index wrote no, but it promptly started back up again when the sentence completed.

Anything.

Why do you seek to pact with me?

To save my friends.

There was to response for a moment.

Very well.

Hugh sighed in relief.

Let's do this, then! I...

No. I'm willing to pact with you, but not without firmly establishing terms and conditions first.

Like what?

Nothing happened for a moment, then a long list started writing itself, actually wrapping over to the next page.

The signer of this contract confirms that they truly are Hugh of Emblin. If a party other than Hugh of Emblin signs this contract, the contract will enforce itself fatally upon them.

Hugh of Emblin will not knowingly put the Index, the Library, or the staff of the Library in danger if it is at all possible to avoid. Violation of this clause is room for declaring the contract null and void. Severe enough violations may be grounds for enforcing this contract fatally.

Hugh of Emblin will be responsible for bringing at least one (1) volume to be added to the Library's collection each year. Said volume must not be already possessed by the Library. If Hugh of Emblin fails to do so, that will be allowable cause for declaring the contract null and void. Reasonable accommodation will be made for this requirement, however- for example, if Hugh of Emblin is traveling and will have difficulty returning to the Library on time, or is ill, or if similar extenuating circumstances occur.

The contract went on and on like that for some time. All told, there were nearly thirty clauses to the contract, establishing allowable behavior, requirements, and the like. At the very end was a single clause that simply read:

Hugh of Emblin will have his mana intermingled with the drafting party of this contract, and will be granted appropriate affinities thereby, as well as training in how to use them.

Hugh smiled and put his pen to paper.

I accept.

Hugh pulled out the second sheet of Index paper and began to copy the contract he'd recorded in his spellbook onto it. He drew a series of spellforms linking the clauses on the first page with the contract, then linked it all together.

The last step was actually signing it. It didn't require actually signing the contract, or signing it in blood, like some imaginative story-tellers had claimed. Instead, it simply required both parties to channel their mana into the two unlinked portions of the contract's spellforms. Normally both parties needed to be physically present, but since they were writing the contract on paper that was physically part of the Index, Hugh was sure that it would work fine.

Hugh took a deep breath and reached his finger towards the spot he needed to touch. Then a single word scrawled itself across the page.

No.

The page jerked itself out of Hugh's hands, flew out over the pond, and ignited. It burned to ash in seconds, which drifted down into the pond.

Hugh stared at the pond in shock, then down at the pages in his hands. Words were writing themselves onto the first sheet below the clauses.

That contract spellform is intended for contracts with demons. Where did you find that? Was it from the demon Bakori you mentioned?

Hugh quickly wrote down the story about finding the volume of forbidden spells.

Fascinating. I have no record of that book. That book should not be shelved there, and should be in a much more secure section. This is a mystery for another time, however. Given the danger of your situation, we should complete your contract quickly. I will provide the contract spellform. Once the contract is complete, you and your

friends need to STAY WHERE YOU ARE. I will send help for you. That being said, know that I sign this contract against my better judgment. If there were any other way to locate you, I would take it, but signing a contract might be the only way to find you.

Hugh watched, fascinated, as a new spellform sketched itself on the final page in his possession. It largely resembled the first contract, but it had a number of key differences, most notably in the manner in which energy was routed between the signatories. In a matter of minutes, the new warlock contract was done, and the empty spellform for the Index's magical signature lit up.

Hugh took a deep breath, trying to calm his racing heart, and pressed his finger against the page, then channeled his mana through it.

Hugh's world went white.

Hugh was sitting in a blank, empty void, with only whiteness surrounding him. He was naked, holding only the warlock contract and the page with the clauses in his hand. He opened his mouth to speak, but before he could say anything, the letters and spellforms began tearing themselves out of the page. They drifted and swirled like a cloud of bugs in front of him for a moment.

Hugh reached out to touch the letters, but the instant he touched one, it burned his skin, leaving a welt. He pulled his hand back, hissing.

And then all the letters and spellforms shot straight at him like arrows.

Each and every one burned worse than anything he'd ever felt before, and he could feel them crawling beneath his skin, writhing and twisting and rewriting themselves. The pain felt like it would last forever, but then it stopped.

Hugh panted, barely conscious. He looked down and saw the spellforms seemed to have tattooed himself on his chest. Even as he watched, the blisters and welts faded away to nothing. He could feel writing on his back as well, and somehow knew it was the contract's clauses.

Slowly, the tattooed contract began to fade. So did the white void around him.

But it wasn't replaced by the cave.

Instead, Hugh found himself being swept up by a mighty river. He couldn't tell which way was up, and found himself being pulled every which way by the powerful currents. His lungs burned, and he frantically tried to swim through the water, only to have it turn into skin tearing wind, and then a suffocating flow of sand, and then writhing vines, and…

"Hugh!"

The vision went on and on, and the powerful forces tearing at him never relented, and never held a single form for longer than a moment.

"Hugh, wake up!"

Finally, just when he thought he was about to succumb to the current, he felt something immensely strong grab him by the arm and haul him out of it.

Awaken, Hugh. Your friends need you.

CHAPTER EIGHTEEN

SOMETHING HUNGRY THIS WAY COMES

Hugh woke with a gasp. He felt… different. He could feel his mana reservoirs like he never could before. There were three new, deep channels leading into and out of them. He…

He sat up abruptly, only to be hit by a blinding pain. He recoiled, only to realize a second later that he'd smacked Talia in the forehead with his own forehead.

"Hugh! You're awake!" Talia tackled Hugh, knocking him back down to the ground and squeezing him so hard that he thought his ribs would break. "We all woke up and you were asleep and having some sort of nightmare and there were spellforms glowing on your chest and we couldn't wake you for hours and…" Talia pulled out of the hug and looked Hugh deep in the eyes, her face inches away from his.

Then she slapped him. Really, really hard.

"What in the name of the ghosts of everyone who ever froze to death did you do to yourself? You had us all scared senseless!"

Talia smacked him upside the head, and Hugh raised his arms to protect himself.

At which point Talia punched him in the stomach. "I thought you cared enough not to worry us like that, Hugh! I…"

A hand reached out and caught Talia's arm before she could hit Hugh again. Sabae bodily picked up Talia, turned away, and set her on her feet.

"What Talia means to say," Sabae said, "is that we're all very concerned and would like to know what happened after we fell asleep."

Sabae offered Hugh a hand up, and as she helped him stand Hugh got a chance to look around for the first time since he'd woken up. He was still in the cave, still by the pond. He had no idea how much time had passed, but…

It was at that point that Sabae wrapped him in a hug, and he realized how much stronger physically she was than Talia.

"Can't breathe. Can't…"

Sabae let him go, and he took a deep breath of the cool cave air in relief.

"Where's mah hug?" Hugh heard Godrick say. Hugh turned around to see Godrick propped sitting up against a stalagmite near the shore. Hugh smiled, happy to see Godrick awake, and strode over towards him. He paused just out of hugging range, however.

"Please don't break my ribs, Godrick," he said.

"Don't think ah can right now, honestly," Godrick said.

Hugh leaned in and hugged Godrick. True to his word, Godrick's hug was gentle- for Godrick, at least. Hugh was sure he'd hardly gotten more than a few bruises from it.

The others joined them, and they all sat looking at the pond.

"I signed a warlock contract," Hugh said.

Everyone's heads snapped to look at him.

"Why would you…" Godrick started.

"Not with that demon?" Sabae said at the same time.

Talia just growled inarticulately at him.

"No, I didn't sign a contract with the demon. I signed it with the Index, and I did it to try and save all of you."

Everyone was silent for a moment, and then Talia spoke up.

"You did WHAT?"

It took Hugh quite a while to explain what had happened, after which they were silent for a time.

"What affinities did yeh get?" Godrick asked.

"I…" Hugh said. "I, uh, don't actually know."

Everyone stared at him.

"You don't know?" Sabae said.

"I didn't think to ask," Hugh said.

"You didn't think to ask?" Sabae said.

Hugh didn't know what to say to that.

"I, uh… I think I have three of them," Hugh said.

"Well, uh… that's nothin' ta sneer at," Godrick said.

"I bet you have an affinity for sheer idiocy," Talia said.

Hugh dodged an elbow from Talia, but she didn't seem to be trying that hard to hit him this time.

"So now all we have to do is wait," Sabae said.

"After all of this, I'm fine with being patient for once," Talia said.

Everyone looked at her in surprise.

"I can be patient when I want. What? Quit looking at me like that!"

They waited for hours and hours without anything happening. They talked for much of that time- of Talia's figuring out her bone affinity on her own, of Sabae's reluctant decision that she should learn to properly use her healing affinity, and of Godrick's desire to simply finish attuning fully, so he'd never find himself so vulnerable again.

Hugh gave the enchanted dagger to Talia and the shield (which probably didn't work) to Sabae. He offered an apology to Godrick for not having anything for him, but Godrick just laughed and said it was fine.

Finally, Hugh found the nerve to talk about what had been lurking at the back of his head for so long.

"I'm sorry I've been a burden for so long," Hugh said. "If I'd had a pact before, maybe I actually could have helped you out more in the tunnels, instead of just being a useless burden."

Everyone stared at him for a moment, and then Talia slapped him in the face again. Even harder than before.

"You're not a burden, you great idiot!" Talia said.

Hugh rubbed his cheek. "I wasn't able to help you all like I should, and maybe you wouldn't have been hurt if I…"

"Talia's right, you really are an idiot," Sabae said. "You're the last thing from a burden. If it hadn't been for your wardstones, we would have taken a lot more in the way of injuries from those imps on the first level. And you saved all of our lives when you stopped our fall down that shaft."

"If it hadn't been for you basically hauling me up Godrick's ladder," Talia said, "I doubt I would have gotten out of the statue room."

"Ah would have died when Talia's bone outcropping exploded if yeh hadn't hauled me away from it, Hugh. Yeh saved my life," Godrick said.

"Hugh, we all depended on each other out there," Sabae said. "If any of us had been absent, none of us would have survived- and that includes you. You need to stop thinking of yourself as worthless, Hugh. You're one of the smartest mages I know, and I'm happy to have you by my side."

"Aye," said Godrick.

"I'm going to beat you black and blue next time I hear one of your damn speeches about how worthless you are, Hugh," Talia said. "They might be the most annoying thing I know."

Hugh grinned weakly and tried to surreptitiously wipe the corner of his eye. The others, thankfully, pretended not to notice.

"Thank you all so much for everything," Hugh said. "I…"

It was at that point that they heard a crunch come from beyond the bone barrier, and then something enormous growling.

Everyone went immediately silent. Hugh cursed himself silently. He'd assumed that they were safe just because he'd gotten in touch with help when he pacted with the Index. He'd just let them all yammer on like fools, even knowing that if a monster down here overheard them it could mean their deaths.

The thing on the other side of the barricade brushed against it, and several bones came clattering down. Hugh could hear the thing breathing raggedly.

To his sides, Hugh could see Talia's tattoos begin to glow, and wind begin to circle around Sabae's fists. Godrick's fingers began to sink down into the stone below him.

The barricade shuddered again, and Talia's tattoos brightened even farther. The bones of the barricade began to rapidly grow, filling the hallway. The glowing cracks followed soon behind. If the creature stayed there, maybe…

The barrier shattered as *something* plunged through it. Hugh's wards detonated, not seeming to affect the creature at all. The extra bone that Talia had grown exploded when it was broken, and the thing was lost in the flame for a moment. It rolled across the ground, putting much of the fire out, and climbed onto its feet again.

It looked like a wolf, if wolves were ten feet tall, covered in scales, and had writhing mouths full of fangs running down their sides. The creature looked around the room for a moment, then fixed its gaze on them.

Then it charged.

Time seemed to slow down for Hugh again. He could see Talia launching dreamfire bolts at the creature to one side, and Sabae readying herself behind her new shield. Several spikes of stone shot up from the floor in front of the creature, but it slammed through them without slowing down or seemingly being injured.

Hugh found himself desperately reaching out with his hands and his mind, and his mind… found something. It latched itself onto one of the new channels running through his mana reservoirs, and redirected the flow outwards. Hugh didn't even try to craft a spellform in his mind's eye- he just let the torrent of mana flow through him, and somehow felt the Aether ripple around him as he did so.

A shaft of molten light tore out of Hugh's hands, slamming right into the charging beast's chest. The air seemed to scream, and waves of heat slammed into Hugh.

The creature simply exploded, splattering across the room in a wave of gore and ichor.

The light blinked out. Hugh stared at his hands for a moment, then looked at his friends in shock.

And promptly fainted.

CHAPTER NINETEEN

AN UNEXPECTED CONVERSATION

THE first thing Hugh noticed upon waking up was that the rock floor of the cavern was oddly soft.

The second thing he noticed is that he didn't remember there being blankets in the cave.

Hugh opened his eyes and bolted upright. He was in an unfamiliar bed in an empty room, with a whole row of beds next to him. Only one was occupied, however. In it lay Godrick, who was heavily bandaged and asleep.

"It's about time you woke up," someone said.

Hugh turned away from Godrick to see Alustin, who was sitting on a chair nearby, reading a book. In fact, he hadn't actually looked up from the book at all- he was still reading.

"Sir, what…" Hugh started.

"How many times do I have to ask you to call me Alustin?" Alustin said.

"Sir, what happened? How did I… we… get here? Where are Sabae and Talia? Why…" Hugh said in a rush.

Alustin held up his hand without looking away from his book, stopping Hugh in his tracks. "Sabae and Talia are fine, they're merely in the girl's wing of the infirmary. As for the rest of your questions, I'll answer them- and many more, I'm sure- in a moment. For now, though, get dressed, and I'll meet you in the hallway. We have somewhere to be."

Alustin reached under his chair and tossed a student uniform onto the bed, then left the room, still reading as he walked. Hugh noticed his spellbook, beltpouch, and Clan Castis dagger were all tucked between the trousers, shirt, and jacket.

Hugh quickly got dressed and followed Alustin out the door.

Alustin tucked his book into his ever-present satchel as Hugh walked into the hallway, and gestured for Hugh to follow him.

“Before I answer any more questions, I’m going to need to hear your version of events down in the caverns,” Alustin said.

Hugh told him everything. About the imps on the first floor, the fight with Rhodes, the encounter with Bakori the demon, the statues, the crabs, and the horrid wolf creature.

Alustin was quiet for several minutes, then finally sighed. During that time, Hugh recognized where they were- they were heading towards the library.

“Ask your questions, Hugh.”

“What happened down in the labyrinth after I passed out?” Hugh asked. “The last thing I remember was blasting apart that wolf creature with… fire? I pacted with the Index, I was expecting a paper affinity or something.”

Alustin sighed. “You tapped into a brand new, completely unattuned affinity, then cast an unstructured spell that not only used up your entire mana reserves, but also drained much of the mana from the Aether immediately surrounding you. It badly overstressed your mana channels and reservoirs, as well as giving you significant burns all over your hands and arms.”

Hugh glanced at his hands. They seemed fine.

“We- that being Artur Wallbreaker, Aedan Dragonslayer, Sulassa Tidecaller, and a few others- arrived less than an hour after you slew the… we have no idea what it was, considering how little of it you left behind, and your friends’ descriptions didn’t shed a lot of light on it. We brought you out of the labyrinth, and you’ve been recovering ever since. You were unconscious for about two days, even with all the healing magic the infirmary healers have been pumping into you.”

They passed into the library, and began heading down the stairs towards the restricted sections. Hugh realized that Alustin had never actually answered the question about his new affinity.

“It’s astonishing that you survived as long as you did down there, Hugh. No one has ever heard of a group of first years that made it down that deep and lived to tell the tale. Most full mages seldom venture much deeper than you went. You were extremely lucky- but you also had help."

"Help?" Hugh said, but he had a suspicion he knew what Alustin was about to say.

Alustin didn't say anything, though. Instead, he walked up to a door, and pressed his hand against a spellform on it. The door cracked open, and on the other side was the immense, cavernous space of the Grand Library.

"Sir, should I be here? You spent all that time warning us about how dangerous it is..."

"You're with me, you'll be fine. Besides, your contracted partner is here, and you need to meet them in person."

They strode out onto the balcony, and Alustin walked them to the nearest index node. He wrote something Hugh didn't see, and the page tore itself out, folding itself into a tiny pegasus in mid-air. Hugh and Alustin followed it as it took off along the balcony.

"Sir, where are we..."

"I've been lying to you for some time, Hugh." Alustin looked somewhat ashamed as he said this.

"Sir?"

"Hugh, when's the last time you've gone outside of the mountain?" Alustin said.

"...Sir?" Hugh replied, genuinely puzzled.

"When's the last time you went outside?" Alustin said.

"Uhhh... I couldn't say for sure, but it's been a while, sir," Hugh said. "I've been pretty busy training for the labyrinth test."

"When exactly?" Alustin said.

Hugh started to open his mouth, then closed it, puzzled. The pegasus flew out into the immense open space in the center of the room, where a large platform assembled itself out of flying cobblestones in midair. It was big enough for a dozen people, so Hugh and Alustin fit easily. The instant they stepped on board, the whole thing began to descend.

"I... I'm not sure," Hugh said.

Alustin gave him a serious look.

"So far as anyone in Skyhold knows, you have not once set foot outside of the mountain since you entered it. You've skipped every class with a field trip and always found ways to dodge going outside with your friends."

Hugh wracked his brain, and realized to his dismay that he actually couldn't think of a single time he'd gone outside since he'd gotten to Skyhold. How had that happened? Hugh loved the outdoors, and had spent most of his childhood in the woods of Emblin.

Alustin pulled a series of rolled-up drawings out of his satchel and handed them to Hugh. Hugh opened them up as they passed a floor that seemed to be entirely filled with books made of glass.

"Sir, these are my wards from my room… and from my old room, too."

"What do the spellforms in blue do, Hugh?"

"They… uh… hmmm."

Hugh couldn't remember what those spellforms did, even though he distinctly remembered adding them to his room wards.

"They're wards meant to protect your dreams from outside intrusion, Hugh."

Hugh stared at Alustin.

"Why would I draw those, and why didn't I know what they were?"

Alustin was silent for a moment.

"Do you remember the first time I told you that you were a warlock, Hugh?"

"Yes," Hugh said cautiously.

"Do you remember that I told you that if I'd even suspected you'd been in contact with a demon, that I'd have taken drastic measures?"

"Yes," Hugh said cautiously again. "But I wasn't, so you didn't."

"I lied," said Alustin. "You have, in fact, been in contact with a demon since the first day you walked into Skyhold."

Hugh stared at Alustin in shock as the platform continued to slowly descend through the immense chamber.

"I… no I haven't, sir!" Hugh said.

"You have indeed, Hugh, though not consciously. Uncontracted warlocks are particularly susceptible to mental manipulation by potential contracting partners. Demons are especially fond of doing so, and by doing so gaining the services of warlocks. Since you first set foot in Skyhold the demon you met below has been subtly manipulating you in an effort to gain a contracted warlock."

Hugh looked away from Alustin and stared out into the space in the center of the immense room. A huge bridge spanned the nearest corner of the room on this level, and it was entirely filled with rows and rows of bookshelves.

"The demon Bakori was the reason that you never left the mountain. If you had, you would have left the range of his mental manipulation, and who knows if you would have willingly returned," Alustin said. "He was the reason you kept isolating yourself socially farther and farther."

"I've always been shy and bad with people," Hugh said. "He didn't make me that way."

"No, but he exacerbated the problem," Alustin said. "He amplified your feelings of loneliness, your despair at your inability to do magic, all of it. All to make you more vulnerable. It was Bakori that led you to the library door with the weakened wards, and Bakori that led you to the volume of forbidden spells in here, not the Index."

Hugh watched an origami golem in the shape of a seagull desperately flap to get away from a pack of hungry grimoires pursuing it through the air. He felt a little sick as he thought about all the gut feelings that kept leading him astray over the last year.

"Once you entered the labyrinth itself, the demon's manipulation grew much more overt. Those gut feelings that led you down specific pathways? Those came from Bakori," Alustin said.

"Sir, maybe you should stop saying his name so much, so you don't draw his attention," Hugh said.

Alustin smiled, but there was no humor to it.

"There's no risk of that, Hugh. You were the only one who he could hear calling his name, and only because of the spells he had placed on you, and those were all broken when you signed a warlock pact. Not many spells can survive that sort of interference."

The blue-white glow from below was growing close now, bathing the lower levels of the room in its light. It didn't seem like they could have dropped that far at the speed they were going, but they had to be miles below the level near the top of the room where they had started.

"It was Bakori who led you to that secret chamber above the mana flume chamber where you found him," Alustin said. "Rhodes was manipulated there as well, but by swarms of Bakori's imps instead. In retrospect, the test should have been stopped as soon as students started reporting imps showing up. It's amazing we didn't have any deaths this year. It was Bakori who amplified your despair as you fought your way through the labyrinth, and it seems Bakori almost had you in that last cavern. But…"

Alustin didn't say anything for a moment.

"But?" Hugh said.

"You fought back," Alustin said. "You've been fighting back this whole time."

"I've been what?"

"You've been fighting back," Alustin repeated.

Hugh could see indistinct shapes in the glow below them. They were orderly, regular, and shifting constantly.

"You might not have consciously known you were being manipulated, but you did subconsciously- and you were fighting it to the point that you were unknowingly drawing wards on your door to try and keep Bakori out of your dreams. In fact, your unusual abilities with wards might be directly related to this- I've never heard of a warlock whose will imbuing abilities apply to wardcrafting. The vast majority of warlocks have those talents apply elsewhere- battle magic, bindings, or banishments, usually. Your subconscious might have forced your will imbuing abilities to apply to your wards in order to help protect you from the demon."

Hugh thought back to the fight he and Talia had when she found his lair, and the nightmares he had the night before he repaired his wards. He found himself nodding slowly. Then a thought occurred to him.

"How do you know all of this, sir?"

"Much of it I've pieced together from circumstantial evidence and the stories of others. I do have to admit, however, than I have been, uh… spying on you for some time. One of my attunements is farseeing."

Hugh stared at Alustin in surprise. He'd never told his apprentices what his attunements were, though they'd suspected he had more than one. Farseeing, however, was a rare attunement for a battle mage. It was closely related to light attunements, but rather than manipulating light, allowed the mage to see visions of far away places- or, at the least, see long distances. It was a highly valued power, but extremely difficult to train and use.

"Was the demon why you haven't told us what your attunements are? What are your others?"

Alustin just smiled and pointed off the side of the platform.

"This is the Index."

They were sinking down into the blue haze. Hugh was sure there was no way that they had approached so closely so fast, but the air was already glowing misty around them.

The haze itself wasn't any particular color- it just looked like incredibly thick mist. The blue glow came from the moving shapes inside the mist. As they drew closer, he reached out and ran his hand through the mist. He could feel a slight resistance, but he doubted he would have noticed it if he hadn't been paying attention.

As they sunk fully into it, Hugh could start to make out shapes within it. Gears, chains, axles, and more arched around them through the mist. They turned, ratcheted, and shifted all about them. They all seemed to be made of brilliant blue light, though Hugh couldn't get a good look at any through the mist. Tiny blue sparks darted about the mists. Whenever Hugh tried to watch one its behavior looked random, but when he looked at the movement of the sparks as a swarm, the order of their behavior became immediately obvious, though he doubted he could explain it. The Index was much quieter than he would have expected, with the rumble of machinery sounding faint and far away, and only a gentle hissing noise from the sparks.

"Hello?" Hugh said. "Index? It's me, Hugh."

Nothing answered.

"Hello?" Hugh tried again. "I made a contract with you through some of your pages?"

Again, no answer.

Alustin finally spoke up again. He looked visibly nervous.

"There's another lie I told to you, Hugh."

Hugh glanced sharply at him.

"The Index isn't alive. It's not sentient to any degree whatsoever- it's merely a mass of information. It was specifically designed, in fact, to not be able to become sentient. Its creators judged it too much of a risk. Instead, it has the ability to be linked to a single, powerful mind at a time, which has the ability to direct it and lend it a limited degree of intelligence."

Hugh gaped at him.

"What… what are you saying, sir?"

The haze was thinning around them as they sank through the Index.

"You didn't form a contract with the Index, Hugh. You formed a contract with the mind controlling the Index. You pacted with High Librarian Kanderon Crux."

CHAPTER TWENTY

THE HEART OF THE LIBRARY

HUGH was still gaping at Alustin in shock when they burst out of the mist (and midst) of the Index. He looked around to see Kanderon Crux waiting for them. She rested atop a massive floating dais made of blue crystal. Hugh couldn't see anything below her dais but darkness and mist like that in the Index, but without the glow of the Index's machinery. Her face was that of a stern woman in middle age as she glanced up from the book she was reading.

Said face was taller than Hugh.

Kanderon Crux was a sphinx, with the face of a woman, the body of a lion, and the wings of an eagle. She was at least seventy-five feet long, not counting the length of her tail, and had proportions similar to, albeit thicker limbed, than those of an actual lion. Her coat was a deep tawny amber, and her eyes were a deep blue.

Her wings were what immediately drew attention, however. Unlike every illustration of sphinxes that Hugh had ever seen, her wings weren't covered with feathers, or even made of flesh and blood- they were solid crystal. They were a shade of blue that closely resembled the blue of the Index's machinery, but that somehow possessed immensely deeper depths. The crystals were cunningly… crafted? Grown? However they were put together, they flexed and moved like true wings, with a faint whisper of musical chimes whenever the crystals brushed against one another.

Though the wings were folded up, Hugh was sure they must have a wingspan wider than Kanderon Crux's body was long. They must weigh more than the rest of her combined. No, more than all the buildings in Hugh's home village.

Their platform slowly pulled alongside Kanderon's immense crystal dais. Kanderon closed her book with a single claw with a loud thud.

Alustin stepped onto the crystal dais, then went down to one knee and lowered his head. Hugh quickly emulated him. The origami pegasus golem that had led them there left, darting back up to the mists of the Index.

"High Librarian," Alustin said.

"Hugh of Emblin."

Kanderon's voice hit him like a ton of bricks, and he almost lost his balance, even lowered to one knee. He felt it resonate inside his mind and mana reservoirs as well.

"**My apologies**," Kanderon said. This time her voice was much quieter. It was still as loud as you'd expect from a being larger than most houses, and Hugh still felt it resonate inside his mind, but it was bearable now. "**I've never pacted with a warlock before, so much of this is new to me.**"

"It's… it's fine, mas… er, High Librarian."

"**Master Kanderon will be fine, Hugh.**"

Hugh finally found the nerve to meet Kanderon's unblinking gaze.

"I am Kanderon Crux, High Librarian of the Grand Library of Skyhold, the Sphinx of Living Crystal, and the last known living Founder of the Academy at Skyhold. I have rejected every single offer to pact with me before this, Hugh. Do you know why I accepted yours?"

Hugh waited for some time before he realized that the sphinx wasn't merely asking a rhetorical question. He was still a little in shock at hearing her claim to be one of Skyhold's founders- that would make her at least half a millennium old. At least. He shook his head.

"No, Master Kanderon."

"Venture a guess."

Hugh racked his brain frantically.

"Because you didn't want me to contract with Bakori?"

Kanderon snorted, and her exhalation hit Hugh like a strong wind.

"Thwarting that wretched demon is quite a bonus, I must admit. I thought that I'd destroyed him centuries ago, so I was displeased to hear that he survived. But no, that's not the reason, Hugh."

She continued to stare unblinkingly at Hugh.

"Then… why? Why me? I'm nobody special."

A horrifying rasping noise came from deep within Kanderon's throat. Hugh was horrified for a moment until he realized that she was laughing.

"Nobody special, Hugh? You fought off a demon's influence almost single-handedly for most of a year. You attracted the attention of one of my most prized pupils, who I was convinced would never take any students of his own."

Alustin snorted at that.

"You and your friends are learning magical skills that few full mages even attempt. Did Alustin ever tell you how rare your skills are? Only one in a dozen dream attuned mages ever learn to reliably manifest dreams, and of those only a tiny handful ever master dreamfire. Your barbarian friend doing so even with the restrictions of her tattoos in just a few short months? It should have been impossible. Your little storm mage friend should never have been able to successfully combine mana layering, formless casting, and a truly impractical set of mana channeling techniques. So far as I know, her developing style of magic is unique."

Kanderon leaned closer.

"And you, Hugh. You were so desperate to prove your worth to yourself that you took on a task generally considered to be the domain of archmages. There are plenty of mages who create their own spellforms. Learning to do it on the fly? There are only a handful of mages on the continent with the knack for it. Alustin isn't even capable of it, and had I known what he was up to, I would have forbidden him from trying to teach it to you for fear of catastrophic failure."

Hugh's jaw dropped in shock, and he shot a glance at Alustin, who was avoiding eye contact with Hugh.

"Hugh's skill with wards didn't just come from his warlock related will imbuing talents," Alustin said. "He was an absolute natural at recombining the spellforms that he was given to craft wards with to get new results. It seemed an intuitive enough leap to follow."

"To teach him how to craft new spellforms in a lab, perhaps. On the fly? Sheer ambition on your part."

For all of Kanderon's criticism, Hugh thought he actually detected a hint of pride in her voice.

"So that's why you chose me?" Hugh said. "My ability with spellforms?"

Kanderon's attention returned to Hugh. **"Warlocks with comparably impressive abilities have tried to pact with me before, Hugh. Impressiveness alone is not enough for me to pact with someone. No, I only brought that up to make it clear that I would not pact with a nobody, and that I most certainly considered you worthy in that regard."**

Hugh looked down at the ground, but a faint smile touched the corners of his mouth.

"No, Hugh, what made me decide to pact with you? It was the fact that you had no idea who I was, what powers I might grant you, or even if the contract would work. You risked everything on the chanciest of bets, and you did it entirely selflessly- not for your own power, but for your friends."

Hugh blushed.

"Actually, uh… I was wondering…"

"Well?"

"What are my affinities? The one I tried to use in the labyrinth was… terrifying."

Kanderon chuckled.

"That is the most offensively oriented of the affinities I've granted to you. It's commonly known as a star affinity, though I prefer stellar affinity as a name. It's closely related to, though distinct from, solar affinities."

Hugh couldn't help but smile and think of Heliothrax, the sun dragon that had been the first entity he'd ever seriously imagined contracting with.

"Once fully attuned to it, you will possess immense destructive capability, but I have to warn you against relying too heavily on it. Spells cast using this affinity are immensely mana intensive, and it will be years before you can use more than a small number of star spells in a day. Even I have to be conservative with their use."

Hugh was a little disappointed by this, but not too much. He'd never even heard of another stellar mage before Kanderon.

"The next should, I hope, be obvious."

Hugh looked at Kanderon blankly, then shook his head.

She sighed loudly. *Very* loudly. **"The second is a crystal affinity, which should have been obvious from my wings, my dais, and the construction of the Index."**

"Crystal affinity?" Hugh said. "Is that to rock affinities like steel affinities are to iron affinities? Just a more focused, powerful version of it?"

"There is… a small amount of validity to that comparison," Kanderon said, **"but it's more incorrect than otherwise. We'll discuss that another time, but for now, suffice it to say that this affinity will be by far the one you use most of your three. It provides numerous defensive options, a few offensive options, and an immense amount of versatile utility spells. It will even provide you with some fascinating new options for your wards."**

Hugh really liked the sound of that.

"The third… the third affinity is complicated. It's closely related to spatial affinities, but is quite distinct."

Hugh had never heard of spatial affinities before. He opened his mouth to ask, but Kanderon pressed onwards.

"It's… sometimes erroneously called a labyrinth affinity, given that it is used in the construction of most labyrinths. I also used it in the construction of this library, and some archmages have been known to use it to create pocket universes. It's also known as a dimensional affinity, but I tend to refer to it as a planar affinity. The most basic use of it is creating extradimensional spaces."

Kanderon leaned incredibly close, until her face was mere feet away. It suddenly occurred to Hugh that while most of Kanderon's teeth resembled a human's, her fangs were both much larger and much sharper proportionally. Her mouth was big enough that she could likely devour Hugh in a single bite, if she so chose.

"It is not a natural affinity, and absolutely no one is born with it. It can normally only be trained. Even with your exceptional skills, you are never, under any circumstances, to even tap into that affinity without my express command. Nine out of ten mages who attempt to develop a planar attunement die in the attempt, and I do not intend to waste my effort and have you be one of them."

Hugh's heart was racing, and all he could do was nod mutely in response.

"Why… why is it so dangerous?" Hugh asked.

"Look over the edge of my dais, Hugh," Kanderon said.

Hugh cautiously walked over to the edge and peered down into the mists.

"How deep do you think that is, Hugh?"

"I have no idea," Hugh admitted.

"Nor do I. I originally intended this room to be a mid-sized addition to a library already lacking in space, but thanks to unanticipated interactions with the magic of the labyrinth, this room has continued to grow every year of its existence. It grows not only when we add new books, but grows on its own, adding books seemingly on its own, books that, so far as we can tell, don't come from our world. Planar magic is terrifyingly difficult and seldom works as intended."

Kanderon stared at him searchingly for a moment, then eased back away from Hugh again.

"Will I gain any other magical abilities from our contract other than the affinities?" Hugh asked.

Kanderon raised an eyebrow at Hugh. **"Perhaps, but if that occurs it will likely take quite some time. We'll discuss your duties and training in more detail later, but there's more we need to discuss today. Alustin, if you would bring out the stone?"**

Alustin pulled something out of his pocket. Hugh immediately recognized it as the stone he'd found on the skeleton in the labyrinth.

"This, Hugh, is known as a labyrinth stone," Kanderon said. **"The stone itself is naturally occurring, though extremely rare. Most specimens are used for the same purpose- when they spend enough time in a labyrinth, they begin to channel the mana of that labyrinth through them. Eventually, they begin to allow the wielder to navigate the labyrinth more reliably, as well as bestowing other, more obscure powers. And this stone lay down in the labyrinth a long, long time. If that were all, it would be an exceptionally valuable find, and would serve you well in the future. However... you had it on you during our contract, and it somehow bonded to you during the pacting process."**

Alustin tossed Hugh the stone. He caught it and felt a curious sense of warmth from it.

"I mentioned that you might be able to form multiple warlock pacts due to your unusually large mana reservoirs," Alustin said. "I didn't expect you to do so until far in the future, and frankly I have no idea what a pact with a labyrinth stone will do, or whether it riding along another pact will allow it to become intelligent, like other pacted items."

"Nor do I," said Kanderon, **"which is not a feeling I particularly enjoy. We will be observing this stone carefully. It would be wrong to take it from you, however, so Alustin will be teaching you the relevant spells for maintaining a pacted item- starting with a spell capable of locating it anywhere."**

Hugh clutched the stone tightly, then tucked it in his beltpouch, next to the scent absorbing stone and the last remaining wardstones.

"Two more things before you go, Hugh. First, do not assume that just because you have broken Bakori's spells upon you, and that because I have pacted with you, that you're entirely safe from him. He will not take your rejection of his deal lightly, and he holds grudges for centuries. Bakori is an exceptionally dangerous foe, and it will be in everyone's best interest to keep you far away from him."

Hugh nodded, suddenly a bit nervous again.

"And the second thing?" Hugh said.

"On your way back, Alustin is going to give you a very, very thorough lecture on the dangers of crafting wards on fast-moving objects without the correct compensatory spellforms. You're exceptionally lucky those stones haven't exploded violently yet in your beltpouch. Throw them off the edge, if you would."

Hugh looked at the wardstones in shock, then gingerly eased them out of the beltpouch and tossed them into the mists below.

"We'll be speaking again soon, Hugh. And a fair word of warning- you'll come to view Alustin as an easy and undemanding teacher."

Hugh gulped.

Hugh rested his arms on the balcony railing and took a deep breath.

He stood on one of the balconies overlooking the sandship port and the Endless Erg. The sun and breeze felt amazing against his skin- he hadn't realized how much he'd missed having more access to the outdoors than a single window.

A sandship was just pulling out of Skyhold's port. Hugh watched it a bit enviously as sand drakes dodged between its masts.

"We're going to be on one of those soon enough when Alustin takes us on that trip he keeps talking about," Sabae said.

"I know," Hugh said, "but I still can't stand the idea of spending more time than I need to indoors.

Talia snorted and elbowed him in the ribs. "I'd always just figured people from Emblin were just normally that pale, and you avoided going outside so as not to burn."

Hugh rubbed his side ruefully as the others laughed.

"What happened then?" Godrick said.

Hugh had been telling them about the meeting with Kanderon Crux.

"Not much. A little more lecturing, then Alustin led me out of the library."

No one spoke for a long time after that. Hugh found, to his surprise, that the silence felt comfortable, not awkward. If you'd told him a few short months ago that he wouldn't just be a mage, but one apprenticed to a battlemage and bonded to a centuries old sphinx, Hugh would have… well, maybe not laughed, he would have been to shy for that, but at least thought you were crazy.

And if you'd told him that he'd actually have friends of his own? Friends who were not only amazing mages in their own right, but who would actually stand up for and stand with Hugh? Who thought Hugh was worth a damn? He definitely would have thought you were crazy.

Hugh took another deep breath, and slowly let it out.

He could get used to this.

JOHN BIERCE
PART 2
JEWEL OF THE ENDLESS ERG

CHAPTER ONE
THE TASTE OF SAND

Hugh of Emblin was good at quite a few things, but he wasn't particularly good at running on sand. Which was unfortunate, because he really needed to be right now.

"You're wasting your energy, Hugh. Sense my attacks, don't merely run wildly."

The massive sphinx that had spoken stared down at Hugh with irritation. She stood at the bottom of the sand dune Hugh was atop, and still towered over him. Kanderon Crux was at least seventy-five feet from nose to the base of her tail.

It had been several weeks since he'd formed a warlock pact with Kanderon, and she'd proven a far less patient teacher than Alustin.

Hugh tried to speak, but he couldn't manage to get words out past his parched mouth and aching lungs. Kanderon narrowed her huge eyes in irritation.

"Again."

Hugh reached out with his affinity sense, seeking the crystals that Kanderon was forming out of the dune's sand. There'd be no hint of them on the surface, so he had to find them before Kanderon launched them out of the sand at him again. This might just be training, but Kanderon was far from a gentle teacher.

The biggest differences he'd felt after pacting with the sphinx were his affinity senses. They allowed you to somehow *feel* whatever you were attuned to. Hugh had thought at first that this should easily allow him to detect the crystals Kanderon was forming out of sand.

Hugh, unfortunately, had never realized that sand seemed to be mostly made up of tiny crystals, so his senses almost entirely overwhelmed him each time he tried.

Hugh carefully tried to filter out the overload of information his senses were bringing him from the sound. Part of the time it felt like he was hearing his affinity senses, and part of the time it felt like he was smelling them. Kanderon and Alustin both claimed that it took time for the human mind to learn to understand an entirely new sense, and that it would be more comprehensible eventually, but right now trying to understand just gave him a splitting headache.

As Hugh tried to sort through what he was sensing, a fist-sized hunk of quartz abruptly hurtled out of the sand and hammered into his stomach. Hugh fell to his knees, feeling like he needed to vomit.

He decided that was probably a smart course of action, and promptly did so.

Kanderon rustled her wings in irritation. They were entirely fashioned— or grown, Hugh wasn't sure— out of blue crystal, with many chunks hovering in the air unconnected, yet holding formation with the rest. As she moved them, Hugh couldn't help but think of the world's largest wind chime.

"I could almost swear you're getting worse." Kanderon said.

Hugh winced. He spent a few moments catching his breath, then responded. "I'm trying, Master, I really am. But…"

He paused.

"But what?" Kanderon demanded.

"Do they really need to be watching?" Hugh asked.

He unwillingly glanced over at the next sand dune over, where Alustin sat with his other two apprentices, Sabae and Talia. They had chairs, a table, and an awning giving them shelter from the brutal desert sun. Sure, Alustin was making them do homework, but Hugh would rather be doing homework than dodging chunks of crystal any day of the week.

"A little humiliation makes the lessons sink in faster," Kanderon said.

Kanderon was at least five centuries old— maybe even older, for all Hugh knew— and her teaching methods were, unfortunately, nearly as out of date.

Hugh sighed and staggered back to his feet.

It was another hour before Kanderon finally decided Hugh had suffered enough for the day. She lectured him for a time, then took off in a blast of wind and sand that knocked Hugh off his feet.

Hugh staggered upright and spat sand out of his mouth. He hadn't managed to dodge a single lump of crystal, and he was bruised, sunburned, thirsty, and all-around miserable. He turned and trudged through the sand back towards the others.

When he arrived, Alustin waved to him cheerfully. "Well done, Hugh! You managed to catch every single one of those crystals. That was your intent, I presume?" The mage was tall and thin, with an unruly head of light brown hair.

Hugh just glowered at him.

Sabae gave Hugh a sympathetic look. "You look awful. I'd offer to heal you, but…"

"No more trying to heal people until you get some proper training," Alustin said.

Sabae shrugged. The tall girl had pale hair, dark skin, and thin, branching scars up her hands and one side of her face. They came from one of her affinities gone awry. She had inherited all three of the traditional affinities— wind, water, and lightning— from her family, the powerful Kaen Das of Ras Andis, but she had also inherited her father's healing affinity, which had wrecked her ability to work magic at a distance. And, as it turned out, lightning wasn't particularly safe at close range.

Talia snorted as she looked up at her homework. "Clan Castis only heals wounds from battles and accidents. How is training supposed to sink in properly if you don't live with the consequences?" The short, pale redhead was covered in intricately detailed blue tattoos- spellforms that had been intended to increase the power of her family's traditional fire affinity. Instead, however, she'd somehow ended up with dream and bone affinities. Up until recently, she'd been unable to control her magic at all.

Before Alustin had chosen them as his apprentices, none of the three had thought they'd had a future as mages. Alustin had changed all of that.

"Can we go back inside out of this heat now?" Talia asked. "It's miserable."

"Of course," Alustin said. "You just need to pack up and carry all of this back inside. And you still have to finish packing for our little expedition— our vessel should be arriving tomorrow."

Hugh groaned.

As the group arrived back at Skyhold, Hugh readied himself to deal with the crowds. They hadn't bothered him quite so much a few weeks ago, but then a few weeks ago no one recognized him when he walked around, except maybe as that inept student who could barely cast a single spell.

Then, during the final test for the first years, Hugh and his friends had ended up falling down to the sixth level of the labyrinth the test was held in. First years weren't supposed to leave the highest level— even ending up down on the second level was often fatal for the inexperienced. Somehow, though, they'd actually survived the monsters and traps of the lower levels long enough to be rescued.

Now, unfortunately, everyone seemed to know who Hugh was. What made it worse was that no one outside of his small group of friends knew how they'd survived— Hugh had signed a warlock contract with Kanderon granting him power, as well as letting rescuers track them down through the link.

Since no one knew what had happened, rumors were flying everywhere, each more ridiculous than the last. Quite a few people thought that the whole thing was exaggerated, and that they'd only fallen to the second or third level. Others had come up with stories about one of them finding some ancient and powerful magical weapon from the Ithonian Empire or the like.

The fact that Hugh was now being tutored by Kanderon Crux, Head Librarian and last living founder of Skyhold and its academy, really just served to fuel the rumors even further.

Sabae seemed to ignore the attention entirely, and Talia seemed to accept it as her due.

Hugh hated every moment of it. He couldn't wait for them to leave on their trip into the depths of the Endless Erg, either. It felt weird wanting to spend weeks in the depths of a deadly expanse of sand, but Hugh would take merciless heat and horrible monsters over crowds paying attention to him any day of the week.

As they entered Skyhold, however, Hugh did see one face that made for a welcoming sight. Godrick was the fourth member of their little group. He was sixteen, just like Hugh and Sabae— Talia would be turning sixteen in a few weeks— but he was already pushing seven feet in height. He had more muscle on him than any three other people Hugh knew. In fact, the only larger human Hugh had ever met was Godrick's father, Artur Wallbreaker. Godrick shared his father's dark skin and curly hair, but he lacked the streaks of white running through the older man's hair.

Godrick waved cheerfully, then strode over and grabbed the poles for the awning from Talia.

"How was trainin, Hugh? Ah meant ta' watch, but me da insisted on lookin through all a' mah luggage to make sure ah was packing everythin' ah needed." Godrick, happily, was coming on the training expedition with them.

"I'd imagine Hugh's happy you didn't make it to watch," Sabae said.

Godrick winced. "That bad?"

Hugh sighed and nodded.

Godrick helped them all carry the awning back to the storeroom Alustin had gotten it from, and then the four of them went to eat dinner at one of the mess halls. Afterwards, Hugh made his way down to the library stacks, where his room was hidden.

Most students lived in the cramped dormitories, unless their masters assigned them better living quarters. Hugh, however, had discovered a hidden room deep in the stacks of the library. It was bigger than the student rooms, and, best of all, had a window overlooking the sandship port and the desert.

Its door was tucked away behind a bookshelf, and Hugh had carefully warded it to make it even harder to find. Unless you were looking for it or were especially perceptive, your attention would most likely drift away from it. And if you somehow did try to open it without Hugh's permission, well… Hugh was excellent at crafting wards. It would be very painful and undignified.

Hugh carefully stepped over the line of spellforms that composed his ward. He flopped down onto his bed for a few minutes to rest, then got to packing.

He planned on traveling light— which should be easy, given how little he owned. Alustin had gotten him a sturdy leather pack, and his clothing— a few sets of mostly-white school uniforms— only took up the bottom half of the bag.

The first things he packed were the gifts his friends had given him for his birthday. First went the work journal of Sabae's great-grandmother, a mage who specialized in building storm wards big enough to shield entire cities. Next in went a small, enchanted glass sphere the size of a marble. Godrick had worked together with one of the Academy's enchanters to create it— the sphere had the ability to absorb the scent of anything it was rubbed on. Hugh mostly used it for his armpits. His other two birthday presents he planned on carrying on his person- a Clan Castis dagger from Talia, and a large, leather-bound blank spellbook from Sabae with a strap meant to go over the shoulder.

Other than that, he packed a few more books and a pair of rope sandals, in case something happened to his boots. He also packed his leather sling and a few slingstones- he hadn't yet replaced the explosive wardstones that he'd made for the labyrinth trip yet, though he intended to soon. His pack still wasn't full when he finished packing- Hugh wanted to make sure that he had room to bring back any books he acquired on their trip.

As he packed, Hugh's hand frequently reached up to touch his chest, where a small stone hung on a leather cord. He still didn't quite understand what the labyrinth stone was supposed to do, but it had gotten caught up in his contract with Kanderon somehow.

When all was said and done, Hugh went back to his window, watching the goose-sized sand drakes flap around the port. He knew he should get to bed early, but he doubted he could sleep— he was just too excited. Last time he'd been on a sandship he had been on his way to Skyhold for the first time, and he'd been too terrified and anxious to pay much attention.

Despite his excitement, however, he dropped off to sleep almost the instant he got into bed.

CHAPTER TWO

THE MOONLESS OWL

THERE were a lot more permanent structures alongside the docks than Hugh was used to from his visits to Emblin ports— but then, with no tides to worry about, why wouldn't there be? Emblin's tides weren't even that bad, most of the time— twenty feet on an average day, sometimes as high as thirty. Hugh had heard of ports that had tides fifty or sixty feet high.

Though there were no tides in the Endless Erg, all the sheds, warehouses, and other buildings still felt wrong to him.

Hugh met Talia, Sabae, and Godrick at the main balcony above the port early in the morning. The balcony was big enough to support a number of teashops, restaurants, and other businesses. Despite Skyhold mainly being known for the Academy, an entire city— home to tens of thousands— was carved into the sides and interior of the mountain.

They all got tea from one of the shops, then snagged a table overlooking the port, spending their time discussing which of the twenty-odd sandships they would be taking. Hugh was arguing for a particularly large, well-armed vessel when Talia elbowed him in the side.

"Look who it is," she said.

Hugh and the others turned to see Aedan Dragonslayer, one of the mightiest mages alive, striding through the crowd like it wasn't even there. Behind him was a tall handsome blond youth that Hugh knew entirely too well— his chief bully over the last year, Rhodes Charax, nephew of the king of Highvale.

Hugh felt his heart speed up. The last time that he'd seen him was in the labyrinth, when Rhodes had started a fight with them that resulted in Hugh and his friends being dumped down into the depths. He swallowed, expecting Rhodes to come over and start something.

As Aedan and Rhodes passed, however, Hugh noticed something- Rhodes looked miserable. The noble was staring at his master's feet as he walked behind him, not looking around him at all. Hugh doubted Rhodes even knew he was nearby.

No one at Hugh's table spoke until Rhodes had passed out of sight.

"Ah heard Aedan's been less than pleased wit' Rhodes," Godrick said. "E' thinks Rhodes was cowardly fer flyin' away rather than helpin' the lot of us. He's making Rhodes' life a livin' hell, trainin' dawn to dusk."

"He should have stayed and continued his fight with us rather than fleeing," Talia said.

Sabae sighed. "He wasn't afraid of us, Talia. He was afraid of whatever lurked in the depths of the labyrinth."

"Still a coward's act," Talia muttered.

Hugh wasn't so sure. He couldn't stand Rhodes- the noble had made his first half a year at Skyhold a hell of its own, until Hugh had been chosen by Alustin as a student and he'd met his friends. Still, he thought that Rhodes might not have done so well had he stayed- the demon Bakori had shown up almost immediately after Rhodes had fled.

Hugh shuddered. He didn't really want to think about Bakori right now, or the fact that he was still lurking somewhere in the depths of Skyhold's labyrinth.

Thankfully, before that particular conversation went any further, Alustin arrived to take them to their ship.

Their sandship wasn't the big one that Hugh had been arguing for, or the sleek one Sabae had liked. It was, in fact, one that hadn't even been visible from the balcony.

The *Moonless Owl* was only about sixty-five feet long, dwarfed by many of the other ships at the port. Hugh had been to Emblin's fishing ports a few times, and he had seen quite a few vessels this size- but where a seagoing caravel, a vessel close to the size as the *Moonless Owl*, was narrow and agile, the sandship looked somewhat like a barge.

The *Owl* was wide, with a broad, flat bottom lacking the ski-like runners of the larger ships. The bottom of the hull, where Hugh could see it, appeared to be polished and treated to run over sand easier. The sides curved up gently to the top of the ship, which was lower-set than

Hugh was expecting- there was maybe room for one or two decks inside. It had two triangular sails on its masts, which at least looked familiar to Hugh. Twin sand-rudders descended along the sides of the ship near the back. It also had a statue of an owl as a figurehead.

It looked to be a well maintained ship, but Hugh couldn't help but feel disappointed. He had been hoping to race along the sands in a sandship like those in the stories, not in… this barge.

Alustin, who didn't appear to have brought any luggage other than his usual over-stuffed satchel full of books and scrolls, gestured for them to follow.

"This is really our ship?" Hugh asked.

Alustin swiveled to face them. He kept walking at the same speed as he did so- it didn't seem to matter which way he faced as he walked.

"It really is! And we couldn't ask for a better one, either- we've been waiting as long as we have to leave specifically for the *Moonless Owl.* I've chartered it just for us for this trip- although the crew will still be doing some trading at our stops."

"Any chance of telling us where those stops are yet?" Sabae asked. Alustin had been closemouthed on that so far, just claiming that they'd play it by ear once they got going. And, true to form, Alustin just grinned and swiveled around to face frontwards once more.

As the five of them strode down the dock, Hugh spotted three figures standing at the top of the ship's ramp— an old woman in robes, a burly middle-aged man, and a girl who looked around his own age. They all shared the same short stature, dark skin, and wavy dark hair (though the old woman's hair had turned mostly white), and were immediately recognizable as a family.

Alustin waved cheerfully to them as they boarded the ramp.

"These your students?" the old woman demanded. Hugh noticed that she wore immense golden hoop earrings.

"They are indeed, Deila!" Alustin wrapped her in a hug. She sniffed and rolled her eyes, then hugged him back. As he stepped away from her, she pinched his arm, hard.

"You're still too skinny," she said.

Alustin winced, then gestured to the students in order as they boarded the ship. "Deila, this is Sabae Kaen Das, Talia of Clan Castis, Godrick, son of Artur Wallbreaker, and Hugh of Emblin. Students, this is Deila of the *Moonless Owl*, her son, Captain Solon, and…"

Deila nodded at the girl. "This here's my granddaughter Avah. She was aboard another Radhan ship for mage training when you rode with us before. She just turned fifteen a few weeks ago."

Hugh tried not to stare. Avah was about his own modest height. Her hair stretched all the way down her back in a braid, far longer than her grandmother or the captain's. She was dressed similarly to the captain- trousers and a shirt that clung tightly at the neck, wrists, waist, and ankles, but billowed out elsewhere. She lacked the huge earrings of her grandmother.

And she might also be the most beautiful girl Hugh had ever met.

He swallowed, then tried to turn his attention back to the conversation at hand.

Despite Deila's son Solon being named as captain, it seemed clear to Hugh who was really in charge on the *Moonless Owl.* When Deila took a breath from lecturing Alustin— apparently she made it quite clear that she wanted no repeats of the gorgon incident, whatever that was— he finally spoke up.

"Welcome to the *Moonless Owl.* Have you all been on a sandship before?" Everyone nodded their heads except for Talia.

When they looked at her, she shrugged. "My brothers escorted me to Skyhold along the foothills of the mountains."

Hugh looked at Talia in surprise, but it made sense after a moment. Clan Castis lived in the northern Skyreach Mountains, the steepest and most brutal mountain range on the continent, and Skyhold was found on the far south of the same mountain range, most of a continent away. The foothills were as difficult as many actual mountain ranges, but they'd be no problem for the clanfolk.

Thinking about how difficult Talia's trip must have been was a welcome distraction for Hugh, at least.

"We've got a few rules," Captain Solon said. "First of all, if a member of the crew orders you to do something- move out of the way, hold a rope, even jump off the side of the ship- you do so immediately. Second, you do not touch the ship's wheel for any reason. Third, and most importantly, do not accidentally destroy this ship while practicing magic. I know how you young mages are."

Hugh felt that last was a little unjustified. Well, maybe not for Talia, but for the others, at least.

"My daughter will show you to your bunks while we get underway," Captain Solon said.

Hugh gulped.

Avah waved for them to follow her, and she led them across the deck, past a number of other sailors that also looked like they could be her family.

"So you're all mages in training too?" she asked.

Even her voice was beautiful.

"We are," Sabae replied. "Are mages common among the Radhan?"

Avah smiled back at them. "Most of the Radhan are mages to one degree or another. Our magic is more focused on speeding and maintaining our ships than on battle, though. My affinities lie in wood and sand— I mostly help smooth out the sand and hull where they touch. What about yours?"

Hugh wondered who exactly the Radhan were for a moment, then realized that Avah had asked them a question, and his mind abruptly went blank. He was still trying to come up with a response when Talia answered.

"You're awfully forward with telling others your powers," she said. "That seems a little risky."

Avah smiled again. "Maybe for a battlemage. For a working mage, though, it's just good business."

Talia eyed her suspiciously, then grunted. "My affinities are in dream and bone."

Avah's eyes widened a bit at that. Both affinities were rare, and looked on with a little distrust by most. The combination of the two was extremely rare. Talia didn't, however, mention how her tattoos warped her powers.

"Ah've got stone and steel," volunteered Godrick. Likewise, he didn't mention his scent affinity.

"Wind, water, and lightning," offered Sabae, leaving out her personal limitations and her healing affinity.

Hugh started to try and answer, but nothing managed to come out of his mouth. Sabae quickly interjected.

"Hugh's affinity is for crystal."

Hugh started to feel affronted at Sabae leaving out his other two affinities that he got from Kanderon— stellar and planar affinities— then remembered that he was supposed to keep those two secret, along with his nature as a warlock and his contract with Kanderon.

He also realized he hadn't actually managed to successfully talk to Avah yet, and he felt his cheeks redden a bit. He moved so he was walking a bit more behind Godrick.

"Watch your heads," Avah said, as she ducked into the stairwell down into the ship.

Hugh followed the others down, finding, to his surprise, that the deck was much shorter than he was expecting. He could still walk upright just fine, but Sabae's head came quite close to the ceiling, and Godrick had to bend down to keep from smacking his. He also had some difficulty navigating his huge sledgehammer through the hallway without hitting anyone.

Talia, of course, had no trouble at all. Hugh often forgot how short she was, given how loud and aggressive she tended to be.

"So Sabae— are you one of *the* Kaen Das family?" Avah said. "The guardians of Ras Andis?"

Sabae nodded, suddenly a bit more reserved. "Yes."

"And I've heard of your father, of course," Avah said, smiling at Godrick.

Hugh felt a tinge of jealousy.

"I imagine you probably all want to get settled in so you can watch the departure," Avah said. "We finished loading and unloading our trade goods already, so I need to go help prepare for casting off. These two cabins are yours." She gestured at a pair of side-by side doors. "The ship's mess, more crew quarters, and the small goods storage are on the next deck, and the bottom deck is dedicated to heavy goods storage. Passengers aren't allowed on the bottom deck unaccompanied."

Avah left to head back above decks.

"Chatty, isn't she?" Talia said. She didn't seem impressed.

"Friendly enough, though," Sabae said.

"Hugh and ah'll take tha cabin on tha left, then?" Godrick said.

"Sounds fine to me," Talia said.

Godrick opened the door to their room and gingerly eased his way in. Hugh followed him in.

Their cabin was tiny. It was less than a quarter of the size of Hugh's room in the library. His bed wouldn't even fit into this cabin. The only furniture was a narrow set of bunk beds, with a narrow floor space between them and the bulkhead.

"Mind if ah take tha bottom bunk?" Godrick asked. "Worried ah'd break the top one."

"Sure," Hugh said, and climbed up to the top bunk. There wasn't a real ladder, but there were several wooden blocks protruding from the wall that Hugh used to scramble up. The mattress was lumpy and hard, but Hugh had slept on much worse before. He took off his backpack and set it up on the bed- it was that or store it below the bottom bunk, and Godrick's pack and hammer already took up most of the space down there. Hugh would have to be careful not to trip on the haft when he entered or exited the room.

"Yeh've been awful quiet, Hugh," Godrick said. His legs were poking off the bed into the tiny walkway in their cabin. Hugh was a little amazed he even fit like that. "Seein Rhodes put yeh in a bad mood?"

"A bit, I guess," Hugh said. "That, and, you know… I'm still not the best at meeting new people."

"We'll be on tha *Moonless Owl* for a while, ah think. Yeh should get ta know tha crew."

"I guess." Something occurred to Hugh. "By the way, who are the Radhans?"

"Yeh've never heard a' tha Radhans? Yeh're on one a' their ships right now."

"But who are they?"

"They're merchants and traders. They all live on their ships as families- all a' tha crew onboard are probably related. Not just on tha Endless Erg, either- their ships range the oceans and rivers, too. They're a fairly private bunch, but nice enough. Ah've traveled with them before."

Godrick was silent for a moment.

"Ah wish me da could have seen us off."

"Why couldn't he?" Hugh asked.

"He hates ships," Godrick replied. "Every time he's ridden one, it's turned out badly, so he said goodbye before ah left."

"I'm sorry," Hugh said. He wasn't entirely sure what else to say.

"Eh, don't worry about it," Godrick said. "Ah want ta watch tha ship leave tha port, yeh in?"

"Definitely," Hugh said.

CHAPTER THREE

THE ENDLESS ERG

THE sandship Hugh had ridden to Skyhold had been near twice the size of the *Moonless Owl,* and far, far noisier. You could barely hear people yelling from a few feet away on the deck thanks to the sound of the runners grinding over the sand and the ship itself rattling and shaking.

The *Owl*, however, lived up to its name. As it pulled out of the port, the only noises to be heard were a whisper as it slid over sand and the sails in the wind that the ship's mages summoned up. The ship was also far faster than Hugh would have expected.

Hugh and the other apprentices watched the port quickly recede. It was easy to forget how huge Skyhold was when you were inside of it, but the mountain it was carved into was massive even by the impressive standards of the rugged Skyreach range. There were hundreds of balconies, towers, and windows all carved into the sides of the granite peak.

"At least this breeze helps cool things off a little," Talia complained.

"Wait until we get going full speed!" said a passing sailor, carrying rope over her shoulder. "Now *that's* a breeze."

Talia grinned. "That's more like it."

The four of them watched Skyhold recede in silence for a few minutes, then the whole ship shuddered.

"What was that?" Talia asked.

"We're getting out of the lee of the mountains," Sabae said. "The terrain is going to get a lot bumpier as we start crossing actual dunes."

Talia looked around uncomfortably at the gently rolling sand. "These aren't actual dunes?"

"In the depths of the Erg, many dunes can grow to a couple hundred feet in height," Sabae said.

Talia's face paled a little bit.

"We'll be avoiding dunes that big, right?"

"No idea," Sabae said.

Talia turned to Hugh, but he just shrugged. He'd only taken the one trip in a sandship before.

Alustin walked up just as Talia asked Godrick.

"We'll likely be going through many of the larger dune fields," he said. "Our first destination is Theras Tel, the fabled jewel of the Endless Erg."

Hugh and the others looked at each other in excitement. Theras Tel was the stuff of stories. It was a city built atop a plateau deep in the heart of the Endless Erg. Its wells were the only reliable source of water for nearly a hundred leagues in any direction. Theras Tel had grown immensely wealthy under two centuries of stable rules by its dragon queen.

"Don't get too excited," Alustin said. "We're still a week of travel away, and we've got a lot of dunes to cross first. And a lot of training to do."

Their excitement fell a bit at that. Alustin, surprisingly enough, had the same training exercise for all of them- a simple levitation exercise.

Considering that it was Alustin, however, it was far from simple. It turned out that levitating an object while both you and the object were in motion was extremely difficult- the spellforms used in simple levitation cantrips weren't designed to handle moving frames of reference. Alustin, of course, wouldn't simply give them a new spell- instead, he put a twist on each of their exercises.

Sabae was forced to not use an actual levitation spell at all- instead, she was forced to hold up a metal sphere using her wind armor, which consisted of her channeling her mana to rapidly rotate wind about her limbs. In order to keep the metal sphere from being sent flying, she had to apply equal force to each side, as well as force the wind to rotate in different directions around each hand.

Godrick's exercise was somewhat more straightforward- he merely had to suspend a stone sphere in front of him. Unfortunately, the spellform Alustin provided him with could only be used to manually adjust for the movement of the ship, forcing him to concentrate without a break the whole exercise.

Talia's exercise, unsurprisingly, was more potentially destructive than the rest of the group's- she was required to suspend a sphere of dreamfire in front of her while sitting in the wind of the prow.

Hugh should have been at an advantage to everyone else for this exercise. He was training in improvised spellform construction- given a few minutes, he could easily design a spellform appropriate for the task. Alustin, knowing this, had added an extra twist to the exercise. He had to levitate his lump of crystal with his eyes closed, using only his new and unreliable affinity sense to observe the crystal.

Hugh should have known this expedition wouldn't be anything like a vacation.

Within an hour, Hugh had learned two very important lessons- affinity sensing was extremely difficult even when Kanderon wasn't pelting him with chunks of crystal, and Talia was extremely prone to... seasickness? Sand sickness? Once the sail was patched where the dreamfire had accidentally gone through it, Alustin asked a sailor, who claimed seasickness was the correct term, though another insisted ergsickness was right.

Hugh, Sabae, and Godrick all wandered below decks to the ship's mess after Alustin let them out of training. Talia was still attached to the ship's railing, trying to void her already empty stomach further, and angrily rejecting any offers of company. It seemed she preferred to suffer alone.

Unfortunately for Talia, they hadn't even reached any of the major dune fields yet.

The ship's mess was cramped, noisy, and overwhelming. Hugh wedged himself into a bench in the corner of the room, with Sabae on one side of him and Godrick across from him. Only ten or so of the crew were in here— he'd heard there were around thirty crewmembers total— but it was much worse than the huge cafeterias of Skyhold, since all the crew seemed inordinately interested in the three of them.

It didn't help that jars and bags of exotic spices and other fragrant ingredients hung everywhere. The galley didn't smell bad, just entirely overwhelming. It was probably for the best that Talia had stayed above decks.

The burly, wrinkled old cook wandered over to them, and dropped three bowls of some unidentified meat with vegetables in a thick sauce. Hugh was fairly sure it smelled good, but it was hard to tell over the smell of the rest of the mess.

Hugh suspiciously tried a bite, and found to his surprise that it tasted far better than anything he'd been served in Skyhold.

"This is good!" Hugh said.

Godrick nodded, not taking time away from eating to actually answer. Sabae, however, was just picking at her food idly.

"Don't you like it?" Hugh asked.

Sabae didn't respond for a moment.

"Sabae?"

"Isn't it weird that Alustin would keep our destination a secret so carefully, then just tell us the instant we left Skyhold?" Sabae looked at the two of them seriously.

"Alustin just likes surprises," Hugh said. "What is this stuff called, by the way?"

Godrick nodded at that, taking another bite from his bowl.

"It's a curry," Sabae said, idly stirring it in her bowl. "If he was waiting to surprise us, you'd think he'd do it in a more ridiculous fashion, wouldn't you? Waiting until we actually arrived at Theras Tel would have been much more his style."

"I'm sure the crew would have leaked the information before we got there," Hugh said. Godrick nodded again, taking yet another bite. His bowl was already almost empty.

"Maybe," Sabae said. "Or, maybe, he didn't want anyone at Skyhold knowing where we were going?"

Godrick swallowed, then spoke up. "Why not?"

Sabae tapped her spoon against her bowl.

"When he first told us about this trip, he claimed we were going to find..." she looked around and lowered her voice, "a contract partner for Hugh."

Hugh glanced around suspiciously, hoping no-one had overheard that. Warlocks weren't well-liked in most places- people tended to assume they all had signed contracts with demons. Which, in fairness, Hugh had been offered the chance to do so, but he'd thankfully chosen not to.

"But then, even once Hugh signed with Kanderon," Sabae went on, "he still kept planning the trip as though nothing had changed. I think..." she leaned closer to them, "that Alustin is on a mission for Kanderon."

Hugh raised his eyebrows in surprise, but it actually made a lot of sense. Alustin was a Librarian Errant, one of the battlemages employed by Kanderon to retrieve rare volumes for the library, as well as very aggressively reclaiming overdue books.

"That's one rare book, if Alustin wants to keep things secret," Godrick said. "Ah wonder what it could be. Some ancient grimoire?"

Sabae just smiled and took a bite of her food.

Godrick went through three more bowls before he was full, much to the amusement of the elderly cook. Afterward, the three of them headed back above-decks to check on Talia, and bring her a bowl.

They found her miserably curled up in the prow of the ship, sheltered from the wind and blowing sand by the solid railing.

"I'm dying!" Talia loudly claimed when they walked up to her. "Make sure to burn my corpse once I'm dead."

"You're not dying, just seasick," Sabae said. "And why would we burn your body?"

"Everyone in Clan Castis is cremated after their death," Talia said.

It made sense to Hugh- Clan Castis was largely made up of fire mages, after all.

"We brought yeh some food," Godrick said, offering Talia the bowl. She eyed it suspiciously, then took it from him. She took a first, cautious bite, then her eyes lit up.

"It's good!" She started shoveling the food into her mouth.

"Make sure to eat all of it. A full stomach might help," Sabae offered.

They told Talia of their suspicions about Alustin's mission while she ate. She listened with a serious expression, then set down her half full bowl after they finished, turned, and vomited over the side of the railing. Sabae jumped up to hold back Talia's long red hair as she did so.

When she finally sat back down again, she shoved the bowl back towards Godrick. "Full stomach does not help." She curled back up in the prow.

"Some folk's stomachs just aren't tough enough to handle ship life," someone said.

Hugh jumped a little in surprise, then scooted back against the railing as he looked back. Avah had somehow managed to sneak up on them without anyone noticing.

"I'll show you tough," Talia growled, but it was less than convincing.

"Hey, Avah," Sabae said.

"Avah," Godrick said, nodding at her.

Hugh managed to nod at Avah.

"We should try and get her below decks," Avah said. "The ship's movement isn't quite so bad there. We shouldn't worry about food so much as water, though— you should try and drink some if you can, Talia."

Talia tried to stand up, but she promptly slid back down onto the deck. "Nope."

Avah gave her a doubtful look, and opened her mouth to say something, when a shout came from atop the mainmast. "Sunlings ahead!"

Avah smiled in delight, and leaned out over the railing. Hugh and the others quickly followed suit. Ahead of them and off to the right side of the ship— Hugh couldn't remember what it was supposed to be called— a flock of strange creatures flew a few feet above the sand.

The sunlings were each around two feet long and a foot across, and they resembled nothing so much as leathery leaves flapping along like wings. Their backs were scattered with curious black scales that seemed to drink in the light.

Talia managed to drag herself up to the railing to look as well. "That doesn't tell us what they are," she muttered.

"They're all over the Erg," Avah explained. "They fly around and drink sunlight all day, then rest on the sand at night."

"They're the foundation of the Erg's ecosystem," another voice added. Hugh whipped his head around to see that Alustin had joined them as well.

"Sir?" Godrick said.

"Most animals that live in the Endless Erg either prey on the sunlings or prey on the things that prey on them."

"There are plants and such at some of the oases," Avah said.

"They're still all connected, though," Alustin said. "What I'm trying to get at is that even in a harsh environment like this, life can find a way to thrive- so long as it has the means to do so. A food source is one of the most critical. The sunlings don't just derive nourishment from sunlight, they also get it from the Aether, as well— one of the only known species to do that directly. No matter where you go, you'll find something on the bottom of the food chain, and it will always be the most common lifeform around."

Alustin paused, then Hugh realized he was waiting for one of them to ask a question. Hugh cleared his throat, making sure not to look at Avah.

"If that's true, then what was at the bottom of the food chain in the labyrinth?" Hugh managed.

Alustin smiled broadly. "Excellent question!" Before he could speak, someone interrupted him.

"There's something above us! To arms!"

CHAPTER FOUR

ON THE NATURE OF CRYSTALS

THE crew frantically scrambled about the sandship, pulling crossbows out of hidden compartments that Hugh never would have noticed otherwise. Large hatches were opened up in the front and back of the deck, revealing two ballistae, each capable of firing their bolts almost straight upwards.

It hadn't been more than a minute since the lookout had raised the alarm, and Hugh still hadn't managed to see what the threat from above was, or even where it was. The sun's glare was…

No, there it was. A massive shadow was winging towards them from the east, high above them. Hugh couldn't make out its shape, but its wings…

Its wings were reflecting blue in the sunlight.

Hugh grabbed Alustin by the arm and pointed. "It's Kanderon!"

Alustin shaded his eyes with his hand and looked. "So it is." He took a deep breath, then bellowed, "Stand down, it's a friend!" Hugh had never heard Alustin yell before, and he was shocked at how loud his teacher could get.

The crew slowed down and looked at Alustin uncertainly. "Put away those weapons!" Alustin yelled again.

"Belay that!" another voice bellowed. Hugh looked to see Captain Solon storming up to them. "Alustin, I don't care what favors you've done for us in the past, you do not give orders on my ship, not when we have an unknown threat winging towards us."

Alustin stared at the captain calmly. "Hugh here has better eyes than your lookout." Hugh flushed uncomfortably at that and shifted behind

Alustin a little. "That 'unknown threat' is Kanderon Crux, Head Librarian of the Academy at Skyhold. She also happens to be a multi-century-old sphinx archmage bigger than this entire ship, who can shrug off your ballista bolts like they were nothing. I strongly suggest you follow my advice."

Captain Solon paled, then he whirled and started bellowing orders to the crew. Almost as fast as the crossbows and ballistae had appeared they vanished again. The crew began putting away the sails, or whatever they called rolling them up, and the *Owl* began slowly grinding to a halt in the sand.

Hugh looked around to see everyone in the prow except Talia staring at him. She was staring at the ballistae.

"How could yeh make out any details this far away?" Godrick asked. "Does it have anythin' ta do with, yeh know…"

Sabae interrupted Godrick, shooting him a glare. "How did you make out any details, Hugh?"

"I saw blue glinting off her wings," Hugh said.

"That's your proof?" Avah said. "There are plenty of dragons out there with blue wings, that doesn't prove anything."

Hugh flushed and looked down at the deck.

"No one has wings like Kanderon," Sabae said.

"We shouldn't…" Avah started, when Talia interrupted.

"It seems awfully convenient that you have ballistae that can fire upwards," she said.

"Most of the predators of the Endless Erg fly," Alustin said.

"Hold on a minute," Avah said.

"It's the most sensible way to get around in a desert like this- moving around on foot is a good way to exhaust yourself in this sand," Alustin said.

"I…" Avah started again.

"Ah thought predators in tha Erg swam under the sand," Godrick said.

The ship finished coming to a full stop. Talia sighed in relief.

"Some, not many," Alustin said. "It's an even more exhausting way to get around than walking, so most of the burrowers are ambush predators."

"We can't risk the ship on the word of some random kid!" Avah said.

Hugh flushed. He was older than she was.

Talia looked like she was ready to fight Avah, but Alustin interrupted.

"That's Kanderon, alright."

Kanderon's immense crystal wings barely seemed to move as she descended into a landing several ship lengths away. She barely stirred up any sand as she landed.

Hugh, without looking at Avah, vaulted over the edge of the ship.

As Hugh fell, he started crafting a levitation spellform in his mind's eye. He started with the spellform foundation, followed by definitive and aiming lines. He also added some compensatory lines to deal with the unstable footing provided by the sand.

When Hugh had first started learning spellform crafting, this would have taken him most of a minute, but the levitation spell kicked in long before he reached the ground- almost as fast as the average mage his age could use a simple memorized spellform.

Hugh couldn't craft just any spell this quickly- levitation cantrips were something of a specialty of Hugh's at this point. This one kicked in immediately upon completion, lowering Hugh to the ground slowly. If he'd had a wind or gravity affinity, he might have been able to make himself fly, but none of his affinities were any use there.

That actually brought up an interesting question- Kanderon's crystal wings looked far, far too heavy to carry her in flight, and he knew sphinxes weren't usually supposed to have crystal wings.

Hugh heard Avah shout something after him just before he hit the ground, but he quickly strode off towards Kanderon, face still burning in embarrassment at being dismissed as just a kid by her.

Kanderon watched him approach, eyebrow raised.

"You seem somewhat less hesitant than usual, Hugh. You usually take your time about approaching. I approve. Let's begin, then."

Hugh suddenly felt a lot less determined as a patch of sand nearby solidified into crystal and launched itself at him.

Talia's stomach felt better now that they had stopped, but she definitely didn't feel like eating again just yet. The heat and sand, however, were still as awful as ever. She missed the cool air and stone of the halls of Skyhold, or the mountain breezes of Clan Castis' territory.

The crew of the *Moonless Owl* pretended to be busy, but most were obviously watching Hugh train with Kanderon. Well, watching Kanderon, at least— not that Talia blamed them. She'd been to quite a few training sessions with Hugh, and still found the sphinx intimidating. The only comparably sized creatures Talia had ever personally seen were dragons, and even then from quite a distance.

Hugh was doing terribly, as usual. Talia was fairly sure that he was somehow managing to sabotage himself again— that boy was his own worst enemy. She didn't understand him— one minute, he could be displaying his genius with wards or his quick reactions to danger, the next he would withdraw straight back into himself.

He'd improved a lot since Talia had first met him, but he still had a long way to go. He still regularly went days without talking to anyone but his small group of friends and teachers.

Talia would very much like to meet the family that had treated Hugh so badly as to make him like this. She doubted they would enjoy it nearly so much.

She spared a glare for Avah. Avah was sitting near Godrick, trying to flirt with him as he focused on his training. Hugh shouldn't have simply taken Avah's insult quietly, he should have confronted her directly. Maybe Emblin was one of those foolish nations that believed men shouldn't fight women? It might be, at that, given how little magic it had to level the field.

Well, if Hugh did think like that, she'd have to beat it out of him.

"Talia, back to work," Alustin said.

Talia snorted, but she obeyed the librarian. She focused back on the paper construction in front of her. It looked like a labyrinth in three directions, and Talia was supposed to be guiding a spark of dreamfire through it without burning any of the paper. It was supposed to teach her delicacy and fine control with her magic.

She didn't much see the value of either. Dreamfire was far harder to summon and control than real fire would have been, but it was also far more destructive.

Why pick a lock when you can just burn down the whole building?

Hugh collapsed on the ground, exhausted and sore. He'd only managed to dodge a single chunk of crystal, and that was purely by accident on his part— he'd just tripped.

The headache wasn't as bad as it had been during yesterday's training session, but his affinity senses were still a jumble of incomprehensible noise firing on all channels. They were maybe a little more focused than yesterday, but not enough to save him from the chunks of crystal.

The problem was that he just couldn't tell the difference between the crystals and the sand around it until they got into the air. Even though the crystals were larger and… purer feeling than the sand, it still didn't seem to make a difference.

Hugh was starting to become convinced that growing up in Emblin had messed up his affinity senses as well, just like it had messed up his ability to cast spells at first.

It didn't help that Avah and the rest of the crew of the *Moonless Owl* were doubtless having a good laugh watching him fail again and again.

"Get up, Hugh. We're not done yet," Kanderon said. The immense sphinx loomed over him.

"What's the point?" Hugh said. "I can't tell the difference between the sand and the crystal. It's like they're the same thing to my senses. Maybe I'm just not cut out for a crystal affinity."

The sphinx narrowed her eyes at Hugh.

"So are you planning on giving up, Hugh?"

Hugh started to say yes, then he slowly shut his mouth. If he'd possessed actual affinities when he'd entered the labyrinth below Skyhold, maybe his friends wouldn't have gotten hurt as badly as they did. Next time they got in a dangerous situation, Hugh wanted to be able to help them.

Hugh shook his head.

Kanderon smiled broadly. Given the size of her fangs, this made Hugh a bit nervous.

"It's about time you realized the problem," Kanderon said.

"The problem?" Hugh said.

"Why you've been unable to sense the crystals. You are, in fact, correct- they're essentially the same as the sand around them. Most of the sand in this desert is made up of grains of quartz- when I consolidate them into crystals, I'm merely growing them from the quartz sand grains and excluding any other types of grains."

That explained why the crystals felt a little purer, though that still didn't help Hugh catch them.

"So how am I supposed to detect them, if they're made of the exact same material?" Hugh said. "Am I supposed to be able to reliably detect the purity of the crystal?"

"That would be a waste of your time," Kanderon said. **"Most crystals you'll be making or running across won't be nearly as pure as mine. No, instead it's time to explain something much more important to you: what a crystal actually is."**

Hugh glanced at one of the crystals lying on the sand near him. Crystals were… shiny rocks? Shinier, more regularly shaped rocks? Somehow, that didn't seem right.

"Crystals are patterns, Hugh." Kanderon said.

"Patterns?" Hugh said, rubbing the back of his neck.

"Patterns. The internal structure of every crystal is made up of countless repeated patterns that mimic the crystal on a larger level, which then, in turn, repeat on yet smaller levels."

"I don't see any patterns in them," Hugh said. "It just looks clear to me."

Kanderon snorted irritably. **"The very patterns and order of quartz are what lets the light travel through the crystal."**

"I feel like this should have been something you explained to me from the beginning," Hugh said.

"Failure is an important part of the learning process. You humans seldom value knowledge until you understand its necessity."

Hugh wasn't entirely sure how to respond to that.

"Most affinity senses merely show you the shape and composition of the substance in question. For crystal attuned, this isn't enough- you

must learn to see the patterns that crystals are made of. The patterns are everything- they are how crystals grow. Crystals grow quite slowly naturally, but once you learn to perceive the patterns, you'll be able to funnel mana into them, growing them further yourself."

"That's how you're growing the crystals out of the sand?" Hugh said.

"That's one of the simpler applications, yes. The quartz grains making up most of the Endless Erg's sand already contain the pattern in them, they merely need to be fused."

Kanderon reached her paw out into midair, where it seemed to simply vanish. Hugh tried to look at the spot where it vanished, but space seemed twisted there, and he quickly looked away.

"When we first spoke, you asked me if crystal affinities were to stone affinities as steel affinities were to iron affinities- a case of a more specific affinity being more powerful but less versatile. It's not the same relationship, though. Stone is not a single substance- it's merely a name for the byproducts of our world's lifecycle. There are stones made of cooled magma, stones made of compressed seashells, stone made of plants compressed over time, and many more. One thing the vast majority of them have in common? They almost all contain crystal, whether tiny grains or larger patterns. Minerals are inherently crystalline."

Kanderon shoved her front paw even deeper into the twisted space.

"Almost all stones?" Hugh said. "There are some that don't?"

"Obsidian doesn't, nor does any other glass. Amber, opal, pearl, jet, and a few others lack crystalline structures as well. Each for their own reasons- I'll provide you with a list to memorize. For now, just be cautious about going up against any glass mages."

Hugh didn't need to hear that advice twice. Glass mages had an absolutely terrifying reputation to begin with.

"There are also many crystals found outside of stone, as well. Ice, for instance, is a crystal. You can often find crystals in living beings—the shells of clams are crystalline."

Kanderon scrunched up her face as she reached even farther into the empty patch of space.

"Ah, here we are."

Kanderon withdrew her paw from the twisted patch of space, which quickly faded away. Between two of her claws she clutched a crystal the size of Hugh's fist.

"Hold out your hands, please," Kanderon said.

Hugh did so.

Kanderon gently moved the crystal between Hugh's wrists, then let go of it. It floated there unsupported for a moment.

"Close your eyes and reach out to the crystal with your affinity sense," Kanderon said.

Hugh obeyed again, and found that the crystal didn't resemble the quartz of the desert at all. It was far, far more complex, yet still felt symmetrical.

"It seems familiar," he said.

"Reach out with your senses to my wings," Kanderon said.

Hugh had tried that before, but always found his senses blocked. This time, however, he was able to perceive Kanderon's crystal wings with only a little resistance.

They were composed of the same kind of crystal, but somehow… altered. Differently symmetrical, a little more… deliberate seeming? Hugh thought he might actually be sensing the patterns Kanderon had been talking about.

"What kind of crystal is this?" Hugh asked, not opening his eyes.

Abruptly, something forced his senses away from Kanderon's wings. At the same time, he felt something cold on his wrists. His eyes snapped open to see that the crystal floating between them had grown massively in size, until it encompassed both wrists.

He started to struggle to free his hands, but Kanderon spoke up. **"Hold still, Hugh. You're not in danger; I'm the one shaping the crystal."**

The crystal slowly expanded until it completely sheathed both wrists. Then, as Hugh watched nervously, it began to thin, narrowing into a thinner and thinner spindle of crystal, until it seemed to flow apart completely into the two thick bands of clear crystal around his wrists.

"There," Kanderon said, **"All done."**

Abruptly, the bands on Hugh's hands seemed to increase in weight tenfold, and they pulled Hugh down face first into the sand.

Hugh slowly hauled himself upright. He could lift his arms, but it took some effort to do so. Keeping this up for long would leave his arms feeling like jelly.

"To answer your earlier question, they're Aether crystals. Mana made solid. Enchanters often use them in more advanced projects, but they're uniquely helpful to crystal attuned mages."

Kanderon reached out and gently tapped a claw against one of Hugh's bracers. Hugh barely felt the impact, which was impressive, given that Kanderon's paw was bigger than he was, but the crystal rang out clearly in response.

"These bracelets are going to keep growing in weight and size until you master them. Not quickly- perhaps a pound a day, depending on the density of the Aether near you, but steadily."

"Why..." Hugh started.

"Consider it an important part of your training. My duties are many, Hugh, and I cannot be flying out into the desert every day to train you further. Alustin is quite capable of helping you with much of what you need, and these will provide the rest. You're going to have to practice continually at holding up the weight of the bracelets using your attunement. A simple levitation spell won't do, either- the patterns inside the crystal will interfere with your spellform. You'll have to use your affinity senses and adapt spellforms specifically for the crystal."

"How long do I need to wear these? When will I be able to take them off?" Hugh asked.

"Take them off? You won't be taking them off, Hugh. They will eventually become your greatest tool as a mage. As you further attune your crystal affinity, these bracelets will further attune to you. You'll be able to shape them, manipulate them, and use them for many other purposes. There aren't many crystal attuned mages out there, but each has found unique uses for their aether crystals. My wings and the Index are both comprised of aether crystals. Others have fashioned theirs into swords, crowns, and more. This crystal will gain something of a life of its own as it grows with you."

The idea of a sword made of living crystal bonded with him rather appealed to Hugh. He conveniently ignored his complete lack of training with swords.

"Your warlock abilities will likely enhance your connection with your crystal even further over time, though it's hard to say for sure how much, or whether you'll be able to pact with it."

"You keep referring to these bracelets as a single crystal— why is that?" Hugh said.

"Because they are a single crystal. Each aether crystal is unique in its underlying pattern. That pattern is what defines the crystal as a single unit, not whether it happens to connect or not. They're incredibly rare, and largely found only in the depths of labyrinths and other places of highly dense aether."

Hugh looked at his new bracelets with a little more respect.

"Eventually, you'll need to fully attune them to yourself. Doing so requires you to channel an absolutely immense amount of mana through them- more than you can count on anywhere but in the densest Aether fields— as in the lower levels of Skyhold's Labyrinth. Since it is too dangerous for you to return down there so long as Bakori lurks there, we'll likely have to send you down into another labyrinth. The gorgons are usually more approachable."

Hugh winced at the mention of Bakori. He didn't want to think about the demon. He was still cautious to never sleep without wards protecting his dreams.

"The spell you channel through the crystal while fully attuning them will alter their pattern irrevocably, determining what its strengths and uses will be. The crystals will allow you to funnel far more mana than usual during the process— attuning aether crystals often result in spells that become the best known act of a crystal mage's career. The attunement will also determine its final color. Don't get your hopes up too far on that one- no one's quite figured out how the choice of spell relates to the final color of the crystal. In addition, the crystals gain other properties based off your other attunements— for instance, a crystal mage that also has a fire attunement might be able to use them to amplify the heat of their fire spells. Yours will almost certainly possess most of the same properties as mine."

Kanderon ruffled her wings. The crystals sounded like a river made of wind chimes as they brushed against one another.

"I have some questions about…" Hugh began.

"Questions will have to wait. We have more training to do. This time, try to focus on feeling the patterns inside the crystals, rather than on trying to find the crystals themselves."

Hugh stared at her, then at the crystals on his wrists.

"But…"

A crystal launched itself out of the sand, slamming against his thigh with a bruising impact.

"Begin."

CHAPTER FIVE
SHIPBOARD ROUTINES

HUGH actually managed to dodge a couple crystals this time around, and he came close to dodging a few more. He also managed to, memorably, block one using one of his new bracelets.

Depressingly enough, Kanderon wasn't even paying much attention to him— she spent most of the time talking to Alustin.

Before she left, Kanderon had given him a thin volume containing a few spellforms for crystal attuned. She'd then taken off in another huge blast of wind and sand that sent Hugh tumbling. He'd had to root around in the sand to locate the book she'd given him.

Even with his better performance in training than usual, he stumbled back to the *Moonless Owl* almost too tired and bruised to think.

Ironically, the moon was already coming up by the time he got back to the ship. It was full tonight, and bigger than his outstretched hand, though still smaller than usual.

Several of the crew started asking him questions immediately after they hauled him back on board, but Sabae swooped in to save him, escorting him to his room to sleep. Hugh was so tired he didn't even look around the deck for Avah.

Hugh did, however, manage to force himself to draw defensive wards for his and Godrick's room. Once he'd clambered up to his bunk, he immediately collapsed into sleep.

Life on the *Moonless Owl* settled into a routine pretty quickly after that. The crew of the ship had their own routine long drilled into them. Hugh did, in fact, find that almost all the members of the crew were family.

Only the elderly cook was unrelated, and he'd been adopted into the ship's family after his own ship was lost to pirates.

True to her word, Kanderon only stopped by twice more for training sessions over the next week. Hugh improved a little bit, but he still ended each one badly bruised and exhausted. While he wasn't dodging the crystals very well, at least his affinity sense was improving in leaps and bounds. He was definitely starting to perceive the patterns in crystals that Kanderon spoke of.

The instant he showed any improvement, of course, Kanderon got him started attempting to fuse the crystals in the sand into larger crystals. It went even worse than his earlier lessons had.

Hugh and his fellow apprentices quickly developed their own routine as well. Breakfast first thing in the morning, followed by various magical training exercises. Lunch came after that, followed by the ship coming to a halt for a couple hours so the apprentices could do physical training in the sand.

After that, it was back to more magical training, then various academic subjects taught from Alustin's seemingly endless supply of books. Hugh could have sworn Alustin had only brought the one satchel onboard, but maybe he'd had his luggage delivered early. Hugh was becoming growingly convinced that Alustin's unknown affinities were somehow involved. Either that, or Godrick was right about the bag itself being magical.

After that was dinner, and then the students were finally given a little free time- assuming they had managed to get their assigned readings done.

The daily classwork and training they'd had under Alustin during their first year had been far easier than this. When they told him as such, Alustin just smiled and told them this was still far easier than their second year would be.

Hugh suspected the physical training breaks in the middle of the day were in large part for Talia, whose stomach hadn't really adjusted to the ship yet. The voyage to Theras Tel would take them almost two weeks, and Talia was only able to keep food down so long as the ship didn't move for at least an hour after she ate.

And, of course, the longer this went on, the more bad-tempered Talia became. She hated being sick all the time, hated the sand, and hated the heat. Hugh tried not to mind too much— he wouldn't be much happier in her position.

Her training, at least, was going well. Her destructive power kept increasing at a steady clip— though her fine control, much to Alustin's chagrin, remained somewhat lacking.

They also spent quite a bit of time experimenting with her bone affinity. No one had quite encountered anything like it before— she could cause bones, so long as they weren't inside a living creature, to grow massively larger, in shapes that resembled flames. Then they exploded. Violently.

Alustin spent hours trying to figure out exactly what Talia was doing to the bones, largely to no avail. They did, however, make a few discoveries. It was possible for Talia to control the rate of growth, as well as, to a small extent, the length of time before the bones exploded. They also found that different types of bones— whether from different parts of an animal's body or a different species of animal entirely— tended to have very different growth speeds, material strengths, and explosiveness.

Godrick, meanwhile, was probably doing the best of all of them in his training. He was already able to partially construct the improvised magical armor his father was famed for— a thick layer of stone and metal that could withstand countless blows and spells. Godrick wasn't there yet, but he could already construct a light shield or breastplate.

It also turned out that there was a good amount of overlap between stone and sand masteries, so Godrick was able to learn to do a few neat tricks with sand from the *Owl's* crew. His favorite was turning sand into sandstone, which he mostly used to get better footing in the sand. It took considerable effort to make the change permanent, but even temporarily shifting it to sandstone was good enough for Godrick's purposes, most of the time.

Sabae, surprisingly to Hugh, was doing fairly badly. She was now able to channel her wind armor across most of her body, so Alustin had pushed forward in her training. Movement techniques and training with her water affinity had been added to her training program.

The movement techniques involved loosening her grip on her wind armor as she stepped or jumped. This was supposed to propel her swiftly in the direction she was going, but more often than not she ended up crashing onto the deck, getting caught in the rigging, or going overboard into the desert. She quickly started to get as bruised as Hugh did from his training with Kanderon.

Her water affinity training was an exercise in pure frustration for her. The first step she had to take was gathering water to herself. Unfortunately, the Endless Erg was renowned for its dryness, and Alustin refused to allow her to use any water from the ship's stores for training. He simply told her that if she could gather moisture from the air in the Endless Erg, she could gather it anywhere.

Hugh, meanwhile, wasn't doing much better. His arms and back were constantly sore from the weight of the crystal bracelets. True to Kanderon's word, they steadily increased in weight daily. With Alustin's guidance, it only took a few days to figure out how to construct spellforms to help support the weight of the crystals, but it was challenging on a level Hugh had never anticipated.

First of all, the motion of his arms and the motion of the ship were constantly throwing off his spellforms. Levitation spells had to compensate for any other forces acting on an object, not just gravity, or it was likely to get thrown in a random direction— not an outcome you really wanted when you were wearing the objects in question on your wrist.

Every time the ship turned, or began moving up or down a dune, or Hugh wasn't paying attention while he was walking on deck or through the inside of the ship, he was likely to be pulled in an unintended direction by his spell helping him hold up the bracelets. Within a few days of this, Hugh's arms, shoulders, and back were perpetually sore, and he had bruises all over his body.

He had to be especially careful not to leave the spells active while he slept.

It didn't help his pride at all the number of times Avah was around to see it happen.

There had to be a better solution than a levitation spell- even one specifically adapted to the patterns of his crystal. He took to spending most of his free time in his and Godrick's cabin, trying to plan out a solution in his oversized spellbook.

He regularly told himself he wasn't doing it to avoid Avah.

They hadn't spoken since Kanderon had shown up. Avah pretty clearly didn't have time for someone she viewed as a child.

It'swasn't like Hugh blamed her, though. She'd taken to hanging around Godrick whenever possible. Godrick towered over Hugh, was good looking where Hugh was average, confident where Hugh was barely able to talk to anyone outside his immediate circle, and unlike Hugh, he was actually allowed to show off his attunements. So far as Avah knew, Hugh only had the single affinity, unlike the others.

Hugh might not be as worthless as he'd once thought he was, but he definitely wasn't a great catch romantically.

Godrick spent a surprising amount of time in the room with Hugh, talking over the problem of his bracelets or just reading while Hugh worked. Hugh didn't know why— if Avah thought he was worth the time of day, he'd be spending all that time with her. He assumed Godrick was just being a good friend and keeping him company.

The bracelets seemed intractable, so Hugh often took breaks from the problem to chat with Godrick, or browse through the book on storm wards that Sabae had given him. He couldn't help but dream about building wards of that magnitude someday— wards were the one thing that he felt truly capable at, and wards of that size would be impressive to anyone.

They were only three days out from Theras Tel when Sabae stormed into Hugh and Godrick's room, looking furious and dragging Talia behind her. Talia also looked miserable, but she had the whole time they'd been on the ship.

"I have had enough of all your sulking," Sabae said.

Hugh looked up from his spellbook in alarm.

"We're not…" Godrick began.

"The three of you have barely spent an instant on deck," Sabae said. "Talia here at least has an excuse with her stomach. What's yours?"

Hugh desperately tried to think of an explanation that didn't make him look terrible. Hiding from a girl didn't exactly sound very courageous.

Godrick reached out with his foot and closed the cabin door behind the girls.

"It's… well, it's Avah," Godrick said. "She won't stop followin' me around and flirtin' with me every time ah'm on deck, and ah'm not interested in her like that. It's makin' me a bit uncomfortable. Hugh's just bein' a good friend and keepin' me company."

Hugh blinked in surprise. Godrick thought that Hugh was the one doing him the favor?

"I could throw her off the ship for you," Talia muttered, but no one paid that any attention.

"Why didn't you say something to her?" Sabae asked.

"Ah'm not good at letting people down," Godrick said.

"Why didn't you say something to us?" Sabae demanded

"I'd have thrown her off the ship for you," Talia said again.

Sabae rolled her eyes. "Why didn't you tell me or Hugh?"

"Hugh can't stand Avah," Talia said. "Ever since she insulted him in front of all of us, he's avoided her. He should just challenge her already."

Hugh furrowed his eyebrows. "What? I don't hate her."

"Why not?" Talia asked.

"Then why…?" Sabae started to ask at the same time. She stopped, and a look of realization came across her face.

"You have a crush on her!" she said.

Hugh blushed.

"Why?" Talia said. "She's no warrior, and she's not that pretty."

Godrick poked his head up over the edge of Hugh's bunk.

"Do yeh?" he asked.

Hugh's face turned even redder. He finally managed a small nod.

Sabae stared at him for a moment before sighing.

"Hiding in your room is literally the worst possible way to do something about that," she said.

"It doesn't matter," Hugh said miserably. "She thinks I'm just some weird kid."

"Based off of what, exactly?" Sabae asked.

"What she said when I spotted Kanderon," Hugh said.

Sabae sighed.

"That was more than a week ago, Hugh. I thought you were going to try to be more outgoing."

"I've been more outgoing," Hugh mumbled.

"Have you literally talked to anyone other than us or Alustin since you boarded the *Owl?*" she asked.

Hugh raised his finger, then slowly lowered it. "Kanderon?"

"I saw him thank the cook once," Talia said.

Sabae glared at him. "That's it- We're all going on deck, right now."

"But..." Godrick started. Sabae shifted her glare to him, and he quieted down.

Hugh sighed, and began crafting a spellform in his mind's eye to try and help him move the crystal bracelets more easily onto deck.

Sabae was quite pleased with herself as she left Hugh and Avah talking in the morning sun. It had been profoundly awkward at first— it turned out that Avah was convinced that Hugh hated her, from the way he'd been avoiding her. It was the type of awkwardness that Sabae, like any sane person, entirely preferred to avoid. She even preferred to skip past those bits in novels. Sabae was pretty sure that neither Hugh nor Avah had noticed that she'd manipulated them into moving past that part quickly, and into a conversation about the similarities and differences between sand and crystal affinities.

Sabae had some doubts as to whether there was any romance to be found there, but at least she had ended Hugh's moping for now. More than an adequate repayment for getting the two past the awkwardness.

She looked around, noticing Godrick and Talia up near the prow. Godrick was clearly relieved to be out of the cramped confines of the cabin, where the huge youth could hardly even stretch out. She wasn't sure why he was so uninterested in Avah— she was certainly pretty enough— but Godrick was surprisingly hard to understand, sometimes. It was easy to just see the friendly, cheerful giant sometimes, and not suspect there was more underneath.

Talia, on the other hand, was about as complicated as a hammer to the face. Prideful and angry with a chip on her shoulder bigger than her entire body, but she was loyal to a fault.

Unfortunately, there wasn't much Sabae could do about Talia's seasickness, especially since she'd been forbidden from using her healing affinity any further without more training.

Sabae felt the back of her neck prickling, and turned to see Deila watching her from the prow of the ship. Sabae had no idea why her friends seemed to have so much trouble remembering nautical terms. The old woman smiled knowingly at her, gesturing with her chin towards Hugh and Avah.

It seemed someone, at least, had noticed Sabae's work. Deila reminded Sabae of her own grandmother, so that didn't really surprise her.

"It seems you managed to get everyone up on deck for once," Alustin said.

Sabae barely managed not to jump out of her skin. She could have sworn that Alustin hadn't been on deck a second ago.

"Good work," Alustin said with a broad smile. "I thought I'd have to take care of that myself. I wasn't really looking forward to spending the time doing that, since we're about to be attacked by pirates."

Sabae gave Alustin a disbelieving look. Alustin merely smiled wider.

Well, at least this should cheer up Talia.

CHAPTER SIX

PIRATES

ALUSTIN had used his farseeing affinity to scry the ships, apparently. Hugh still wasn't entirely clear how that worked, but Alustin had quietly informed Deila and Captain Solon of the danger, and the crew had prepared for battle surprisingly quietly and efficiently. They brought back out the crossbows and ballistae just as fast as Hugh had seen them do it before. Avah and the other sand mages all moved to the bottom deck, to get close to the sand and keep them moving as quickly and smoothly as possible.

There were three pirate ships in total, according to Alustin. Two were slightly smaller than the *Moonless Owl*, while the third was near twice its size.

The *Owl* had been cruising in a valley between two rows of dunes, and the pirates had used those dunes to sneak up on either side of the *Owl*— the larger on one side, the two smaller on the other.

Each of the smaller pirates had four ballistae apiece, and the larger had ten.

Captain Solon had pulled out a cutlass entirely engraved in intricate spellforms. Hugh had no idea what it was supposed to do, but it had even more spellforms than the dagger he'd found for Talia in the labyrinth, or the buckler he'd found for Sabae. The latter, sadly, was too damaged for her to use without extensive repairs— she'd been forced to leave it with Skyhold's enchanters for repair for the length of the trip.

Alustin, of course, had decided that this was an excellent learning experience for his students. Rather than instruct them on how to help defend the ship, however, he merely grinned and told them to "be creative." He then returned to go confer with Captain Solon about something else.

Hugh really hated it when Alustin smiled like that.

Talia had taken up a position at the back of the ship, seasickness largely forgotten and replaced with a terrifying smile. Godrick and Sabae had taken up positions on the side of the ship nearest to the small vessels.

Hugh, however, had no idea what to do to help.

If he'd manufactured any more of his exploding ward-carved slingstones, those might have come in handy— though, considering how much his bracelets weighed down his arms, he likely wouldn't be able to use his sling correctly.

Hugh was more than competent enough with cantrip spellforms, but cantrips weren't particularly useful for combat, even with his ability to improvise new ones. He wasn't good enough with his crystal affinity for use in combat yet— or, really, use in anything. As for his other two affinities, Kanderon and Alustin had strictly forbidden him from even trying to use them.

So what did that leave him with? What he always resorted to.

Wards.

Hugh was, without a doubt, the best wardcrafter his age at Skyhold. He was, he was fairly certain, better than most adult mages. It was partially due to his nature as a warlock— most warlocks could imbue a certain class of spells with their will, allowing for greater control, and for Hugh that class of spells was wards.

Mostly, however, Hugh could thank his own hard work and natural talent with wards.

Of course, drawing wards on a moving object was miles more difficult than drawing them on something stationary. Wards had a tendency to decay and fail explosively when physically moved around too much. Hugh had begun studying how to build wards that were more resistant to movement, but only just— so he was much more limited than usual in his choice of ward.

There was also the fact that this would be by far the largest ward he'd ever attempted to craft. Even with his studies of large-scale wards from the stormward book Sabae had given him, it would be daunting, and Hugh wasn't sure how he would be able to craft a large enough ward in time to be useful.

Hugh stared at the one stick of chalk he had been carrying in his pocket. He doubted he could craft a ward around the entire ship with it in the time he had, even if…

Hugh grinned. He didn't need to craft a ward around the entire ship.

Hugh dashed for the front of the ship— no, Sabae had told him it was called the prow at least a dozen times already— as the pirate ships crested the tops of the dunes, then slid down them towards the *Owl* with a noise like an avalanche.

The instant the first smaller ship pulled alongside the *Owl,* both let loose with bolts from crossbows and ballistae, as well as all sorts of magical assaults.

Every single one of them was deflected by shields of wind that rose up around the ships. It was standard practice for wind mages on a ship to do so- most assaults early in a battle would be easily deflected by the wind gusting rapidly around the ships.

The problem, of course, was that maintaining wind shields large enough and powerful enough to protect an entire ship was incredibly draining. Even ships with an outsize number of wind mages, like the *Moonless Owl,* could only maintain them for a few minutes— even less when actively under attack. On top of that, windshields significantly reduced the amount of wind making it into the ship's sails, slowing them quite a bit.

Hugh frantically drew spellforms on the prow of the ship. He needed to get this ward done before…

A lightning bolt slammed through the wind shield, hardly affected, and shattered a portion of the railing on the right side of the ship. Hugh flinched, almost ruining his spellforms.

Not all magic was troubled by windshields.

He needed to get this ward done before the windshield went down.

Talia glared at the pirate ship behind them. Its windshield had easily dispersed every bolt of dreamfire she'd sent at it.

She'd hoped that with as strange as dreamfire behaved in other ways, it would be less vulnerable to strong winds than regular fire. If there was a difference, however, it was hardly noticeable.

Well, there were ways to deal with windshields. Clan Castis had fought more than its fair share of wind mages in its time, and Talia's family had often told her of techniques they'd used.

The *Owl's* windshield wasn't a problem— any decent windmage could craft a shield that detected and parted for spells coming from the inside. You could perform an extremely basic enchantment on your bolts and arrows to allow them to pass through as well. The sand blowing in it mucked with her aim a bit, but not enough to mess her up entirely.

The whole ship lurched, and Talia's stomach tried to climb up out of her mouth. She managed to hold it down through sheer force of will, but it was a close thing.

Talia grimaced, and manifested dreamfire in front of her. The spellforms to do so were far, far more complex than a simple fire summoning spellform— dream spells could only summon something the caster had seen in a dream, so the caster had to use the spellform to draw on a memory of a dream.

That had been the hardest part of training the attunement in the first place— training her mind to remember her dreams clearly, while avoiding lucid dreaming. Lucid dreams made poor fuel for dream spells.

Thankfully, Talia dreamed of fire quite often, as was right and proper for a scion of Clan Castis.

Rather than launch a dreamfire bolt immediately, Talia began focusing more and more mana into the purple-green flames. She kept the dreamfire focused in as small a sphere as possible. That sort of thing wouldn't be possible for most people— Talia's tattoos didn't just enhance the power of flame spells. They also increased her range, control, and even the flexibility of her spells. Talia was far, far more flexible than other attuned mages- so long as she was trying to destroy things with fire.

Talia was glad Alustin hadn't decided that she needed to learn spellform improvisation as well as Hugh. While it gave Hugh even more flexibility than her tattoos gave her, it just didn't seem worth the effort when all you wanted to do was incinerate something.

Once Talia was sure she couldn't pack the slightest bit more mana into the dreamfire bolt, she began envisioning a second spellform in her head. Alustin had been training her to hold more and more spellforms active in her mind's eye at once— he claimed that it would be essential to her as a ranged combat mage. Talia wasn't so sure about that, but Alustin had seldom steered her wrong before, and some of the members of her clan practiced similar disciplines.

The second spellform wrapped a thick sphere of dreamfire around the first, with a thin gap of air in between the two. It wasn't nearly as mana dense as the one in the center, but it didn't need to be. This was the trickiest of the spellforms she was planning, since it needed to maintain a uniform density of mana, even as it lost some.

Talia could feel herself start to sweat from the strain of holding two spellforms at once. Doing her best to ignore the strain, her nausea, the Radhan mages and crossbowmen beside her, and a series of crossbow bolts and firebolts slamming into the windshield in front of her, she began work on a third spellform— this one a cone of dreamfire wrapped around the other two, pointing forwards towards the enemy ship.

Finally, Talia envisioned a relatively simple spellform connecting the other three. Once she pumped mana into it, all three of the others would launch simultaneously.

Just as she prepared to do so, the ship lurched harshly to the side as the larger pirate shipped rammed its shield against the *Owl's.* Her spell accelerated forwards towards the pirate ship. The *Owl's* windshield parted to allow it through, and it slammed into the enemy windshield.

The cone on the outside hardly lasted any time at all before it got dissolved in the windshield, but it did get the others several inches through. The next layer began dissolving just as fast, but thanks to its mana density maintenance, it stayed largely intact through the rest of the windshield, only dissolving into a shower of sparks at the very end.

The dense core of the compound dreamfire bolt punched through the last part of the windshield, hardly losing any of its dreamfire. If the *Owl* hadn't lurched, and Talia's aim had been true, it would have slammed right into the mainmast.

Instead, it hammered right into the forward ballista. If Talia had used regular fire, it likely would have just exploded. Dreamfire, however, was seldom so predictable.

Instead, it began to hum. The strings began vibrating like they were on a harp instead of a siege engine, and the whole thing began to shake. It went from barely audible to deafening in seconds. Its crew lurched away from the weapon, clutching their ears.

Just when it seemed it couldn't grow any louder, the noise stopped. The ballista just sat there for a moment, then began to split apart. Every piece of wood on the thing collapsed into fibrous strands, leaving a curious pile of fibers with a few bits of metal jutting out of the pile. The decking around it looked somewhat fibrous as well.

Talia, however, saw none of this, as she was puking off the back of the ship. The windshield, unfortunately for her, did not recognize vomit as a spell.

Godrick barely caught Sabae before she fell over the side of the ship. He turned to see that the bigger vessel across the deck from them— on whatever the right side of a ship was called— had crashed its windshield against theirs. Several of the *Owl's* windmages had dropped down to their knees in exhaustion, but none had dropped out of the fight.

Sabae caught her balance, and Godrick let her go. "Should we switch over ta tha other side of the ship?" he asked.

Sabae looked at the other mages on this side of the ship, then nodded. "Neither of us is going to be a lot of good in a long-range fight," she acknowledged.

Godrick nodded, then followed her over, clutching his sledgehammer. He still wasn't entirely used to its balance— it was heavier and sturdier than the one he'd left in the labyrinth. He also hadn't gotten used to maintaining the armor spells that shaped stone and metal around him— unlike Sabae, who was getting better and better with her wind armor daily.

The pirate ship kept trying to force its way through the *Owl's* windshield, and Godrick could see several spots where the two windshields had begun to weaken and cancel each other out. Attacks would begin raining through the gaps soon.

Godrick could feel the aether around them thinning noticeably as so many mages drew on it to refresh their mana reservoirs. If the ships came to a halt, they'd likely drain it nearly completely in their immediate surroundings. At least, until more aether flowed in from farther away, but that could take quite a while.

Though his father's training mostly focused on close-range combat, Godrick had still been taught a few ranged spells. One of the most useful, he'd found, was also one of the simplest— a spell that simply pushed a target piece of steel away from him. It was quick, simple, and he could envision the spellform in a fraction of a second. All he had to do was know what steel he wanted to target.

Godrick closed his eyes and began reaching out with his affinity senses. His father could do this with his eyes open, but Godrick couldn't sort out the sensory confusion well enough yet. He ignored anything on this side of the windshields, seeking out pointed bits of metal aimed their way. As he did so, he kept the spellform up in his mind, focused on the heads of the crossbow and ballistae bolts.

The instant one began moving forwards, Godrick triggered the spellform. Mana drained out of his reservoir, and the crossbow bolt tumbled to the sand between the ships harmlessly.

Godrick could feel the strain— he hadn't expected blocking crossbow bolts to be so difficult the first time he tried it, given how small they were compared to his hammer or some of the other objects he'd moved in the past, but they packed a lot of energy when fired. He could only stop a relative few before they drained his mana reservoirs. He wasn't even sure if he could handle any ballista bolts.

If he had reservoirs the size of Hugh's, Godrick was sure he could block as many as he wanted. Hugh had more mana available to him than many adult mages— he'd actually managed to slow the fall of six people with a cantrip in the labyrinth. Most mages without a wind, gravity, or force affinity were lucky to be able to slow the fall of a single person.

Godrick missed a crossbow bolt thanks to his spacing off. He was always doing that. Luckily, it missed any of the growing holes in the windshield. He focused back on the battle, just in time to catch another crossbow bolt. His reservoirs were draining rapidly, and there were so many people drawing so heavily on the aether around them that he could actually feel the rate at which he channeled mana from the aether into his reservoirs slow.

Then, to his horror, a gap opened up right in front of a ballista about to fire. Godrick focused all of his attention on the bolt, preparing to try and block it…

Wait, why was he waiting for them to fire? Godrick grinned, and pushed on the head of the bolt as the ballista's crew prepared it to fire. Since it was higher up than him, the front of the bolt flipped up into the air, which in turn managed to release the drawstring of the ballista. The drawstring caught the twisting base of the bolt, somehow managing to send it twirling backwards. It ended up slamming point first into the mainmast, where it stuck, trembling.

Godrick would never have believed that had happened if he hadn't done it.

With a grin, Godrick began reaching out for other crossbow and ballistae bolts, knocking them loose from their mounts. It took barely any mana compared to stopping them in flight, and the enemy rate of fire slowed to almost nothing.

Which, of course, was when the enemy mages took notice of him. Before Godrick could react, the lightning mage fired a bolt of lightning straight at him.

Captain Solon was too far away from him to block the lightning bolt, and Godrick would have been turned to ash if Sabae hadn't stepped in front of him, deflecting the bolt with both hands. She might not be able to safely use her lightning affinity offensively yet, but she'd been constantly drilled by Alustin to be able to deflect lightning safely since the labyrinth.

"Watch yourself, kid!" the captain called. He hurled the lightning bolt back against the side of the larger ship, then knocked an enemy firebolt out of the air with his cutlass.

Godrick nodded. Then, to his horror, several crossbow bolts came flying straight for Sabae and him. The brief seconds he'd stopped paying attention had been just enough. He frantically reached out with his affinity senses, pushing against one, then two bolts, but the third one slipped just past him. His heart seemed to stop as he watched it hurtle towards Sabae's chest.

It slammed into her personal windshield, and deflected off easily.

Sabae glanced down at her torso. "Huh." She glanced back at Godrick. "At least I can block stuff."

Godrick smiled weakly at her. Sabae turned around to see another crossbow bolt flying at her, which she almost casually punched out of the air.

He turned his attention back to preventing crossbows from being loaded. Godrick really, really needed to start paying better attention.

The larger pirate swerved directly towards the *Owl*, and the whole ship shuddered as their wind shields collided.

"What are you working on, Hugh?" Alustin said.

Hugh picked himself up off the deck, not answering. He wasn't really equipped to help much in this fight otherwise, so he had to do *something.*

"Generally, wards are expected to be crafted before a battle begins," Alustin said.

Another bolt of lightning flashed over from the larger pirate vessel, but Captain Solon somehow deflected it harmlessly into the sand with his cutlass.

"Not much else I can do right now," Hugh said.

"What, exactly," said Alustin, looking over Hugh's ward, "is this intended to do? I'm fairly certain I didn't teach you most of these runes, except for the ones that stabilize moving wards."

Hugh finished the last of the spellforms for the ward, but he didn't activate it just yet. All told, the ward would have been almost fifteen feet long if it had been stretched out. Instead, it curved in a V-shape, coming to a point in the prow.

"They're going to redirect the wind hitting us from the front upwards. According to the book, that should create a patch of lower density in the air ahead of the ship, and we'll actually get pulled into it. I got the spellforms from the Kaen Das stormward book," Hugh said.

"Have you somehow developed a farseeing affinity too, Hugh?" Alustin said.

Another lightning bolt struck the side of the ship, charring it. The enchantments the Radhan traders had worked into the sides of their ship apparently worked quite well, thankfully, preventing any more damage. The larger enemy ship's windshield, however, was steadily dissolving into their own.

"No, why?" Hugh said.

"No reason." Alustin stared at the ward for a moment longer. "Ah, I see. How clever."

"Shouldn't you be helping fight off the pirates?" Hugh said.

"We'll be able to escape quite handily once the sandstorm hits," Alustin replied.

"Sandstorm?" Hugh asked.

Alustin just smiled. "You should see about extending that ward further along the sides."

Talia had mostly cleaned the vomit out of her face when the *Owl's* windshield collapsed for a moment. Enemy bolts and spells promptly began making their way through from the ship behind them. One of the Radhan crossbowmen next to Talia went down with a bolt in her shoulder, crying out in pain.

The windshield flickered back into existence, but it looked much smaller and thinner than it did before. Several spells and bolts hit it, nearly punching through.

Her stomach still clenching, Talia levered herself up on the railing. The pirate behind them still had its windshield up, and Talia didn't trust her stomach or the *Owl's* windshield to hold for long enough for her to manifest another dreamfire bolt capable of piercing the enemy windshield. There had to be some sort of way to…

Talia smiled, and dug into her belt pouch, pulling out a handful of small, jagged white objects.

Shards of bone.

Talia reached into her mana reservoirs. Manifesting dreamfire was still difficult, but she'd been able to do it reliably for some time now. Her bone affinity, however… The mana felt sluggish, angry, and full of knives. It *hurt* to draw on those reservoirs, and she still wasn't sure exactly what was going on when she did.

More terrifyingly, Alustin had no clue either.

When she pumped the mana into a piece of bone, it grew and grew, far faster than it should be able to with the amount of mana she could handle. Growing solid objects was one of the most mana-intensive tasks for a mage, far more than merely reshaping them.

It felt like the bone was trying to be a fire when it grew, but it couldn't move freely like a fire. It couldn't twist and dance, it just grew and grew and strained against itself until the heat of imprisoning itself grew to be too much.

Talia took a deep breath and envisioned a spellform. It was incredibly, incredibly basic- all it did was direct her mana into the shards. This prevented her from draining herself as badly as channeling the mana uncontrolled had in the Labyrinth.

It was more than enough, though. The bone shards immediately began to grow and heat up. Talia threw them behind the speeding ship.

By the time they were a foot from her hand, they'd each grown to the size of her fist, tendrils in the shape of flames reaching out in all directions.

By the time they entered the *Owl's* windshield, they were each bigger than her head.

By the time they hit the sand, they were the size of her torso.

By the time the enemy windshield passed over them, they were each bigger than she was, and they barely rocked in the wind.

And by the time the pirate ship ran over them, barely a couple of seconds after she threw them, they were each the size of Godrick.

They gouged into the bottom of the pirate ship, cutting long, horrifying gouges into the bottom. Goods and supplies began tumbling out, but only for a moment- because that was when the massive hunks of bone exploded in flames. Smaller shards of bone scythed out through the ship, carving channels and holes before they, too, exploded.

The pirate's right runner gave way completely, and the whole ship seemed to *crumple* forwards. Jagged chunks of wood tumbled through the air along with panicked, injured pirates.

The mainmast tore itself loose from the ship entirely, falling into the sand and carrying several pirates with it.

Talia smiled, then she grabbed onto the railing again and began vomiting once more.

That was, thankfully for Talia if not for anyone else on board the ship, when the *Owl's* windshield failed for good.

CHAPTER SEVEN

STERN CHASE

SABAE was busy protecting Godrick from enemy crossbow bolts and spells when the shield failed for the second time. The pirates had seemingly figured out that he was the one preventing most of their crossbows and ballistae from firing, and they were concentrating most of their fire his way.

Sabae's wind armor, however, was proving surprisingly up for the job. The pirates only seemed to have the one lightning attuned mage, the wind mages maintaining their shields, and a few fire mages. Their crew might have drastically outnumbered the *Moonless Owl's*, but that didn't do them any good when the windshields kept them from boarding.

The first time the shield went down, it was only for a moment, and it went back up again in time to keep the enemy ship from slamming into them. Sabae didn't know how well the *Owl* would stand up to that— a normal sandship its size would have its runners collapsed and wreck, but since Radhan ships like the *Owl* didn't have runners, it might be more resistant to ramming.

The second time it went down, however, it stayed down. Sabae immediately let loose a powerful gust strike, correctly anticipating an entire flight of crossbow bolts and fireballs. The gust strike knocked most of them harmlessly out of the air, but it took a lot out of her. Sabae had to struggle to keep up the momentum of her wind armor.

While she could stop those, she could only stare helplessly at the enemy ship and its windshield as they bore down on the *Owl*. The Radhan ship had immediately started to pick up speed when its windshield went down, but it was far from enough to get them away in time.

Time seemed to slow down as the pirate vessel bore down on them. Sabae slowly turned towards Godrick, hoping to somehow tackle the huge youth out of the way, when the whole ship jolted forwards, knocking both of them entirely off their feet.

The expected impact with the pirates never came.

Sabae stood up again and looked around. Somehow, the *Owl* had accelerated forward at an absurd rate, putting them far ahead of the three…, no, two remaining pirate ships. Sabae saw the third crushed and burning far behind them.

"What was that?" Godrick asked. "Ah felt like tha ship was gettin' pulled out from under me."

Even as Sabae watched, the pirates began falling farther and farther back, their bolts and spells falling far short of the *Owl.*

"I have no…" Sabae began as she helped him up, then she looked towards the bow of the ship. A thin vertical curtain of white light, like a bleached aurora, was rising up in a V-shape in the prow, and just behind it was…

Sabae smiled. "That was Hugh."

Godrick looked towards the bow of the ship and grinned as well. "Ah shouldn't be surprised. Ah'm going to go check on Talia."

They split up, Sabae heading towards the prow. Hugh appeared to be frantically searching his pockets for something. Alustin stood next to him, curiously poking his finger into the curtain of light.

"There you go, saving the day again," Sabae said to him. "Though I'm not exactly sure how you did that?"

Hugh glanced up at her and smiled shyly, still searching his pockets.

"I never could have done it without you," he said. "I got the idea from your great-grandmother's journal. This ward redirects the wind hitting the ship from the front upwards, though I'm not entirely sure why it pulled us forwards as fast as it did. Reducing the wind resistance shouldn't have made this much of a difference."

Sabae didn't feel like she deserved that much credit, but at least Hugh was keeping some for himself this time. "You made it so there was less air in front of us," she said. "That hole in the air pulled us forwards. It's how wind-mages fly."

Hugh finally pulled a new piece of chalk from his belt pouch. "Really? I thought they pushed themselves with gusts of wind," he said.

"Takes too much effort, and it's too hard to control," Sabae said. "Pulling works much better."

"Each of the affinities that allow for flight work in fairly unique ways," Alustin said. "Wind mage flight works quite differently than the way gravity mages fly. And force mages don't fly so much as jump absurdly far."

Hugh started drawing on the deck with his chalk again, apparently extending the ward farther back.

"What are you doing?" Sabae said. "We're already moving too fast for the pirates to catch up with us."

"I'm not worried about the pirates," Hugh said. "I'm worried about the sandstorm."

"The what?" Sabae said.

Alustin pointed past the bow as they crested a short dune. Sabae looked forwards to see that the horizon appeared to have been turned black.

"Oh," Sabae said, her throat suddenly dry. "That sandstorm."

The sandstorms of the deep Endless Erg were legendary. They could arise with little to no warning, growing to immense size. They swept through the desert like a scourge, entirely reshaping the dunes in their path.

You didn't go toe to toe with the sandstorms. You found somewhere to shelter from them or you fled ahead of them.

They were, above the predators, the lack of water, or even the heat, the biggest reason why no-one crossed the Endless Erg on foot or on mounts. Anyone caught in the deadly winds would have their fleshed stripped from their bones by the blowing sand.

The ships that crossed the Endless Erg had different ways to survive. Most of the larger ships simply took down their sails, battened down the hatches, and waited them out. So long as you had a wood mage to repair any damage and a sand mage to dig your ship out of the reshaped dunes, you'd probably be fine.

The faster ships tended to try to outrun the storms. The storms were swift, but the winds that blew ahead of them could be navigated by a skilled captain for long enough to get them out of the past of the worst of it.

For smaller, slower ships… well, there were a few options. The best was to hope a sandstorm didn't show up during your trip. Sabae had heard of other ships that carried extra-large complements of sand mages, in order to bury their entire ship, with plant mages to keep the air from going stale.

"Are we planning to run ahead of the storm?" Sabae said.

"Our mages are exhausted," Captain Solon said. "It would be incredibly risky." Captain Solon, his mother, and his daughter had joined them on the prow of the ship as the sandstorm grew steadily larger on the horizon.

"Bury ourselves?" Sabae asked.

Delia shook her head. "The pirates might not be able to catch us right now, but they haven't given up yet— and aren't likely to, since the little redhead destroyed one of their ships. The big ship looks sturdy enough to wait out the storm on the surface and attack us when we dig ourselves out— not to mention we don't have any plant mages on board."

Sabae was still a little shocked by the destruction of the pirate sandship. Talia was by far the most dangerous of the four apprentices, but destroying an entire sandship would be astonishing even for most fully trained battle mages.

She glanced back at the pirates. They'd regained some of the lost ground now that they'd dropped their own windshields.

"We run through the storm," Alustin said.

Everyone stared at him in shock.

"That's ridiculous," Captain Solon said. "The *Owl* is a tough little ship, but its rigging can't handle those winds."

Alustin just pointed at Hugh. He'd continued the ward about halfway down the port side of the ship, though he hadn't activated any of it beyond the initial bit in the prow.

"An apprentice's trick is supposed to…" Captain Solon began, but his mother raised her hand to interrupt him, staring at Alustin intently.

"Hugh has my full confidence," Alustin said.

"Can Hugh really do it?" Avah asked Sabae quietly. She'd been silent up until now, obviously exhausted from her work smoothing the sand and the hull for speed.

"Of course he can," Sabae said, more confidently than she felt. Hugh was a marvel, but that sandstorm was immense. Even from miles away across the horizon, it looked like a black wave rolling across the gold-white sea of sand, preparing to wash away the first shore it came upon.

Still, Sabae wanted to make Avah think it was a sure thing. Impressing Avah like that couldn't hurt Hugh's chances.

Sabae noticed Delia eying her again. The old woman cocked an eyebrow slightly at her.

Delia definitely reminded her of her own grandmother, though perhaps a little less terrifying.

"We just need to give Hugh enough time to finish the ward," Alustin was saying. "Can your mages run us in front of the storm for that long?"

Captain Solon considered for a moment, tapping his fingers on the hilt of his cutlass. "It seems like our best option," he said. "And if your apprentice's ward doesn't work, we can try to keep running the front as long as we can."

By the tone of his voice, it didn't sound like he thought that would be for very long. Sabae really, really hoped Hugh had studied her great-grandmother's journal well.

Hugh drew on the deck so quickly his wrists ached. He'd already gotten several splinters from the battle-damaged deck, and he hadn't paused long enough to remove them. His stick of chalk was almost out, so he hoped Godrick returned from their room quickly with the extras he'd sent him for.

This was, without a doubt, the single most challenging ward Hugh had ever drawn, and it was with far less preparation than he was used to.

First off, it was far larger than any ward he'd ever attempted before. Wards tended to be fairly mana efficient, but as they got larger, their mana requirements grew more and more rapidly. Hugh was fairly sure he could sustain this one, but it would be a real challenge.

Then there was the sheer complexity of the ward itself. Sabae's great-grandmother had been an absolute master of wardcrafting, and Hugh barely understood most of the wards in her journal. This was one of the simplest ones in the book, and it still stretched his abilities.

If that weren't enough, he couldn't even copy the ward out of the journal exactly— the original design was meant to be powered by someone with a wind affinity, rather than being designed to handle any sort of mana, like most wards, so Hugh had to alter the spellforms to allow him to channel his crystal mana in— Hugh knew better than to try and access his starfire or planar reservoirs. He also had to add in the spellforms that stabilized the ward while it was in motion, so it didn't randomly explode.

He couldn't make the ward uniform, either, or the wind-redirection effect would slow them too much. He had to slightly decrease the power of the ward as it went farther and farther back down the ship. He also had to make sure the ward would curve over the top of the ship— Hugh doubted that the winds inside the sandstorm would be polite enough to only blow horizontally.

Of course, the biggest challenges were his crystal bracelets. Hugh couldn't trust any of the spells he'd devised to help support them not to mess up his spellforms, so he was having to drag them along the deck, and his arms ached fiercely.

"Ah've got yer chalk!" Godrick called. Hugh paused long enough to accept a new stick, then he kept drawing. He was nearly to the back of the ship— whatever sailors called it.

Hugh made sure not to look up at the approaching sandstorm. He couldn't afford any distractions.

Sabae spun up her wind armor as the storm front approached the *Owl*. The sandship had tacked so that they were moving away from the storm at an angle, albeit a much shallower one than normal. The pirates had kept up the chase, apparently still determined to avenge their fallen comrades, but they had taken a steeper angle than the *Owl* had.

The sandstorm was only a couple miles off the port side of the ship at this point, and it dwarfed everything as they raced northwards. The storm towered into the sky, pitch black and all-consuming. Even this far away, sand had started to whip around the deck, stinging skin and eyes. Captain Solon had ordered all unnecessary personnel below decks, so Sabae had taken over Godrick's role carrying Hugh's chalk as he drew, depending on her wind armor to shield her from sand. Irrick, a Radhan mage a couple years older than them, followed as well to shield Hugh with his wind and sand affinities.

Captain Solon shouted something at the ship's pilot, but Sabae couldn't make out any words over the roar of the storm. Sabae had *never* heard anything this loud before, and she'd watched her grandmother lead the mages of her family in turning aside entire hurricanes from Ras Andis. As she watched the storm nervously, a flash of light lit up inside of the abyssal cloud, swiftly followed by another.

There was lightning inside the sandstorm.

Sabae's stomach constricted a little, and she ran her fingers along the scars on her cheek from where her early experiments with her lightning affinity had burnt her. She was getting more comfortable deflecting lightning spells, but those were nowhere near as powerful as actual lightning bolts. She glanced over to the helm, and noticed Captain Solon clutching the hilt of his cutlass, knuckles white.

Sabae turned her attention back to Hugh. He had less than a quarter of the circumference of the ship to go.

"Are…" Irrick began to shout, but Sabae glared at him. Hugh didn't need any distractions.

Sabae felt her wind armor flex and twist as the winds of the storm increased even more. The whole ship was shuddering now, like it wanted to shake apart at the speeds they were traveling. Sabae didn't think she'd ever moved this fast in her life. If she fell off the ship now, even her wind armor and the softness of the sand wouldn't protect her from the impact.

The storm was less than a mile away now, and it filled half the sky. The dunes between the storm and the *Owl* looked like they were dissolving.

The ship slowed slightly as the pilot turned to avoid a particularly large dune. Traveling up it would slow them even more than avoiding it.

Hugh's hand reached out, and Sabae dropped the wind armor on one hand to reach into the bubble Irrick had crafted around Hugh. In the fraction of a second before her hand went inside it to give Hugh the next piece of chalk, the blowing sand left her skin red and painful.

The ship shuddered and picked up even more speed as the storm grew closer again. Sabae was almost knocked off her feet, and Hugh cursed as he messed up a line. He frantically erased it, then resumed his drawing.

Sabae was desperately trying not to think about what would happen if Hugh didn't make it in time.

Something flashed in the corner of Sabae's eye, and she looked over to see a flock of sunlings flying ahead of the storm front. Even as she watched, they seemed to give up the chase and dove down into the sand, burrowing deeper.

The roar of the storm was deafening, even through her wind armor. She could see Captain Solon bellowing right in the pilot's ear, but couldn't even detect a hint of it.

As she and Irrick followed Hugh slowly across the deck, she glanced back at the pirates. They were still following, but were nearly a mile farther away from the storm and considerably farther back now— they weren't foolish enough to sail as close to the sandstorm as the *Moonless Owl* was.

The top of the storm front was actually *above* them, now. Sabae wanted to laugh hysterically— the deck of the sandship was still in brightly lit, golden daylight from the sun in the east, but the sky straight above her was pitch black.

The base of the storm looked like it was about to swallow them whole when, abruptly, it began to pull away. Sabae looked around to realize that Captain Solon had ordered the angle they were running in front of the storm steepened. Slowly but surely, the ship started to pull ahead.

Sabae desperately tried not to see how exhausted all of the wind mages on the ship were. She also tried not to feel ashamed that she couldn't assist them. That wasn't her fault at all.

She only partially held off the shame.

Hugh's hands and wrists felt like they were going to fall off. They'd never hurt this badly in his life, and he was shocked he hadn't dropped the chalk yet due to the cramps.

To keep his spellforms from being scoured away by the wind, he'd started channeling mana into them. Not enough to activate the ward, but enough to keep it stable. This wasn't something most wardcrafters could do- it was part of his will imbuing talents that came from being a warlock. It was just one more irritating distraction.

He didn't even dare look up. It was just him, trapped inside a bubble of calm as he moved forwards. He tried not to extend out of the bubble the Radhan sailor— whose name he hadn't caught— was crafting for him. Earlier he'd accidentally stuck his head out, and it took precious seconds to clean the sand out of his eyes.

Hugh just kept drawing.

Talia held the empty chamber pot in front of her and dry-heaved. Godrick held her steady as the ship shook, lighting up his and Hugh's room with a simple cantrip.

"Ah yeh sure yeh need that?" Godrick asked. "Ah don't think yeh've got anything left in yer stomach."

Talia tried to glare at him, but then she heaved again as the ship hit a bump of some sort. Godrick should tell that to her stomach.

Hugh only had a single hand's width worth of ward left to draw, and he couldn't do it.

Not because he couldn't move his fingers anymore— Hugh actually wasn't entirely sure he could drop the chalk if he wanted to.

No, Hugh couldn't finish it because he'd misjudged the circumference of the ship. He'd finished a full unit of the spellform a full hand's width from where it needed to end— he couldn't fit another spellform in between the two ends he needed to connect, and he didn't dare adapt the active ward in the front of the ship while it was helping speed them up.

He could draw simple ward extender lines there, but that would act as a weak spot in the ward, and make the whole thing consume far more mana— more than Hugh thought he could handle providing to the ward, even with his large mana reservoirs.

Hugh had doomed everyone. He should have just told everyone that he couldn't do it, instead of listening to Alustin. He should never have gotten it in his head that he was worth…

"Hugh!" Sabae shouted. She'd stuck her head into his bubble, which had shrunk to the point where Hugh was having to huddle nearly into a ball. "What's wrong? You've been staring at that section for ages now!"

"I miscalculated! There's no room for another full spellform here!" Hugh shouted. "I'm…"

"Isn't there something else you could put there?" Sabae shouted.

Hugh stared at her for a second, thinking furiously. You didn't just add components to a ward to make it longer, they had to serve a function that didn't interfere with the rest of the ward. Hugh had already planned out everything he needed to maintain the ward through the storm.

He stopped, then he felt a grin slowly creep across his face.

There absolutely was something he could put into there.

He quickly drew a series of spellform lines running perpendicular to the gap, intersecting them in. He drew the new spellform line almost a foot farther inside the deck, where he quickly drew a circular spellform about a foot across.

Hugh had been originally planning to power the ward himself for however long he could. His massive mana reservoirs were at least useful for that.

But he'd specifically constructed this whole ward to be able to accept any type of mana, since he couldn't use the wind mana the ward was originally designed for. So what he'd done was create a mana tap— a place in the ward where anyone could add mana to it. Better yet, since it was a fully functioning spellform on its own, it wouldn't act as a weak point.

Hugh drew the last line and took a deep breath. If he'd gotten even a single line wrong, the whole ward might fail.

All he could do was hope he'd gotten it right.

Hugh took another deep breath and channeled his mana into the tap.

Sabae moved back and forth between watching Hugh draw, watching the approaching storm, and watching the pursuing pirate ships. They were trapped between a rocky shore and a stormy sea here— move too far from the storm, the pirates closed in; move away from them, risk the storm. Until Hugh finished that ward, they were the next best thing to dead in the water.

She watched Hugh finish the odd circle jutting farther into the deck, take a deep breath, and then place his finger into its center— and then it lit up.

Light raced through the chalk lines around the ship, glowing unbelievably brightly. Thin wisps of white light began to rise from them, rapidly congealing into a curtain that arched over their heads, intersecting the top of the mainmast. As it thickened and solidified, the buffeting wind and noise seemed to die down inside the ward. Sabae noticed that the ward was distinctly weaker at the back, allowing a fixed amount of wind in for the sails.

Everyone on deck looked around in shock, like none of them really expected the ward to work. They were all silent for a few moments.

Finally, Captain Solon broke the silence. "Hard to port. We're heading into the storm."

CHAPTER EIGHT
SANDSTORM

COMPARED to the *Moonless Owl's* previous turns, this one seemed slow and cumbersome, as though the ship itself feared to enter the storm. Hugh kept his hand on the mana tap as they accelerated. It wasn't strictly necessary for him to touch it to channel his mana into it, but Hugh did it anyways.

Where before they couldn't approach directly at all, except at a wide angle, now they seemed to be rushing head-on into the storm. The harder the wind buffeted against them, the faster they seemed to pull forwards.

Behind them, the pirates seemed to hesitate, then they slowly turned away, unwilling to follow the seemingly insane merchants.

The storm rushed at them at terrifying speed, now that they weren't running in front of it any longer. As they moved farther and farther towards the cloudwall, the ship shook harder and harder, slowing as it forced its way directly into the wind. Even with Hugh's ward pulling them forwards, the wind resistance against their hull was hard to overcome.

As they plunged forwards into the storm, the dunes once more seemed to dissolve around them in the wind. The *Owl* shuddered and shook like it was about to fall apart. At one point the sand blew out from under the hull, and the whole ship fell several feet straight down, knocking over half the crew on deck and staggering the rest.

The sun stayed disconcertingly bright and cheerful until they were nearly into the storm. Finally, the choking sand and dust began to dim the light ahead of them as they approached the base of the stormwall.

Hugh tried to swallow, but he found his throat completely dry.

The *Owl* passed into the storm, and the world went dark.

Hugh couldn't see anything at all, at first. He could only hear the thunderous howl of the storm, the shaking of the ship, cracks and creaks from the masts, and, almost entirely drowned out by the rest, the shouting of the crew.

The *Owl* was shaking so badly Hugh could hardly lift himself to his hands and knees.

Ever so slowly, Hugh's eyes adjusted to the murky darkness, and began to make things out in the dim light of his ward.

The crew desperately clutched onto lines, masts, and whatever else they could clutch. The pilot was only on his feet by virtue of holding onto the ship's wheel— not, at this point, that Hugh really suspected the ship's rudders were really doing much to steer them.

Beyond the wards, he could see blowing, swirling sand for a few feet, and then nothing at all.

Hugh felt abruptly fatigued, and looked inwards. His mana reservoirs were draining far, far more quickly than he had anticipated— the winds inside the storm were far more powerful than he'd imagined. There was nothing to do but hold on for as long as he could.

Suddenly, Hugh's vision vanished in a flash of light. He cried out in fear, but couldn't even hear himself over the din of the storm and an abrupt rumble.

Lightning. It had been lightning. Slowly, Hugh's vision cleared, and he saw that the ship was untouched. The lightning had been nearby, but not close enough to strike the ship.

In the distance, lightning struck several more times. That was the closest Hugh came to having any idea where the ground lay— for all he could see, there was no world other than the swirling sand around them. He looked behind them, but there was no trace of the sun in the sky, nor did Hugh have any idea of whether they'd kept to their course or not.

Hugh felt a hand on his shoulder. He turned to see Sabae, also on her hands and knees, looking at him with concern.

"Are you alright?" she shouted in his ear.

"I'm fine!" Hugh shouted back. "I'm just worried about how long I can maintain the ward! I built it so that anyone could channel into it through this mana tap, though, so we can take turns!"

Sabae nodded, then shouted back in his ear. "I'll pass the word around!" She crawled off towards a cluster of nearby crewmembers.

Hugh took a deep breath, trying to focus on the ward and not the storm around him.

Godrick gently patted Talia's back as she retched miserably. Despite being below decks the whole time, he knew he could pinpoint exactly the moment they'd entered the actual storm— what they'd gone through before was nothing compared to the shaking and howling they were feeling now.

They'd been going for hours, now, and the storm had never quieted long enough for a conversation. There had been momentary lulls here and there, but that was all.

At one point, Godrick had staggered out into the hallway to see if he could help on deck, but two of the Radhan sailors were guarding the hatch to ensure that no one else opened it— in case the ward collapsed, the only chance of survival for the people inside the ship was keeping all hatches shut.

When Godrick had asked about the "else" part of "no one else", the answer he received was, unsurprisingly, that Alustin had already gone up onto deck some time ago, somehow distracting the guards and slipping past them.

More than once the ship had fallen unsupported— whether ramping off the side of a dune, having it collapse out from under them, or even being carried a distance up into the air by the wind, Godrick couldn't begin to say.

So he just waited, comforting Talia in her misery by the light of his lonely little cantrip.

Their entrance into the storm was an abrupt, terrifying affair, but their exit was a gradual one. They'd spent an unknown number of hours in the storm.

Hugh had kept funneling power into the ward the whole time, running his reservoirs nearly empty again and again. Others contributed as much as they could, taking the strain off him, but most of the Radhan mages were still exhausted from the battle and the chase. Sabae did what she could as well, and though her mana reservoirs were considerably larger than average, she still found herself drained quite quickly.

They gave him as much time to rest and refill his reservoirs as they could, but Hugh felt almost entirely wrung out and bone tired just a few hours into the nightmarish trip, long before they were out.

Even with all that, the ward still would have failed, without Alustin. The librarian mage had appeared on deck what felt like a couple hours into the storm, just when it seemed they couldn't maintain the ward any longer.

Alustin had crawled over to the mana tap, seemingly without anyone needing to tell him anything. (Hugh suspected Alustin had been scrying events on deck the whole time.) It was then that Hugh realized the difference between his mana reservoirs and those of a fully trained battle mage.

Hugh's reservoirs might be impressive- two to three times larger than those of the average student mage— but Alustin's mana reservoirs were, apparently, many times more than that in size. He was able to maintain the wards unassisted for several hours after coming on deck, giving all the other mages time to recuperate.

It also helped that the aether was considerably thicker inside the sandstorm— approaching the density of Skyhold at times.

Unlike the wind shield, Hugh's ward actually blocked lightning bolts— but each time one hit, it drained an immense amount of mana from the mage powering the ward. They had to be careful to always keep extra mages nearby, just in case.

The first sign that they were beginning to pass through the storm was the sun. Hugh saw a faint red dot in the sky, and it took him quite some time to realize that the sun was starting to peek through the storm. When he turned to tell Sabae, he realized that he could actually hear himself a little more than he could before, though he still needed to yell.

Gradually, the sun grew brighter and brighter, and the storm around them was illuminated with an angry red glow. The lightning grew less frequent, and eventually the red began to fade to orange, then a pale amber.

Then, almost before they knew it, the sky was blue again, and the world had changed from night to late afternoon.

Hugh turned around to look for the storm. From behind it resembled nothing so much as an immense golden cloud resting on the ground- wispy and peaceful looking, as deceptive as that might be.

"We're out!" he said to Sabae. His voice still sounded muted, but from the ringing in his ears, not the howl of the gale.

"I noticed," Sabae said wryly.

Hugh called out to Captain Solon. "Is it safe to drop the ward?"

The captain looked contemplatively back at the storm. "It should be, aye."

Hugh, with a deep sigh of relief, stopped channeling mana into the tap. The ward dissolved into motes of white light that drifted gently upwards before vanishing.

Hugh laid back down on the deck, closed his eyes, and enjoyed the sun on his face. He was asleep in seconds.

Captain Solon had ordered the ship to a halt while Hugh was sleeping so that everyone could rest. The captain seemed more exhausted than anyone except Hugh himself— using the cutlass apparently took quite a bit out of him.

They didn't even know where they were, and it seemed the odds of the pirates finding them again were low, but a watch was set nonetheless.

Deila had come up on deck and woken Hugh from his slumber before he got sunburned— "Hardly a fitting reward for the hero of the day," as she put it. The old woman made Hugh eat a quick meal in the galley— which was wrecked from the storm, pots and pans everywhere— then sent him to his room to sleep. Talia was curled up in Godrick's bunk, and Godrick was nowhere to be seen. Hugh was too tired to wonder where he'd gone, though, and instead just struggled to climb up into his bunk. He didn't even remember falling asleep.

Hugh slept for more than half a day, not waking again until the next morning was close to over. The ship was still motionless, but he could hear voices and activity around the ship. He got up to see what had been going on around the ship and found he was alone in the cabin.

Amazingly, no lives had been lost during the battle— there had been several sailors badly wounded, but all would heal in time.

The *Moonless Owl* had taken a lot of damage during the battle, and the storm had only made it worse. It had stripped the varnish from much of the ship, leaving it battered and splintered. The falls and drops the sandship had also taken during the storm had Captain Solon worried, so the Radhan wood mages were poring over every inch of the structure of the ship, healing any cracks or weaknesses they found.

The cargo, even as bound down as it was, had been badly jostled around, so many of the other Radhan who weren't resting were busy inventorying and repacking it. On any other ship, Avah had told Hugh, the captain would need to be there to make sure the sailors didn't steal anything, but everyone on this ship was family. The Radhan didn't steal from each other.

That comment from Avah hadn't just been a passing one— as he wandered about the ship, Avah took quite a few opportunities to talk to him, both about the activity on the ship and how amazing his ward had been, despite her being below decks for the entire storm. Hugh definitely didn't have any complaints about that.

Alustin, apparently, had taken the other apprentices off the ship for some training, but he had left orders for Hugh to rest and take it easy. Hugh couldn't say he minded too much.

The elderly cook had only cleaned up some of the mess in the galley when Hugh wandered down to get something to eat, but he gladly took a break from cleaning to praise Hugh and whip him up a quick meal. It was some sort of finely chopped meat mixed with vegetables, all wrapped up in thick flatbread, and just as heavily spiced as everything else Hugh had eaten onboard. He was just finishing it when Avah came running down into the galley.

"Hugh, your sphinx is here!" she said.

Hugh stood up and brushed bits of food off his uniform. "I'm more Kanderon's human than she is my sphinx— I don't think she'd appreciate that description." He strode out of the galley, flashing Avah a shy smile on his way out.

So much for taking it easy and resting.

CHAPTER NINE

SUNBURN

"But why do they only use crossbows?" Talia demanded. "Crossbows are terrible!"

"They're also much, much easier to train with," Alustin said, "and easier to store onboard a ship. It takes years to master a longbow, and anyone can just pick up and use a crossbow with a relatively small amount of training."

Godrick trudged through the sand behind Talia and Sabae. Alustin walked in front, facing back towards the apprentices. Godrick had no idea how Alustin was walking up a dune backwards without falling over.

Talia tripped in the sand, falling to her knees again. She'd done that about every twenty or thirty feet, and Godrick reached down and pulled her to her feet automatically at this point.

"Why do we need to walk this far?" Talia demanded. "In sand, at that. Sand is terrible, you can't walk in it, it feels awful, and it gets everywhere. And the sun and the heat don't help anything, either."

Godrick rather liked the heat. And he minded sand a lot less now that he had learned a spell to firm it up while walking on it.

Sabae glanced back at Godrick and rolled her eyes. This was a bit much even for Talia, but Godrick couldn't say he blamed her— she'd had a fairly awful couple of weeks on the ship.

"Like I said, we're here for some important lessons."

"I don't…" Talia started.

"Lessons in what, exactly?" Sabae interjected.

Alustin crested the top of the sand dune and looked around for a moment while the others made it to the top. Godrick, who had been carrying a pack of water and assorted other supplies, gratefully dropped it onto the sand, along with his sledgehammer. This was the tallest dune around for some distance, though he still couldn't make out the *Moonless Owl* from here.

Godrick could also smell something… metallic. His sense of smell had been massively improved by his scent affinity— that was, apparently, normal for any sensory affinity. Sound affinities gained improved hearing, for instance, and he suspected that Alustin's vision had been improved by his farseeing affinity.

Alustin took off his huge, floppy hat. Godrick had no idea where the mage had gotten it from, but he'd been wearing it when they set out from the sandship earlier.

"Lessons in practical ecology," Alustin said, then he fell over backwards, sprawling out into the sand. He shifted position a few times to get comfortable, and then dropped his hat atop his face.

"Ah'm not sure exactly what that's supposed ta mean," Godrick said.

The scent had grown significantly stronger.

"It means," said Alustin from beneath his hat, "that we're about to be attacked by one of the more unusual predators of the Endless Erg. I recommend you all duck."

"What?" Talia asked.

The smell was much stronger now, and…

Godrick's eyes widened, and he tackled Talia and Sabae to the ground. He felt the wind from the passage of something huge above him as he did so.

"What was that for?" Talia yelled.

Godrick scooped up his sledgehammer and climbed to his feet. Fifty feet away, something that looked like a massively oversized sunling with claw-tipped tentacles trailing from its edges circled around the dune, regaining altitude for another dive.

"That," said Alustin, who hadn't moved at all, "is a sunwing, which is a terrible name, given how easy it is to confuse with sunling. The two sounded nothing alike in the language they were originally named in, apparently. Thankfully, they're more often referred to as sunmaws these days. Still an awful name, but much easier to distinguish."

The sunmaw turned in flight, giving Godrick a glimpse of a massive, circular mouth lined with jagged teeth. The leaf-shaped creature had to be at least fifteen feet long, and eight feet across.

"Like the sunlings, they rely primarily on the light of the sun, but unlike the sunlings, sunmaws like to supplement their diet with meat. They don't need to eat often, but it seems now is one of those times."

Godrick doubted that timing was a coincidence.

Talia hurled a series of dreamfire bolts at the creature. Most of them missed, but a couple hit— and did nothing.

The apprentices all stared in shock.

"Oh, and they're quite magic resistant, as well." Alustin said. "They seem to create turbulence in the aether around them. I'm guessing it's somehow related to the aether harvesting sunlings do, since sunmaws are clearly close relatives."

Godrick rolled his shoulders and adjusted his grip on his sledgehammer. "Ah don't think that'd be especially effective against mah hammer."

"How are you going to hit it?" Talia asked. She'd pulled a shard of bone out of a pouch, and was staring intently at the sunmaw.

"I have an idea," Sabae said. She'd begun spinning wind armor around herself. "Talia, I'm going to need you to blind it. Dreamfire might not be able to hit it, but it should be able to distract it."

Talia glanced at Sabae,and then at the shard of bone in her hand. She nodded, and slowly put the shard away.

"Godrick, I'm going to bring the sunmaw down to the ground. When I do, I'm going to need you to hit it with your hammer. A lot."

"That ah can do," Godrick said. He grinned.

"Here it comes!" Talia said.

The sunmaw had regained enough altitude, and had turned back towards the group again.

"How are yeh plannin' ta get it on tha ground, Sabae?" Godrick asked.

"Well, I have been learning those new movement techniques," Sabae said.

"You're terrible at those!" Talia said.

"I can do it this time," Sabae said.

"Ah have an idea, hold up a second," Godrick said. He envisioned the spellform to temporarily firm up sand, and channeled mana into it.

"There, now yeh should have a better spot ta jump from," Godrick said.

Sabae tested it and nodded.

Talia had manifested a large bolt of dreamfire between her hands, which was steadily growing it in size. Sabae's wind armor had thickened and sped up around her legs. Godrick tightened his grip on his sledgehammer.

"Alright— On three," Sabae said. "One, two, and… three!"

Talia launched the dreamfire bolt straight at the sunmaw. Before it came too close to the creature, it detonated in a bright burst of sparks.

Sabae leapt, releasing a massive burst of air as she did so. It hurled her twenty feet into the air, then thirty. The burst of wind knocked Talia over entirely, sent Alustin's hat flying off his face, and actually staggered Godrick a little.

Unfortunately, Sabae went flying off in the completely wrong direction.

Godrick was about to throw himself to the ground as well, since Sabae's plan had failed, but then he realized that the burst of dreamfire had caused the sunmaw to drop considerably in altitude. Instead, he pulled back his hammer and envisioned a spellform. This was the first one his da had taught him— it amplified the momentum of any already moving piece of steel. In this case, Godrick's hammer.

Godrick felt the momentum spell collapse as the hammer approached the creature, but it had already done its job. The sledgehammer hit the sunmaw in the face like an avalanche.

Godrick found himself thrown entirely off his feet, dazed and winded. He pulled himself into a sitting position to see Talia run up onto the belly of the upside down sunmaw, lying atop the dune with them. She had a chunk of bone in her hand that was rapidly growing in size and glowing an ominous orange color.

Talia tossed the bone chunk, which tumbled through the air towards the creature's mouth. Godrick thought it would miss, but it bounced off the edge and tumbled in between the gnashing teeth. As it drew close to the creature, Godrick could see the bone's growth become chaotic and irregular, but it didn't stop.

Talia, meanwhile, had thrown herself to the side, narrowly tumbling off the creature between two flailing tentacles.

For a moment nothing happened. Then, with a wet ripping sound, the creature's abdomen tore open, spraying ichor up into the air and all over Talia.

Godrick pulled himself to his feet, and then looked around for Sabae. He walked in the direction she'd been heading, and saw a long furrow leading down the dune. Sabae was standing at the bottom of it, trying to brush sand out of her pale hair.

"And that," called Alustin down to Sabae, brushing off sand from his hat, which he'd recovered while Godrick wasn't looking, "is why you don't count on suddenly mastering a technique in the middle of battle that's been giving you trouble, just because you need it all of a sudden. Improvising using already learned techniques is to be encouraged, but learning mid-battle? Not so much."

"You're teaching Hugh to do that exact same thing!" Sabae shouted back.

"No," Alustin said, "I'm teaching him a set of skills that he can easily improvise with. It's the difference between knowing how to use a tool for a lot of different tasks and having a lot of tools for different tasks that you don't know how to use."

"Now," said Alustin, turning to Godrick. "We're going to need to flip over the sunmaw. The sun harvesting scales on its back are quite prized by enchanters."

"I really, really hate the desert," Talia said, futilely trying to wipe off the ichor.

Kanderon was waiting for Hugh about a half-mile away from the ship, patiently reading a book as he trudged out into the sand. The sphinx tucked the book away into a fold in space as Hugh clambered atop the sand dune nearest to her. His climb wasn't particularly aided by the clumsy spells he had helping him support his bracelets, and the bracelets kept catching on the spellbook slung over his shoulder.

"It seems you've had quite the adventurous couple of days, Hugh," she said.

Hugh nodded. Kanderon said nothing for a few seconds, and then she raised an eyebrow. Hugh realized she wanted him to recount everything that had happened, and he did so.

When he'd finished, Kanderon nodded thoughtfully. **"Well, at least your wardcrafting skills continue to improve at a reasonable pace. How are your crystal affinity skills advancing?"**

"I've figured out some simple spells that help me move the bracelets, but they're as likely to knock me off balance as they are to hold them up," Hugh said.

"Draw the spellforms in the sand," Kanderon said.

Hugh did so, and Kanderon examined them carefully.

"These are hardly simple, Hugh. There are enough extraneous lines in them for controlling unwanted movement that I'd be annoyed having to envision them all day long."

"So what should I be doing, then?"

Kanderon contemplated that for a time.

"If I had my way about it, I'd leave you to batter away at the problem, but I'm not going to be around to teach you for a while."

"Why not?" Hugh asked.

"Theras Tel and its environs are the territory of Indris Stormbreaker. I avoid entering her territory without permission, just as she avoids Skyhold without mine."

Hearing that Kanderon and Indris Stormbreaker, the legendary dragon queen of Theras Tel had some sort of standoff was immediately humbling to Hugh. Even in Emblin they'd told tales of Indris. He'd known Kanderon was incredibly powerful, but…

"So while we have this opportunity, I suggest we get to work," Kanderon said. She reached out with a claw and delicately began to draw a spellform in the sand.

"This is the spell you will use to move your aether crystal bracelets more easily."

It looked like no spellform Hugh had ever seen. The foundation line was curved with waves in it, rather than angular, and he recognized almost none of the other lines. It was one of the most complex, difficult spells he had ever seen.

"I'm supposed to hold this in my mind all day? This is far more difficult than the spells I've been using."

Kanderon shook her head slightly in amusement. **"You won't need to hold this spell. It will establish a constant link between your mana reservoirs and the aether crystal. You'll have to manually turn off that link with another spellform."** She quickly sketched out another, much simpler spellform in the sand.

Hugh noticed that both the original spellform and the new one she was drawing were holding much more stable than you'd expect from sand, and when he touched the first spellform, it didn't give— Kanderon had partly fused the sand into crystal.

"Copy these down into your spellbook, Hugh."

Hugh sat down and carefully did so, then turned it around so Kanderon could inspect his drawings. She took her time doing so, and Hugh was much more aware than usual of how enormous the sphinx was, with her face only a couple feet away from Hugh's.

"Acceptable," Kanderon said. **"Now, very carefully envision this spellform and cast the spell. Do *not* get this wrong, or it could end quite disastrously."**

Hugh swallowed and nodded. Kanderon was not the type to give idle warnings. He carefully began envisioning the spellform in his mind's eye. It was even more difficult than he anticipated, since he had grown accustomed to assembling spellforms from scratch in his head, rather than merely memorizing their shapes like most mages. He had no idea how the construction of this spellform worked, so he merely had to replicate what was on the page, like the greenest student.

After what felt like ages, he had the spellform assembled to his satisfaction. Hugh took a deep breath and began channeling mana from his reservoirs into it. To his shock, the instant he poured a little in, his reservoirs opened like floodgates, pouring mana into the spell at an astonishing rate. He desperately tried to control the flow, but the mana just kept pouring out.

Finally, the rate slowed to a trickle, and his reservoirs began to refill at a much slower rate than usual, counterbalanced by the continuous trickle of mana. Hugh followed that trickle with his mind, and…

He could *feel* the bracelets. Not around his wrists, but as though they were an extension of his nerves. As though they were part of him.

Hugh didn't realize he'd spoken aloud until Kanderon answered him. **"This spell is known as a proprioceptive link. It is an extension of the same sense that allows you to touch your nose or elbow with your eyes closed. Rather than having to manually adjust the spells holding much of the weight, you should automatically channel mana to the aether crystal to move it. Give it a shot."**

Hugh nodded and slowly moved his arm. He could feel the mana traveling through the crystal as it effortlessly moved along with his arm. The mana wasn't pulling the aether crystal in the fashion his muscles pulled his limbs, it was more like… it was holding the bracelets in relative position against his wrists.

He stood up and moved around a little bit more. He found that they hadn't become weightless, and there was still some resistance, but they were actually moving!

"The spell doesn't actually support that much of the weight yet. It merely distributes it over your body, so you'll still gain the physical benefits of wearing them," Kanderon explained. **"As your bond with the crystal grows, the spell will become more and more a part of it, and it will be entirely locked in when you cast the spell that seals them to you. As an added benefit, the mana to control it won't come from your mana reservoirs, but rather from the mana you convert as you're refilling those reservoirs. Most mages only convert mana from the aether when refilling their reservoirs, but you'll be doing it constantly now. It'll result in even more massive growth in your mana capacity, at the cost of slower refilling."**

A sudden suspicion came over Hugh. "How was I supposed to develop a spell to do this? I didn't even know that a prioperceptive..."

"Proprioceptive," Kanderon corrected.

"I didn't even know that a proprioceptive link was possible," Hugh said. "How was I supposed to solve this problem.

Kanderon smiled broadly. **"You weren't. It was an exercise in problem solving and spellcraft. It might not have led you to a correct solution, but you most certainly pushed your skill forwards quite a bit."**

Hugh was not the biggest fan of Kanderon's methods sometimes.

"Now it's time for training. I hope your dodging has improved."

Hugh really, really wasn't the biggest fan of Kanderon's training methods.

To Hugh's shock, he dodged the majority of crystals Kanderon fired at him, and blocked most of the rest with his bracers. He'd still have a few bruises, but fewer than usual.

"Is it the proprioceptive link letting me dodge?" he asked Kanderon. "It feels oddly like it."

"No, the link only works with your aether crystal. What you're describing is your affinity sense finally maturing. It seems your mind is interpreting the new stimuli proprioceptively as well. Not the

most common method, but hardly the rarest, either. Alustin's affinity senses work that way as well."

"Do yours, Master?"

Kanderon gave Hugh an appraising look, as if considering whether or not to answer. **"No, mine do not. My mind interprets my affinity sense in the same manner that my kind feels changes in air pressure while flying."**

Hugh couldn't even imagine what that would feel like.

Kanderon glanced up at the sun. **"I must leave soon, but I have one more thing to teach you before we go. Do you have the volume of crystal spellforms I gave you?"**

Hugh nodded, and he pulled the thin, hand-sized volume from his trouser pocket.

"Turn to the third from last page."

Hugh did so. He'd looked at all the spellforms in the book already, but mostly just in passing, paying more attention to their descriptions in hope of finding one that helped him move the bracelets. This one, notably, lacked any description or name beyond two words: "Pattern linking."

The spellform itself seemed strange to Hugh. It wasn't especially complicated, but its shape was…

Hugh blinked as he realized that it somewhat resembled a far, far simpler version of the prioperceptive link, at least in regards to the foundation line. The other lines made no sense to Hugh whatsoever.

"This, Hugh, is the spell I've been using to grow the crystals below the sand. It is, in fact, the only spell I use to grow crystals at all, or to shape them, or to bind them together, so long as they're crystals of the same type."

"How's that possible?" Hugh asked.

"The pattern linking spellform lets you focus mana through your affinity senses directly into the pattern. It then… Making it grow is the wrong way to describe it. It alters the conditions around the pattern so that the pattern grows, as a crystal does in a solution."

Hugh still felt puzzled, and Kanderon seemed to see that in his face. She frowned, then reached out into her invisible fold in space again. She rummaged around for a time, then smiled and pulled out a dense tome. She tossed it on the ground in front of Hugh.

The book, *On the Nature and Growth of Crystalline Solids,* appeared to be made entirely of crystal itself. Even the pages appeared to be opaque crystals the shape and thickness of sheets of paper. Despite their thinness, Hugh gained the impression that he wouldn't be able to break the pages with his hands even if he wanted to. And even being made of crystal, it was hardly much heavier than Hugh would expect a normal book of that size to be.

Hugh picked up and opened the book, to see it filled with tiny text, intricate diagrams, and highly technical vocabulary.

He groaned slightly to himself.

"The fundamental philosophy behind much of crystal attuned spellcasting is one of making spellforms unnecessary," Kanderon said. **"Spellforms may be the most easily accessible method of shaping mana for humans and most other sentients, but it's far from the only method. Crystal attuned mages have, over the centuries, developed methods to use as few spellforms as possible, as well as making the ones we do use as versatile as possible."**

"Like the formless casting Sabae uses?" Hugh asked.

"Very similar, at least philosophically," Kanderon said. **"Most battlemages seek out one method or another of reducing their reliance on spellforms. Formless casting is among the most common of methods— though not in the way Sabae does it— but there are quite a few other ways as well. It's one of the reasons there are so few mages trained to improvise spellforms, as Alustin is training you to do— finding ways around spellforms or ways to minimize them is usually just easier."**

"Won't my spellform improvisation be useless with crystal affinity spells, then?"

Kanderon snorted, sending a cloud of sand at Hugh. **"Not in the slightest. Most of the crystal spellforms in that first book operate under the same basic spellform construction principles Alustin taught you in the first place. You'll be able to devise variants and new versions of those to your heart's content. As for the more versatile crystal affinity spells, such as pattern linking, I will consider teaching you how to alter and design spells like that someday."**

"Just consider it?" Hugh said.

Kanderon narrowed her eyes, and her pupils started shifting towards slits.

"Master," Hugh added quickly. Kanderon was fine answering as many questions about the material she would teach as Hugh wanted, but she was, for all her patience, less than fond of having her decisions questioned in the slightest.

Kanderon's eyes slowly went back to normal. **"I will consider teaching you these things if, and only if, you display both a sufficient mastery of spell improvisation, your crystal attunement, and a certain degree of maturity I seldom encounter in any human, let alone in ones your age. Meddling with the structure of these spells is considerably more dangerous than the spellform improvisation you have done so far."**

Hugh nodded acceptance. Kanderon seldom sheltered Hugh from danger, so if she really thought it was too risky, it was probably absurdly so.

"Now, Hugh— it's time for you to grow your first quartz crystal from the sand."

It only took three hours for Hugh to succeed at growing his first crystal. It was ugly, lumpy, and weirdly colored, but Hugh stored it in his belt-pouch like it was the greatest of treasures.

Unfortunately, however, Deila's kindness in preventing Hugh from getting sunburnt went to waste. Kanderon merely told Hugh that he wouldn't have gotten sunburned if he had learned faster, and took off in a blast of wind and sand.

As Sabae and the others trudged back to the ship, they were just in time to see Kanderon off. While Alustin and Kanderon spoke, the apprentices compared sunburns.

By acclaim, Talia's was by far the most impressive. All of them were miserable. Sabae and Godrick's darker skin had protected them a bit more than the other two, but even he still winced whenever he shifted the pack on his back.

They traded stories about their training sessions and the sunbeast on the way back to the sandship. Alustin had put them to training for most of the day after the sunbeast attack. Sabae had drilled in her movement techniques for the entire day, and she was sore and covered with sand from crashing into the ground again and again, even with her wind armor.

Still, by the end of the day she had started to be able to consistently travel in the general direction she wanted to. Precise trajectories were still out of her reach, as were landings any more graceful than a full crash, but she felt far less frustrated than she had before.

When they got to the ship, Sabae could hear voices, but she couldn't make out anything they were saying. She frowned, wondering if she'd hurt her ears somehow, but as they ascended the ship's ramp, she realized that the voices were speaking in a different language.

When she climbed off the ramp onto the deck, she spotted Irrick and another crewmember talking to each other, looking like they were gossiping. Both of the sailors were only a couple years older than Sabae, and Irrick looked quite pleased about something. They froze the instant they saw Alustin and the apprentices, a look of fear in their eyes.

"Idiots!" someone shouted. Sabae glanced over to spot Delia storming over to the two. "You know better than to…"

Delia glanced at the apprentices and closed her mouth. She grabbed the two sailors by the ears and hauled them below decks, the two trailing behind the little old woman like leaves in a storm.

"What just happened?" Sabae asked Alustin. She noticed that Hugh was staring at the ground again in that way he did when he thought he was in trouble. Or when he was feeling shy. Or anxious.

Alustin removed his floppy hat and began to fold it. "The Radhan are forbidden by custom from speaking their language around outsiders. It was one of the only languages on the continent other than Ithonian to survive the Ithonian Empire's purges. You're not in trouble at all, the responsibility lies with the sailors for speaking it with you around."

"The what?" asked Sabae.

Alustin raised his eyebrows at them. "Have none of you heard of the language purges?"

Everyone shook their head.

"Well, that's a lamentable gap in your educations," Alustin said. His face grew more serious than usual. "It was one of the main tools the Ithonians used to cement their rule— they'd eliminate the languages of other peoples on the continent, making them far easier to dominate."

"Did they make laws against speaking the languages or something?" Hugh asked. He'd relaxed quite a bit when he realized no-one was mad at them, though he was still a little tense.

"No, I was speaking literally when I said they eliminated them. They actually destroyed the languages themselves. The Ithonians weren't the most inventive lot— they mostly adopted the technologies and magics of other cultures, though they usually perfected them beyond what the originators had. One of the few things they mastered on their own were language affinities and attunements. We have no idea how they did it— it's one of those affinities that no one is born with, and can only be developed deliberately, like planar affinities. They took the secrets of how to develop language attunements to their grave as a civilization. They used the language attunements to develop countless strange spells, but the most powerful of them was known simply as the tongue eater. It was an insanely difficult piece of grand magic, taking dozens or hundreds of mages to cast each time, but when it was cast, the spell would, well, begin to eat the language it was targeted at."

Sabae raised her eyebrow. She'd read countless tales from the days of the Ithonian Empire when she was young, and she'd never heard of anything like this.

"The Ithonians cast it again and again on other cultures. Destroying a language did more than just force people to speak Ithonian. It seemed to… disembowel the cultures that lost their languages. Their customs, traditions, and histories just began falling apart. It's as if a vital part of their culture was lost this way. Interestingly, civilizations that had joined the Ithonians before they developed the tongue eater didn't have their cultures fall apart the same way, even when their own languages were destroyed— it was as if culture can transmit between languages, but takes time to do so."

Alustin's face grew even more serious. "That wasn't all, though. Anyone who only spoke a language targeted by the tongue eater lost language entirely, and they became little more than feral beasts. No one was ever capable of teaching them another language after they lost it. And people who had learned Ithonian, but lost their first language to the tongue eater… they were lessened, somehow. They became less intelligent, less motivated, and more obedient. It was as if they'd had some vital spark of life taken from them. Many mages afflicted this way, interestingly, often lost some of their attunements, or even all of them."

Sabae gulped. She'd never heard of anything capable of removing an attunement from a mage before.

"This wasn't even close to the only weapon the Ithonians had in their arsenal of terrifying magics, but it was almost certainly the most effective. It's part of why almost everyone on the continent of Ithos speaks Ithonian today— that, and they seem to have somehow used the language attunements to make Ithonian more stable, and less prone to changing over time. The Radhan only kept their language alive by hiding it, and making the Ithonians think they'd willingly adopted their language entirely. The tradition has become part of their culture to this day— they speak Ithonian around strangers, but only Radhan among themselves."

Alustin stretched. "Now, I'm sure you've had enough lessons for the day— go get something to eat."

Alustin strode across the deck to confer with Captain Solon as the apprentices filed below decks. They could hear Delia shouting somewhere below them, but they were all silent for a time. Sabae had never even thought about it before, but given the stories she'd heard about the profusion of languages on other continents, it did seem strange that she would speak the same language as Hugh, Talia, and Godrick, all of whom came from regions hundreds or thousands of miles away.

Talia cleared her throat. "Sabae…"

"Yes?"

"Is there any chance you could use your healing affinity of yours on our sunburns?"

Sabae looked around. "I'm not supposed to use it until I get more training."

She opened the door to her and Talia's cabin and quietly gestured for the others to go in.

She might not be supposed to use it, but that was for fear of messing up on a serious injury— she'd caused nearly as much damage as she'd fixed when she'd healed Godrick in the labyrinth.

A sunburn, however, should be relatively straightforward, based on what she'd been reading on healing, and what she remembered her father telling her.

And there was no way she'd be letting herself or her friends walk around in this much pain for days.

Sabae was buying a hat the instant they arrived in Theras Tel.

CHAPTER TEN
THERAS TEL

THEY saw their first dragon a day out from Theras Tel.

The storm had driven the *Moonless Owl* farther off course than anticipated— after repairs were finished, they had a four and a half day trip to the desert city.

The days passed much more quickly, now that Hugh wasn't hiding in his room. The apprentices spent most of their free time with Avah. Hugh, to his own surprise, managed to not make an idiot out of himself too much with her. He did notice that Godrick had grown much more comfortable with Avah since they'd talked to Sabae— probably not least due to Sabae usually sitting in between them.

For most of the crew and passengers, they were pleasant days as well, especially once Alustin informed them that he could no longer scry the pirates within his range.

The exceptions, of course, were Talia (thanks to her seasickness) and Irrick and the other sailor, thanks to their ongoing assignment to all the worst jobs on the ship.

The dragon didn't come particularly close to them— you had to squint to even see it wasn't a bird— but Hugh had never even seen a dragon from a distance before. He was standing in the prow with Avah when it flew overhead, while Godrick and Sabae grabbed lunch for them to share on deck. (Which had been a suggestion of Sabae's.)

"Is that Indris?" he asked.

"Doesn't look like it," Avah replied. "I don't think it's big enough, and she doesn't leave Theras Tel that often. It's probably one of her children— they do most of the work patrolling the area around the city. There are supposed to be dozens of them still living in the city."

She turned back to the sand she held in her hand, and began trying to craft a sandcastle out of it. The spell she was using, however, tended just to make a vaguely castle shaped lump.

"How can you tell? It's so far away," Hugh said.

"I can't for sure," Avah said, "I'm just guessing. Indris is supposed to be over two hundred feet long, though."

Hugh blinked. Kanderon was by far the biggest creature he had ever encountered before, and she was only around seventy-five feet long.

"Did you have dragons in Emblin?" Avah asked.

"Huh?" Hugh replied, and winced internally.

"When you all boarded, Alustin introduced you as Hugh of Emblin. I thought there weren't any mages from Emblin."

"Not… not really, no." Hugh said.

"I've heard there's no magic there at all," Avah said.

"Not much of it, but a little," Hugh said. "It's an aether desert, so it's hard for mages to convert any to mana."

He didn't really want to talk about Emblin— people usually tended to make some unpleasant assumptions about him because of that, usually along the lines of his abilities as a mage.

"It would be awfully boring not to be able to do magic," Avah said, as her spell failed to build a castle in her hand again. "Is that why you left?"

"Something like that," Hugh said. Then, quickly, to forestall that line of questioning, he added, "and I've heard stories about dragons that live in the far reaches of Emblin's mountains, but I think that was mostly my cousins trying to scare me. The only magical beasts I've heard of in Emblin are a few giant rats and spiders, and none of those are bigger than a dog."

"Weird," said Avah. Her sandcastle spell failed again.

"Can I see the spellform you're using?" Hugh asked. He unlatched his spellbook, and opened it to a blank page. He pulled out a quill and ink for her to use.

Avah gave him a curious look, but she dumped her handful of sand over the railing and took the quill in hand. She spent a couple of minutes sketching out the complicated spellform.

"I can get it to work on the ground, but I've never been able to get it to work off the ground," she admitted.

Hugh stared at the spellform. He didn't understand a lot of the markings— some were pretty clearly specific to sand affinities, while others…

"Does it make the same castle every time, or do you have to envision it?" Hugh asked. He was fairly sure it was the latter— the former would take an absurd level of complexity to describe in the spellform, while the latter was the method used by illusionists and artists with countless different attunements. It wasn't very mana efficient, but it worked.

"The same shape every time," Avah said. "Otherwise, I'd just use a standard sandsculpting spell."

Okay, so there was a *lot* going on with this spell that Hugh couldn't understand.

"Could you draw the standard sandsculpting spellform for me?" Hugh asked.

Avah gave him a bit of a weird look, but did so. It resembled Godrick's stonesculpting spellform much more than it did the sandcastle spellform.

Hugh turned his attention back to the sandcastle spell, looking for the pieces he did recognize. Foundation line, definitive lines… there. There was a set of lines specifically describing the quantity of sand to be used. Since there wasn't enough sand in Avah's hand, the spell kept failing.

Why was there such a strong quantity restriction on the sandsculpting spell? Maybe… Hugh shook his head, then he started drawing a new version.

And then stopped.

Alustin had repeatedly warned him to never modify a spellform with pieces he didn't understand. Every line of a spellform modified all the others, and the spell could react in unforeseen ways if Hugh wasn't careful.

Since Hugh was being trained to improvise new spellforms on the fly, this was doubly important— even Alustin, an exceptionally skilled spellcrafter, generally avoided improvising spellforms. He'd told Hugh he never would have even considered training him this way if he hadn't seen Hugh already doing it with his wards untrained. (Though, admittedly, there had been a lot more to the situation than that.)

But… how impressed would Avah be if he fixed her spell right then and there? Hugh was on the verge of resuming drawing when he was thankfully interrupted by the return of Godrick and Sabae with lunch. They'd even managed to haul Talia back on deck with them.

Theras Tel was immense. The city was built into a plateau of volcanic stone that rose out of the sand with shocking abruptness— the massif was easily over a mile in height at its lowest point, and at least four miles in width. There was a noticeable slope to the top of the plateau— the south end was at least a mile taller than the north.

The city itself flowed over the plateau like moss over a tree stump. Buildings stood atop any surface that was even the slightest bit closer to the horizontal than the vertical, and more buildings were carved into the very face of the cliff itself, descending at least a half mile downwards from the top.

There were at least two dozen other sandships in sight, both leaving and arriving at Theras Tel. After the weeks in the Endless Erg, with the pirates the only other ships they'd seen, it was something of a shock.

Above the city wheeled four or five dragons, all a muted brown color.

"How many people live here?" Hugh asked, a little breathless.

"Well over a million," Alustin said. "It's one of only six cities on Ithos this large, and is likely the greatest city in the southwest of the continent."

Sabae coughed purposefully, raising her eyebrow at Alustin. All the apprentices and Avah were gathered with Alustin in the bow to watch the approach— even Talia was actually showing interest in something other than her own misery.

"Except, of course, with the possible exception of Ras Andis," Alustin acknowledged. "Another of the six great cities."

Sabae smiled faintly.

"How do they feed that many people?" Hugh asked.

"They grow quite a few mushrooms in the basements and caverns below the city, but the vast majority of their food is shipped in," Alustin said. "The city spends an absolute fortune every day. If trade ever faltered, the city would collapse in weeks, if not days. And it's all thanks to their wells— they're the only source of water in hundreds of leagues, making them a vital stop on trading voyages across the Endless Erg."

"And all the wells," Sabae interrupted, "are owned by Indris, making her possibly the wealthiest individual on the continent."

"How wealthy are we talkin' about, here?" Godrick asked.

"Her yearly personal income is estimated by the staff of the Skyhold library as greater than the entire holdings of many individual city-states across the continent," Alustin said.

Everyone was silent at that for a few moments as the city drew closer. The dunes shrank as they grew closer to the plateau, and the ride grew smoother.

The *Owl* slowed as they approached the city— apparently Indris' government had rather strict rules about the speed at which sandships could travel in proximity to the city. It took them almost an hour to round the plateau and arrive at Theras Tel's harbor.

During that hour, Alustin lectured them on the history and economics of Theras Tel— water might be the heart of their economy, but there were still vast fortunes coming from the mushroom farms, from the copper mines Theras Tel owned in another volcanic remnant forty leagues away, from the continual need for ship repairs, from the thriving trade in desert monsters— both from their salable parts, meat, and even live captures. According to Alustin, there were more different ways to make money in Theras Tel than there were mages at Skyhold.

Most of all, though, there were fortunes to be made in trade. Everything crossing the Endless Erg came here. Spices from the southern coast and other continents, wine and silk from Tsarnassus and its neighbors in the northeast of the continent, magical items from Skyhold, ironwork from Highvale, and even, to Hugh's surprise, immense cargoes of lumber, wool, and dried fish from Emblin. Hugh had never realized it before, but Theras Tel was the single biggest buyer of Emblin's exports— both for its own purposes, and for resale in farther ports.

Thanks to all this, Theras Tel's coinage, apparently, was both the most stable and most valuable in the region. No matter the fluctuations of other currencies, Theras Tel's coins always held their value.

During the hour, Avah continually interrupted Alustin, explaining points she'd felt he'd glossed over, adding details, and even arguing with him. It turned out that Avah had a passion for every sort of economic detail— she wasn't just born into the life of a merchant, but was genuinely passionate about it.

The harbor on the north side of the plateau was every bit as impressive as the rest of the city. The natural indent in the side of the plateau was small in comparison to the rest of the massif, but it absolutely dwarfed the dozens and dozens of ships docked inside of it.

Like Skyhold's ports, there were a considerable number of permanent structures at ground level, and it still felt wrong to Hugh.

Still, though, it kept to the most important rule of ports— always build atop cliffs or something else tall near the sea, unless you wanted to be washed away. Even if this sea was made of sand without tides.

No roads led up the side of the massif— the only way up was via a series of massive lifts. Alustin told them how once they had been moved by muscle— both man and dragon— until Indris had spent a mind-bogglingly huge fortune investing in enchanting them. Most of the expense had come from making the huge lifts efficient enough not to overburden the aether around the city— while it was quite thick here, it didn't even come close to the densities near Skyhold.

It took another half hour for the *Owl* to be guided into a docking spot— the harbor walls largely blocked the wind from entering, so the harbor mages created winds to guide ships around the harbor. Ship mages were strictly forbidden from doing so themselves.

Customs officials met them at the dock. Hugh didn't pay much attention to them, watching other ships loading and unloading. After a couple minutes, though, Sabae started muttering under her breath in their direction.

"What's going on?" Hugh said.

"They're charging us a docking fee," Sabae said.

"Don't ports usually do that?" Hugh asked. Emblin's small fishing ports certainly did.

Sabae shook her head. "Theras Tel doesn't need to. They've always been a free port. They make more than enough money from water sales and tariffs to get by. So why are they charging us?"

"They are a free port, to everyone except the Radhan," Avah said. "We're the only ones they charge."

"Why would the Radhan be the only ones charged docking fees?" Sabae asked, but Avah merely scowled, shook her head, and walked away to help prepare cargo for unloading.

Sabae turned to Hugh and shrugged.

The lift started upwards with a jerk. It was much quieter than Hugh would have expected— the only noises coming from it were the creaking of the cables and faint humming noises.

Alustin had quickly ushered all the apprentices onto the lift the instant he'd finished paying the docking fees for the sandship. No sense in sticking around waiting for another lift, apparently.

Onboard the lift, they were joined by several merchants, a couple dockworkers, and a pile of crates and barrels, but the lift was large enough that they could have a corner to themselves out of anyone else's earshot.

"Alustin, why does Theras Tel charge the Radhan a docking fee?" Sabae asked.

Alustin smiled, then he walked over to the edge of the lift, leaning on the platform's railing.

"Look at all the newly docked ships and tell me what you see," Alustin said.

Hugh and the others joined him at the railing. They'd already traveled a surprising distance up the cliff, giving them an excellent vantage.

Hugh stared out over the harbor. He saw ships docking, unloading, loading… but other than the differences in the designs of the ship, he couldn't see anything that might cause the Radhan ships to be charged when others couldn't.

"Sir, is it the design of the…" Hugh began, when Alustin interrupted him.

"How many times do I need to tell you that it's not necessary to call me sir? Alustin is fine, Hugh." The mage sighed. "And it's a good guess, but no, it's not the design of the Radhan ships."

The apprentices stood there silent for a couple minutes as they lifted higher and higher into the air. Then Godrick spoke up.

"It's the water! They're loadin' barrels of water onta every ship except' the *Owl*!"

Alustin smiled. "Exactly so. The Radhan don't need to buy water from Theras Tel, and so they threaten its monopoly on water."

"So the Radhan have a hidden supply of water?" Sabae asked.

"If I were Indris, I'd track any Radhan ships to find and destroy any other water sources, to help preserve my control over it," Talia said. She looked considerably better already.

"She's tried that dozens of times over the decades," Alustin said. "And yet she and her children have never found anything."

"How could they possibly hide something like that from a nest of dragons?" Sabae asked.

"They can't, and don't," Alustin said, leaning forwards over the railing. Hugh felt a little queasy watching him. "There is no secret water source."

"Then how…?" Sabae began.

"Like I told you before," Alustin said, pulling himself back fully onto the platform and smiling at her, "If you can gather moisture from the air in the Endless Erg, you can gather it to yourself anywhere."

Sabae looked like she'd tasted something sour for a moment, then her face gradually turned thoughtful.

The lift slowed as it reached the top. Godrick whistled in amazement as the edge of the cliff came close enough for him to see over. Sabae looked equally impressed once she could as well, and Hugh promptly raised himself on the tips of his toes to look over.

He found himself staring into a shockingly crowded street. Merchants haggled heatedly with one another, seemingly unconcerned about the mile long drop only feet (or, in one particularly alarming case, inches) away from them.

As Hugh looked farther up, he saw an absurd cluster and tangle of buildings. Almost all of them were built of the same stone as the plateau, many as tall as four stories. The streets twisted and tangled with one another as they steeply rose towards the other end of the plateau. Hugh could see places where street edges dropped down to the roof of houses below. Every street Hugh could see was filled with bustling crowds.

Here and there, immense towers rose out of the tangle of buildings like trees among shrubs. The towers had huge arched entrances along their sides and tops, and Hugh could see dragons basking in the sun inside and atop many of them.

At the very top of the plateau was an immense palace, covered in arches, domes, and walkways. There were a pair of massive dragon statues flanking the entrance, which Hugh could easily make out even miles away. Down from the palace ran tangles of aqueducts through the city, standing far above the buildings, though shorter than the towers.

Hugh echoed Godrick's whistle.

He tried not to smile as he heard a faint exhalation of air as Sabae tried and failed to whistle as well.

"What?" Talia demanded. She still couldn't see over yet. A few moments later, as the lift continued to rise, she stopped grumbling as well. "Oh."

"Well, come on then," Alustin said, as the lift drew level with the street and the attendant unlocked the gate.

"Where are we going, anyways?" Talia demanded. "Are we getting a proper inn?"

Alustin shook his head. "No, we'll be coming back to the ship to stay there again tonight. Hiring an entire ship is expensive, so we might as well keep using it as our base of operations. And as to where we're going, you'll see."

As Hugh prepared to step off the lift, he turned around to look out at the desert one more time. The view made the one from his hidden bedroom in the library pale in comparison— Hugh could see farther than he'd ever seen before in his life. Ships sailing the sands looked like mice and beetles slowly crawling about from here.

"No dawdling, Hugh!" Alustin called.

CHAPTER ELEVEN

WHERE THERE'S SMOKE...

Hugh had never experienced crowds this thick in his life. Alustin, somewhat surprisingly, didn't even try to walk backwards through it. People were constantly jostling them, seldom even looking to see who they'd bumped into.

Talia had it the worst— she was almost knocked over time and time again in the crowd. She repeatedly expressed her dissatisfaction that Godrick hadn't brought his sledgehammer with him.

Going was particularly slow until the apprentices just piled behind Godrick and let him clear a path for them. Even in a city the size of Theras Tel, Godrick stuck out of the crowd like a lighthouse, and people were quick to get out of his way.

Alustin, unsurprisingly, navigated the crowd like he'd been born to it. He seemed in a particularly cheerful mood.

As they walked, Hugh gawked at everything around him. He knew he must look like a country bumpkin, but for once that didn't bother him. There was just too much to look at.

They walked through spice markets so pungent that Hugh took the glass scent-absorbing sphere out of his belt-pouch to hold by his nose so he wouldn't sneeze himself silly. They walked past tailor shops containing outfits in every color imaginable— and some Hugh was fairly sure he'd never imagined at all.

Hugh gawked as a group of naga slithered past them. They were fairly common in the south, but Hugh had never seen one of the snake-people before— the tails they had in place of legs had to be at least fifteen feet long, if not longer. They were all different colors— one naga's tail was the color of the desert sand, another's was brilliant emerald, and a third scarlet with azure stripes running lengthwise.

There were fountains every couple of blocks, ranging from pools fed by the aqueducts above to fountains enchanted to play out scenes that repeated over and over again with moving sculptures of water. Hugh's favorite had a pair of dancers endlessly twirling around inside the pool of the fountain, and the splash of the water sounded like music, though the tune always just escaped Hugh's grasp.

Restaurants and streetside cafes were absolutely everywhere. Teacarts cluttered every corner, and Hugh had to struggle not to run off into a bakery whose windows were filled with pastries and cakes.

That was another thing, too— glass was everywhere. In Emblin, glass was expensive, generally shipped in from afar. Most people just had wooden shutters in their windows, rather than actual glass panes. Here, however, almost all the windows were glassed in.

Alustin explained that glassblowing was one of the major industries of the city— something helped by the large numbers of sand and glass mages living here. Sand mages could help sort the sands of the desert for the perfect mixture for glass, while the glass mages could smooth along every part of the production process, resulting in the highest quality glass on the continent. Hugh started seeing more and more luxury glassware for sale as well.

There were also, of course, far more mages than Hugh had expected to see. They couldn't go a block without seeing at least one storefront for an enchanter, or a healer, or some other sort of mage. Many of them had signs in their windows proclaiming that they were trained in Skyhold.

As they continued farther up the city, shops, restaurants, and houses grew more and more expensive, as did the clothes on the steadily thinning crowds. Oddly, Hugh hadn't seen many beggars or other signs of poverty.

When Hugh asked Alustin about it, the mage gave him a serious look. "There's plenty of poverty in Theras Tel, but for the most part, Indris' city guard keeps the beggars and thieves away from the midline, closer to the edges of the city. The houses carved into the faces of the cliff nearest the harbor are the poorest in the city— people are crammed in there like animals. Towards Indris' palace they're the residences of the servants and guardsmen who work for the wealthy on that end of the plateau."

Alustin looked contemplative for a moment. "Still, though— it's far from the worst city in the world to be poor in. Water is guaranteed to every resident of the city by Indris, there's little disease thanks to the city's desert environment, and there's always plenty of work to be found."

Hugh was going to inquire further when he heard yelling.

"Ah smell smoke coming from that way," Godrick said, pointing in the direction of the yelling.

Alustin, not even missing a step, turned down the street Godrick had pointed down. "Let's go take a look," he said.

Alustin and the apprentices had to fight their way through a crowd of gawkers to get to the site of the fire. They only went a few blocks in pursuit of the commotion, but Hugh could already see how much poorer this neighborhood was than the midline streets they'd been walking on before.

It was the contents of a large tenement building that were on fire. Smoke billowed out of the windows, and the heat was oppressive even in the desert. There was, thankfully, little risk of it spreading, given that the building and its neighbors were constructed of stone. As they got closer, Hugh could see that the front door appeared to have been blasted inwards— the wall was crumpled in on either side of it for some distance.

"What happened here?" Alustin asked a bystander.

"An invisible cult was meeting in secret here, apparently. Dragon cultists must have caught wind of things and burnt them out," the grizzled butcher replied.

"There's more than one cult in this city, it might not have been dragon cultists," an old woman said.

"If there are other cults, they're hiding even better than the invisible cult was," the butcher said. The two quickly fell to arguing.

Alustin stared contemplatively at the fire for a moment, then he turned away and gestured at the apprentices to follow. As they left, Hugh could see a couple of the dragons had started circling over the building and the fresh column of smoke.

Once they'd gotten out of the crowd of gawkers, Hugh asked the question that had been bothering him. "What's an invisible cult?"

"Crazy, is what they are," Talia said.

Sabae nodded. "Pretty much."

"Invisible cults," Alustin explained, "believe in an invisible, omnipresent deity that watches over everything. There are a few different flavors of them, but none tend to stick around long— so far as anyone can tell, if their invisible deity actually exists, it doesn't provide them with any benefits.

Alustin shook his head. "And given how competitive cults tend to be with one another, the ones gaining actual material benefits from worshiping a dragon or other being powerful enough to protect them tend to wipe them out fast and hard."

"So when those people were talking about a dragon cult, they were talking about Indris Stormbreaker's cult?" Hugh said.

"Indris isn't especially interested in having worshipers," Alustin said. "She tolerates them, and she quite enjoys their tribute, but given that she's likely the wealthiest dragon on the continent, she doesn't need the ego boost. She doesn't particularly push for more worshipers. Still, she will come to their defense when they need here."

He gave Hugh a serious look. "She's also rumored to have more than a few warlocks in her cult by those in the know, but their identities are the sort of information that she keeps very, very close to the chest— warlocks are both a significant advantage and a large investment to any being that pacts with them. You can expect any non-invisible cult to likely have warlocks, moreso when their target of veneration is especially powerful."

Hugh understood the warning in that statement very clearly. He'd been warned often enough to keep his warlock pact with Kanderon a secret— if it became public knowledge, it was quite likely others would strike at him to inconvenience her, or try to gain information on her from him.

They returned to the midline streets and resumed walking steadily uphill. Hugh was lost in his own head for quite some time before Sabae spoke up— he'd been wondering about the lives of the warlocks in Indris and others' cults, as well as wondering why invisible cults had never showed up in Emblin, where there weren't any other cults to compete with.

"We're heading to the palace, aren't we?" Sabae demanded.

Alustin turned around to face them as he walked and sighed. "You just had to ruin the surprise, didn't you?"

"It's not that hard ta guess," Godrick said. "We've been headin' straight uphill towards the palace the whole time."

Alustin sighed even harder and turned to face forward again.

"Why are we heading to the palace?" Hugh asked.

"We're going to introduce you to Indris Stormbreaker," Alustin said with a smile.

CHAPTER TWELVE
HERE BE DRAGONS

Hugh could hardly believe how extravagant the mansions got as they moved farther and farther uphill. While all were constructed out of the same hard volcanic stone as the plateau, other than that they had remarkably few similarities.

One mansion resembled the harbor forts of Emblin, with similar crenellations and towers— this, however, was clearly an aesthetic choice, not a defensive one, considering the size of the massive glass windows everywhere in it.

Another mansion was a series of linked-together domes with what at first looked like vines growing all over them. When Hugh looked more closely, however, he realized that the vines were carved right onto the stone and painted to look alive.

Not all of the mansions were so flamboyant— a great many merely resembled manor houses. Still, however, Hugh felt he could easily tell the difference between each one.

He forgot all about the mansions when they reached the palace gates. The two dragon statues he'd seen from the top of the lift were absolutely massive up close— they were considerably larger than even Kanderon. The gate in between them was smaller than Hugh might have expected— though it was still huge, and he was sure half a dozen wagons could go through side by side at once, but it was dwarfed by the statues.

No one stopped them as they strode through the gate. There was a massive crowd pouring in and out of the gate, and Hugh supposed it would be impractical to stop them all for questioning.

The wall the gate ran underneath had to be at least a hundred feet thick— long enough that glow crystals were needed to light the center of it, and noticeably cooler than the hot desert air everywhere else. Talia let loose an incredibly dramatic sigh.

Hugh noticed that unlike the mansions, this was definitely built for defense— murder holes lined the ceiling the whole way through the arched tunnel.

Hugh wasn't entirely sure why they'd bothered— capturing the plateau seemed like it would be nearly impossible from below, even if someone actually managed to supply and transport an entire army across the Endless Erg.

After they passed out of the tunnel, they found themselves in a massive courtyard, surrounded by numerous large buildings, all apparently serving some sort of governmental function. Guards were scattered all around the square, both to keep the peace and offer directions. The crowd around them split in several directions— apparently quite a bit of business was conducted in the palace.

Alustin confidently led them deeper into the palace complex without asking any directions from the guards. They quickly found themselves walking amongst a group of people who were obviously wealthy, even at a glance. Hugh wouldn't be surprised if some of the outfits he saw around him were worth as much as his entire home village, back in Emblin.

Sabae seemed to be the only one of the apprentices at ease among these people— Godrick and Talia both looked uncomfortable amidst all this wealth, and Hugh couldn't shake the feeling that everyone they walked past knew with certainty that Hugh didn't belong there, that he really was just some country bumpkin. Hugh looked down at the ground in shame and felt his face start to flush.

Then, to his surprise, he felt a hand on his arm. He looked over to see Talia giving him a concerned look. Hugh took a deep breath, then another.

"I'm alright," he whispered. "Just a little intimidated by all this. But… thank you."

Talia smiled at him. "Just don't forget, these people shit like everyone else."

Talia most certainly was *not* whispering when she said that, and quite a few passerby gave her offended looks.

"Nonsense," said Sabae, looking back at them with a wicked grin. "I lived around people like this for years, and I can tell you with certainty that they are far, far too wealthy and dignified for that. They have hirelings to shit for them."

Godrick and Talia both burst into laughter at that, and Hugh felt a grin spread across his face. He also could have sworn that he heard Alustin snort as though repressing laughter.

They finally arrived at their destination after another few minutes of walking. It was immediately obvious to Hugh that this building was the heart of the city.

"Welcome to Indris' Throne," Alustin said.

Indris' Throne was a truly massive edifice, dwarfing any structure they'd encountered thus far in the city, save for the wall around the palace complex. Rather than being assembled from masonry, it was a single, solid piece— as though it had either been shaped entirely by stone mages or hewn from the stone of the plateau itself.

On the walls were carved massive friezes, depicting more scenes than Hugh could take in. Just in a quick glance he saw scenes of dragons in flight, sandships sailing across the Endless Erg, great battles, depictions of construction sites, and more.

Over a dozen of the massive dragon roosting towers scattered throughout the city below jutted out of the top of Indris' Throne. Hugh could see several dragons resting in them, one of which was idly watching the people entering and exiting the building. Hugh forced himself to look away from it, not wanting to meet its gaze, even if it was still hundreds of feet away.

As if that weren't enough, the building seemed to be the source for all of the city's aqueducts as well. They twisted and turned about one another, branching apart as they spread out over the city.

As they walked up to the doors of Indris' Throne, Hugh took a deep breath. He'd survived Skyhold's labyrinth, he could survive this.

"State your name and business," the clerk said.

Unlike the great gates into the palace complex, everyone was stopped and questioned on their way into Indris' Throne. A row of bored clerks sat behind a counter, making note of everyone that passed them. Several guards monitored the area as well, but less than Hugh would have thought.

"Alustin Haber, Librarian Errant of Skyhold, and apprentices," Alustin said.

The clerk raised his eyebrow at that. "And your business?"

"Paying a courtesy call to Indris to let her know we'll be in her city for a time," Alustin said.

The clerk rolled his eyes. "The queen hardly cares what a few mages are up to, when we already have hundreds in the city."

"Curious," said Alustin, "I hadn't realized the standing order regarding the High Librarian's emissaries had changed."

The clerk's eyes narrowed, and it looked like he was about to respond with some biting comment when another clerk whispered something in his ear. The first clerk gave the new one a disbelieving look, but the new clerk ignored him and turned to Alustin.

"If you'd care to follow me, I'll escort you from here."

It was a long, long walk to Indris' throne room proper. The halls in the palace were enormous— clearly designed to allow dragons to move about freely inside the structure, not that they saw any. There were quite a few people moving about the hallways on various business, but it still felt empty and hushed thanks to their huge size.

The sounds of rumbling and moving water were present throughout half the corridors they moved through. "That's the machinery that pumps up the city's water from below," Alustin said. "It puts a far greater strain on the aether than the rest of the city combined, even including the lifts."

Hugh reminded himself to read up more on enchanting— wards could mimic some effects of enchantment, but for the most part they were radically different disciplines of magic. He had more than enough on his plate right now, but it still sounded interesting.

They were handed off by the clerk to a new functionary, who led them for a few more minutes before handing them off yet again— this time to someone of actual importance.

"Apprentices," said Alustin, "this is Eudaxus Scalesworn, High Priest of the Cult of Indris. He serves as one of her chief ministers." He introduced them to Eudaxus, and then the two of them moved ahead of the group to talk quietly to one another. It was clear that they knew each other already, and were on quite friendly terms.

Hugh studied the priest as they walked. Eudaxus was a spry, friendly, bald, and energetic man that looked to be in his early seventies. He wore long, flowing blue robes engraved with intricate geometrical designs. He had one feature, though, that stood out far above the others.

"His nose is enormous!" whispered Talia.

Sabae shushed her, but Talia wasn't wrong. Hugh had, to the best of his knowledge, never seen a nose that big in his life.

Eudaxus escorted them past crowds of servants, guards, and ministers, all clustered around a massive pair of open, bronze-plated doors.

On the other side was the throne room. It was nothing like what Hugh had expected— there were no heaped piles of gold, immense firepits, or anything of the sort. Instead, it was merely a massive stone hall, largely unadorned with the exception of a few tasteful tapestries depicting scenes of dragons in flight and the like.

The most unusual part of the room's architecture was the far wall— or, rather, the complete lack of one. It opened up entirely to the outside, revealing a vista overlooking leagues and leagues of the Endless Erg. There was no railing or wall of any sort— the palace merely ended at the edge of the volcanic plateau.

Hugh was paying very little attention to any of this. All of that was being taken up by the dragons. There were three in the room. The two smaller ones— clearly Indris' children— were only about fifteen feet long.

The two smaller dragons were impressive enough in their own way. They were brown like the rest of the dragons Hugh had seen from afar, but were less graceful than Hugh had expected— their heads more shovel-shaped and their necks thicker than the illustrations in his books. They gave the impression of brute force more than grace.

Indris Stormbreaker was another matter entirely. It took Hugh at least a solid minute to be able to start understanding her as a single creature— his brain simply didn't want to believe anyone could be that big.

The rumors of Indris' size, if anything, didn't do her justice. The dragon queen easily measured over two hundred feet in length, and her limbs were far wider around than her children's torsos— for that matter, her head alone was bigger than the two of them combined. She took up a significant chunk of the hall on her own. When she shifted her weight, Hugh felt the movement through the floor.

Hugh gulped.

Eudaxus patted Hugh's shoulder and smiled. "I felt the exact way the first time I saw the queen as a lad."

The others, save for Alustin, seemed just as cowed by Indris.

The old priest led the way across the throne room. Hugh barely noticed the richly dressed crowd around him. The throne room was surprisingly full, and felt more like a busy market. The guards appeared to largely be there in case of disputes between courtiers— though, in fairness, Hugh had trouble imagining how much use they'd be if someone powerful enough to seriously threaten Indris arrived.

Hugh felt himself trembling a little as Eudaxus brought them to the clear space in front of Indris.

"Ah, who have you brought before me today, Eudaxus?" Indris' voice had the same overwhelming quality as Kanderon's. Hugh could feel it in his bones.

"My queen, this is Alustin Haber, emissary of Kanderon Crux, and his apprentices." Eudaxus said, bowing.

Indris's massive head shifted so she could train one eye on Alustin.

"We have met before, librarian, haven't we?" Indris said.

"We have, Indris," Alustin said, bowing as well. "Five years ago."

Did Hugh need to bow? He glanced at Sabae, but she was staring intently at Indris.

"Ah, the incident with the gorgons? That was resolved quite tidily, thanks to you librarians," Indris said. **"I hope nothing similar has brought you to my city today."**

Alustin shook his head. "Nothing like that. I just brought my apprentices here to train and gain experience of the world outside Skyhold."

Indris turned her eye onto the apprentices. Hugh could *feel* her gaze, as though it were an actual physical force.

"Very well, librarian. Pass my regards onto Kanderon when you speak to her next. Now, Eudaxus, my children tell me of a fire in the city."

Indris appears to have dismissed them from her thoughts already, and Hugh was more than happy to follow Alustin away. Eudaxus nodded pleasantly at them as they left Indris' presence.

"That was it?" said Talia. "That was all we came for?"

"It's considered good manners for the servants of one of the great powers to pay these sorts of courtesy visits, Talia," Alustin said.

As they left the throne room, Hugh glanced behind him. Indris seemed to have all of her attention focused on Eudaxus, but both of her children in the throne room with her were staring intently in their direction.

Hugh shuddered, and quickly looked away.

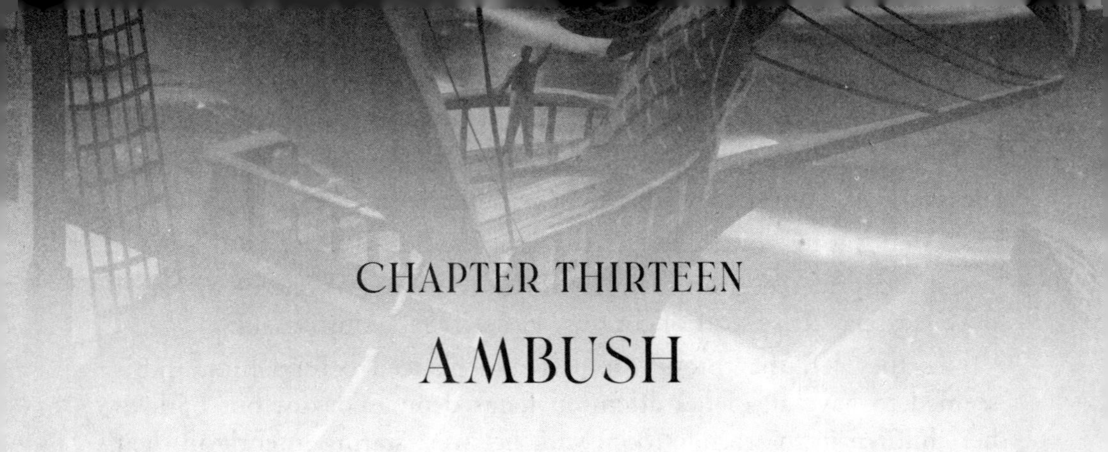

CHAPTER THIRTEEN

AMBUSH

THE next few days were some of the best Hugh had ever had. Alustin gave each of them a small pouch of coins and told them to enjoy themselves.

Avah joined them on their wanderings through the city. Despite the fees charged to the Radhan, the *Moonless Owl* still stopped there several times a year, so she was quite familiar with the city, and happy to serve as a guide.

They visited all sorts of shops, teashops, and restaurants during those days— including the bakery that Hugh had noticed before.

One of the first places they visited was a millinery at Sabae's insistence, where they all bought hats for the sun.

As they wandered, Avah spent hours telling them tidbits about the city's economy, supply chains, and trade. It hadn't been something Hugh was especially interested in before, but Avah was passionate about the topic and quite talented at making it more interesting.

Of course, as Talia teased him when Avah was out of earshot, Hugh would probably find literally anything Avah said interesting.

They also visited quite a number of bookstores at Hugh's insistence— he'd grown into quite a bookworm since moving into his secret room in the library. None of the others minded, of course— all of them, especially Talia, were keen readers. Hugh found quite a few books he wanted to buy, though he restricted himself to a couple of books on wards and an adventure novel set after the fall of the Ithonian Empire.

One of Hugh's most amusing finds was a copy of Galvachren's Bestiary lying on the floor in one of the bookstores. He had his own copy of it back at Skyhold, which he hadn't brought with him— it weighed a similar amount to Godrick's massive sledgehammer, if not more. He could only imagine that its own weight was the reason it rested on the floor— it couldn't be good for bookshelves.

Talia's birthday happened to fall on one of their free days.

Hugh had spent weeks of his free time crafting her a reusable ward. It was a long circular band of leather with a protective ward inscribed on it. It could easily be rolled up and stored away. The user would have to charge it up with mana before each use, but Hugh had made it extra mana efficient.

Godrick had gotten Talia a set of hairpins that would reshape themselves into keys if you channeled mana into them while they were in a lock. Each could only be used once, but there were at least a dozen of them.

Sabae had gotten Talia a history of some of the bloodier battles from the Ithonian Empire's wars against the northern mountain clans. Clan Castis hadn't existed then, but Talia was still extremely pleased by the gift.

They were heading back towards the lifts down into the harbor after their last day of freedom when the ambush struck.

It was already night, and the city was being lit by countless glow crystals. Most of the fountains had crystals of their own in them as well, which made for a beautiful sight whenever they walked past one.

They were taking a bit of a shortcut back— the midline roads, despite their name, didn't actually strictly follow the middle of the plateau. Instead, they curved and twisted, often trending off to one side or the other a bit. They were cutting through some of the neighborhoods alongside the midline roads when the ambush hit.

Hugh probably would have died if Avah hadn't been there.

He was trying to convince Avah that no, in fact, Kanderon did not eat people (he was pretty sure) when she abruptly shoved him out of the way of one crossbow bolt and directed two others against the stone street with a spell.

Talia and Sabae both immediately whirled to face the alley where the bolts had come from. Hugh and Godrick were just a moment behind them. A crowd of robed figures armed with spears burst out of it.

Sabae had already begun spinning up her wind armor, and she managed to block another crossbow bolt. Before any more shots from the ambushers could be fired, there was a series of abrupt splintering cracks, and Avah sagged to the ground, clearly exhausted.

"I took care of the crossbows," she said.

"Good work," said Sabae, before charging towards the robed figures. Godrick followed close behind. As he did so, rock tore itself from the road, forming itself onto him in the form of a breastplate.

Talia manifested a series of dreamfire bolts, launching them past Godrick and Talia into the crowd of robed figures. At least two of them went down— one with a hand that shrank away into nothing, the other who simply gained a hole in the middle of their chest that didn't bleed at all.

Hugh was still feeling stunned. He'd fought against quite a few monsters in the labyrinth, but he'd never seriously fought another human being before.

Sabae snarled as she plunged into the crowd of assailants. One swung his spear at her, but she easily blocked it with one wind-armored forearm. She retaliated with a gust kick that sent him flying back into a group of his fellows, sending them all to the ground.

Next to her, Godrick swept two attackers off their feet with a low swing of his hammer, then stopped a thrown spear in midair with his steel attunement.

Sabae was never teasing Godrick for hauling that huge hammer around everywhere with him ever again.

Sabae unleashed a gust strike at the next assailant to approach her. It clearly affected the muscular woman, but instead of being thrown backwards, she merely slid a few inches back.

Sabae frowned, then abruptly staggered as her weight seemed to double.

The woman was gravity attuned.

If Sabae hadn't been training physically for months under Alustin and Artur's training regimes, she would have fallen to the ground at once. As it was, she barely managed to block a spear strike by the gravity mage.

Sabae frantically tried to remember what she could about gravity mages. They were one of three types of attuned that could most commonly fly, along with force and wind attuned, but flight for them was considerably more difficult to master. Since this mage was fighting on the ground, she likely wasn't overwhelmingly powerful.

Sabae backpedaled, dodging another spear thrust.

Gravity mages could alter the weight of themselves and others. The more they altered the weight, the more mana the spells used. They frequently increased their own weight for purposes of physical training.

A simple levitation spell would counter the gravity spell somewhat, but it would be far less efficient, and would drain Sabae's mana reserves far too quickly.

Sabae felt her mana reservoirs deplete as she took several more blows on her armor from the gravity mage. Godrick, thankfully, was holding off the attention of several others, while Talia had more of them pinned down in the alley.

Gravity magic had relatively few direct offensive abilities beyond messing with the weight of opponents, so gravity attuned tended to rely on other attunements for offense, or if they only had the one, physical combat. Massively increasing your opponent's weight could end a fight incredibly quickly, and…

Sabae smiled.

Sabae waited for the next spear strike, then she dodged forwards inside the spear's reach. The haft of the spear harmlessly deflected off of Sabae's wind armor as Sabae grabbed the gravity mage.

Then Sabae simply leaned on her.

The gravity attuned staggered, trying to hold up both of their weights. She'd also increased her own weight, to keep Sabae from tossing her around with gust strikes, but even her massively over-developed muscles couldn't hold up both of their combined enhanced weights. Just as the woman started to topple, Sabae felt the extra weight vanish off them.

While Alustin had largely made his point regarding trying out completely untested techniques in the middle of combat, Sabae couldn't resist this one time, as she, for the first time, delivered a gust strike with a head-butt.

It worked perfectly.

"Hugh, snap out of it!" Talia yelled.

Hugh shook himself. He'd just been standing there as his friends fought. He frantically reached into his beltpouch for his sling.

It wasn't there. He'd left it on the ship.

He needed that sling. It was the only reliable combat...

His hands closed on an angular, irregular lump.

Hugh pulled it out of his pocket. It was the ugly chunk of quartz he'd grown from the sand.

Hugh smiled, and quickly cast one of the levitation spells he'd tried to use to support his bracelets on his own on the chunk. He'd abandoned this one because while he could control the direction it pushed the bracelet with a thought, it had the nasty tendency to throw him a considerable distance in whatever direction he aimed it.

If he wanted a piece of crystal to go flying, though...

With a thought, the chunk hurled itself out of Hugh's hand, straight into the stomach of a spearman about to swing on Godrick. The man dropped his spear with a groan, clutching his gut. As he was still in the process of letting go of the spear, Hugh redirected the crystal off to one side, where it slammed into the meat of another man's thigh with bruising force, sending him down to one leg. The instant it impacted, Hugh redirected it again, breaking a spearwoman's wrist with it.

Hugh smiled. All of a sudden, he didn't feel so useless.

Talia frantically hurled several more dreamfire bolts at the wind mage in front of her. The mage smiled, almost casually spinning his sword-staff, generating a windshield in its wake that easily dispersed her dreamfire.

This mage seemed to be in a weight class above the rest of the attackers. They all had simple spears and rather unimpressive magic, while this man was highly trained with his unusual weapon and was quite capable with his wind attunement.

She didn't have time to generate a shield-piercing bolt while still keeping out of the way of his spear, and he just kept dispersing her regular bolts. Talia didn't dare use her bone affinity in this melee, for fear of injuring one of her friends.

The mage, seeing her pause, lunged forwards with his sword staff. At the same time, he summoned a burst of wind behind Talia that pushed her towards him.

Talia, rather than fighting the wind, lunged forward with it, rolling under his thrust. As she did so, she manifested a dreamfire bolt.

She'd love to see him generate a wind barrier at point blank range.

To her surprise, he didn't even try. Instead, he sent a powerful, uncontrolled gust of wind at the ground directly in between them. They were thrown away from one another, Talia's dreamfire dissolving harmlessly.

As Talia climbed to her feet, she surreptitiously drew one of her daggers. Not her Clan Castis dagger, but the one Hugh had found for her in the labyrinth.

The wind mage, who had pushed himself back to his feet with a gust of wind, snarled and charged her, pushing himself forwards with a gust of wind. Mobility techniques for most wind mages, unfortunately for Talia, were far easier than they were for Sabae.

As he swung his sword-staff at her, Talia pulled the spellform-engraved dagger out from behind her. The mage smiled derisively as she moved to block the sword with it.

The instant before the two weapons made contact, Talia channeled her mana into the dagger.

The dagger could only be used by a mage— it didn't store or gather any of its own. Instead, when a mage channeled mana into it, it triggered its own unusual magic effect— a kinetic anchor spell.

The sword-staff slammed into the dagger, then simply bounced off. Talia hardly even felt a tremor through the hilt of the dagger.

When enough mana was being channeled through it, the dagger wouldn't be moved by anything. Talia had been able to block blows from Godrick's warhammer with it in training, though that took a massive amount of her mana reservoirs to do. It was a bit of an odd enchantment for a dagger to have— it would be much more useful on a weapon big enough to block safely and more consistently with. Even if the dagger could block powerful blows with ease, it could only do so if Talia could get it in front of the blow, which was no trivial matter with a weapon this small.

Still, Talia loved the little weapon.

The wind mage stared at her in shock, but he quickly recovered and swung again, this time powering his blow with a wind spell. Talia stopped channeling mana through the dagger and dodged forwards. She reached up to parry again, channeling mana into her dagger. As she did so, she immediately let go of the hilt of the dagger, but kept channeling mana into it. Talia lunged into a forward roll on the ground as she did so.

The haft of the sword-staff collided with the dagger, which hung in midair. With the mage's strength and the wind spell behind it, the haft slammed into the dagger with far more force than it had before.

The dagger didn't move in the slightest, it just hung in midair as it cut the sword-staff in two, sending the blade and the rest of the pole clattering down the street.

Meanwhile, Talia came up from her roll, manifesting a dreamfire bolt in her hand as she did so. As the windmage stared in shock at his broken weapon, still confused what had happened, she shot the dreamfire bolt into his stomach at point-blank range, too close for his armor to disperse it all.

He never even knew what hit him.

Just as quickly as it started, the fight ended. The ambushers fled, leaving their dead and those too wounded to walk. Hugh called the chunk of quartz back to his hand. It smacked into his palm unpleasantly hard, but he ignored the stinging.

The whole fight must have taken less than a minute.

"Who for the sake of frostbite were they?" Talia demanded.

"And why'd they attack us?" Hugh said.

"Were they trying to rob us?" Avah asked.

"Ah can't say they were that impressive," Godrick said, letting the stone breastplate fall from him.

Sabae ignored them all and started searching one of the fallen attackers. After a moment, she pulled a necklace from around his neck. She frowned at it, then she moved to search another body, pulling a necklace off that one as well. Then a third body— which, when it turned out not to be dead, punched them in the face, then removed a necklace from them as well, leaving them groaning on the ground.

"We should get back to the ship," Sabae said, staring at the necklaces.

"What did you find?" Talia asked.

"Now." Sabae said, in a voice that brooked no argument.

They set off at a run.

They got back to the lifts out of breath but without further incident. They were the only passengers on this descending lift, so the instant they were out of earshot of the top, Sabae pulled the necklaces back out of a pocket.

They were unadorned leather bands, each with a small golden ornament hanging from them in the shape of some sort of insect. It looked like the child of a scarab and a mantis— much sturdier and heavily armored than a mantis, with far bigger jaws, but far more articulated than a scarab, with the claws of the mantis.

They looked really familiar to Hugh for some reason.

"What are these supposed to be?" Talia asked.

"Bad news," Sabae said. "I think they're holy symbols, markers for the faithful."

"Indris' cult get a silhouette of a dragon tattooed on their shoulder," Avah said, "they don't wear weird bug necklaces."

"That's because they're not dragon cultists," Sabae said. "I think another cult is making a play for the city."

Everyone was silent for a moment, staring at her in shock. Finally, Godrick spoke up.

"Ah think we need ta tell Alustin immediately. This is way, way over our heads."

Everyone just nodded at that.

Alustin heard them out silently on the deck, only interrupting to confirm that none of them had been injured. Once they finished, he sat quietly for a time, staring at the necklace he held in his hands.

"Your conclusions are logical, Sabae, but I wouldn't take them for certain just yet. It's possible that they're just a gang who use this insect as a symbol." Alustin didn't look away from the necklace as he spoke, however.

"Do you think they were the ones who burnt down the invisible cult?" Talia asked.

"Probably not," Alustin said. "That was most likely the dragon cultists, under Eudaxus' orders. A new cult infiltrating the city wouldn't want to risk coming to the attention of the dragon cultists until they were ready"

"But… he seemed so friendly," Hugh said.

"He's a good man, and I consider him a friend," Alustin replied, never taking his eyes off the golden insect, "but he's also fiercely devoted to Indris, and he can and will be ruthless against those he sees as encroaching against her."

The mage was silent for a while, contemplating the necklace even further. Finally, he broke the silence.

"We're going to need to tell Eudaxus about this tomorrow. Even if it turns out to just be a local gang or something, he'll likely still want to know. In the meantime, you should all get some rest. One last question before you go, however."

Alustin finally looked up from the insect, giving them a serious look. "This doesn't seem like a random attack at all. Why would a cult trying to stay hidden attack the five of you? Why would anyone in Theras Tel, for that matter?"

No one had an answer for him.

CHAPTER FOURTEEN
CONSEQUENCES

NEEDLESS to say, none of them went to bed when Alustin told them to. The five of them sat on crates in the small goods storage cargo deck, talking over the events of the night.

"I'm pretty sure Talia was the only one who killed anyone, Hugh," Sabae said. "The worst any of the rest of us did was break a few bones."

Hugh felt a curious mixture of relief and disappointment at that— it's not that he *wanted* to kill anyone, but he was training to be a battle mage, after all. He felt like a proper battle mage wouldn't be so bothered by the idea. Killing monsters in the labyrinth hadn't bothered him, but so far as he knew, nothing they'd killed down there could talk.

"Why aren't you freaking out about killing people, Talia?" Avah asked.

Talia shrugged. "It's not even close to my first time. Clan Castis gets raided by other clans plenty, and I've had to take up arms before."

"Why didn't yeh wreck the pirate's crossbows like yeh did earlier, Avah?" Godrick said.

"It wouldn't have worked," Avah said. "None of our ambushers had wood affinities, but the pirates had plenty."

"So?" said Talia. "Just overpower them."

Avah shook her head. "It doesn't work that way for wood affinites. Your ability to affect wood when opposed by another mage is determined by your familiarity with the particular piece. The weakest wood mage on the planet could overcome the strongest if they were fighting over a walking staff the former had used for decades. It's like that for any attunement to do with living things— the effect is even stronger for mages with attunements for living plants, and animal mages have trouble affecting animals they don't know or understand even unopposed."

Talia stared at her for a moment. "You could have just said that it's really easy for wood mages to block one another," she said.

Avah blushed.

"I guess it makes sense, though— probably related to why I can't affect living people's bones," Talia said.

"Wait, how can yer family all affect the *Owl* at once if yeh all have years of experience with it?" Godrick asked?

"When you're cooperating, the situation is reversed— the effects are more powerful than what you'd expect by simply adding them together," Avah said. "The Radhan also specialize in cooperative magic."

Godrick looked thoughtful at that.

"Seriously, though," Sabae said, "what could they possibly have against us specifically?"

"Maybe they actually were behind the destruction of the invisible cult?" Hugh said. "They could have seen us watching the fire, maybe?"

Sabae seemed to mull over that for a second, then she shook her head. "Lots of people were watching, though— why'd they single out us to target."

They spent a couple hours longer endlessly debating the ambush. At one point, while Talia was debating Godrick and Sabae about some inane detail of the fight, Avah caught Hugh staring at her. He quickly blushed and looked away.

"What is it?" Avah said.

Hugh felt his face redden even further, but he made himself look back up at her. "You saved my life tonight. If you hadn't pushed me out of the way of that crossbow bolt…"

It was Avah's turn to blush. "You were the reason that we all survived the sandstorm, so I'm just returning the favor."

It seemed like Avah was about to say something else, but they were promptly interrupted by Talia demanding their opinion on how part of the fight had played out.

No one noticed Sabae glaring at Talia.

Sabae and the others were exhausted the next morning as Alustin dragged them to Indris' palace again. They'd only gotten a few hours of sleep each. Thankfully, Alustin let them stop at a tea shop on the way.

Eudaxus was in a meeting when they arrived, but the instant he got out of it and heard what they were there for, things moved astonishingly fast. Within twenty minutes, Sabae was telling their story in front of an assembled group of councilors and high ranking guardsmen. The others, except for Hugh, contributed whenever they felt it was needed. Not that Sabae particularly expected Hugh to talk in front of a group like this, of course.

Two of the necklaces Sabae had recovered were passed around the table. She couldn't help but notice that Alustin had kept one for himself.

One of the guard captains informed them, after consulting with some underlings, that no such bodies had been found in that district.

The meeting resolved after about an hour, leaving only Eudaxus and two other councilors with them. One was Bandon Flame-hair, one of the three captains of the city guard. Like his name implied, the dark-skinned captain's hair was, somehow, even redder than Talia's— something Sabae never would have believed if she didn't see it. The other was Pale Lisan, the middle-aged minister of trade for the city. So far as Sabae could tell, there was nothing pale about Lisan— she was darker-skinned than Sabae, and wore dark grey robes.

"Why in the name of fallen Ithos were your rivals attacking my apprentices, Eudaxus?" Alustin said. His normally cheerful, pleasant demeanor was gone entirely— he hadn't even looked this upset when he'd caught the apprentices sneaking into the Great Library.

"We don't know that they're a rival cult..." Bandon began.

"They are," interrupted Eudaxus with a sigh. "We've suspected their presence in the city for a few months now, but it's only in the past couple of weeks that they've started acting against us. We've lost a dozen of Indris' Chosen in nighttime ambushes so far."

Bandon shot him a glare that Sabae interpreted as the guard captain being very displeased at not being told about this threat sooner. To his credit, however, he didn't say anything— breaking ranks in front of outsiders was bad form, even if they were allies.

"We've been trying to track them down, but we've had no luck so far," Eudaxus said. "We still have no idea who they worship— these pendants are the first clue we've had so far. It seems they didn't think the five of you were enough of a threat to dedicate many resources to."

Sabae saw Talia smiling broadly at that from the corner of her eye.

"And the invisible cult?" Alustin asked. "It seems rather surprising that they'd just randomly show up at the same time as well."

Eudaxus looked uncomfortable at that. "We… actually knew about the invisible cult for some time," he said. "We chose to let them be, in order to keep our eyes on them."

"Better the viper you can see than the one you can't," Sabae said.

Eudaxus nodded at her.

"So why'd you choose now to root them out?" Lisan asked, fixing Eudaxus with a cold stare.

"Some of our… more fervent younger members got it in their heads that maybe the invisible cult was… responsible, or at least connected, and decided to take action" Eudaxus said, even more visibly uncomfortable. "They've been reprimanded appropriately."

Sabae strove to keep her face blank. Maybe that was actually the case, or maybe Eudaxus didn't have as firm a hand on the reins of Indris' cult as he'd like to pretend.

Sabae hoped it wasn't the latter. She didn't want to be in a city about to break out in religious war in the first place, let alone when the dominant cult was unstable. And, for all of Theras Tel's wealth, they were in a quite precarious situation in many ways. They were almost entirely dependent on trade for food, and if they grew unstable enough that traders kept away… The stability Indris had brought was the only reason that the city had grown to its current position of wealth and power.

"Does this pendant give you any better idea who they worship, at least?" Alustin asked. "It's clearly got to be some being powerful enough to challenge Indris herself in order for them to be this confident."

Eudaxus shook his head at that. "I've never seen anything like these things," he said, holding up a pendant.

Everyone was silent for a moment at that. Eventually, Bandon shook his head. "I've already issued orders to increase patrols at night," he said.

"I'll have my clerks begin poring over all the city records for any clues," Lisan said. "I'm sure they'll be less than pleased at that, but a little work will be good for them."

The two exchanged farewells, then they left the table together, talking intently. No one said anything until they were out of sight, at which point Eudaxus ran a hand over his bald pate. Sabae was pretty sure he was about to say something else, but instead he just shook his head.

"I'll keep you updated on the investigation, Alustin. In the meantime, however, you might want to consider getting out of the city."

That sounded good to Sabae.

"I'll take that under consideration, Eudaxus." Sabae couldn't get a read on Alustin's expression as he said that.

They said their farewells, and then went their separate ways.

As they walked through the palace, Sabae walked up alongside Alustin. "He knows something, doesn't he? Or at least suspects it?"

Alustin gave her an appraising look, then he simply nodded.

On the way back to the ship, Sabae pulled Talia aside so that they trailed the others.

"You should be careful not to interrupt Hugh and Avah," Sabae said. "They were having a moment last night before you dragged them back into the conversation."

Talia gave her an odd look. "Are you still trying to make that happen? I'm not sure what Hugh even sees in her, other than her looks. He barely knows her. And she's only interested in him because she thinks he's a great mage— before the sandstorm, she only had eyes for Godrick."

Sabae rolled her eyes at Talia. "I doubt he'd really need more than her looks— have you looked at that girl? And, to her credit, she's actually friendly and interesting. And she thinks Hugh is a great mage because he is."

Talia started to open her mouth again, but Sabae cut her off. "Even if she didn't have anything else going for her, I'd still tell you to give them space," Sabae said. "This is the first time we've seen Hugh withdraw from his shell enough to actually notice anyone romantically. Even if nothing happens, this will be good for him. It's hardly the first time a pair of teenagers have started falling for each other out of shallow reasons, Talia."

Talia's expression was still doubtful, but she nodded. "If you say so."

Sabae clapped her on the back. "Let's see if we can get Alustin to let us stop by a bakery on the way back."

Talia grunted irritably.

CHAPTER FIFTEEN

AVOIDING TROUBLE

To Hugh and everyone else's surprise, Alustin decided that they should stay in Theras Tel, rather than leaving. It actually devolved into an argument on deck between Alustin and Deila, with Captain Solon standing awkwardly between them.

"That's gotta be one hell of a book Kanderon wants 'im ta get," Godrick muttered to the other Skyhold apprentices, once no one was around to hear.

"At this point," Sabae said, "I'm fairly convinced that this is all over something bigger than just a book."

Everyone stared at her. Sabae rolled her eyes. "You really hadn't figured it out yet? Alustin and the other Librarians Errant are more than just glorified treasure hunters specializing in books, they're Skyhold's intelligence service."

Hugh opened his mouth, then shut it again. That made a disturbing amount of sense.

"Then why is he taking so much time to train us?" Talia said. "Are we just supposed to be some sort of cover for him?"

Sabae shook her head. "According to my grandmother, most of spycraft is just waiting around. I think Alustin is quite serious about our training for its own sake, without it interfering with his other duties at all."

Not for the first time, Hugh wondered at exactly what type of person Sabae's grandmother was.

"So the attack on us..." Hugh said.

"Almost certainly has to do with whatever game Alustin is playing at," Sabae said.

Hugh really didn't like the thought that he was merely caught up in currents outside his control, and, by the expressions of the others, he wasn't alone in that.

Alustin almost immediately set them to more training. Even though Hugh was pretty sure he'd sworn never to be surprised by Alustin making them train more, he was still a little shocked that they were staying in the city.

Their training actually took them outside the city most days. They took a little rented sandskiff out onto the sands— it'd be a waste of time and effort to take the *Moonless Owl* itself out. The crew was greatly enjoying their shore leave— especially since they were getting paid for it. They could always find one of them to pilot the skiff out onto the sands for them, even so.

Godrick could really train anywhere, so he wasn't an issue, but the others had more specialized training needs.

It was probably best to keep Talia's training outside the city where it couldn't hurt anyone or damage any property. Alustin actually largely had her working on her cantrips, in an effort to be able to use them without them setting them on fire. So far… well, she'd even managed to make a cantrip designed to put out candles and other small flames instead cause a candle to explode.

Sabae was primarily focusing on her mobility techniques— the sand gave her softer landings when she crashed, which was most of the time at first. She started to show rapid improvement within a few days, however.

Alustin also started training her on spellformless water manipulation techniques, though she hadn't yet figured out how the Radhan actually gathered it in the erg, and they weren't telling. So Sabae mostly ended up hauling waterskins out onto the sand to practice with.

Easy access to sand helped Hugh immensely— he spent most of his time practicing growing crystals out of it. There was far, far more to crystal growing than he'd ever anticipated, even with Kanderon's warnings. *On the Nature and Growth of Crystalline Solids* was one of the densest and most difficult books Hugh had ever encountered, but it seemed like everything he read in there was somehow relevant to his crystal affinity.

He just had to figure out how.

Avah took over sailing the sandskiff for them a few times, and she actually even trained with them a bit— it turned out that both Hugh and Godrick could, to a limited extent, manipulate sand— Hugh could manipulate the crystalline grains, though not very dexterously, and Godrick could manipulate all of it, though it generally just clumped together when he did so.

After a few days of training, Hugh asked for Alustin's help with the sandcastle spellform that Avah had shown him— though, admittedly, on a day when she didn't come with them. He'd spent hours poring over the books they'd brought with them, trying to figure out how it worked— he'd never seen anything like this spellform before.

Alustin stared at it for quite a while, his brow furrowed. Then, just when Hugh was convinced he didn't have any idea either, Alustin burst out into a smile.

"Hah, I knew it would come to me!" Alustin said. "It's been a while since I've seen them, but these are... well, translating the word is difficult, but *unuot* marks. The literal translation is *the unfolding of the bud into the flower.* Essentially, it's a shorthand for encoding highly complex structures into spellforms."

"Translated from what language?" Hugh asked. "And how does it work?"

"The language is Osolic," Alustin said, "which is spoken in the Thousand Tears of Uos. A Radhan trading vessel must have picked it up there."

Hugh just gave him a blank look.

Alustin sighed.

"We really need to work on your knowledge of geography, Hugh. There's a lot more to Anastis than just the continent of Ithos, and we're very, very far from being the center of things."

"Yes, sir," Hugh replied.

"Don't call me..." Alustin sighed, then went on. "The Thousand Tears of Uos are a massive archipelago stretching across the entire west coast of the continent of Gelid. Each island is essentially just a mountain jutting up from the sea, and most rule themselves, squabbling and trading with the others constantly. The powerful live closer to the peak, while the poor scrabble around near the tide line, hoping not to be washed away. Their mages and warriors are all expected to be artists as well, so their spells tend to value beauty as much as effectiveness."

"This," Alustin said, tapping the page, "seems to be a training spell, or perhaps a spell to amuse children. It's much less complex than most of the *unuot* spells I've seen before. As for how it works, though… I have no idea."

Hugh gave him a disbelieving look, but Alustin just shrugged.

"I can't know everything, Hugh, and there are countless ways to craft spellforms. There's a reason that spellforms are overwhelmingly the most common method of manipulating mana— they're by far the most energy efficient method, and you can design them for nearly any purpose. It more than makes up for their lack of speed and versatility in most situations. *Unuot* marks are a particularly challenging field of study. From what I do know, however, it should be safe to alter the lines that control the quantity of sand used— the actual *unuot* marks are quite stable, and the other lines in their spellforms can usually be altered easily enough."

To Hugh's pleasure, the modified spellform worked perfectly the next time Avah joined them. It formed a dainty little castle in the palm of her hand, with gates, turrets, and all. The walls were so thin that when Avah held it up to the sun, you could actually see through the castle— the bits of quartz in it gave the sunlight a faint rainbow shimmer.

Avah was watching Hugh grow quartz crystals in the sand, sometimes magically reshaping the sand he was working with to amuse herself.

"You haven't had time to go into the city proper for a couple of weeks, have you?" she asked.

Hugh shook his head, trying to concentrate on his task.

"Things are getting tense. There are far more guards patrolling than usual, and they're reinforced with dragon cultists."

Hugh gave up on his current attempt, too interested in what Avah had to say.

"There have apparently been quite a few more attacks from those mysterious cultists as well," Avah said. "There are also a bunch of rumors of weird monsters creeping around, though most people don't put much credence into that. The rumor mill in the city doesn't know what's going on exactly, but everyone seems to know that something's up. Even the dragons are on edge."

"I'm not sure I want to know what a dragon on edge is like," Hugh admitted.

"They're far more active than usual," Avah said. "They're sleeping less, keeping a watch on strange activities in the city more, and even descending into the streets at times."

"Hey, I hadn't decided if I wanted to know yet," Hugh said, mock-glaring at Avah.

She rolled her eyes at him, then she shaped a chunk of sand into the shape of a crystal. "Hey, look, I'm doing better at your training than you are."

It was Hugh's turn to roll his eyes at her.

Hugh was a little shocked how comfortable he felt around Avah. He still caught his heart racing at times when he looked at her, but being alone around her didn't send him into a near panic anymore— he supposed that her saving his life might have helped with that a little.

Besides, they were only about fifty feet away from Godrick and Sabae. Though, admittedly, about four times that far away from Talia.

Better safe than sorry.

"Wait," Hugh said. "Should you really be going into the city on your own? How do we know it wasn't you the cultists were after?"

"I didn't go on my own," Avah said, frowning at him, "I went with some of my family's mages. And we weren't ambushed, so I don't think it's me they were after."

That figured. Knowing Hugh's luck, it was probably him they were after.

A terrible idea surfaced in the back of Hugh's head. What kind of being would be willing to challenge Indris? How about something that even Kanderon considered a rival?

Had Bakori escaped the labyrinth?

It made a sinister amount of sense to Hugh. The rumored monsters wandering around could be his brood of imps, and the insect necklaces could just be Bakori playing tricks to fool Indris into thinking she faced a different enemy.

It would also explain why they'd been ambushed.

"Still here, Hugh?" Avah asked.

Hugh turned back to Avah, trying to drive the wild speculations out of his head.

Godrick trudged back towards the sand skiff, with a complaining Talia beside him. So far he'd been treated to long rants about the heat and sand, as well as jabbing fingers in his side whenever she thought he wasn't paying attention.

In fairness, he actually hadn't been paying attention most of the time.

Alustin had kept them out later than usual, and worked them considerably harder as well. Even Avah was exhausted, and she'd spent more time talking with the others than actually training— not that she was required to train, but Alustin had been quite willing to help her improve her cantrips.

Thankfully, Talia's new hat had helped quite a bit, so she wasn't complaining about the sun anymore, at least.

Talia jabbed Godrick in the side again. "Are you listening or not?"

"Ah'm sorry," Godrick said, "Ah was off in mah own little world again."

His father used to lecture Godrick all the time to pay better attention to his surroundings. Godrick had definitely gotten quite a bit better at it these days, but ever since they'd left on this trip, he'd just constantly been distracted like he used to.

Maybe it had something to do with keeping secrets from his father and his friends.

All of a sudden, he realized that Talia had stopped talking. Expecting a jab in the side from her, he looked up from the sand at his feet.

Talia didn't poke him in the side, though.

She was too busy staring at the dragon that had just landed next to the skiff.

Hugh had tried to suppress his paranoia about Bakori escaping all day. Finally, though, on the way back to the skiff he confessed his fear to Alustin.

Alustin seemed to consider for a moment, then he shook his head. "No, I shouldn't think so. Skyhold has all the entrances to their labyrinth secured tightly."

"Couldn't Bakori have tunneled out, then?' Hugh asked.

Alustin shook his head and smiled. "You could dig a hole straight through Skyhold and it would never intersect the labyrinth. You could level the whole mountain and never intersect the labyrinth at all, and the entrances would just be hovering in midair. Likewise, you can try and dig out of the labyrinth all you want, but you'd never reach anywhere. If Bakori hasn't made it out of the labyrinth entrances, he's still trapped down there."

Hugh just stared at Alustin for a moment, and he found himself toying with the labyrinth stone around his neck. "What… how does that…"

It was as Hugh was trying to formulate a complete sentence, however, that the dragon landed near the skiff.

Hugh, to his surprise, recognized the dragon immediately. It was one of the two smaller dragons that had been with Indris in her throne room. It still dwarfed the skiff, but it didn't fill Hugh with the sense of impossible size he got from Indris.

Alustin simply walked right up to the dragon. Hugh and the others, however, stayed well away from it.

"Greetings! I don't believe we've been formally introduced yet," Alustin said. "I am Alustin Haber, Librarian Errant of Skyhold."

"I know who you are," said the dragon. "I haven't earned my name yet."

"I'm sorry to hear that," Alustin said. "What can I help you with today? Did Indris need something from me?"

The dragon shook its head. "No, I was just curious. I've seen you all coming out here for a few days now, and I wanted to get a closer look at you. And no need to apologize, Mother is just being overprotective. She'll let my sister and I go on our Naming Flight once she has another clutch of eggs and we're not the youngest anymore."

Alustin turned and waved the apprentices closer. Talia immediately approached, but it took a bit longer for the others to follow. Avah took the longest, and when she did approach, she hid behind Godrick.

The nameless dragon eyed them all curiously, before nodding. Without another word, it spread its wings and took off. Hugh staggered a little in the wind of its takeoff, but he didn't fall.

"That… that was seriously it?" Talia asked. "It really just wanted to look at us and go?"

Hugh shrugged, and moved to climb into the skiff.

There was a sealed scroll lying on one of the benches. Hugh grabbed it, examining it more closely. It was addressed to Alustin in an elegant hand, and the wax seal had a ward spellform embossed into it. Hugh could tell that the ward would destroy the scroll if opened improperly, but there were also a number of other marks that Hugh didn't recognize in the ward spellform— he was guessing they determined how the ward was supposed to be opened.

Hugh held out the scroll to Alustin. "Sir, this is addressed to you."

Alustin took the scroll, an interested look on his face. "It seems our visitor didn't merely come to satisfy his curiosity."

Alustin strode off a distance from the others to open the scroll.

"Did the scroll say who it was from, Hugh?" asked Sabae. Hugh shook his head.

Alustin spent a solid ten or fifteen minutes poring over the contents of the scroll. When he returned to the skiff, he merely shook his head when asked about it.

As they prepared to sail back into the city, Hugh made eye contact with Sabae, who shot a glance at Avah and shook her head slightly. Hugh didn't like it, but Sabae was probably right about not discussing the scroll around Avah.

By the time the skiff was ready to go, twilight was already turning towards night. As they sailed back around the city towards the harbor, lights began coming on in the city.

There were no torches or bonfires in Theras Tel— wood was far too precious. Even oil was seldom used. Instead, even as expensive as they were, glow crystals adorned Theras Tel. They ran up and down the streets, were found in shop windows, studded the edges of the aqueducts, and even ran down along the paths and ladders connecting the cliff dwellings.

The entire plateau lit up like the world's biggest candle at night.

Always before, they'd been either in the city proper or down in the harbor at night— and while the city lights were certainly beautiful enough from inside, they were nothing like the view from outside the city.

"It's beautiful," Hugh whispered.

Godrick let out a low whistle, and Sabae and Talia looked just as impressed.

"I've seen this sight dozens of times," Avah said, from where she was controlling the sail, "and I still never get tired of it."

Alustin seemed lost in his own little world as they glided over the sands, clutching the scroll in his hands.

"Definitely about more than just a book," whispered Sabae.

CHAPTER SIXTEEN
STORMBREAKER

A SANDSTORM struck Theras Tel the next day.

The five of them had all taken the lifts up into the city—Alustin judged it safe enough for them to be up there during the day, so long as they stuck together. The mystery cultists hadn't attacked during the day yet, and they were unlikely to start now.

Hugh did notice, however, that Alustin made doubly sure that Godrick brought his hammer with him.

The bells started ringing while they were eating at a food stall that sold some sort of pastry filled with candied ginger and peppers. Talia, ironically, had proven the least capable of handling spicy foods, and she had opted for one that just had ginger.

The bells, located in Indris' palace, were apparently magically enhanced to echo around the city- no normal bell could be this loud. As soon as the bells started ringing, dragons took off from every one of the roosting towers. The sky was suddenly filled with dozens and dozens of the massive beasts— Hugh was shocked they didn't crash into one another.

Strangely, the people of Theras Tel didn't seem alarmed in the slightest.

"You're going to want to see this," Avah said, then she rapidly shoveled the rest of her pastry into her mouth.

"See what?" Godrick asked.

"Sandstorm," Avah somehow managed to mutter around a mouthful of pastry.

Avah led them to the base of one of the dragon roosting towers. A large crowd was already filing into the base of it, to Hugh's surprise.

"The towers are generally closed to the public, but they open them up before a sandstorm," Avah said.

"Do they lock up the dragon treasure beforehand?" Hugh asked, visions of mounds of gold coins dancing in his head.

"Dragons keep their money in banks like everyone else," Avah said. "Hoards don't accrue interest."

Hugh opened his mouth, then shut it again. That made a lot of sense, actually. Plus, a dragon wouldn't have to worry about guarding its hoard all the time that way.

It took them a solid half hour to file up the narrow staircase towards the open floor where the dragons roosted— there were just too many people in the tower already.

Most of the crowd was clustered all to the west side already when they got up there— apparently that was the direction storms usually came from this season.

Godrick eyed the crowd, then smiled. "Ah've got an idea," he said, before turning and walking away from the crowd towards the nearly empty east side of the roosting area.

Godrick walked over to one of the columns holding up the roof and placed his hand on it. He closed his eyes, assuming an expression of concentration. After a minute or so, he opened his eyes back up and walked around to the edge of the platform.

Then he winked, and apparently stepped off the edge of the platform behind the column.

Hugh and the others rushed to the edge, only to find Godrick hanging off a stone ladder he'd shaped into the back of the column.

"I bet you think you're clever as a snowcat in a tree," Talia said.

Godrick just chuckled and started climbing.

The others, making sure no one was paying attention, climbed up after him. Once everyone was up, Godrick smoothed away the ladder, to make sure they'd have the roof to themselves.

Once he'd finished that, Talia promptly kicked him in the shin. "That's for scaring me like that!" she said.

Godrick feigned a mortal wound, much to the amusement of the others.

The roof was as flat as the floor below, and offered a truly spectacular view of the city and the surrounding desert.

"I don't see a sandstorm," Hugh said.

"It'll likely be at least another hour until it gets here," Avah said, "if not longer. Indris has quite a few scrying mages of various sorts watching for sandstorms."

"Windtalkers, mostly," Sabae added.

When Hugh looked at her questioningly, Sabae just shrugged. "Indris is probably the most powerful weather mage on Ithos outside of my family. We keep tabs on her."

"Where'd all the dragons go?" Talia asked.

Hugh looked around, realizing that Talia was right— there were only a few dragons left in the sky.

"All of Indris and Ataerg's children are accomplished wind mages in their own right," Avah said. "They fly out to all ships within range of the city and defend them from sandstorms, just as Indris does for the city itself."

"Ataerg?" Talia asked.

"Indris' mate," Sabae explained. "He's enormous for a male dragon, almost two thirds of Indris' length. They've mated exclusively with one another for over a century. His territory is in the deep northwest of the Endless Erg, with his lair in a huge maze of stone pillars and caverns. Half their children live with him, and half here with Indris."

"I thought dragons changed mates just about every mating flight," Talia said.

"Most do," Sabae said, "but not Indris and Ataerg. They don't even have a hard and fast border between their territories, which is almost unheard of."

Witnessing a sandstorm approach from this height was a completely different experience than from on a ship among the dunes.

Hugh could see many times farther from the top of the tower, and he caught sight of the sandstorm long before it even came close to the city.

It started as a faint smudging on the western horizon, but rapidly grew larger. The center resolved into recognizable clouds first as the storm approached.

If anything, the higher vantage point made the storm more impressive, not less. It extended as far north and south as the eye could see, without a hint of weakening in either direction. The great height of Theras Tel was still dwarfed by the storm— as it grew closer, it became more and more apparent how far the stormwall towered above the city.

Hugh could see quite a few ships running before the storm, each escorted by a dragon of Indris' brood. From what Avah and Sabae had told them, though, most would hunker down, each protected by one of the dragons. While a properly prepared ship could usually survive the storms well enough, having one of Indris' children to shield the ship with its magic would be enough to prevent damage entirely.

The distant rumble of the storm slowly grew deafening, and the wind grew steadily stronger and stronger, to the point where Hugh needed to lean against it. The storm was still miles away, and even though he knew better, it looked like it would swallow them in a heartbeat.

Hugh could feel the aether thicken as the storm grew closer. One of the best indicators of the power of a storm was, apparently, the change that could be felt in the aether.

Judging by what he felt, this storm was going to be far more powerful than the one they'd faced before.

Indris waited for what seemed like the last possible moment before taking to the sky. He didn't see her take off, but Avah shook his shoulder, yelling into his ear over the noise, and he turned to see the dragon queen lift into the sky above the city. Several of her children returned to her side as she did so.

They looked like sparrows beside an eagle. Hugh was struck again by how astonishingly massive Indris was— if she were to crash inside the city, she would probably demolish several city blocks before she came to a stop.

For that matter, if she were merely to try and walk around inside the city streets she would obliterate countless buildings beneath her. It seemed a little ironic to Hugh that Indris was a queen that could never walk the streets of her own city.

Then the howl of the wind just… stopped. Hugh staggered forwards when the wind he was leaning against disappeared, and the noise of the storm dropped from a roar to a muted rumble.

Hugh could hear cheering from below and in the streets.

At first Hugh couldn't see what had changed— the storm was still coming, the dunes dissolving just ahead of it. Then he saw what looked like a wall raising up from the sand about a mile out from the city, but spinning.

Suddenly, Hugh realized what he was seeing.

Indris Stormbreaker had raised a miles long wind-shield around the entire city.

The wall was raising itself farther and farther around the edge of the city. It was sand being lifted upwards farther into the cyclone of the windshield. When the windshields had gone up around the *Moonless Owl* and the pirates, they'd filled with blowing sand almost immediately. Theras Tel's windshield, however, was so massive that the sand would take several minutes to get all the way to the top.

People started pouring out into the streets when the noise of the storm muted. Hugh could hear shouting, cheering, and even music. Street vendors were rolling out kegs of ale, wine, and spirits— it was clearly apparent that this was very familiar territory to the inhabitants of Theras Tel.

The stormwall hit with a crashing rumble that seemed to vibrate the city, and everything went completely dark. The sound faded quickly, however, and the cheering resumed, even in the pitch-black of the storm.

Within moments, a lightning strike landed near the city. It wasn't blinding like it had been on the *Moonless Owl*— instead, it was like seeing it through a cup full of ale. Indris' windshield was so thick and sand-laden that the light could barely penetrate through it.

Several more lightning bolts struck, each giving off that same diffuse glow. It was really quite beautiful.

Slowly, Hugh realized that it was growing light again— the glow-lights of the city were coming on in response to the fall of darkness. They shimmered upwards against the sand-laden windshield, which glittered and shifted like some strange fluid in the city's light.

Soon, the city and the desert contained within the windshield looked as though they were in a bubble at the bottom of some strange, alien sea.

Seeming quite satisfied with herself, Indris slowly descended to the courtyard in front of the palace, just in front of the two massive stone dragon statues. Hugh was slightly surprised to see that they weren't even as large as Indris was.

"That… that was…" Hugh began.

"Ayup," Godrick said.

Everyone was silent for a bit.

"I think I kinda understand why people join Indris' cult now," Talia said.

"That… was a rather more impressive sight than my family made it out to be," Sabae said. "Indris might not be able to steer the paths of storms, but this… this takes an absurd amount of raw power."

No one spoke for a few more minutes, watching the windshield swirl and glitter in the city's light. They all lay down on their backs to watch the shield and the lightning strikes. When the lightning bolts struck now, they appeared very differently than they had before— now they were equalizing the light on both sides of the shield, so lightning flashes gave glimpses of the swirling storm outside.

Below them, the impromptu festival seemed to have filled the entirety of the city's streets. Bards and bands played on every corner, and dances had formed up everywhere.

"We should head back down and join the party," Avah said, climbing to her feet.

Hugh immediately felt his shoulders tense. He was decent at handling crowds when he didn't feel like anyone was paying attention to him, but he'd never been in a crowd even close to that dense or worked up before.

"I kind of like it up here," he started, but Avah reached out and grabbed him by the hand, trying to haul him up as well.

"It'll be fun, I promise!" Avah said.

Hugh's hand tingled where Avah held it, and he groaned and let himself be pulled to his feet.

"Alright, fine," he acquiesced.

"Ah'll remake the ladder," Godrick said, climbing to his feet as well.

"I've got a better idea," Talia said, a wicked grin on her face. "Let's have Hugh get us down."

Hugh's eyes widened at that. "I'm really fine with going down the normal way."

"What are we talking about?" Avah asked.

"Ah like this plan," Godrick said.

"Sabae, what do you think?" Talia asked.

Sabae smiled widely. "Let's do it."

Hugh let out a deep sigh.

CHAPTER SEVENTEEN

THE CALM DURING THE STORM

THEY all leapt off the top of the tower together on the count of three, holding hands. A few people screamed in the crowd below until Hugh's levitation cantrip kicked in and their fall slowed to a slow downward glide.

Hugh had refined the basic spellform quite a bit since he'd first used the spell, he was only slowing the fall of five, rather than six, people, and his mana reservoirs were larger than they used to be, but it was still exhausting to cast.

They gently landed in the space the crowd had cleared for them to general cheering. Avah was laughing hysterically. "Let's do that again!" she shouted.

The crowd clustered back in, and someone pressed a wineskin into Hugh's hand. "As thanks for the show!" the man shouted, before turning back to dance with a woman wearing stilts.

Hugh eyed the wineskin suspiciously. He'd had a glass or two with dinner often enough before, and in one of the rare moments of closeness he'd had with his cousins, they'd stolen a small cask and drank entirely too much of it, but…

"Are you going to drink, or just stare at it?" Talia shouted over the crowd.

Hugh stuck out his tongue at her, then he popped open the wineskin and took a swig. It was possibly the worst wine he'd ever tasted in his life, but he took another and passed the wineskin to Talia.

They passed around the wineskin as they wandered around the crowd. They passed dancers in all manner of costume (and more than a few who had more of a lack of costume), acrobats, musicians, and jugglers. Talia was particularly taken with a fire mage who was acting out entire battles in the street with flame soldiers less than an inch tall.

Dragon cultists were everywhere, preaching the glories of Indris. Hugh thought that Indris holding back the storm was probably far more effective at inspiring converts than anything that the cultists had to say, but the fact that they were giving out free food and drink made their sermons quite popular.

After the first wineskin, they found an impromptu outdoor tavern where ice mages were creating slush-like alcoholic confections. Hugh got one that tasted overwhelmingly of mint.

They spent who knows how long wandering the streets and enjoying the festival. The locals of Theras Tel were old hands at organizing these impromptu celebrations. The Cult of Indris didn't have any other holidays, other than a festival celebrating the laying of each new clutch of eggs Indris and Ataerg had. It made the celebration a sort of wild abandon that Hugh had never experienced before— everyone was throwing down their responsibilities on only a couple hours' notice.

Overhead, the storm roiled and twisted, not relenting in the slightest. Lightning bolts regularly pounded into Indris' windshield, but according to Avah, they never made it through— the sheer amount of sand carried by the shield absorbed all the hits, fusing into fulgurites, or lightning-glass. The sand near the base of the shield would be littered with them by the end of the storm. Given how often enchanters used lightning-glass, it would all be gathered up and sold by entrepreneurial members of the city's population at the end of the storm.

Avah would have continued in this vein for quite a while longer if Godrick hadn't interrupted to point out a street where gravity mages were working together to lower everyone's weight, and dancers were leaping fifteen feet into the air with their partners.

"Let's go dance!" Avah said, pulling on Hugh's arm.

"I don't know how," he admitted, his stomach twisting. She'd probably just go ask Godrick to dance instead, and...

"It's easy, I'll show you!" Avah said, pulling him even harder. Hugh relented, letting her pull him into the area of lowered gravity.

In retrospect, that might have not been the best place to learn. Hugh managed to crash them into at least three other pairs of dancers in mid-air, getting them both kicked out of the area. Thankfully, Avah seemed more amused by that than anything. They stood on the sidelines, watching as

Talia danced with Godrick and Sabae danced with a boy their age with hair even longer than hers.

Hugh was, however, paying a lot less attention to their friends than to the fact that Avah hadn't let go of his hand yet.

Everywhere they wandered, Hugh saw mages at work— creating entertainments of every sort for the crowd. Illusions, magically enhanced foods, and more.

A slightly more sober part of Hugh (admittedly, at this point, a rather small part) marveled at the density of the aether the storm brought them. He would have expected Indris' windshield to take up most of the available mana, but even though Indris mana use was so demanding on the aether that he could actually feel it swirling towards Indris, it was still far more available than usual in Theras Tel.

Most of Hugh, however, was focused on Avah. They'd wandered the festival hand in hand, following behind the others and talking. (And trying to ignore the ridiculous kissing faces Godrick and Talia kept making at Hugh whenever Avah couldn't see them. Sabae, thankfully, did her best to keep that to a minimum.)

"Hugh, look! It's yer fountain!" Godrick called back.

Ahead of them was Hugh's favorite fountain in the city, the one with the dancers made entirely of water endlessly twirling about. The street they were in was a little quieter than many of the others they'd wandered through— it was still packed with people, but most were eating or talking amongst their friends, rather than dancing or celebrating. A few musicians idly played in front of a closed up shop.

The five of them sat down on the edge of the fountain for a breather. None of them were even remotely sober, and they'd all been on their feet for hours.

It was probably thanks to the alcohol, but when the idea came to Hugh, he didn't even feel remotely nervous about it. He let go of Avah's hand, took his spellbook off from over his shoulder and handed it to Godrick, then he darted over to the musicians.

Hugh whispered his request to the lead musician, tossing a handful of Tel Theras coins into the hat in front of her. She tipped her enormous feathered hat at him, then re-situated her lute to a more comfortable position and started giving orders to the rest of the band.

Hugh darted back to the fountain as the band readied their instruments, and gave his best attempt at a court bow to Avah. "May I have this dance?" he asked.

She giggled. "That was the worst bow I've ever seen, but yes, you may." She stood up and offered him her hand.

Hugh, swollen with the confidence and drink, somehow managed to ignore Godrick's whistle, as well as Sabae's terrible attempt at one.

Hugh took Avah's hand, but rather than put his arms around her, stepped past her into the fountain. His boots immediately filled with water, but he didn't pay that any attention.

"What are you?..." Avah began, then her eyes lit up, and she hopped into the fountain next to him. The two of them waited at the edge of the fountain for the perfect moment, then strode farther in.

The band began to play a tune that perfectly matched the movements of the fountain's water dancers. Hugh and Avah carefully matched the poses of the dancers, then began mirroring their every move.

It felt like they danced for hours, the crowd around them laughing and cheering, many of them starting to dance as well— though no one else hopped in the fountain. Hugh ignored everything going on around them, staring into Avah's eyes the whole time.

He knew he should kiss her, but even the alcohol wasn't giving him enough courage. Hugh swallowed, feeling his stomach start to knot up.

Avah, to Hugh's great surprise and pleasure, was much more confident than he was. The crowd cheered even louder.

They stopped dancing as they kissed, until the water dancers danced right into them, soaking them both completely.

Hugh woke up slowly, his head feeling like it was filled with wool. He felt a heavy weight on his right arm, and looked over to see Avah snoring gently, leaning on him.

Above them, the storm still blew, but Hugh could visibly see that it was weakening.

Hugh gradually came fully awake. Had… had that kiss really happened? It felt a bit like a dream, but Hugh was pretty sure it actually had.

After the dance in the fountain, they'd wandered the streets for a few hours longer as the festival continued around them. The last thing Hugh remembered, someone had handed them a flask full of something made of apples.

Mostly apples, at least.

Hugh looked to his left, where Sabae and Talia both slept propped up against Godrick, who, in turn, was propped up against the same thing that Hugh… wait, what were they resting against? It was warm, smooth, and *moving* faintly.

Hugh sat bolt upright. Avah lost her balance, and she awoke with a startled squeak.

The naga's tail he'd been leaning against twitched, and he woke up from where he was lying, cuddled up with a half-eaten cake. The naga glanced at him, seeming barely awake. "Thanks again for the cake," he said, shifting his tail again, then he lowered his head back down and went to sleep.

Hugh had no idea what that was about.

He slowly stood up, helping Avah to her feet as well. The others, woken by the naga moving around, started moving as well. Hugh patted his side, finding his spellbook slung over his shoulder— he'd apparently taken it back from Godrick at some point.

His clothes were dry, at least.

They were lying on the side of a city square. There were several other passed-out revelers scattered about near them, as well as one fellow aimlessly staggering about. Hugh could see crowds of revelers down several streets, but the party seemed to be dying with the storm.

"Ow," Avah said, clutching her head with her hands. "What the hell happened last night?"

Hugh froze, afraid that Avah had completely forgotten their kiss.

"The last thing I remember was Godrick trying on the stilts after that drink that tasted like apples," she said.

Hugh definitely didn't remember that. To his great relief, Avah leaned forwards and gave him a quick kiss.

"I had a lot of fun last night," she said.

Hugh blushed, and mumbled something. Avah chuckled.

The storm ended completely as the five of them slowly staggered back towards the port. It had lasted a full day, and it was early afternoon when the sun was revealed again.

Indris, visibly exhausted even from this distance, rose back into the air as the shield began to fall. The shield didn't fall all at once, but instead began to retreat downwards away from the top of the dome it had formed. Shockingly little sand fell onto the city below as the shield swirled down to the ground.

The enormous dragon queen slowly gained altitude, then began gliding around to her palace.

The five of them idly tried to piece together what had happened towards the end of the night with mixed success. Godrick seemed to have vague recollections of the five of them riding a dragon as drunk as they were through the streets, but they all agreed that was absurd. Talia muttered something unflattering about ink mages and tattoos, but wouldn't elaborate further.

They'd been walking for around an hour and were about halfway back to the port when they heard Indris scream in rage. Even from miles away and shielded by the bulk of the palace, it was by far the loudest noise Hugh had ever heard. It hit him with physical force, sending him staggering.

Indris tore through the roof of her palace as though it were paper, sending chunks of masonry the size of houses hurtling through the air. Hugh could feel the whole city shudder.

Indris' shoulder tore through a major aqueduct like it wasn't even there, sending a river of water pouring down into the city streets. She spread her wings and took to the air, bellowing again.

Hugh and the others covered their ears and braced themselves against the sound. The roar completely drowned out the sound of the masonry chunks raining down on the city, crashing into mansions, streets, and even a roosting tower, which cracked, but didn't fall.

Indris' entire brood seemed to take to the air at once, swirling wildly around the dragon queen.

"My egg!" bellowed Indris. **"My egg has been stolen!"**

As Hugh's hearing slowly returned, he heard the screaming begin.

CHAPTER EIGHTEEN
THEFT MOST FOUL

THE five of them desperately jogged through the city. Citizens rushed everywhere, panicked and confused. At one point they were stopped by a chunk of palace masonry that had blocked the street. They could only drag Sabae away from trying to heal people injured by rockshards thrown by the impact when a team of trained healers showed up on the scene.

Indris' brood swirled wildly through the air, bellowing and searching. Several times the five of them had to take a different turning to avoid a dragon stalking down a city street, angrily shoving its snout into doors and windows.

City guardsmen and dragon cultists swarmed everywhere as well, seeming to question citizens almost at random. The five of them were somehow overlooked each time— a group of hungover teenagers apparently weren't high on the list of suspects.

What should have been the walk of less than an hour to get to the lifts down to the port ended up taking them almost four. Things had settled down a little bit, but largely just because most of the citizens had retreated inside. Several store owners offered to let the five of them in, but they'd refused each time, convinced that getting back to the *Owl* would be best.

Despite the increasingly deserted streets towards the end of their trek, they found a shockingly huge crowd at the plaza with the lifts down to the harbor. Merchants and travelers clamored to get down to their ships, while locals were standing around and gawking.

Unable to work their way through the crowd, Hugh and the others found a narrow combination stairway and alley with a view of the plaza.

The lifts themselves were being blocked by a small army of guardsmen and cultists, as well as no less than four of Indris' brood, one of which even surpassed Kanderon in size.

When the crowd pressed forwards, one of the dragons let loose a gout of flame over their heads, and the crowd frantically drew backwards.

Only one of the lifts was moving, and it was slowly creeping upwards. As it drew into sight, Hugh could see that it was packed with guardsmen and cult mages, all clustered around a single prisoner.

At the front of the pack on the lift was a figure with a bald shining head that Hugh recognized immediately— Eudaxus, High Priest of the Cult of Indris.

The guardsmen in the plaza forced the crowd farther back as the group stepped off the lift and marched out into the plaza. They moved slowly, since there was only so fast the scared and shouting crowd could get out of the way.

Eudaxus' group was halfway across the plaza before Hugh finally caught a glimpse of the prisoner. He could hear all of his friends make noises of shock at the same time.

It was Alustin.

Talia and Hugh lunged forwards at the same time. Talia was snarling, while Hugh was absolutely silent. Before they could plunge forwards into the crowd, however, their friends grabbed them— Godrick grabbed Talia, and Avah and Sabae held back Hugh.

"We need to help him!" Hugh yelled.

Talia yelled something inarticulate, then bit Godrick's arm. He winced, but held on.

"There's nothing we can do!" Sabae said. Hugh kept struggling, and Sabae shook him. "There's nothing we can do!" she yelled.

Hugh slowly stopped struggling, trying to catch his breath. Sabae let him go and strode over to Talia, who was yelling and kicking Godrick's shins repeatedly.

Sabae slapped her in the face.

"Are you trying to get us all killed?" she yelled.

Talia froze, glaring murder at Sabae. Slowly, however, she let out a long breath and seemed to relax. Godrick let go of her, rubbing his arm where she'd bitten him.

"Ah think yeh drew blood," he said reproachfully.

Hugh noticed that a few people at the back of the crowd were staring at them curiously.

"There's nothing we can do to help Alustin right now," Sabae said. "If we try to break him loose right now, we'll be taken captive immediately, if we're lucky. More likely we'll just be incinerated or eaten by one of those dragons. We need to retreat and find somewhere to hunker down until we know what's going on."

Hugh nodded. Talia glared a moment longer, then she begrudgingly tilted her head.

They set out at a brisk walk, without any specific destination in mind— just trying to avoid guardsmen and dragons. No one spoke for a long time— Hugh, even though he knew Sabae was right, couldn't help but feel angry at the whole situation, as well as at himself for not being able to do more. After everything Alustin had done for Hugh, he couldn't do a single thing to help him in return.

If Avah hadn't been there once again, they likely would have died. All of the apprentices were too lost in their own misery and not paying attention to their surroundings when the first flight of crossbow bolts and spears came hurtling at them from the windows and doors on either side of the street. Avah, the only one of them really paying attention, somehow managed to block the entire flight of projectiles. She staggered to the ground as she did so, almost entirely drained.

Robed members of the mystery cult that had attacked them before came pouring out of the nearby buildings, as well as out of the nearby alley.

"Take the Kaen Das girl alive!" one of them shouted. "Kill the rest!"

Godrick frantically backpedaled and worked at the straps holding his sledgehammer to his back as a cultist jabbed his spear at him. Why hadn't he just been carrying it, given how tense things were? If he'd already had the hammer out, he could have blocked the…

Godrick cursed himself for a fool. He didn't need his hammer to block with. He envisioned the steel-repelling spellform he'd used against the pirates. As the cultist prepared to jab at him again, Godrick poured mana into the spellform. The cultist's spear slid back through his hands, cutting them open as it did so, then it slammed butt-first into the stomach of another cultist behind them.

Another cultist charged at him from the side, but a lump of quartz shot out of nowhere and knocked the front third of the spear off in a spray of splinters. The cultist stared at it foolishly for a moment before Godrick's fist obstructed his view.

Avah seemed to be blocking most of the crossbow bolts, but while Godrick had a second, he reached out with his affinity senses looking for more crossbow bolts. He quickly disarmed several crossbows being loaded in the buildings above them by pushing against their steel points, as well as scattering the contents of several quivers.

Godrick finally got the straps untied, and began the spellforms to craft his stone breastplate. In a melee like this, it would have been wonderful if he could construct the full armor like his father did, but…

A pair of cultists attempted to flank Godrick, while a third came at him from the front. Godrick swung out with his hammer at the cultist on his right just as he finished crafting his breastplate spellforms. The front cultist's spear was knocked out of his hands by the breastplate as it formed out of the stone of the street and flew to Godrick's chest, and the cultist on the right had his calf broken by the hammer.

The cultist on Godrick's left was struck in the head by a dreamfire bolt, and Godrick winced at the sight and looked away.

Hugh helped Avah stand as he frantically smashed the lump of quartz into wrists, ankles, and spears. Thankfully, most of the cultists were focusing more on the other three, who made more obvious threats. Talia in particular had drawn the attention of a pair of fire mages, and the three were locked in a long-ranged duel.

"Hugh, I don't think I can block many more crossbow bolts," Avah said.

"You can't shatter their crossbows this time?" Hugh said.

Avah shook her head as she deflected several more crossbow bolts. "I already shattered as many as I could, but the rest seem to have been enchanted to prevent wood mages from doing that. I'm not a battlemage, Hugh, I don't know what else to do."

"You can still sense their crossbows, right?" Hugh asked. Somewhat to his shock, he managed to block a thrown spear with one of his crystal bracelets. He barely even felt anything from it— the weight of the bracelets had grown enough over the past few weeks that Hugh was fairly sure he wouldn't be able to lift them at all if he deactivated the prioperceptive link.

"Yes," Avah said, "but…"

"So use your senses to locate where the strings connect to the wood, then burn them with a fire-starting cantrip," Hugh said, launching his chunk of quartz into a cultist's stomach.

Avah blinked, then she furrowed her eyebrows in concentration. Within seconds, a series of snapping noises and curses came out of the nearby windows.

Hugh nodded, and focused on keeping cultists back from the two of them with the chunk of quartz.

Sabae backhanded a cultist with a gust strike, sending him flying.

They wanted *her*? Why did they want her? Sure, she came from one of the most powerful and wealthy mage families on the continent, and…

Vines came whipping out of a cultist's robes straight at her, and Sabae detonated her wind armor near her feet, sending her flying upwards and backwards.

That had been her real hang-up with the mobility techniques Alustin had been trying to teach her— she kept trying to release the wind in a controlled fashion in one direction, which seemed logical. Counterintuitively, however, the means to control her jumps had come from releasing the wind in a chaotic fashion. At least, somewhat chaotic— by detonating the wind armor in a very specific manner, she could actually launch herself accurately.

By the time she landed, she'd already spun the wind armor around her feet back up, and it took most of the impact for her.

The plant mage was still charging her direction, vines latching onto posts and doorframes to pull her towards Sabae even faster. Sabae could see that the vines all led to a backpack filled with dirt on the woman's back.

Who would have expected to encounter a plant mage in the desert?

Sabae blasted off to her right again— she couldn't let herself get separated from the others any more than she already had.

Midleap, however, something curled around one ankle, and Sabae felt herself crash into the ground.

Sabae twisted to see the cultist smiling as her vine wound its way around Sabae's ankle. Sabae desperately launched a gust strike against the vine, but it held firm. Another vine lashed out, catching her other leg.

"I've got her!" the plant mage shouted, as a third vine shot towards Sabae.

It never reached her.

A figure with brilliant red hair came hurtling out of the sky, slicing all three of the vines apart. The ones on Sabae's legs went limp immediately.

For a brief moment Sabae thought that Talia had picked up a pair of shortswords somewhere, until she recognized the figure.

It was Bandon Flame-Hair, the city guard captain they'd met at the meeting.

Bandon glanced at her and nodded, then he shot forwards towards the plant mage like he'd been fired out of a ballista.

The tides of battle turned swiftly with Bandon's arrival.

He was everywhere in the battle— and not just figuratively. The instant he planted a sword in the chest of the plant mage, he seemed to split into a half-dozen copies of himself, each of which launched themselves into the crowd of cultists.

For a moment Hugh thought that Bandon actually somehow copied himself, until he saw a cultist's spear pass harmlessly through one of the Bandons— they were just illusions.

Still, it was absurdly impressive. Each illusion seemed to act completely independently of one another, and Hugh couldn't even start to keep track of them all as they hurtled around the battlefield. It was like one of those roadside games where a gambler hid a coin in a cup, then shuffled around a whole group of identical cups, leaving the player to guess where the coin was.

And, like the people who played that game, the cultists never won.

Bandon pretty clearly had a force attunement as well— those absurd leaps were entirely normal for a force mage, though more powerful ones were able to fly. Bandon also regularly used it to send cultists— or entire groups of cultists, flying uncontrolled into the air as well.

Within a few short moments of entering the battle, he'd cut down nearly a dozen cultists, sent even more flying, and put the rest into confusion. It quickly turned into a rout, the cultists fleeing en masse.

Only one stayed and tried to fight— one of the fire mages that had been dueling Talia. He sent firebolts hurtling into all six copies of Bandon, but to the mage's shock, they passed harmlessly through all of them.

Then, to everyone else's shock, the fire mage's head seemed to just fall off.

The six copies all faded away, and then the real Bandon shimmered into view from where he'd been standing invisibly behind the mage, swords dripping blood.

The red-headed guard captain glanced at his blades, and the blood just ran off them all at once— Hugh guessed that he'd used a cantrip of some sort. Bandon slid his swords back into the sheaths on his back almost casually, then he turned to the teenagers.

Bandon raised his hands, palms out. "I'm here as a friend; no need for us to fight as well."

"What do you want?" Sabae demanded. "Why is Eudaxus arresting Alustin?"

"Several of Indris' cultists reported seeing Alustin in the palace during the storm," Bandon said. "He's the prime suspect for the theft of the queen's egg. You four apprentices are wanted for questioning as well."

Hugh tensed up again, ready to fight if need be. He could see the others doing the same.

"I'm not here to take you in," Bandon said. "I'm a friend, like I said."

"So what do you want, then?" Sabae asked.

"I want to help, and it's pretty clear who the actual culprits are," Bandon said, kicking the corpse of a cultist with his foot. "I've got a safe-house you can hunker down in, like you were planning to do, until we know what's going on and can clear Alustin's name. I'd rather not put teenagers into the custody of the dragon cult right now, as riled up as they are— they weren't entirely under Eudaxus' control even just with the threat of the mystery cult, let alone with this."

The five of them glanced at each other, then Sabae turned back to Bandon and nodded. "Fine. We'll come with you for now."

"Good," Bandon said. "We should get moving quickly— someone will be here soon to investigate the noise from the fight."

As they followed him into an alleyway, a momentary whim took Hugh, and he grabbed one of the cultist's necklaces from around their necks.

Bandon managed to scrounge up cloaks for all of them from an empty tailor's shop. He had to pick the lock to get in— apparently you picked up a lot of interesting tricks working in the city guard— and he actually left money for the cloaks as well.

He'd told Avah that she didn't need to come with the others— only the apprentices were being looked for, and she'd probably avoid a lot of trouble that way. Avah seemed torn, but when Bandon told them that the lifts were locked down so that no one except the guards and cultists could ride them, and that all ships were being kept from leaving the port until the egg was retrieved, she quickly decided to stick with them.

No one spoke as Bandon— the only uncloaked member of their group— led them through the city. He mostly took them through alleys and narrow side-streets, hoping to avoid as many guardsmen and cultists as possible, not to mention the large numbers of dragons walking the streets.

Indris and the majority of her brood still swept the skies above them. Indris frequently roared and bellowed, demanding her egg back. Each time, they had to cover their ears and brace themselves.

Despite all of Bandon's precautions, a group of guardsmen still came across them unexpectedly. Hugh readied himself to fight, feeling a strange tingling on his skin. He glanced over to check on his friends, only to realize that they'd all vanished.

Then he glanced down and realized that he couldn't even see himself.

"Captain Bandon!" one of the guardsmen called. "Any news?"

"I heard they captured the bastard that stole the egg," Bandon said, "but no word of the egg itself," Bandon said. "What about on your end?"

The soldier shook his head, looking frustrated.

Bandon seemed to consider for a moment. "Why don't you soldiers report back to the West Undertunnel guard post? It seems like most of the city's guards are swarming around up here— if the egg's down in the undertunnels, I doubt they have enough men to search them right now."

The soldier nodded, then the whole group turned and marched away.

The moment they were out of sight, Bandon sighed, and the tingling on Hugh's skin ceased. The five teenagers all faded back into view.

Bandon led them through more and more twisting alleys. The streets and buildings got shabbier and shabbier as they moved farther and farther west, and they caught glimpses of beggars huddling in doorways and behind piles of trash, none of which they'd seen towards the midline of the city.

Indris' flight seemed to grow more erratic and enraged as time wore on and her egg still wasn't found. They'd been following Bandon for over an hour when they came to a street that dead-ended at the edge of the cliff.

Bandon sighed in relief. "We're almost there," he said. "The safe house is in one of the cliff dwellings below us, it's just a short climb down."

As they strode forwards towards the edge, Indris gave another bellow. This one seemed… different, though. It was weaker, shriller, and more anguished than the one before.

Everyone turned to look.

Indris was lurching around through the air like an unsteady drunk. She missed a beat and dropped through the air before recovering.

Bandon audibly drew in a breath, his eyes round with fear.

"What is this?" he whispered audibly. "What's going on?"

Indris let loose another pained shriek, then she went limp in midair. Her children frantically dove out of her way as she plummeted out of the sky towards the city.

The impact was so powerful that it shook the whole plateau, actually throwing everyone except Bandon and Godrick off their feet. A massive cloud of dust and rubble rose into the air.

The whole city was completely silent for what felt like an eternity as the dust rose. Then, in an unbelievable cacophony, Indris' brood began to scream at the top of their lungs.

CHAPTER NINETEEN
SAFEHOUSE

BANDON started to sprint towards the impact site before any of them had even stood up, but then he came to a skidding halt. He looked back at them, then back at the pillar of dust, and then back at them.

Finally, the guard captain seemed to sigh. Hugh couldn't hear him over the dozens of enraged dragons, but Bandon gestured for them to follow, heading toward the cliff.

They descended a steep stone staircase down the side of the cliff. There was no railing between them and a drop of over a mile. Hugh didn't have much of a problem with heights, but he still felt a little bit of vertigo.

Several times he caught glimpses of terrified faces looking out from behind the curtains in the doors and windows of the cliff dwellings they passed. No-one was out and about, however, clearly terrified by recent events.

The noise slowly dimmed as they descended, but only from deafening to painful.

Bandon took them down several rickety ladders, another few sets of staircases, and even through a cliff dwelling at one point. Finally, he stopped at what seemed to be a dead end— a landing at the end of a staircase with nothing past it.

"Here," he said. He reached out, and to Hugh's shock, dispelled an illusion there, revealing a ladder that appeared to have been shaped from the rock itself. Bandon hopped down onto the ladder and began to descend.

They followed him down.

Bandon's safehouse was surprisingly roomy. It was hidden under an overhang, and was completely invisible from above without any sort of spell whatsoever. The ladder had taken them a considerable distance, much farther down than any other cliff dwellings had been built so far.

Bandon only stayed long enough to show them where the food, bedding, and other supplies were located, before telling them not to go anywhere, and that he'd be back as soon as he could to check on them. Then he clambered back up the ladder. A few minutes later, the ladder rippled and vanished again.

Leaving the five of them alone.

Sabae healed a few minor cuts, bruises, and burns, but no one said much after that.

They assembled a quick meal of dry rations, then all of them curled up and went to sleep. It was only late afternoon, but they were all exhausted, both by the festivities the night before and the events of that day.

It was almost two days before Bandon returned, and the news he bore was less than encouraging. The wait hadn't been an enjoyable one— Talia was still furious about them not going after Alustin, Hugh had withdrawn into himself, and even the normally cheerful Godrick and Avah barely said a word.

Of course, Sabae really wasn't being much more communicative than the rest of them.

"Indris was poisoned," Bandon said. "Holding back a sandstorm always leaves her exhausted and hungry, so her priests prepare her a massive feast for the end, usually involving a dozen oxen. It was partway through her feast when one of her priests noticed that the egg was missing. If it hadn't been for that, she'd likely have finished the feast, which would have been enough poison to kill her twice over."

The guard captain looked like he hadn't slept or bathed since he'd seen them last. Sabae was honestly a little surprised that he'd even made it down the ladder without falling, considering how unsteady on his feet he looked.

Bandon ran his hand through his hair. "She's near-comatose, and when she does awaken she's barely lucid. They haven't been able to move her from where she crashed into the city. They're trying to recover all the corpses and wounded from the wreckage, but without much luck—every time she thrashes in her sleep, more of it collapses."

"What about Alustin?" Talia demanded.

Bandon sighed. "He's being kept prisoner in the holding cells of the palace," he said. "There's a sizable group of Indris' cult that just wants him executed on the spot, but the rest of the cult and Eudaxus, the guards, and most of the other factions are holding off until the egg is recovered. So far as I can tell, I'm about the only one who actually thinks he might be innocent. Most of the arguments now are about whether Alustin is working with the mystery cult, Kanderon, or Sabae's family to try and overthrow Indris. Even Eudaxus seems convinced of his guilt, and the two of them have been friends for years."

"My family wouldn't be behind something like this!" Sabae said angrily. Her family had its faults, but something like this would be completely… well, at the very least they wouldn't attempt a takeover using methods like this.

"Ras Andis is the biggest economic rival of Theras Tel in the region, and your family rules Ras Andis in all but name, Sabae," Bandon said.

"Any idea why the mystery cultists wanted me prisoner?" Sabae asked. "Were they hoping for a ransom, or?…"

Bandon shrugged. "I honestly have no idea. That seems as likely of an explanation as any other, but…"

"What about my family?" Avah asked.

"They're fine," Bandon said. "Still trapped at the docks like every other ship that was here or has been arriving, but no one seems to want to lay any of the blame on them."

No one else seemed to have anything to say. Eventually, Bandon awkwardly took his leave, making sure to remind them that there was nothing they could do, and not to go anywhere.

They all sat silently for some time after that. Talia angrily stared out the window. Godrick repetitively sculpted a lump of stone between his hands. Hugh sat and stared down at the cultist's necklace. Avah repeatedly trying to start conversations, only to stop talking almost before the words were out of her mouth.

Sabae sighed and stood up.

"Bandon's wrong," she said.

Everyone looked at her. Well, most everyone— Hugh just kept staring at the necklace in his hands. He was probably in one of his funks again— Sabae would have to try her best to pull him out of it later. Or, at the very least, offer what kindness he'd accept from her.

If Talia wasn't so angry at everything right now, she'd probably have better luck. Talia might be perpetually belligerent towards the world, but somehow she was always the best of them at dealing with Hugh's moods, and she seemed to know instinctively when Hugh just needed a friend or when he needed a kick to the shin.

"About what?" Avah asked.

"About there being nothing we can do," Sabae said. "It seems to me that we're about the only ones out there who really want to help Alustin other than Bandon, and he's not enough. We need to try and prove that he's not behind the theft of the egg or the poisoning."

"And how do you expect us to do that?" Talia asked. "We're just a bunch of teenagers, and we can't even leave this rat's nest."

Sabae stared at her for a moment, then she turned to Hugh. "Hugh, toss me some chalk?" Hugh always had chalk on him for wards.

Hugh didn't look at her, but he dug into his beltpouch for a stick of chalk and tossed it to her.

"Alright, so let's write down what we know," Sabae said. "First off: suspects. We've got a mystery cult infiltrating the city, and presumably they want to seize it for their patron, who I'm guessing is some sort of giant intelligent insect or something, judging by their necklaces." She wrote *mystery cult* on the wall in chalk.

"If they're behind poisoning Indris, the motivation is pretty clear— they want their patron to take over the city, and poisoning her is a clear move in that direction. That being said, I have no idea why they haven't moved yet or why they would have stolen the egg. Or why they want me alive."

"Next, we've got..." she hesitated here for a moment, then wrote *Ras Andis* on the board. "The city of Ras Andis and my family. I'm fairly confident that they aren't behind this for a few reasons— we're still recovering our strength after the Blue Death, we've never had any sort of expansionist policy in the past, and I don't think grandmother would move against the city if they knew I was here. No idea why they'd want to steal the egg, either."

"If yer family was behind the mystery cult," Godrick said, "They might have ordered them ta get yeh out of the way."

"That's… possible," Sabae admitted. "But I don't think they would have ordered your deaths. Grandmother wouldn't have sent the book of stormwards to Hugh if she didn't think of him as something of an investment already, and I'm sure she's already looking for uses for the rest of you."

"Except me, of course," Avah said.

"I'm sure she'll start trying to find a use for you if she ever hears about you," Sabae admitted.

Sabae moved a little farther down the wall. This time, she hesitated even longer, but finally wrote *Alustin* on the wall.

"Alustin didn't do it!" Talia said immediately, almost shouting.

"Even if he did," Sabae started, but Talia interrupted again, looking like she was about ready to fight.

"He didn't!"

"Even if he did it," Sabae continued, "do you know what I'd want to do then?"

Talia just glared.

"I'd say we'd either frame someone else or break him out of prison," Sabae said. "Alustin matters a hell of a lot more to me than Indris does."

Talia opened her mouth to reply, but then she shut it again. Her gaze softened, and she nodded. "That's alright then, I suppose."

"And if it's your family?" Avah asked.

"They matter a hell of a lot more to me than Indris does too," Sabae said. "I'd hope you'd all side with me if we need to act against Indris' government to break Alustin out, but I can't ask you to do the same if it's my family."

Avah shook her head. "I can't risk getting anyone mad at the Radhan. If you end up turning against the city, I'm staying out of it. And you know you all have no chance against an entire city, right?"

"That's fair," Sabae said. "And with things as they are now, I wouldn't be surprised if the government and the dragon cult are falling into confusion, so I highly doubt we'd be facing any significant resistance in breaking Alustin out."

"Of course ah'm with yeh," Godrick said. "Ah mean, ah sure hope we don't have ta go against Theras Tel, but if we need to, we're with yeh."

Talia nodded. "Just point me at what you want me to wreck."

Hugh looked up long enough to catch Sabae's eye, then he nodded at her before looking back down at his lap.

"So what's the case against Alustin?" Talia asked.

"First," Sabae said, "Kanderon and Indris have butted heads before, and likely the only reason it hasn't come to actual blows is probably Kanderon having to work with the rest of the Skyhold administration. Given that Alustin is her most trusted agent, it gives him a definite motive, if Kanderon has decided to make a move."

"And Alustin's definitely here on a mission," Talia noted. "We've known that much for a while."

"Second," Sabae said, as she wrote in chalk on the wall, "is the fact that there are actually witnesses in the palace claiming he was there at the appropriate time."

"Couldn't an illusionist have just mimicked Alustin's appearance?" Talia asked. "Bandon copied his own appearance easily enough."

"It's supposed ta be much harder ta copy someone else's look," Godrick said. "Somethin' about anchorin' the illusion ta the actual image, or it looks like a bad paintin'. Even turnin' invisible is much easier."

"So possible, not probable," Sabae said, noting it down.

"And what would Alustin or Kanderon want with a dragon egg?" Talia asked.

"That's up in the air too," admitted Sabae. "So far as I can tell, there doesn't appear to be any motive for stealing the egg for any party. Plus, that's what interfered with Indris' poisoning."

"There is a piece of evidence against Alustin being the culprit," Avah said. "Normally when Indris and Ataerg are having another clutch of eggs, they make a huge announcement about it, and Indris throws a festival in Theras Tel. She didn't this time. So far as I know, there was no public announcement about the egg at all."

"How's that evidence against Alustin?" Godrick asked.

"I'm guessing that Indris knew there was a threat to her egg, which is why she hid it away," Avah said. "If she had an idea of what the threat was, and it had been Alustin, don't you think the meeting with her you told me about would have gone very, very differently?"

"What about the message Alustin got from that dragon?" Godrick asked. "How does that fit in? And what would Kanderon and Alustin have ta do with the mystery cult?"

No one had an answer to Godrick's questions. Everyone just stared at the suspect list.

"Can anyone think of any other suspects?" Sabae finally asked.

"Eudaxus," Talia said immediately.

"Why would Eudaxus poison Indris or steal her egg?" Avah asked. "He's in charge of her cult."

"It's always the High Priest that's guilty in novels," Talia said. "Plus, have you seen that nose? No decent person could have a nose that big."

Everyone except Hugh just stared at her.

"Does anyone else have anything to add?" Sabae asked, not adding Eudaxus' name to the list.

"I do," Hugh said, finally looking up.

Everyone looked at him in surprise.

"I think I know who the mystery cult is worshipping," Hugh said.

CHAPTER TWENTY

INVISIBLE LADDER

ALUSTIN Haber, Librarian Errant of Skyhold and chief agent of Kanderon Crux, the Crystal Sphinx herself, was feeling quite talkative.

This wasn't unusual for Alustin, but it was rather unusual for a prisoner in Indris' dungeons. Normally, the jailers had to work quite hard to convince prisoners to talk.

Alustin, however, they couldn't get to shut up.

A big part of that came from the fact that he was imprisoned in the mage cells. They couldn't casually enter his cell to kick him around a little bit, since breaking the seal on his cage would give him a chance to refill his mana reservoirs and escape.

The cages didn't block the aether entirely— nothing could do that. Nor would they last for more than a couple of weeks before needing to be replaced. But they were enough to keep most mages imprisoned for a time, at least.

It was usually much easier to kill a mage than to imprison them.

Killing Alustin was out of the option, as was leaving him unguarded. So Indris' jailers had the dubious pleasure of listening to Alustin ramble on about whatever subject interested him at any given moment.

The jailers often woke prisoners up repeatedly throughout the night to keep them tired and suggestible, but they'd even stopped doing that with Alustin— every time they'd tried it, they'd end up getting a multiple hour lecture immediately.

As Eudaxus entered the jail, the topic today seemed to be agricultural uses of magic in Highvale, specifically in relation to crafting and maintaining terraces in their steep valleys.

"Ah, Eudaxus!" Alustin said, looking surprisingly cheerful. "Come to join our lecture?"

Eudaxus wanted to snarl at the man. He wanted to kill him and feed him to his queen. He'd considered Alustin a friend, despite his status as Kanderon's pawn, and to be repaid like this was betrayal of the worst sort.

"I'm giving you a chance to talk, Alustin," Eudaxus said. "I highly advise you to take it."

"I am talking," Alustin said. "About agricultural magic. It's a surprisingly interesting topic."

"Why does a battlemage even need to know about..." Eudaxus stopped himself. He was not going to let Alustin get him off topic today.

"I want to know where you hid the egg, and what you used to poison Indris," Eudaxus said.

"I did neither," Alustin said, "Though I did once have to carry a hatching hydra egg through ten miles of snake infested jungle. That wasn't much fun."

Aggravatingly, Alustin was probably telling the truth about that one.

"Tell us how to access the hidden extraplanar pockets of your bag," Eudaxus said. By their best guess, the egg was still in Alustin's shoulder bag— it was famous in certain circles for being able to store massive amounts inside, and it was supposed to have been a gift from Kanderon. Eudaxus had heard a story of Alustin hiding an entire wagon in there once.

"It's just a bag," Alustin said. "Nothing magical about it." He smiled broadly at Eudaxus.

The high priest prided himself on his ability to tell when people were lying to him, but he couldn't get the slightest read on Alustin right now. He'd played cards with Alustin before, and had never had any trouble picking out all of his tells and easily winning. Had that all been just a bluff? Though, to think of it, being bad at cards was probably more useful to a spy than being good at them.

"Alustin, I can only hold off those who want your head for so long," Eudaxus said. "I might be able to convince Indris to merely exile you from the city and the desert if we've recovered the egg by the time she's healed. I don't believe you had anything to do with the poisoning— I think your theft just got caught up at a bad time. I'm trying to help you, my friend."

Eudaxus actually was sure of nothing of the sort, but his first priority wasn't punishing Indris' poisoner. That could wait until after he'd recovered the egg.

Even with all the drama and intrigue this particular egg had already caused.

Alustin just smiled and shook his head. "Anyhow, most of the slopes in Highvale are far too steep to water crops on— it would just result in extensive topsoil erosion. The terraces they've constructed instead…"

Eudaxus snarled at his one-time-friend, then he turned and stalked away.

Hugh blushed as everyone kept staring at him. "At least, I know how to find out," he said.

"How?" Avah said.

"I've seen these before," Hugh said, holding up the necklace. "In Galvachren's Bestiary. There was an illustration of one in it."

"What is it?" Sabae asked.

"I… uh, don't actually remember what it is," Hugh said. "Just that it was in the Bestiary."

"That doesn't help us much, does it?" Godrick asked. "Yeh left yer copy at Skyhold, cause it weighs as much as Talia does." He glanced at her and grinned. "Not, yeh know, that she weighs that much."

Talia punched him in the side.

"I distinctly remember running into a copy in one of the bookstores we've visited here," Hugh said.

"Do you remember the specific bookstore you saw it in?" Avah asked.

"I… think I do. At least, I remember the general neighborhood," Hugh said. He was fairly sure he could find it again.

"So… we're supposed to sneak into a city under martial law to find a book you casually encountered at a bookstore that you may or may not remember the location of?" Sabae asked.

Hugh paused for a moment, then nodded. "Uhhhh… yeah, basically."

They'd forgotten at least one major difficulty to the whole thing—Bandon had left the ladder invisible, and they had no way to fix that.

So they had to climb an invisible ladder.

Hugh desperately tried not to look down. He wasn't afraid of heights, but climbing an invisible ladder with nothing underneath him for at least a mile was *not* okay.

The fact that the wind had picked up didn't help either.

With every single step upwards he took, Hugh carefully felt upwards for the next rung. Several times he jammed a finger into the underside of rungs.

Eventually, he made it to the top of the ladder. He spent several seconds just sprawled out on the top catching his breath, then he turned to help Avah up.

"That was the absolute worst thing ever," Avah said.

In the end, they'd decided to just send Hugh and Avah. Everyone else was too distinctive in appearance— Godrick's size, Talia's hair and tattoos, and Sabae's scars. Talia had been furious about having to wait in the cliff dwelling, but in the end, she'd... mostly seen reason. She had insisted that Hugh bring her magic dagger.

Things were still obviously tense, but not as bad as they had been. The swarming dragons were still winging about the city searching for the missing egg or watching over their mother, but they weren't flying about roaring in panic any longer. People were actually moving out and about a bit, though there still weren't a ton of them moving around near the cliff dwellings.

That number increased marginally as they reached the top of the cliff and entered the streets, but it was still far, far quieter than Hugh was used to Theras Tel being.

They'd only gone a couple of blocks when Avah reached out to grab Hugh's hand. Despite everything going on, Hugh couldn't help but grin at her. Sabae had specifically warned them that this did not count as a date, and not to act like it.

Talia, of all people, had thought that a covert mission in a city under martial law sounded like a good date idea, though she'd seemed oddly grumpy about it.

Actually, in retrospect, that sort of made sense to Hugh. He'd never seen Talia express any sort of romantic interest before, but he was pretty sure that anyone who attracted Talia's interest would have to be at least as insane as she was.

Avah grinned back at Hugh, then she gave him a mock serious look. "This isn't a date, it's just… camouflage. We're camouflaging ourselves as teenagers on a date."

Hugh was pretty sure that a lot of his better mood was due to Avah, but just as much of it was from him actually *doing* something. He'd been miserable just sitting around doing nothing while their teacher was being held in prison.

They'd talked over everything that could go wrong for hours, but one possibility that the four of them had never discussed was, well, nothing going wrong. A few passing guards glanced at them curiously, but never tried to stop them.

An even greater surprise was that Hugh easily found the bookstore, and it was actually open.

"Well, I live upstairs, and you're here, so it's clearly not a waste of my time," the shopkeeper said, putting down her own book. She kept court in the bookstore from a massive old armchair and footrest with books sticking out from the sides of the cushions.

Hugh had trouble arguing with that logic.

Galvachren's Bestiary cost him quite a lot— enough that Avah cracked a joke about the shopkeeper charging by weight. The old woman just snorted at that.

The way back was just as easy. No one followed them, and hardly anyone looked at them. A few people eyed them curiously as they went down the ladders and stairs of the cliff face, but nothing more than that.

In fact, the only really difficult part of the trip was climbing down the invisible ladder with the book. They ended up having to send Godrick up to do it— he was the only one who could carry the immense tome one-handed, and his stone affinity sense meant he didn't need to be able to see the ladder.

Of course, Hugh was then faced with the problem of finding the entry in question.

Galvachren, whoever he was, had enchanted all the copies of his book to update whenever he updated his master copy. Over the years, it had apparently grown in size massively, and entries were perpetually moving about and being edited.

It took hours to find the entry in question. It didn't help that the others kept getting distracted by other entries— the one on the Living Eclipse, a sunbeast the size of a ship that supposedly lived in the depths of the Endless Erg, especially caught Avah's attention. She insisted on reading the whole thing, just in case.

Eventually, however, Hugh tracked it down. The drawing looked almost identical to the necklace— a curious scarab/mantis hybrid.

> ***Issen-Derin:*** *These insects have only been encountered a few times in the history of the Ithonian continent. No one is entirely sure where they came from— they certainly don't seem natural. While the individual members of a hive aren't overly imposing, they reproduce and grow at an absolutely terrifying rate. A single queen can grow an army of tens of thousands of drones in mere months. Issen-Derin queens are highly intelligent, making them even more threatening of a foe. They're only naturally known to be found in labyrinths, but a few times in history they have escaped those unusual ecosystems. When uncontained, they reproduce and consume until they completely collapse the biomes they find themselves in, usually quickly dying off themselves. Despite the intelligence of the queens, this fate has proven universal to Issen-Derin hives.*
>
> *Their queens usually establish their hives underground, raiding aboveground for food. Issen-Derin consume nearly anything organic, from fungus to wood to meat.*
>
> *Two centuries before the fall of the Ithonian Empire, a major Issen-Derin outbreak occurred during the middle of a rebellion of one of Ithos' territories. The rebels, who had actually been winning, at least temporarily, set aside their grievances to unite forces with the Ithonians to stamp out the Issen-Derin. Despite the rebel forces being too badly damaged in the extermination to continue the rebellion, the Ithonian Emperor actually granted them limited self-rule in gratitude, something unique in Ithonian history.*

The entry continued on for several more paragraphs, detailing further incidents of outbreaks. The general idea was clear, however— if you didn't crack down on an outbreak immediately and aggressively, Issen-Derin swarms could be absolutely devastating.

And, assuming the cultist's necklaces actually meant they were worshipping an Issen-Derin queen…

"We need to tell someone about this. *Now*," Sabae said.

CHAPTER TWENTY-ONE

UNFORTUNATE TIMING

"I HATE this plan," Talia said.

"You hate every plan that involves waiting," Sabae said.

"No, I hate every plan that involves me waiting while others take all the risk," Talia said. "I'm fine with waiting if I'm trying to ambush someone."

"I hate this plan too," Hugh said.

"It was yer idea in the first place," Godrick said.

Hugh just kept pacing back and forth across the cliff dwelling.

They'd sent Avah to go find and bring the ripped out page of Galvachren's Bestiary bearing the information on the Issen-Derin to Bandon. It made the most sense— Avah was the only one of them not being hunted by the guards, and unlike before, Hugh wouldn't be able to go with her, since there would be no way to avoid attention while actively looking for a guard captain.

It had been hours since Avah had left, and Hugh had been pacing almost the entire time. There really wasn't that much else to do in the cliff dwelling safehouse— it was that or read through the Bestiary, which Godrick and Sabae had been doing for a couple hours now.

"Oooh, look at this one!" Sabae said to Godrick. "It's a mile long catfish!"

"That can't be real," Godrick said.

"It says here it is," Sabae said, jabbing a finger at the book.

"Ah thought of a name for yer jumpin' spell, by the way," Godrick said.

"What's that?" Sabae asked.

"Windjumpin'," Godrick said.

"That's not exactly very creative," Sabae said.

"Accurate, though," Hugh said.

"I hear someone coming," Talia said.

"Is it Avah?" Hugh asked.

"Not unless she turned into at least a dozen people wearing armor," Talia said.

Sabae and Godrick scrambled to their feet, and Godrick readied his warhammer. They were ready for a fight, but they weren't at all expecting to see Eudaxus appear, not at the entrance, but at the window.

On the back of a dragon that was clinging to the cliff.

"I strongly suggest you stand down, children," the elderly high priest said.

Hugh glanced at Sabae. She hesitated for a moment, then nodded.

"Your girlfriend sold us out," Talia hissed at Hugh.

"She did not," Hugh hissed back. "She wouldn't do that."

They might be in training to be battlemages, but there really wasn't much they could do against a dragon yet— especially not when the dragon had had them pinned down in a room without any other exits.

So they'd gone with Eudaxus. The soldiers were escorting them through the city streets to the palace, with the dragon walking just behind them. The walk had taken twice as long as it should have, thanks to the need to avoid both rubble and Indris' impact site. Eudaxus had sent a dragon cultist messenger ahead of them to prepare prison cells for them.

"The Radhan girl didn't even mention any of you," Eudaxus said. "You were foolish enough to send her with a page from Galvachren's Bestiary, rather than the whole thing. The page retained a magical link to the rest of the book, which my cult's mages were able to track back to you. We might not have been after her, but we were certainly aware of your affiliation with her. Now, if you please, answer my question."

"We told you," Sabae said, "We found that safehouse on our own. No one showed it to us."

"Your little Radhan friend came looking for Captain Bandon," Eudaxus said. "It's quite obvious he's the one who helped you, I just want to know why."

"My grandmother has a name for people who prefer to believe their own stories over reality," Sabae said.

"Is your grandmother supporting these attacks on Theras Tel?" Eudaxus asked.

"Is the name your grandmother has for them idiot?" Talia asked.

"It's like you know her without having met her," Sabae said.

"My mother calls them the same thing," Talia said. "Though with a lot more cursing."

"Honestly," Sabae said, "There's quite a bit of cursing involved with my grandmother, too."

"*Enough*, children. Quit attempting to distract me and answer my questions."

"Which questions?" Godrick asked.

"What do you mean, which questions?" Eudaxus demanded.

"Ah wasn't really paying attention," Godrick said, "on account of the dragon."

Hugh desperately tried not to laugh as Eudaxus spluttered. He was absolutely terrified, and he was fairly sure his friends were too, but when Eudaxus had refused to listen to their pleas about the Issen-Derin, instead repeatedly interrogating them about Alustin, they'd swiftly responded by acting like this. Hugh had mostly stayed quiet, but the others more than made up the difference. He sort of understood why they were doing it—it definitely made him feel a little more confident, and it clearly did the same for them.

It was a brittle sort of confidence, though.

"We'll see how funny this is when you're all locked up separately from one another," Eudaxus said.

"How funny is it going to be when giant insects devour the city?" Sabae asked.

"There are no Issen-Derin in the undertunnels," Eudaxus insisted again. "It's quite apparent that Kanderon, your family, or both are acting against us. The necklaces are a trick to keep our eyes off the real threat."

"And who's the real threat supposed to be?" Sabae asked.

"That's what you're going to tell me soon, girl," Eudaxus said.

"I think the real threat is you deserving my grandmother's insults," Sabae said.

"I've had enough of this," Eudaxus said, turning red in the face. "If you're not going to answer my questions, be silent."

None of them said anything after that.

There were, to Eudaxus' apparent surprise, several high ranking dragon cultists awaiting them at the entrance to the palace. With them was a cult mage covered in fresh bandages. His robes had even more rips in them than he did.

Eudaxus quickly strode over to confer with the others. As they spoke, Eudaxus' face grew more and more concerned, several times shooting glances back at them.

While they waited, Hugh inspected the palace. The damage Indris had done when she burst out of it was more than he'd expected— chunks of masonry littered the courtyard in front of the wall, and one of the two dragon statues was missing its head.

"Something's happened," Sabae said.

"Obviously," Talia said.

The high priest began sending guardsmen out on errands. It was several minutes before he was done. When he was, however, he sighed heavily, then trudged over to them.

"It seems," Eudaxus said, "that I owe you not only an apology, but an admission that I am, in fact, indeed an idiot. The Issen-Derin have been found in the tunnels below Theras Tel."

Sabae gave him a serious look. "I think that admission might at least disqualify you from being a *complete* idiot."

Things got very busy after that. Hugh and the others were bustled from meeting to meeting to discuss the two ambushes they'd suffered, though taking Sabae's lead, none of them mentioned Bandon in the second. The various rooms they were taken to had varying levels of damage to them— one even had an unplanned new window looking straight into a washroom.

The assembled guardsmen and cultists, however, didn't seem to notice the omission— most of their interest seemed to be in the armaments and mages of the Issen-Derin cultists. The fact that they were largely using spears and crossbows was apparently quite encouraging— both were weapons that could be used with relatively little training, indicating that the enemy cultists didn't have a great amount of military expertise on their side. The number and quality of mages they had weren't especially impressive, either.

That somewhat deflated Hugh's own opinion of their victories.

It was obvious that Eudaxus very much noticed the omission of Bandon from the story. Curiously, he seemed to be helping them deflect the conversation away from Bandon.

To Hugh's relief, Eudaxus had given orders for Avah to be escorted back to the *Moonless Owl.* She'd probably be safer there than anywhere in the city right now.

It wasn't entirely clear if the four of them were guests or prisoners. They were treated politely, and well fed, but Hugh couldn't help but notice that there were guards on them at all times, and Talia's daggers and Godrick's hammer had been confiscated.

And, on top of that, their pleas on behalf of Alustin— even their requests to talk to him— were all summarily denied.

CHAPTER TWENTY-TWO

BELLS

Alustin was, despite all appearances to the contrary, extraordinarily upset about being in prison.

He was rather good at contrary appearances.

It wasn't that Alustin wasn't an eccentric, slightly excitable scholar with a love of both learning and sharing that learning— he most certainly was— but he'd found that exaggerating those aspects of his personality tended to be quite disarming. Even those who knew of his duties to Kanderon Crux and what he was capable of often underestimated him when he began rambling on about forest husbandry in Tsarnassus.

Though, honestly, he did find it slightly perplexing that people didn't find Tsarnassian forestry management more interesting. It was one of the major reasons why they were one of the wealthiest nations on Ithos, as well as being the main reason that they didn't have the same soil erosion and flooding problems as many of their neighbors.

His current guards were prime examples of this. One had even begged him to stop talking about it.

Alustin hadn't paid the slightest bit of attention to the begging. This was, in large part, because he had much better things to pay attention to than his surroundings.

Most people believed that farseers had to close their eyes and focus silently to use the gift, and for most farseers, that was true— it was too hard to sort out the competing images otherwise.

For Alustin, however, it wasn't a problem. It was just a matter of multitasking, and that was his specialty. He could ramble on about whatever topic he wanted for hours while barely paying attention to it.

It had taken nearly a day to figure out how to scry from inside the mage prison— it was a well-built one, to be certain, but there was no such thing as a perfect mage prison.

Of course, then he'd had to find a way to defeat the wards against scrying in the prison, but they were more intended to keep people from scrying in than out— a major flaw, in Alustin's mind.

Once he'd figured out how to get past the prison and the wards, he'd begun scrying non-stop, save for his need to sleep.

One of the weaknesses of farseeing— at least the farseeing attunement Alustin possessed— was its inability to carry anything but images. It was, in fact, a variant of the standard light attunement. There were mages with attunements that let them scry sounds over long distances— usually related to wind or sound attunements, as his was to light— but they couldn't scry images. The mage who possessed both types of scrying attunement was far rarer and more valued than any battlemage.

Alustin had considered attempting to develop the other type of scrying attunement, but he ultimately decided it was easier to learn to read lips.

So much of what had been going on in Theras Tel was utterly baffling, but Alustin was starting to piece them together. Kanderon had sent him to Theras Tel for many reasons— the sphinx never had just a single motivation for anything she did, and Alustin doubted he understood half of them this time.

Alustin couldn't help but feel proud of his students. They'd done remarkably well for themselves so far in a situation way over their heads. Not, unfortunately, as well as Alustin would have liked, but…

Alustin ran his attention over the troops marching down into the undertunnels. Apparently the reason they'd been unable to find the Issen-Derin cult for so long had been due to a truly clever choice of hiding place. Rather than picking a secluded, out of the way place, they'd somehow managed to infiltrate one of the most secure regions of the city— the great underground water reservoirs directly beneath the palace itself.

Alustin found what he was looking for rapidly. Directions through the maze-like (though definitely not labyrinth-like) tunnels below Theras Tel to the reservoirs were carefully guarded, and, unlike stories about farseers, they couldn't simply view whatever they wanted at will. They either had to search it out or be quite familiar with it.

Most of the city guardsmen had never been to the reservoirs either, and so directions would need to be shared. Alustin could follow those to find the reservoirs.

They made it easy for him— they'd brought maps of the tunnels with them. He quickly memorized the layouts, sending his vision winding through the tunnels until he reached the reservoirs. The insect cultists were supposed to be in one of the lower, half empty reservoirs, camped along its edges.

Oh. Oh, that wasn't good.

Alustin withdrew his vision from the reservoir, sending them instead into the depths of the palace.

Well, that was even worse.

Several things fell into place in Alustin's mind all at once, and he rapidly sent his vision ranging northwest across the Endless Erg.

The guards were rather shocked when Alustin stopped lecturing them about the stages of a Tsarnassian forest's growth cycle after a forest fire and started cursing like a dockworker.

They were even more shocked when he pulled a sabre covered in spellforms out of midair and hacked through the cage's lock in a single blow.

When the sword vanished again and thousands of pages of paper came flying, so far as they could tell, out of Alustin's right hand, well, it didn't seem likely that they could get *that* much more shocked, yet they accomplished it.

The paper wrapping and suffocating them into unconsciousness still managed to surprise them the most, somehow.

The apprentices had, as the preparations for battle continued, been relegated to some sort of diplomatic waiting room in the heart of the palace. There was only a single door and no windows, with guards both inside and outside the door. They didn't look pleased to have been left out of the upcoming battle.

There was, at least, an amply supplied buffet table. The rations in the safehouse had been less than appealing.

Hugh was staring at the door when it happened. A large, unsealed envelope came sliding underneath. The guards started, then one leaned down to pick it up. The other guard leaned over to look.

The instant the first guard opened it, several sheets of paper flew straight out and plastered themselves to the guards' faces.

The guards promptly began cursing and trying to pull the pages off, but the paper somehow molded even closer to their faces. Within seconds their cursing had turned to muffled noises of panic.

Not long after that, they crumpled to the ground. As soon as they did so, Alustin strode into the room, smiling broadly.

"You know, I used to find it disturbing how often guards fall for the mysterious letter under the door trick, but it honestly gets funnier every time now."

The apprentices all stared at him in shock.

"Are… are they…" Hugh began.

"They're still alive," Alustin said. "Just unconscious."

"You're a paper mage?" Talia asked, incredulous. "You can't be a paper mage, they can't be battlemages!"

Alustin just raised an eyebrow at her. "It wasn't too long ago that none of you thought you could be battlemages, either. And I did mention that no one thought I could be a battlemage, didn't I?"

Talia started to respond, but Alustin shook his head. "Questions later. For now, we have work to do."

"Work to…" Sabae started, but Alustin just kept talking. As he did so, he stuck his arm into midair, where it promptly vanished.

"Godrick, Talia, I'm going to need the two of you to gain access to the main valves for the palace water pumps and make sure nobody does anything with them until further notice. In a little over an hour, dragon cultists are going to try and flood the lower reservoirs. They've already seized the valve controls, so you'll need to find a way to get past them. You need to stop them however you can."

"Wait, what?" Godrick said.

"Sabae, I need you and Hugh to get to the *Moonless Owl* as fast as humanly possible. We've got maybe an hour, hour and a half before a sandstorm hits, and if we don't shield the city in time it's going to wreck half of Theras Tel. I've already sent an origami golem to let Captain Solon to know to be ready to sail the instant you get there."

"I'm not my grandmother," Sabae said. "I can't just shield an entire city like that."

"No, that's Hugh's job," Alustin said.

Hugh spluttered. "How am I supposed to do that?"

"You're going to ward it," Alustin said, pulling his arm back out of midair, holding a sheet of paper. Hugh noticed a spellform tattoo glowing bright blue on Alustin's arm— the exact blue of Kanderon's wings— that rapidly faded into invisibility.

"How'd you do that?" Talia demanded.

Alustin glanced at his arm. "Oh, Kanderon gave me that. Tattooed an extradimensional storage space onto my arm. I just let people think my bag is the extradimensional storage space."

"Wait, go back to the part where I'm supposed to ward an entire city from a sandstorm in an hour," Hugh said.

"Less than an hour once you get to the *Owl.* And you'll basically be warding the city just like you warded the ship during the sandstorm. Same ward and everything."

Alustin flicked the paper towards Godrick, and it gently drifted to the air towards him, coming to a stop a foot in front of his face. "Here's a map of the palace, with routes to the main valves marked on it." Alustin promptly stuck his hand back into the air.

Hugh stared at him in shock. "It took an entire ship's worth of mages just to power that ward through the storm!"

"That's where Sabae comes in," Alustin said, pulling out the magic dagger that Eudaxus had confiscated from Talia and tossing it to her. "She's going to show you some Kaen Das family secrets."

"I'm going to *what*?" Sabae said.

"How am I supposed to draw the ward around an entire city?" Hugh asked. "I don't have nearly enough chalk or time!"

"Kanderon did tell you that your crystal affinity would be useful for wards, didn't she? Add that in with your ability to imbue your will into wards, and we're golden."

"That..." Hugh started, then stopped, frantically trying to understand what Alustin was saying.

"This map is pointing out quite a lot of defenses on the way to the valve controls," Talia said.

"I'm sure you'll figure out some clever way to completely circumvent them that doesn't involve excessive violence and explosions," Alustin said.

Talia gave him a flat look.

Alustin pulled Godrick's sledgehammer out of the extradimensional space with a look of strain on his face, and didn't try to toss it. He merely set it on the ground in front of him. Godrick reached his hand out, and the hammer flew into it.

Hugh's mind was racing frantically. He thought he knew what Alustin was suggesting, and he was fairly sure it would work, but even just for laying the ward, Hugh wasn't sure he would have enough mana in his reservoirs. The whole thing would have to be miles long without a single break or error. He could repeat the pattern, but that still didn't give them a power source for the ward even if he could manage to...

"No," said Sabae flatly.

Alustin looked at her, seeming surprised. "Pardon?"

"I said no," Sabae said. "We're not doing anything until you explain what's going on."

"We really don't have time for..." Alustin began.

Sabae crossed her arms. Hugh looked uncertainly at her, then at the others.

"I just need you to trust me for long enough to pull this off, and then I'll explain everything" Alustin said. "Do you think I'd lie to you?"

"Yes," Sabae said.

"Yep," Talia said.

"Definitely," Godrick said.

"I mean, it wouldn't be the first time," Hugh said.

Alustin looked vaguely offended for a moment, but then he seemed to consider for a moment and shrugged. "I suppose that's fair. Alright, very, very quick version: Ataerg is leading his half of his and Indris' brood in an attack on the city, and they've raised and harnessed a sandstorm to do so. A lot of Indris' brood has abandoned her to join him as well. There never was a second cult, it was a rift within Theras Tel's dragon cult, with who knows how many of them covertly joining Ataerg. They were the ones who poisoned Indris and stole her egg, and they're the ones who falsely reported the Issen-Derin below the city in order to lure the army down there so they could release the upper reservoirs into the lower chambers and drown the Indris loyalists marching against the imaginary Issen-Derin cultists. I've already sent origami golem letters alerting Eudaxus and other influential members of Indris' government, but we can't count on them believing me."

Everyone stared at him in shock.

"Admittedly, everything past the bit with the reservoir and the fact that Ataerg and his half of the dragon brood are attacking the city and bringing a sandstorm behind them is pure speculation," Alustin said.

"How do we know that you're even telling the truth about..." Sabae began, when she was interrupted by the noise of bells ringing.

"And that'd be the sandstorm, right on schedule," Alustin said. "Do you believe me now?"

"So much of this still makes no sense whatsoever," Sabae said.

"It does explain why the fake cultists were trying to capture you," Hugh said. "They must have been worried your presence meant your family intended to interfere."

"And why they delayed until you were in custody," Alustin continued. "They were worried you'd interfere with the storm. The instant you were captured, they kicked off their plans."

"Which means that Ataerg's plan was always ta wreck Theras Tel, not ta conquer it," Godrick said.

"And it definitely explains how they framed you for the theft of the egg," Sabae said to Alustin. "The traitor cultists didn't even need to find an illusionist that could copy you, they could just lie and say they'd seen you, which threw everything into confusion. It still doesn't explain exactly why they wanted the egg, though— if they hadn't tried to steal it, Indris would already be dead. It's a gaping flaw in their plan."

"Honestly, I'm not entirely sure why they would be motivated to steal the egg," Alustin said. "If they hadn't, though, things would be much, much worse. I still don't understand why Ataerg would turn against Indris after all these years, either. We've still got a chance to keep Theras Tel from collapsing, but only if we *get a move on, please.*"

Sabae stared at him for a moment, then nodded. "We'll do it."

Alustin smiled broadly. "Excellent!" He turned and started walking out of the room.

"What are you going to be doing?" Hugh asked.

Alustin turned back to face them, but kept walking out of the room. "I'm going to slay a dragon!"

They all silently stared at the empty door Alustin had just left through for a moment before Talia spoke.

"He does know that dragons breathe fire, right? And that paper doesn't do so well against fire?"

CHAPTER TWENTY-THREE

TERRIBLE PLANS ALL AROUND

"So how exactly are we supposed to get down to the *Moonless Owl* in time?" Hugh said, panting slightly as they ran down the corridor.

"I've got a plan," Sabae said, sending a gust strike into the chest of a cultist who rounded the corner at a very, very unlucky moment.

"Is it a good plan?" Hugh said

"It's actually something of a terrible plan," Sabae admitted.

"I don't suppose there's a backup plan that's better?" Hugh asked. He sent his quartz crystal shooting like a punch into the stomach of another cultist down the hall, who promptly started vomiting.

"The backup plan is catch a dragon and try to ride it," Sabae said, dodging past the vomiting cultist.

"Ah. No, I think I like the first plan," Hugh said. "What's the first plan?"

"Well, you know how all the streets in Theras Tel tend to be twisty and windy and full of switchbacks?" Sabae asked.

Hugh just nodded cautiously.

"Well, there is one route that's more direct," Sabae said, as they burst out of a door into a courtyard.

"What's that?" Hugh asked.

Sabae just pointed upwards. For a moment, Hugh had no idea what she was talking about until he realized what she was pointing at.

The aqueducts.

"The dragon's already sounding better and better," Hugh said.

"So how are we going ta get in past the defenses?" Godrick asked, as he punched a cultist into a wall. "I really hope yer plan isn't just 'go straight through'."

"Well..."

Godrick stared at Talia in exasperation as they ran past a hallway completely blocked off with rubble from Indris' destructive exit from the palace. "Yer plan is just ta go straight through, isn't it?"

An evil smile crossed Talia's face. "Well, yes, but we're not going straight through the defenses."

"What are we going straight through, then?" Hugh asked.

"The floor," Talia said, coming to a halt in an intersection and pointing at the floor. Godrick glanced at the map, and realized that they were standing directly above the valve chamber.

Godrick stared at her, then he reached out with his affinity senses. "There's too much rock in the way. There's no way ah can get through that much in time."

Talia raised one eyebrow at him. "At this point, your stone affinity is nearly fully attuned, and we won't just be using your stone affinity," she said.

"What do yeh..." Godrick started, then fell silent as Talia manifested a bolt of dreamfire, and sent it hurtling into the floor. A chunk of it the size of his head dissolved into bubbles that floated up into the air before popping.

"That still won't be enough ta make us a hole big enough ta get down in time," Godrick protested.

"It doesn't need to be big enough for us to get down there," Talia said, her smile getting even bigger. She pulled out several shards of bone from her pocket.

"Oh," said Godrick. "Lovely."

Hammet the Diceless was an extraordinarily unlucky man. He lost every game of chance he played. He got assigned all the worst shifts. He'd fallen into Theras Tel's sewers on no less than three occasions. And now he'd been assigned to stay and guard the palace during the first real battle Theras Tel had ever seen during his lifetime.

And now the Skyhold battlemage accused of stealing the queen's egg had burst out of a door right into the courtyard Hammet was stealing a quick smoke break in.

"That's awful for your health, you know," the battlemage said. "Ask any healer about it." A huge swarm of paper started swirling out from his hand.

Hammet frantically grabbed for his sword. He was probably about to die, but he was going to do his duty regardless.

To Hammet's surprise, the paper didn't even approach him. Instead, it swarmed around the battlemage, plastering itself all over his back, and slowly forming some sort of structure…

Hammet blinked, his grasp on his sword loosening involuntarily. The shapes were wings! Four of them, like the ones on the dragonflies you could see in the greenhouses, only longer than the mage was tall!

"Have a nice day, and seriously think about quitting smoking," the battlemage said. The wings started moving at blurring speeds, and he shot upwards into the sky.

"What?" Hammet said.

He must have just stared upwards for a solid minute, when he saw something else.

A teenage girl carrying a terrified looking teenage boy through the air in a massive thirty-foot leap, with her legs surrounded by what looked like miniature cyclones.

The girl slammed feet first into a wall, and the cyclones seemed to explode off her legs, sending the two vaulting even higher. She landed on a nearby roof, then launched upwards once again, coming down for a landing atop a nearby aqueduct, where the two vanished out of sight.

Hammet's pipe fell out of his mouth and broke on the courtyard floor.

As soon as Alustin made it over the palace walls, he promptly dove back down to street level. There was too much risk of one of Indris' loyal dragons spotting him in midair. He wasn't too worried about handling any of them individually, but he simply didn't have time for that— and he definitely didn't have time for a swarm of them.

Alustin couldn't help but survey the damage as he flew. If Indris had just taken the extra thirty seconds to fly out the usual exit, he was sure that dozens of lives would have been saved at the very least, if not more. The damage was greatest close to the palace and towards the midline of the plateau.

It was, Alustin reflected, one of the only times he'd ever seen the wealthier neighborhoods of a city worse-affected by disaster than the poor ones.

He shifted his attention back to scrying Ataerg's oncoming swarm of dragons, then to the sandstorm. They maybe had half an hour before the dragons arrived, and not much more than that before the storm followed in behind them.

Alustin darted around a tight intersection, only to find a Kanderon-sized dragon directly in front of him.

In fairness, it seemed much more surprised to see him than the other way around. It was definitely surprised when he flew between its legs rather than over it, just barely missing hitting its tail on the way past.

It wasn't, sadly, surprised enough not to chase him.

Sabae hadn't learned to use her water affinity to any great degree, and they had no time to build a raft or get any sort of flotation device up into the aqueduct.

So instead, Hugh was casting a levitation cantrip modified to work like a buoyancy spell on them.

This made the aqueduct only slightly less terrifying. The water running through it this close to the palace was comparable in size to a small river back in Emblin, and it was running extremely fast down a very, very steep slope. Not to mention the walls were high enough that he couldn't see anything but the sky overhead.

"Keep us from hitting the walls!" Hugh shouted, as they shot downstream and began drawing close to one wall. They were hugging one another front to front to keep together, which under other circumstances he might have found extremely awkward. Right now, however, he was simply too terrified to care.

Sabae let loose a gust strike at the wall, which succeeded at pushing them away, but also set them to spinning. For a few seconds, Hugh had no idea what was going on as they whirled about, almost sinking underwater even with the buoyancy cantrip.

Thankfully, they stopped spinning fairly quickly.

Hugh really, really hoped the water resistance enchantment on his spellbook worked.

"There's a fork in the aqueduct coming up," Sabae shouted. "I'm going to push us to the right of the channel!"

The aqueducts were an absolute maze of branching channels running throughout the city, like the branching of a bush from the common stem of the palace. Hugh and Sabae hadn't jumped immediately into the water when they'd gotten on top of the aqueduct— they'd spent a few moments trying to memorize the twists and turns that would take them to the harbor.

Sabae let loose another gust strike, this one softer than the last. It still sent them spinning, but they stopped sooner, well in time to watch as they went into the right hand branch of the fork.

"Two lefts next in rapid succession," Hugh shouted. He was already starting to shiver— this water was *cold.*

Sabae sent them left with another gust strike, then even farther left almost immediately after they stopped spinning.

Hugh's stomach was starting to churn, and he was gaining a lot more sympathy for Talia's seasickness.

"Hugh, we've got a problem," Sabae said.

"What?" Hugh said.

"Remember the spot where one channel of the aqueduct went over the other?"

"What about it?" Hugh said, nervousness at her tone of voice adding to the roil in his stomach.

"There's a drain right underneath it," Sabae said. "Hold on tight!"

Hugh frantically tightened his grip onto Sabae as they spun around and the drain came into view. The drains filled the smaller neighborhood reservoirs, and could be open or shut. Unfortunately for them, this one was currently open.

All of a sudden, a massive force seemed to accelerate them upwards, and they actually launched out of the water. Hugh could, to his horror, see straight down the drain as they passed over it before they crashed back down into the current on the other side.

The buoyancy cantrip couldn't stop them from plunging underwater as they came down, and they stayed down for several seconds.

After they came back up, it was at least ten seconds before Hugh could see or talk again.

"There was a turn right after the overhanging channel!" Hugh said, coughing up more water.

"I know!" Sabae said.

"Did we go down the right channel?" Hugh said.

"I'm pretty sure we did!" Sabae said.

"Pretty sure?" Hugh asked.

"Pretty sure!" Sabae said, and sent them shooting off down a left fork.

"Maybe we should get out and check," Hugh said. To his discomfort, the channel was getting much, much narrower.

"We don't exactly have a lot of time," Sabae said, then she launched them down another left fork. "If we did it correctly, we should just have one more left and then we're there!"

Sabae didn't even use a gust strike to correct this one— they were already on the left side of the channel, and it posed a real risk of slamming them into the wall.

Hugh could hear a growing roar of water.

"I really, really hope you're right!" Hugh shouted.

"Me too!" Sabae shouted.

The channel twisted one more time, then vanished ahead of them. Hugh could see for miles and miles across the desert. Hugh really hoped he was imagining it, but it looked like there was a faint smudge on the horizon. Right ahead of them, however, was the drain that dropped a full mile down into the water storage for the port.

"Really, really hold on tight!" Sabae shouted.

Hugh felt a brief moment of vertigo as they began to tip over the edge. Below him, he could see the ships crowded into the harbor, unable to leave while the city was under martial law.

Then Sabae blasted them out of the water and into the air above the harbor.

They immediately began plummeting.

"This isn't going fast enough!" Talia said. "We have no idea when they're going to release the flood into the caverns!"

"We've got time," Godrick said.

"Are you sure, or is that just wishful thinking?" Talia said.

"Little a' both," Godrick admitted.

Despite Talia's complaints, the work was going much faster than Godrick had expected. It had been maybe five minutes, and they were over halfway there.

Still, a little extra speed couldn't go wrong.

"Ah'm going to narrow the spell more," Godrick said. He was using a fairly simple stone-breaking spell focused in a narrow column. It wasn't anything fancy, but it was effective. In combination with Talia's dreamfire, it was making short work of things. And the narrower they drilled, the faster it went.

Godrick wasn't particularly happy about the enhanced sense of smell his scent affinity gave him— the stone the dreamfire destroyed tended to give off a truly awful stench.

Wait a second.

Godrick took another deep sniff, despite the awful smell. "Talia, I smell company."

"You keep at it; I'll fight them off," Talia said. "Which way are they coming from?"

"Not them," Godrick said. "It, and I doubt it will be happy we're drilling a hole in the floor."

The click of large talons on stone became audible over the sound of their drilling.

"You couldn't have waited two minutes longer," Talia muttered, just as the dragon came around the corner. It was a relatively small one— only about thirty-some feet long.

Relatively left a lot of room for getting bit in half.

Talia manifested a rapid sequence of dreamfire bolts, at the dragon, almost before it could react to them. Godrick winced, not really wanting to see any more of what dreamfire did to living flesh.

The dreamfire bolts hit dead on, and the dragon barely flinched. A few of its scales were charred or cracked, but not badly.

The dragon seemed amused more than anything.

"Godrick, dreamfire burns stone, that should have worked. Why didn't it work?"

A low wheezing noise came from the dragon, and after a second Godrick realized that it was chuckling.

"Who could possibly dream of fire burning dragons, little mage?" the dragon said in a deep rasp.

Godrick frantically thought while Talia scrabbled in her beltpouch— if dreamfire wasn't going to work, his hammer wasn't going to do anything, nor would any of his spells be able to punch through…

No. Just because Godrick was big didn't mean he needed to brute force his problems.

"Would you like to see what true fire looks like, little mages?" The dragon visibly inhaled.

Godrick's frantically envisioned a spellform as the dragon inhaled, pumping as much mana as he could into it. Out of the corner of his eye, he saw Talia toss something into the borehole.

The dragon abruptly stopped inhaling, and started trembling.

Then it vomited all over the floor in front of itself.

"What did you do?" Talia asked.

Godrick grabbed her hand and started running. "Ah cast a stink bomb right in its face!"

"Stink mages are the best!" shouted Talia, laughing madly.

"What did yeh do?" he asked Talia.

"I dropped boneshards down the hole, and I'm charging them as we speak!" Talia said, looking immensely proud of herself.

"What did you do to me, little mage?" the dragon demanded, coughing and spitting. It started stalking towards them, clearly distressed. The smell of the stink bomb had started to reach Godrick, and he immediately understood why it had vomited. It was like a skunk had taken offense at a full latrine that had spent a full day in direct sun.

"Ah thought we were going to wait until we drilled all the way through, and drop the bones right into the valve room?" Godrick said. He tried not to show his nervousness— the first time Talia had used her bone affinity, it had saved his life, but it had almost killed him as well.

"Close enough," Talia said.

Godrick glanced back to the dragon, only to see that a spire of bone was growing out of the hole, glowing like iron fresh from the forge from its cracks. The dragon had slowed down and was eyeing the bone spire curiously.

"Talia, yeh might want ta stop pumping mana into it now," Godrick shouted.

As she was turning to look back, the bone started to crack apart, growing even more brightly. Godrick immediately tackled Talia.

They hadn't even hit the ground when the shockwave sent them tumbling. Godrick felt like someone had punched every one of his organs at once, and then he slammed into the ground, Talia on top of him.

Thankfully, it didn't hurt even a fraction as bad as last time.

Godrick groaned, and he slowly opened his eyes. The air of the corridor was filled with dust and smoke, and bone and stone fragments were scattered across the floor. It took a few seconds for Godrick's vision and the dust to clear enough, but the dragon soon came into view as well, lying next to a much-expanded hole in the floor.

Well, the dragon's corpse, at least. A spear of bone had blasted its way through the dragon's skull.

"You know," Talia said, "my oldest brother killed a dragon once."

"Yeah?" Godrick said, groaning a little.

"Apparently after he hit it with a fireball, it said basically the exact same thing to him as well, about true fire and all that," Talia said.

"How'd he kill it?" Godrick asked.

"Cut down a tree with a flame lance. It fell on the dragon and broke its spine."

"Huh."

They both stared at the dragon's corpse for a time.

"It was still alive until he mercy-killed it, and I guess he had some excellent one liner about Clan Castis already knowing true fire," Talia said.

Godrick felt the floor shift underneath him.

"Ah think," Godrick said, "that ah might like his method a' dragon slayin' more."

"Me too," Talia said.

"Do yeh think this one would've even attacked us if yeh hadn't attacked first?"

Godrick felt the floor shift again.

"I might," Talia admitted, "have been a bit too aggressive."

"Ah think Indris might be less then pleased when she finds out we killed one a' her kids," Godrick said.

"You're probably right about that," Talia said.

The floor gave out beneath them.

CHAPTER TWENTY-FOUR

LET SLEEPING DRAGONS LIE

IT took several minutes to shake off the dragon's pursuit— ironically, it had been the dragon taking to the air that had let him get away, as Alustin had immediately darted beneath an aqueduct to get out of sight once it was in the air, then stopped and let the dragon fly ahead.

Alustin slowed a bit as he approached Indris' impact site, scrying ahead of him as he went. There were at least a dozen of Indris' children guarding her as she slept, and over a hundred cultists and guardsmen.

Indris was breathing, but it was still ragged and uneven. Alustin could hear it from blocks away.

For that matter, his own breathing was a little ragged. He'd been in plenty of dangerous situations before, but flying into the middle of a swarm of dragons that suspect you of poisoning their mother and stealing the egg of their youngest sibling?

It was less than optimal.

Alustin hovered for a few moments to gain control of himself, then he raised his altitude and headed straight towards Indris at a steady pace. Go too fast, he might come across as aggressive. Go too slow, he might come across as afraid.

Most of the dragons immediately fixed their attention on him as he flew into the impact site. They were lounged atop buildings, sitting in streets with their tails wrapped around their legs like cats, and several circled in the air above their mother.

The site itself was nothing but wreckage. Indris had skidded and rolled when she impacted the city, annihilating block after block of buildings.

Indris herself looked significantly the worse for wear. The flesh between her scales and the membranes of her wings were a sickly shade, and her chest rose and fell slowly and irregularly. She had several scabbed over wounds from the fall that Alustin could see, and he suspected she had more he couldn't see.

Alustin came to a halt, hovering in the air. "Eudaxus," he called.

No one responded for a long moment. Finally, Alustin spotted Eudaxus' bald head making his way out of a crowd of cultists.

Alustin cracked his neck, then he slowly descended towards the high priest. He stopped several feet above the ground, hovering.

The two faced each other silently for a time until Eudaxus spoke.

"Do you really expect me to believe these absurd claims of yours?" Eudaxus said, holding the letter Alustin had sent him in hand. The paper seemed oddly dark, and when Alustin reached out to it with his affinity senses, there seemed to be something in the way.

Well, that would have been too easy.

"You heard the bells, Eudaxus. Do you really believe that I'm faking the sandstorm, too?" Alustin said.

"I think you're using a natural sandstorm as an opportunity to turn things to your advantage, to finish what you started," Eudaxus said. "I just don't understand why. You poisoning Indris makes sense if Kanderon has decided to make a grab for power, but why steal the egg? I can't see a reason she'd want it."

"Kanderon isn't…" Alustin started, but Eudaxus spoke over him.

"Unless, of course, she didn't order you to steal the egg. Perhaps you're doing it of your own accord," Eudaxus continued. "Perhaps it's part of your little vendetta against Havath."

Despite himself, Alustin scowled. With effort, however, he managed to calm himself.

"Why didn't Indris celebrate the laying of this egg?" Alustin asked. "Why did she keep it a secret?"

Eudaxus' face grew uncertain for a moment, then hardened. "The queen's business is her own. She doesn't answer to the likes of you and I."

"And why did she only lay one egg this time?" Alustin said, lowering his voice.

Eudaxus said nothing, his face a rigid mask.

"I have a theory about that," Alustin said, drawing closer to Eudaxus. "Dragon egg clutches are supposed to be quite a bit larger when both parents are the same breed of dragon, as Indris and Ataerg are. When they're different breeds, well, single egg clutches are quite common."

Eudaxus stared at him silently for a moment, uncertain. "Indris and Ataerg are loyal to one another, as no other dragons are," he said. "This is one of our core tenets. This is part of why Indris deserves praise above all other dragons."

"And how many members of Indris' cult revere Ataerg for that?" Alustin said. "How many of them would join Ataerg if he turned on Indris for, say, mating with a different dragon?"

Eudaxus began to look uncertain. "I would have known if the faithful were breaking away," he said. "And if they were, I would have been able to stop it."

"Eudaxus, you couldn't even stop your underlings from burning down the invisible cult," Alustin said. "They don't worship you, they worship Indris— and for many of them, Ataerg as well. And for her to betray him, to betray part of what sets her apart from other dragons?"

Eudaxus' face wavered even more for a moment, then it hardened once more. "I cannot believe that so many would break the faith, and in such a manner," he said. "And I cannot believe that Ataerg would turn against Indris. This is nothing more than a trick on your part, and this is nothing more than a natural sandstorm. Our contingency plan will be adequate."

"Your contingency plan? Indris's combined loyal brood won't be enough to protect even half of Theras Tel for the duration of the storm," Alustin said. "And that's without Ataerg attacking."

"There is no better option," Eudaxus said. "Only Indris has the power to protect the city."

"I know how to protect the city," Alustin said. "It can be done, if only you'll listen to me."

Eudaxus stared at him, then he shook his head. "I don't know what trickery you seek to accomplish, my friend, but I will not be party to it. I will give you one chance to surrender peacefully, but I cannot afford the time or effort to have you captured. If you resist, I will merely have you killed."

"Eudaxus," Alustin started.

"Choose," the old priest said.

Alustin stared for a moment, then sighed. "I'm telling you the truth. I'm sincerely trying to save both Indris and Theras Tel."

"Then surrender peacefully," Eudaxus said, "to prove your sincerity."

Alustin considered for a moment, then he slumped. "I can't," he said.

"I'm sorry, Alustin," Eudaxus said, "that this is the way it must be."

Eudaxus' shadow twisted and writhed, and spears of darkness shot out of it towards Alustin. Alustin's wings barely pulled him back out of the way in time, and the spears passed inches in front of his face.

"Kill him!" Eudaxus bellowed. "For Indris!"

A dozen dragons and a hundred men roared as one.

Hugh had read a lot of stories that involved someone taking a second to realize that they were the ones screaming, but he knew he was screaming from the very beginning of the fall.

It did, however, take him a second to realize that Sabae was screaming as well.

"This is insane!" Hugh yelled, only slightly coherently.

"You agreed to it!" Sabae screamed back.

Sabae's first windjump had taken them a solid fifty feet out past the aqueduct drain. The cliff walls were rapidly moving past them as they fell.

"I wish I hadn't!" Hugh said.

"Here we go again!" Sabae said, then she windjumped in midair, firing them even farther forwards, startling a passing sand drake soaring nearby. The goose-sized reptile hissed at them as it backwinged away.

This kicked off an entire sequence of five more windjumps forwards, as Sabae carefully steered them towards their target. She then swiveled the two of them until their feet were pointing downwards.

"Get ready!" she yelled.

Sabae sent one last burst of wind straight downwards, slowing their fall. As she did so, Hugh cast a levitation cantrip on the two of them.

They actually seemed to stop in midair for a moment before slowly descended the last hundred feet or so. It was still quite a drain on Hugh's mana reservoirs, but he only used the reservoirs from the two affinities Kanderon had forbidden him to use yet.

With a light thunk, they came to rest on the deck of the *Moonless Owl.*

"That," Captain Solon said, "might be the second craziest way to board a ship I've ever seen."

Hugh and Sabae staggered away from one another. With a sigh, Sabae sagged down on a coil of rope, exhausted from her heavy use of mana, while Hugh just stood there waiting for his heart to slow down. He absently cast a cloth drying cantrip on himself and Sabae as he did so, and water pooled up around his feet, where it was immediately absorbed into the wood.

Something about that bothered Hugh, but he couldn't figure out what.

"Second craziest?" Sabae asked.

Before Captain Solon could answer, Avah came sprinting across the deck towards Hugh. He barely managed to stay on his feet as she hugged him. He opened his mouth to say something, but she promptly kissed him, driving any thoughts out of his head.

Well, most thoughts. There was a good bit of anxiety about kissing in public while sober.

"Does kissing your daughter in front of you raise it to the craziest way?" Sabae asked. Most unhelpfully, in Hugh's opinion.

Captain Solon hesitated before answering. "No, your teacher still has you beat with the whole gorgon incident. And I'd really say Avah kissed him, not the other way around."

Avah let Hugh get a breath, as she glared at her father and made a rude gesture. The sailors on deck— who, to Hugh's embarrassment, he realized had been watching the whole time— burst into laughter and catcalls.

"Where's Godrick and the angry redhead?" Irrick called from the rigging.

"So," Captain Solon said, waving a hand to shush the crew, "I got a letter from Alustin saying you needed our help to save the city, or something like that?"

As the floor gave out from underneath them, Godrick reached out with his steel affinity sense while envisioning a simple spellform in his head. The enchanted dagger on Talia's belt shot out of its sheathe and into his hand as he wrapped his other arm around her.

They only fell a couple of feet before Godrick managed to pump mana into the dagger, which came to an immediate halt in midair.

They hung in midair as the hallway floor collapsed down into the valve room below them. The valve room was massive— not as big as Indris' throne room, but still far, far larger than any other room they'd encountered in the palace. It was enough of a drop that Godrick doubted they would have survived.

Massive pipes rose up from the floor along the sides of the room, rising up into the ceiling. Only a relatively small area in the center of the room had been demolished by the collapse.

The rubble from the hallway lay scattered across the floor. The corpse of the dragon had been carried downwards by the collapse as well, and had been largely crushed by the debris. Godrick could see quite a few other corpses scattered about, presumably from the cultists that had been in the valve room. He didn't see anyone moving.

"Now what?" Talia asked.

Godrick took a deep breath. "Hold on tight," he warned her.

He quit channeling mana into the dagger, and they immediately fell again. After just a few feet, Godrick channeled mana back into it. They came back to a halt with a jerk.

Godrick continued slowly lowering them downwards all the way to the rubble-strewn floor below in this staccato manner. By the time they reached the bottom, his shoulder felt like it wanted to come out of the socket, but they touched down without injury.

"Where are the controls?" Talia asked.

Godrick pulled the map out of his pocket, looking it over for a moment. "I'm pretty sure we're standing on the control platform," he said, gesturing to the rubble pile beneath them.

Talia smiled. "There we go, then. Mission accomplished."

Godrick clambered off the pile of rubble and strode over to the massive steel doors leading out of the valve room. He put his ear against them, and heard faint yelling and arguing on the other side. They shuddered as something slammed against them.

"Ah don't think it's gonna be that easy, Talia," Godrick said.

Hugh rummaged frantically through his belongings in his cabin, trying to find…

There. Sabae's great-grandmother's stormward journal. She had been a ward specialist too, but her smallest wards were ship sized— she was better known for constructing wards the size of entire cities. Many of her wards were built to last months or even years.

Hugh would be happy if his lasted hours.

There was theoretically no real difference between the ward Hugh had crafted around the ship during the sandstorm and the ward Hugh needed to craft around the city except for size. Both were, at their core, simply a repeating series of the same roughly three foot long ward over and over again.

The theoretically bit was the rub, however. A ward of any sort had to be constructed incredibly precisely, else it was likely to fail explosively. Chaining wards together to create larger wards required even higher precision in the ward's construction.

Hugh was going to have to create a miles long ward encircling Theras Tel, and if there was even a single flaw in it, it would fail. And a ward on that scale failing explosively…

Theras Tel would eventually be able to recover from the damage an Endless Erg sandstorm would do to it. The stone structures of the buildings would survive just fine, but over two centuries of safety, the citizens had installed progressively larger and larger windows, greenhouses, patios, and other structures unsuited to the desert. Many of the cliff dwellings descending the sides lacked doors and windows entirely, often having only curtains if they were lucky.

Theras Tel would, however, be significantly less likely to survive the catastrophic failure of a ward powerful enough to hold off a sandstorm, so Hugh really, really needed to not mess up while crafting it.

He could feel the ship shudder below him as it began to pull out of the harbor. The dragons on guard had all abandoned the port when the bells began ringing, but no one else had tried to leave yet— none of them were even rigged to try. Alustin's warning had given the *Moonless Owl* time to prepare, however.

Hugh carefully drew out his ward plan into his spellbook. He double, then triple-checked it. Then checked it a few more times.

"Hugh, are you ready?" Sabae asked.

Hugh started. He hadn't even heard her come to the cabin door.

"All except for knowing how to power the ward," Hugh said.

Sabae seemed conflicted, then with a sigh, she reached for Hugh's quill. Hugh handed her the quill and his spellbook, and she neatly sketched a spellform onto the page.

It vaguely resembled the mana tap he'd drawn onto the ship sized stormward, but diverged in a number of ways. First of all, it was clearly intended to handle a far, far greater amount of mana than the mana tap had. Second, it had a sequence of markings in it that Hugh didn't understand, except that they seemed to indicate that the spellform was designed to handle affinity-less mana.

Most unusual of all, however, it didn't seem designed to draw energy from mages.

"What is this?" Hugh asked.

"It's one of my family's closest kept secrets," Sabae said. "We call it the windlode spellform. A lot of storm mages have something similar, but none of them possess anything nearly as efficient as the windlode."

"That doesn't tell me what it does, though," Hugh said.

"So you've felt how much denser the aether is during storms, right?" Sabae said. "A truly big storm can make the aether even denser than a volcanic eruption or earthquake. The windlode glyph is designed specifically to tap into the types of aether currents storms produce to power spells. I can't use it safely, thanks to my… difficulties, but you should be able to fit that into your ward— great-grandmother was supposed to have done so as well."

Hugh stared at the spellform hungrily. No wonder the Kaen Das family was so important, if they had spells like this available to them. Something had clearly been missing from Sabae's great grandmother's journals before— he'd been unable to figure out why until now.

Normally, Hugh just charged up his wards when he created them, recharging them when needed. This, however, would keep the ward going as long as it was needed— and, thanks to the nature of the windlode spellform, it would only gather power when an actual storm approached, meaning the ward would turn itself on and off with the storms.

At least, it would if he were building something more permanent than what he was planning. He just needed this ward to work once.

"Hugh," Sabae said, looking serious, "You need to be really, really careful with this. Do *not* let anyone else see it. You need to memorize this right now, before you go on deck. And when you're crafting the ward, you need to make sure to conceal it somehow. If the windlode gets out into the open, not only could it result in mages wreacking havoc on the weather trying to use it without understanding it, it would also get me in an absurd amount of trouble with my family."

Hugh nodded, then he bent down to the task of memorizing the spellform. The instant he was done, he ripped the page from the book and handed it to Sabae, who smiled gratefully at him, then used a cantrip to light the page on fire.

As much as Alustin hated to admit it, perhaps his preferred strategy of keeping people off balance through audacity had been poorly thought out this time around.

Largely in that it had failed to knock Eudaxus off balance. In fact, he seemed to have been quite prepared for it.

The instant Eudaxus had ordered the attack, the dragons had jointly summoned up a massive windshield surrounding the impact site— this one, however, designed to keep things in, not out.

And Alustin, unfortunately, was on the inside, airborne with nowhere to go.

"You're making a mistake, Eudaxus!" he yelled, dodging out of the way of a flight of crossbow bolts and one of the high priest's shadow-spears.

A nearby dragon inhaled, then spat flame at Alustin. Spat in quite a literal sense— dragons didn't actually breathe flame, they spat a highly flammable and viscous liquid from their mouths, igniting it as it left. They actually forced it out in a jet by pushing the air in their lungs out through specialized channels in their throat. The nasty stuff was nearly impossible to get off, and even harder to put out— even submerging it in water didn't work.

Amputating a limb it had gotten on wasn't an uncommon response.

Alustin managed to get out of the jet of flame in time, but several droplets of the burning spray hit his paper wings, and they rapidly caught on fire.

Cursing to himself, Alustin shot upwards, then he dissolved his wings. As he fell, he rapidly reassembled the wings from new paper he drew from inside his extraplanar storage space.

The already burning paper he sent straight towards Eudaxus. The high priest cursed, then vanished into his own shadow, reappearing a moment later fifty feet away in a dragon's shadow. The burning paper hit the ground in a shower of sparks.

The main jet of dragonflame slammed directly into the windshield surrounding them, where it immediately got caught up in the revolving winds, without getting put out.

Lovely.

The biggest dragon inside the shield inhaled, clearly preparing to spray fire at Alustin as well. Alustin redoubled his speed, at the same time reaching deep into his extraplanar storage with his senses for a specific small stack of papers. He pulled one from the top, plastering it to his own throat as he barely kept ahead of the jet of dragon fire that was being swept along behind him like a sword.

None of it hit him, but all of it was promptly sucked up by the windshield, where it began to break apart into burning clumps being swept around and around the impact site.

Alustin could already feel the temperature rising. He dodged another one of Eudaxus' shadow spears, then funneled mana into the piece of paper wrapped around his throat— more specifically, into the spellform glyph drawn onto it.

"Eudaxus," Alustin's voice echoed out, magnified by the glyph. Glyphs operated on similar principles to wards and enchantments— they were all spellforms given physical form. While wards and enchantments had much more extensive functionality of their own, however, glyphs were merely spellforms drawn out so that mages didn't have to memorize them, or so that they could just pump mana into them, allowing them to cast more spells at once, or both. Less mana efficient, but there were always trade-offs.

"Eudaxus, I don't want to fight," Alustin said. "I'm trying to help right now. What do you think Ataerg is going to do when he gets here? He already ordered Indris' poisoning, do you think he's here to apologize?"

"I have only your word that he's even coming," Eudaxus said. Alustin shouldn't have been able to hear him at all from across the impact site—

even over Indris' ragged breathing, let alone over the sound of enraged dragons and cultists. Eudaxus' voice, however, seemed to echo out of every nearby shadow.

There was always more than one path to achieve your desired effect, both in magic and life.

"What do I really have to gain from lying about this?" Alustin said, reaching into the depths of his extraplanar storage for another stack of papers. This one, he began pulling out en masse. "Not escape, certainly— I could have easily done that without ever coming close to the impact site."

"To finish the job you started, perhaps?" Eudaxus said. He wasn't shooting shadow spears at Alustin, however, so that was an improvement.

Still, Alustin made sure not to slow down. So long as his shadows stayed scattered by movement, Eudaxus shouldn't be able to strike him through it.

"Let's be honest," Alustin said, "If Kanderon wanted Indris dead, she'd have simply attacked Theras Tel personally, and there's precious little doubt about the outcome. Why would she go about things in such a convoluted fashion?"

On second thought, maybe that hadn't been the smartest thing to say. Several of the smaller dragons, content to sit on the ground and spit flame at him up until now, took to the air after him, apparently enraged at the suggestion of weakness on their mother's part.

Alustin carefully redirected the papers he was pulling out of his extraplanar storage out of their way, continuing to place them carefully across the impact site.

"I doubt the fight would be as straightforward as you claim," Eudaxus said, echoing out through the shadows, "but perhaps you really aren't involved in Indris' poisoning. You remain, however, the chief suspect in the theft of her egg."

"Isn't it interesting how the accounts of me being seen in the palace all apparently came to you from your cult?" Alustin said. "No guards, no servants, no dragons— it was just cultists who saw me. And they have, of course, proven themselves quite trustworthy of late."

Alustin dove towards the roof of one of the buildings inside the windshield to avoid a stream of dragonfire, only to come face to face with another dragon climbing up onto its roof. He tried to dodge to one side, but crashed and rolled on the roof of the building instead.

The instant he stopped moving, Alustin felt ephemeral bonds of cold wrap around him. He looked down to see that his own shadow seemed to have grown tentacles that had wrapped themselves around his legs, arms, and torso.

The dragon in front of him inhaled to breathe out fire. At the same time, the shadow bonds began to constrict.

Alustin closed his eyes as tightly as he could.

"I'm sorry, Alustin," came Eudaxus' voice out of Alustin's own shadow.

"I am too," Alustin said in a normal tone of voice, as he pumped mana into the glyphs on the hundreds of pages he'd been scattering around the impact site.

Light glyphs.

Each of the glyphs on their own was about enough to light a room. Hundreds of them together, however, were like staring into the sun.

Alustin felt the bonds around him disappear along with his shadow, and he heard screams from men and dragons alike as the light blinded them in the seconds Alustin left it on before he stopped pumping mana into the glyphs. Alustin rolled to his feet, blinking away afterimages even though his eyes had been closed.

A dragon nearby staggered, crashing into a half-ruined building. As it collapsed, Alustin noticed something important.

The dragons had stopped maintaining the windshield. Alustin could escape.

Or, at least, he might have been able to, if the collapsing windshield weren't dumping a rain of burning dragonfire.

CHAPTER TWENTY-FIVE
STORMWARD

HUGH settled down in the prow of the ship as the *Moonless Owl* exited the harbor and began to pick up speed, heading in a straight line outwards. He looked over his stormward plans one last time, then he took a deep breath and closed his eyes.

He envisioned a spellform then. Not any part of the stormward, but instead a spellform from his crystal affinity— the pattern linking spellform that let crystal mages fuse and grow crystals.

Holding that spellform in mind, he reached out towards the desert sand ahead of the ship, and began fusing the quartz grains together.

The ship promptly ran over the crystals, shattering them.

Blushing and hoping no one else had heard that, he reached deep into the sand ahead of the ship, and once more began to fuse the crystal together.

Hugh had been confident he'd be able to do that, but his greatest fear had been whether his crystal growing could keep up with the ship or not. To his great surprise, he was able to keep up easily— in large part because he was growing thin threads of crystal underground, rather than heavier chunks like before.

Once Hugh had made sure he could turn, split, and reconnect the paths of the crystal thread, simply by envisioning what he wanted to happen, he let go of the pattern linking spell and opened his eyes. "I'm ready," he called to Captain Solon. The captain nodded at him and started yelling orders to the crew.

The *Owl* started turning until it was running parallel to the curve of the plateau. Hugh reached out with his affinity senses and began pattern linking once more.

This time, however, he kept his eyes open, and focused on the stormward plans in his spellbook.

Hugh took a deep breath to calm himself, then he began crafting the ward beneath the sand.

The ward almost seemed to want to spring into being. Wards had always been easy for Hugh— they were, for a long time, the only spells Hugh was really capable of casting. He'd worried, however, that the scale of this project would somehow make this different, or the fact that he'd never crafted a ward with threads of crystal before.

He shouldn't have worried about any of that. This was, to Hugh's great shock, the easiest time he'd ever had drawing a ward. He wasn't having to rely on his manual dexterity at all— instead, the threads of crystal simply grew exactly as he envisioned them.

What he should have worried about, however, were his mana reservoirs. Even with the unusual size of Hugh's reservoirs, his crystal mana was draining quickly.

It really didn't look like he'd be able to make it half a mile, let alone around the entire plateau.

Alustin desperately tried to rebuild his paper wings before the plummeting dragonfire hit him, even though he knew there wouldn't be time. To his surprise, however, it simply never hit.

"What, exactly" Indris said, **"is going on here? How long have I been unconscious?"**

The plummeting dragonfire had been caught by a new windshield, hovering in midair. As Alustin watched, it contracted, until it was only around twenty feet across. The flame stayed lit, and the whole thing took on the appearance of a writhing ball of liquid flame.

Which, in fairness, it essentially was.

Indris' massive head rose up out of her crater, glancing around. Finally, to Alustin's distress, she focused on him.

"Kanderon's servant," Indris said. **"It shouldn't surprise me to see my children and servants blinded while you stand there unaffected."**

"The blindness is only temporary," Alustin offered nervously.

Indris just stared at him.

"So..." Alustin said, "What exactly is the last thing you remember?"

"My egg was stolen," Indris said.

"Ah," said Alustin. "Well, to make a long story short, Ataerg suborned part of your cult to put poison in your food, he and his half of your brood have harnessed a sandstorm, and they're on their way to kill you and destroy your city right now."

"He lies, my queen!" Eudaxus shouted. His voice came out of the shadows once more, but Alustin's shadow, thankfully, didn't attack him again. "He's the thief that stole your egg. This is all a plot of Kanderon's..."

"**No,"** Indris said, turning her head towards the northwest. **"He speaks the truth, at least about Ataerg and our children. They wing ahead of a sandstorm as we speak."**

Indris shuddered and tried to stand, only to collapse back onto her stomach. Alustin barely kept on his feet as the building he stood atop shuddered.

"It seems, however, that there is little I can do about it," Indris said. **"I cannot stand, let alone fight, and I do not have it in me to stop the storm."**

"I actually might be able to help you with that," Alustin said.

Indris turned a skeptical gaze on him. **"Let me guess— I only need invite Kanderon into my domain, and in exchange, she only wants my submission."**

Alustin shook his head. "Actually, I'm the one that's going to solve your problem, and my price is rather lower than that— I just want a single book from your collection."

Indris snorted. **"Am I to seriously believe that you can stop my former mate from slaying me and destroying my city, little librarian? Leaving alone the accusations that you were the one to steal my egg."**

To Alustin's alarm, the burning sphere was definitely drifting closer to him.

"Ataerg is truly attacking the city, Your Majesty?" Eudaxus said, his voice echoing from the shadows once more.

Indris didn't reply, but merely stared at Alustin.

"In that case, I believe him," Eudaxus said.

Alustin's head snapped in Eudaxus' general direction, as he focused on him with his farseeing. Indris' head turned as well, though at a more measured pace.

"I wasn't willing to believe that Ataerg or your faithful would turn against you, my queen," Eudaxus said. "But if Ataerg has truly done so, then Alustin seems to have been entirely truthful with us. It must have been those cultists that betrayed you who seized the egg."

"Be as that may," Indris said, **"That doesn't particularly help our chances of survival."**

To Alustin's relief, however, the ball of fire started to draw away from him.

"If Alustin says he can take Ataerg, I believe it," Eudaxus said through the shadows, then he gestured to himself and the dragons around them. "He just fought all of us to a standstill, and do you remember the gorgon incident?"

Indris seemed to consider for what seemed, to Alustin, to be an eternity.

"Ataerg alone is mightier than the entirety of our brood. If I were hale, I could defeat him easily, but… very well," she said. **"It doesn't seem like I have many options."**

The sphere of fire hurtled into the sky, on a path out into the desert. Alustin sighed out loud in relief.

"What, precisely, is your plan, little librarian?" Indris asked.

Alustin began pulling a particularly large stack of blank paper from his extraplanar storage as he talked, along with several pots of fast-drying glue. He also pulled out a pair of particularly special quills— each was bound with paper, so that Alustin could manipulate them with his affinity, and each held an extraplanar reservoir entirely filled with ink.

By the time Alustin had finished, Eudaxus' face had paled significantly. Indris, however, seemed quite amused. **"Audacious, little librarian. I approve."**

Alustin bowed, then he began drawing.

Before Talia had really gotten to know Godrick, she'd thought he was as carefree as he was friendly. She'd realized since that Godrick was unnecessarily prone to worrying about the future.

"We've got two problems, as ah see it," Godrick said. "Most urgently, the turncoat cultists outside are going ta break in here before long. Less urgently, we need ta hide the body a' that dragon— Indris isn't going ta like it that we killed one a' her brood."

Talia smiled. "Let's solve the one problem with the other. We move the dragon corpse to the door, wait for them to burst through, then I explode the dragon bone."

Godrick stared at her. "That's a terrible idea. Yeh just droppin' bone down from a hole in the ceilin, that's not a big deal. Blows up the controls, everythin's fine. Yeh detonate an entire dragon worth of bones, well… Ah'm pretty sure it'll take half the room with it, and probably flood the palace. Besides, have yeh ever even tried yer trick with dragon bone before? Do yeh know how it'll react?"

Talia opened her mouth, then shut it again. Those were all very good points, honestly.

"Alright, so we switch. You hide the body, I'll block the door," she said.

"How am ah supposed to hide a thirty foot long dragon," Godrick said.

Talia shrugged. "Sink it into the stone of the floor?"

"Ah can't just sink it inta the stone," Godrick said. "There's be a big lump over it."

"So carve the lump off the top, and make it look like more rubble," Talia said. "It's not like they're going to check to make sure there's exactly the right amount of rubble later."

"That… could actually work," Godrick said. "How're yeh going to block off the door, though?"

"Just trust me," Talia said. Godrick looked like he wasn't too sure about that idea, but he started towards the dragon's corpse.

"Oh, wait!" Talia said. "Save me some of its bones?"

"Nope," Godrick said. "I think someone might find you carrying around bits of dragon bone around when there's a missing dragon a little bit suspicious."

Well, it had been worth a try.

Talia strode over to the massive steel doors. She took a few moments to inspect the edges. They were next to perfectly flush with the walls and floor, so that nothing other than air could get through.

No matter.

Talia manifested a ball of dreamfire no bigger around than her finger. She slowly pushed it into the steel door, which it burned a tunnel straight through.

Well, turned it into little flowers, but to the same effect.

Talia pulled a shard of bone from her belt pouch and pressed her mouth against the door to blow the little hole clear of flowers. She could hear the yelling and arguments on the other side get louder.

Well, this should shut them up.

Talia flicked the shard of bone into the hole. It didn't go all the way through— the door was nearly two feet thick— so Talia ended up casting a simple force cantrip to push the bone the rest of the way through.

The cantrip didn't explode, at least— Alustin had her casting her cantrips a lot more safely these days. It did char the bone a bit, but that didn't bother her any.

She started pumping mana into the shard of bone immediately. It had grown to three times its size before it even hit the ground.

Deciding that it might be good not to stand too close to the doors, just in case, she stepped back a few feet. Then a few more. Then a few feet to the side, so she wasn't standing directly in front of the hole she'd drilled.

The timbre of the arguments changed quite a bit as the bone shard grew and grew in size. Talia would have quite enjoyed hearing what, exactly, they were saying, but, alas.

The doors shook in their frames when the bone exploded. They were well built, however, and didn't fall.

It had been smart of Talia to not stand by the hole. Fire and bone shards came belching through it, spraying twenty feet into the room.

Talia gave things a minute to settle, then she strode up to the door, putting her ear against it.

Nope. No arguing.

Hugh's head had started to ache from the effort of constructing the ward. The *Owl*'s bouncing and shuddering wasn't helping his focus, either.

Crafting the repeating pattern of the ward was almost second nature to Hugh, even after only a few minutes. It almost reminded him on some level of the patterns that fashioned crystals.

He could feel his crystal mana reservoir draining still. The aether had started gradually increasing ahead of the storm, but his reservoirs weren't filling fast enough to stay ahead of constructing the ward.

He had a few options. He could have the *Owl* take breaks during the process, but there was no way they'd get the ward complete in time that way. He could try and break the prioperceptive link to his aether crystal to boost his mana regeneration, but there would likely be some sort of spell backlash doing that, and he wasn't sure how it would affect him.

Hugh knew better than to try and use mana from one of his non-crystal reservoirs. He'd been warned about that time and time again— the best case scenario would be having his spell distorted like Talia's were.

Given that his other two affinities were stellar mana and planar mana, the results would probably be catastrophic— for himself, at the very least.

Even with all its risks, breaking the prioperceptive link seemed like his safest bet. It…

No. There was another option. Kanderon would be absolutely furious, but there was another option.

He could attempt to attune his aether crystal by channeling the ward spell through it. The aether crystal should start actively drawing mana from the aether around him, powering the spell.

Hugh started to shift his affinity senses to route through his aether crystal, then he forced himself to stop. He had a few more minutes before his reservoirs would run out; he had time to consider his other options. Besides, it was probably a good idea to wait for the aether around them to get a little denser as the storm approached before he tried attuning his aether crystal.

Sabae leaned against the ship's railing as she recovered from the aqueducts. She'd never windjumped that many times, that quickly before, and it had taken it out of her, both physically and magically.

The crew of the *Owl* bustled around her as they worked. From their attitudes, you wouldn't imagine that they were dangerously exposed in the path of a gigantic sandstorm.

For a few minutes Sabae just watched their surroundings. She could see figures climbing up from the cliff dwellings above them— it seemed most of the cliff dwellers were moving into the city proper, apparently not believing that their homes would be safe from the oncoming storm.

Sabae glanced back in the direction of the storm. It was still nothing more than a smudge on the far horizon, but she knew that was deceptive— it would look like that until a relatively short time before it hit the city. Endless Erg sandstorms moved *fast.*

A shadow fell across Sabae.

"We need to talk," Deila said.

Sabae shot a glance at the old woman. "About what?" Sabae asked, though she was fairly sure she knew.

"About my granddaughter and your friend there," Deila said. "Don't think I didn't notice your meddling there."

"You also didn't interfere," Sabae said.

The corner of Deila's mouth quirked upwards at that.

"The Radhan generally arrange marriages for our children, almost always from other Radhan families," Deila said. "Though not until after allowing them a few years to… be young."

Sabae nodded at that. She'd basically figured as much— she'd never really considered Hugh and Avah to have much long-term potential.

"So tell me, what exactly are the odds that your little redheaded friend is going to set my granddaughter on fire in a fit of jealousy?" Deila asked, her eyes sharp and piercing.

Sabae was taken aback at that. That… that was not the direction she had been expecting the conversation to take. Talia was over-protective of Hugh, but Sabae was fairly sure she wasn't interested in him romantically.

She shot a look at Hugh, motionless in the prow of the ship, the spellbook she'd given him still slung over one shoulder and open in his lap. Then she looked around for an escape from the conversation.

It didn't surprise Sabae that none of the crew was anywhere near them. She might have even been alright with an enraged dragon or two as an excuse to escape.

Sabae wasn't sure if Deila's expression or the fact that the wind had started to pick up was scarier.

Hugh waited as long as he could before he resorted to trying to attune his aether crystal. He had just a few minutes left in his reservoirs as he started.

He carefully shifted his affinity senses. He needed to stay focused on the crystal threads taking shape below the sand while simultaneously shifting his perception so that it ran through his aether crystal.

At first it felt like trying to run through mud, but the closer and closer his affinity sense drew to the aether crystal, the more difficult it became. Soon, it felt like he was pushing against a stone wall, but he didn't stop.

Hugh felt short of breath, but also curiously disconnected from his body— it was as though his body were no different than the crystal threads he was growing beneath the ship or the aether crystal on his wrists. He strained against the wall, and finally, with a feeling that was less breaking through, and more having the wall grow around him, his senses began running through the aether crystal.

It was… bizarre. He could still sense everything he had before, but he felt even farther away now. His mind seemed to float inside an endlessly repeating sequence of polyhedrons, a seemingly infinite space, yet paradoxically one in which he could sense the boundaries. He tried counting the sides of one of them, but they seemed… wrong, somehow, as though part of them extended in a direction he couldn't see.

Mana started flooding out of his reservoirs. Not just his crystal reservoir, but his other two, as well. Hugh knew he should probably feel alarmed at that, but all his attention was being pulled towards the polyhedrons, which had begun to slowly change shape as his mana flowed into them. His stormward seemed to resonate with his mana and the polyhedrons as well— it almost felt like the stormward was the bank of the river that was his mana.

Suddenly, the river of mana seemed to swell, as a fresh influx of mana came into it— pure, affinity-less mana. The aether crystal had begun drawing in the aether around them.

He wasn't simply feeling like a passive observer anymore. Now, he had to struggle to stay in place, as though the river had grown turbulent and swollen. The mana flowing in from the aether might be pure, but it was also strangely chaotic, moving very differently than he was used to— he understood what Sabae had meant when she referred to the aether moving differently during storms. It wasn't as though the wind were blowing the aether about— instead, it was as though more mana was being added to the aether by the storm sporadically.

Another surge of mana hit Hugh. He could barely hold himself above the current now, and he was having trouble focusing on the stormward or the interlocking, shifting, *growing* polyhedrons. His body felt even more distant and hard to feel than it had before.

Slightly panicked by that, Hugh tried to reach out towards his body once more. He felt… wind? The sting of blowing sand? Someone… yelling?

As his attention drifted back towards his body, however, a sudden surge in mana slammed into him, and he found himself being sucked down into the current, being dragged into and through the polyhedrons, which began to tremble as though they were about to fall apart.

Hugh shouldn't have attempted this. He'd been foolish enough to attempt this off a few short lectures with Kanderon, rather than trying this while supervised by her. Whatever final form his aether crystal took on would likely be near-useless— it'd probably end up as a chair that muddled his spells or something of the sort.

As Hugh was swept deeper and deeper into the pattern of the aether crystal, he began to struggle less and less. What was the point? He barely made himself hold onto the shape of the stormward in his mind's eye.

Unbidden, a vision of his friends eating dinner together came to mind. Hugh tried to ignore it, but it just inserted itself into his attention more loudly.

Wait, why could he see what looked like his own chin near the top of the vision?

Hugh felt a sense of warmth coming from his chest, and looked down to see a glow coming from it.

No, coming from the labyrinth stone.

Hugh tried to ask if the stone was sending him the image, but he couldn't seem to form words in this strange pattern-space.

Somehow, though, he was sure that the labyrinth stone understood him.

What was more, it seemed to want to help him.

With what felt like the last of his strength, Hugh reached out to the stone through the bonds of the warlock contract, hoping for enough strength to fight the current.

Instead, the instant he opened himself to the stone, the current... stilled.

No, it hadn't stilled. It was just as chaotic and turbulent as ever. It was the way Hugh saw it that had changed.

Before, he'd seen only chaos— now, he began to glimpse the order that chaos brought to the pattern. The pattern of a crystal was not built through orderly means— matching components of the growing pattern met by sheer chance, but the more random the movement of the mana grew, the more rapidly the crystal seemed to grow. The randomness and chaos were providing far more opportunities for the pattern to grow than any possible orderly flow could.

Hugh stopped fighting the turbulence, and began to drive it farther and faster. He didn't do so purposelessly, though— he began to see how different turbulent flows would alter the growth of the crystal in different ways. He didn't understand a fraction of what effects the different turbulence would have, but he understood immediately what he needed to do for the sake of the stormward.

Hugh was moving through the pattern more swiftly than ever, and yet more purposefully than ever.

At the same time as he moved through the pattern, he felt someone else moving alongside him. The labyrinth stone was doing... something... to the pattern of the aether crystal, as well as to the stormward. Hugh started to get anxious for a moment, then decided to ignore it. The labyrinth stone had saved him once, he was going to have to trust it.

Sabae had to endure quite a few long, uncomfortable minutes of interrogation from Deila about Hugh before she could escape. She actually gained the impression that the old woman had apparently decided that Hugh had quite the future in store for him, and wouldn't mind… binding Hugh to the Radhan.

Sabae really, really didn't intend to accidentally help arrange a marriage for Hugh.

Her escape from the conversation, however, wasn't quite under the circumstances she would have liked.

Mostly because it was just due to the wind getting strong enough to carry away their words before it reached the other's ears. Blowing sand started abrading against her skin, and with an internal groan, Sabae spun her wind armor back up again. Her mana reservoirs had recovered enough to do so, but it was far more difficult and exhausting than usual.

The sandstorm finally cresting over the horizon and looming over Theras Tel like a malevolent rogue wave didn't particularly contribute to Sabae's desire to chat, either. They'd long since rounded the curve of the city, and were heading northwards towards the port again. Sabae knew the storm was coming from the northeast, but it still felt like they were suicidally rushing into it head-on. Of course, entering it at an angle wasn't any less suicidal than entering it head-on.

The storm didn't make up the whole reason for the conversation's end, however— Hugh was the rest.

Partway through the conversation with Deila, Sabae had noticed Hugh's crystal bracelets were starting to glow with a faint, flickering light. They steadily grew in intensity, and began twitching on his wrists.

At the same time, the aether began flowing towards Hugh, in volumes large enough that Sabae could actually feel it rushing towards him. She had no idea how that was possible— Hugh had large mana reservoirs for his age, but they weren't even close to large enough to draw this sort of mana.

The whole time, he hadn't opened his eyes or moved a muscle.

Deila had generated a windshield around him to shield him from the blowing wind and sand, but he never even reacted— it was as if he hadn't felt the blowing sand pelting him, or even it stopping.

Under her wind armor, Sabae clenched her fists. They'd be cutting this close, but it would work. She'd never met anyone better with wards than Hugh. Her faith in Hugh came from more than that, though. Hugh might be terrified of failure and every new social situation he found himself in, but in so many other regards he was one of the bravest people Sabae had ever known. He'd proven himself more than willing to throw himself into danger for the sake of his friends. He was terrifyingly capable at times, though he seemed incapable of admitting that to himself.

Hugh's ward *would* work.

CHAPTER TWENTY-SIX

PAPERWORK

Ataerg and his forces arrived just minutes before the storm, and Alustin flew out to meet them.

Alustin had armored himself entirely in paper— his eyes were the only thing visible, and only through a thin slit bordered in a ward to keep the blowing sand out. The armor looked like full plate, but sleeker and more streamlined. It wasn't just a single sheet over him, but layers and layers of sheets, with thin spaces filled with honeycombed folds of paper. Nearly every visible sheet of paper was layered in spellforms— both wards and glyphs. No enchantments, but even Alustin didn't have the time to learn enchantment along with everything else he needed to know.

Alustin had found that knowing how to fold things the right way was just about the most important part of being a paper mage.

He was the only one in the sky above Theras Tel. Indris had grounded all of her children as a last line of defense— she was willing to let Alustin attempt this plan, but she didn't trust her children to it.

Alustin was entirely fine with that. He'd had to hold back before— killing any of Indris' brood would have enraged her beyond reason. Ataerg's half of the brood, however… Well, mothers were mothers in any species, but attempting to kill her and destroy her home seemed to have cost them a good bit of favor in her eyes.

Quite understandably, Alustin thought.

He encountered the leading edge of Ataerg's dragon swarm a mile north of the city. There were dozens of dragons in the flight that he could see, and he didn't doubt that even more were out of sight closer to the storm. It wouldn't surprise Alustin if a few of Indris' brood had joined their father after their mother was poisoned.

Ataerg dwarfed his children almost as much as Indris had. He was only around a hundred and fifty feet (Alustin couldn't help but snort at himself derisively for that *only*), but he still looked like a whale swimming through a pod of dolphins. Ataerg was wirier than Indris, and had a truly massive pair of horns sweeping back from his skull. While they were mostly mating displays, Alustin knew better than to underestimate the damage they could do— especially considering how many times longer they were than Alustin was tall.

Alustin spared a final moment to check on his students before plunging into the dragon swarm. Godrick and Talia had seized the valve control room, and were… dismembering and hiding a dragon corpse? Alustin's stomach clenched at that. He had no idea why they would have been foolish enough to fight a dragon at their level of training, let alone how they'd actually managed to kill it. Still, at least they were being smart enough to hide the evidence.

He switched his attention to the *Moonless Owl.* The sandship was close to completing its circuit of the city, and… Hugh's aether crystal was glowing? Alustin's stomach clenched even harder at that. Kanderon had surely warned him against attempting to attune his aether crystal this soon, right? The odds that it would actually succeed were, well… Alustin almost turned for the sandship right then and there, but he forced himself to stay on track. If he didn't stop Ataerg's forces now, almost everything that Kanderon had sent him to accomplish would be in vain.

Hugh had surprised him over and over again in the past. Alustin desperately hoped the same would be true again today.

Alustin had thought about diving at the dragon swarm from above and targeting Ataerg directly, but he doubted he could kill Ataerg with a simple ambush like that— the wyrm was nearly as durable as Indris. Brute force wouldn't be enough to take down Ataerg. He needed to use subtlety and surprise.

Which, of course, was why he charged straight into the swarm from the front, drawing a massive cloud of paper from his extraplanar storage.

The first dragon to see him, a fifty footer, lunged for him immediately, without even bothering to give Alustin more than a cursory inspection.

He honestly found it more than a little offensive to be dismissed so easily. He easily dodged to the side, then sent a portion of his paper swarm straight at the dragon. More precisely, at the dragon's eyes.

The dragon's scream was shockingly loud as the cloud of paper razored through the transparent inner lid and into its eyes. It immediately lost control of its flight, plummeting nearly a hundred feet before it steadied itself, screaming and bleeding the whole time.

That got their attention.

Nearly the entire swarm focused on Alustin, quite a few bellowing and turning course for him. Ataerg, however, looked to his child first before looking to Alustin.

"WHO DARES INJURE MY CHILD?" Ataerg's voice would have easily been the loudest Alustin had ever encountered, if he'd never encountered Indris. That didn't really calm his nerves, though. The dragon swarm halted their approach towards him

Alustin pumped mana into the spell glyph on his paper gorget. His voice boomed out over the noise of the dragon swarm, though not as overwhelmingly as Ataerg's had. "My name is Alustin Haber, Librarian Errant, last loyal son of Helicote, and servant of Kanderon Crux. My master judged you to be too much of a worthless lizard to warrant stirring herself from Skyhold, so she sent me to dispose of you instead."

The entire dragon swarm seemed to pause for a moment as they wrapped their heads around what Alustin had said.

With a deafening roar, the entire swarm dove at him.

Alustin smiled and charged straight at them.

The *Moonless Owl* shuddered as it plunged forwards. The crew had been forced to raise the windshield against the oncoming storm as the waves of pelting sand grew to the point where they could hardly even see the storm advancing on the city.

The dunes below them had begun to dissolve and flow already, and the whole ship creaked and groaned as it struggled to find footing.

The only reason they were even moving forwards at all was thanks to the crew's wind and sand mages forcing wind into the sails. Sabae doubted, however, that they were going at more than a walking pace.

If only Hugh's chalk stormward had been maintained on the *Owl*'s deck, they could have kept moving forwards just fine. With the crew struggling to maintain the windshield, their ability to push against the wind had slowed to a crawl. Even tacking back and forth in the wind was barely helping.

Sabae might be confident in Hugh's ability to craft the ward, but she wasn't confident in the *Owl*'s ability to carry him where he needed to go.

There had to be something Sabae could do. She was a Kaen Das, for tide's sake! Her family were the greatest storm mages alive, and they'd defended Ras Andis and the southwestern coast of Ithos for centuries. Her grandmother regularly turned entire hurricanes off course.

Any true Kaen Das could easily shepherd a single ship through a storm, on sand or water. Sabae… Sabae could just punch things and jump.

She quickly went through the options in her head. Release a series of gust strikes at the sails? It'd drain her too quickly, and wouldn't make enough of a difference. Charge up a single, incredibly powerful gust strike? It would probably just rip a hole in the sails.

If only there was some way to take over part of the task of blocking some of the incoming wind. There was no way for Sabae to expand the size of her wind armor that far beyond her body, no matter how much wind she absorbed into it. She…

Wait. No. That was it.

Sabae sprinted over to Captain Solon, grabbing him by the sleeve. "You need to pull back the windshield a couple feet. Not enough to expose Hugh, but at least enough to expose the figurehead!"

"What?" Captain Solon yelled over the storm. "That makes no sense, girl! That'd just slow us down even more!"

"I'm a Kaen Das, Captain!" Sabae shouted back. "We know the wind better than anyone. You need to trust me!"

Captain Solon gave her a doubtful look, but nodded. Sabae sighed with relief, then turned and sprinted for the prow, spinning up her wind armor as she went.

Hugh was losing control again.

Despite the clarity the labyrinth stone had brought him, the mana rushing through him and the aether crystal just kept growing and growing. It was simply too much for Hugh to handle.

He could barely even perceive anything from his own body anymore, but he could tell from the stormward construction that they had slowed. They kept veering off course as well, forcing Hugh to stretch farther and farther afield to keep the crystal threads of the ward growing in a roughly circular shape.

He could feel the dunes dissolving with his affinity senses as they reached downwards to the ward. The wind hadn't dug deep enough to expose or damage the ward yet, but if they didn't move quickly, it would sooner than later.

Hugh couldn't fail. People were depending on him.

As Alustin dove into the swarm, he began folding paper. One of the biggest advantages paper mages had over other mages was their ability to replicate spell effects across large numbers of targets— so long as all of those targets were identical sheets of paper.

Alustin folded a thousand sheets simultaneously. He didn't go for anything fancy— a simple triangle should do the trick.

It took three seconds to fold the triangles. During that time, Alustin dodged three jets of dragonfire and a diving thirty-footer.

The instant the triangles were done, Alustin sent them flying forwards. They looked almost like a flock of birds drawn by a child.

Most birds, however, didn't shoot through the membranous wings of a dragon like arrows through paper.

Paper arrows through paper? Hmm. Alustin should probably have put more thought into that metaphor.

The first dragon hit by the storm screamed in pain as a thousand rips opened up in his wings. They quickly tore and expanded, and the dragon simply began plummeting towards its death on the sand miles below it.

Alustin had already sent the paper triangles scything through the wings of two more dragons before the first had even begun to fall.

Pages swirled in the wind around Alustin as he danced through the sky. He plastered them onto the faces of dragons, sliced open the eyes of any dragons foolish enough to not close their scaly outer eyelids at their approach, and dodged among them like a hummingbird. He threw masses of paper into the path of dragonflame, blocking it again and again.

Alustin might be the physically weakest creature in the sky right now, but he was by far the fastest and most agile.

He hadn't stopped slicing the triangles through dragon wings, either. With each pass he lost a few more triangles, either by slamming into wing membranes too thick to cut through or by dragonfire, but he continued knocking dragons out of the sky with them.

He hadn't stopped pulling paper out of his extraplanar storage tattoo, either. He pulled a special stack of glyph-covered pages out, folding them into paper arrows as he did so. He sent them shooting into the mouths of three dragons trying to flank him, then pumped mana into their glyphs— simple fire-starting spellforms.

Two of the dragons' heads simply exploded, while the third screamed in pain as dragonflame gushed in a wave out of its mouth.

Dragons didn't light their liquid dragonflame until it was already *out* of the glands in their throat for this exact reason. Their outsides might be entirely fireproof, but their insides were considerably less so.

Ataerg bellowed something incomprehensible over the cries of wounded dragons and the oncoming storm, and suddenly Alustin found all the nearby dragons fleeing him.

Alustin smiled to himself. He'd been fighting for no more than three minutes, and he'd already downed more than a dozen dragons.

At this rate, he should see about claiming Aedan Dragonslayer's title.

Alustin's smile vanished, however, as Ataerg surged forward far, far faster than anything that size should be able to move, jaws open wide as the wyrm prepared to bite Alustin out of the air.

He'd carefully gone over Ataerg's capabilities and preferred tactics with Indris and Eudaxus before he'd left the impact site. Ataerg was a powerful mage in his own right, with deeply attuned affinities for wind and stone. One of his favorite tactics was accelerating himself forwards with wind at astonishing speeds to take opponents by surprise.

Indris had thought that Ataerg's wind mana would be too drained by harnessing the storm to use that tactic. She'd clearly been wrong.

Ataerg was, for that brief moment, moving far, far faster than Alustin. He was moving faster than almost any living thing Alustin had ever seen.

Any *living* thing.

Alustin's swarm of pages shot back towards him in an instant, overlapping as they did so. In a fraction of a second, his four long, delicate wings grew into a single massive sheet of paper, extending in a circle fifty feet across.

One that was facing right into the wind of the storm. It caught Alustin's new sail, sending him flying backwards. He moved so quickly that the blood rushed forward to his face, making him think he was about to pass out.

Even so, Ataerg's jaws closed mere feet in front of Alustin. He could clearly smell Ataerg's foul breath.

As the sail launched Alustin back over Theras Tel, he sent the remaining paper triangles towards Ataerg's wings.

Every single one of them bounced off like he'd sent them into a block of solid steel. Ataerg didn't even seem to notice.

Well, it had been something of a longshot.

"KILL YOU!" Ataerg screamed.

Alustin sent a cloud of pages at Ataerg's face. They hit his transparent inner eyelids, at the perfect angle, and…

Did nothing.

Cursing, Alustin sent the last of his fire-starting glyph pages towards Ataerg's mouth.

Ataerg didn't even seem to notice when they went off.

Well, actually taking Ataerg down in direct combat had always been a longshot.

Ataerg was still pursuing him, but starting to fall behind. Seeing that, the dragon inhaled deeply.

Alustin dissolved his sail completely. He plunged downwards immediately as a column of liquid dragonfire a dozen feet thick blasted above him. Even fifty feet below it, parts of his paper armor blackened and charred.

Alustin rebuilt his wings after he'd fallen fifty or so feet. He dodged to the side to stay out of the way of any falling droplets of dragonfire, and then he shot forwards.

His wings weren't as fast as the sail in this wind, but then, he didn't need to go as fast as the sail took him.

He just needed to go fast enough to keep ahead of Ataerg without losing him.

CHAPTER TWENTY-SEVEN

DRAGONSLAYER

SABAE spun up her wind armor tighter and tighter as she sprinted towards the front of the ship. She leapt around and dove straight into the ship's windshield just as it contracted.

Her wind armor almost shattered plunging through the windshield, but thankfully both it and the windshield held as she passed through it. Sabae landed right at the base of the owl-shaped wooden figurehead of the ship, barely managing to keep the wind from blowing her off the front.

Ahead, she could see the storm looming. They had only minutes before it hit Theras Tel.

Sabae started to spin up her wind armor again. This time, however, she didn't try to keep the wind flows neat or well structured.

She only focused on concentrating as much wind as possible into the armor, and making sure that every drop she pulled in towards her came from ahead of her.

Her mana reservoirs began to dip precipitously as she pulled more and more wind. Sabae took a deep breath. She knew she shouldn't do this, that it was far too dangerous with her mana control problems.

Screw playing it safe. She wasn't going to let her family name down.

Sabae drew the windlode spellform in her mind's eye and pushed the little mana she had left into it.

Wind began spiraling in towards her armor at an insane rate— far faster and in far greater amounts than she should ever be able to spin up on her own.

The *Moonless Owl* lurched forward wildly as the winds that had been slamming against the front of its windshield began flooding into Sabae's armor. She almost fell off the figurehead, but barely managed to grab on in time.

Sabae could feel the strain of holding onto the armor pull at her. She simply wasn't ready hold this much wind in her armor, or be flooded with as much mana as the storm had to offer.

She didn't have to hold onto it for long, though. Just long enough for Hugh to finish his work.

Hugh felt immense relief as the *Owl* surged forwards again. He'd tried pushing forwards on his own, but he quickly reached the limits of his affinity senses. All the extra power hadn't done anything to extend their range.

Hugh kept growing the crystal threads, but he reached forwards with his affinity senses at the same time, searching for the other end of the ward. He wasn't going to get screwed by miscalculating the length of the ward like he'd done before the first sandstorm.

There. It was still distant, but approaching rapidly.

Hugh could tell that *something* was happening inside the aether crystal's pattern space, but at this point he wasn't even trying to guess what. It was still an unending motif of repeating polyhedrons, but it otherwise looked nothing like it had before. The polyhedrons were a completely different shape, connected in completely different ways, and seemed to reach into even more directions that Hugh simply couldn't see.

The labyrinth stone was still up to something as well, but Hugh wasn't sure what. He didn't spare it any thought.

Hugh carefully focused on the design of the last segment of the stormward. This one blended seamlessly into the windlode spellform at the end, which was sized exactly to fit into the space between the two ends of the circular ward.

He'd spent as much time as he'd been able to spare trying to figure out how to conceal the true shape of the windlode from anyone looking for it. He'd considered sealing the whole thing in a huge block of crystal, but instead he had settled on turning the ward into a complete mess of intersecting lines. He just had to make sure to include imperfections in the crystal threads at all the right point so that mana wouldn't flow into the false lines.

With a final surge of effort, Hugh grew the ends of the ward together, crafting the windlode spellform and its concealment in a last burst of effort.

As he did so, the labyrinth stone seemed to push something into the ward as well.

Then his mana drained from him completely, and he fell out of pattern space into his own body.

Hugh couldn't understand what was going on for a moment. His own limbs and senses seemed completely alien. Everything snapped back to him after a few deep breaths, however, and he looked up just in time to see his stormward ignite.

Shafts of white light thicker than any tree speared up from the ground, piercing the sky above them. Hugh could actually see several of them pierce the cresting edge of the sandstorm as it rose above them.

Webs of white light began to grow between the shafts. Then the whole thing flashed, congealing into a rippling curtain surrounding Theras Tel.

The winds inside the curtain simply stopped. The blowing sand started settling downwards. The *Owl* was the only thing still moving as the crew maintained their wind spells for a few moments.

The winds outside the curtain battered at it for a few seconds, then visibly began to rise upwards. The air outside the curtain turned into a rising waterfall of sand and wind, vanishing upwards at shocking speed.

The crew let their spells lapse, and the *Owl* began to grind to a halt on the sand.

The upward flows of wind outside the curtain started tilting to one side, then circling.

Hugh took a second to realize what was happening. The winds of the sandstorm weren't striking the city head on, and the rising wind was creating instability in the storm.

The ward had created a gargantuan stationary tornado around the city.

He'd done it. He actually done it! Hugh couldn't believe that…

Hugh saw something on the prow of the ship out of the corner of his eye and turned towards it.

It was Sabae, still in her wind armor.

The wind armor looked nothing like its usual appearance, however. It was swollen and misshapen, and he could hardly see her through it.

Sabae looked at him and mouthed something, but he couldn't hear her through the thrumming of her wind armor. Then she windjumped off the figurehead.

The blast was so strong it shattered the wooden owl off the front of the ship. Hugh covered his eyes with his arm to block the splinters.

That was when he realized that the bracelets were no longer on his arms.

He didn't spend time thinking about that, however. He pulled his arm away from his face and looked for Sabae.

She'd crashed onto the ground several hundred feet away from the ship, and was staggering around like she was drunk. Her wind armor was bending and twisting out of control.

Hugh vaulted over the railing, casting a levitation cantrip to lower his fall as he did so.

Nothing happened. Hugh's reservoirs were completely drained. He hit the sand hard, landing on his face, his spellbook bruising one hip.

He didn't even pause. He immediately pulled himself to his feet and started sprinting towards Sabae.

Hugh was still a hundred feet away when Sabae's armor detonated. Sand shot two hundred feet into the air from the blast, and Hugh was knocked off his feet by a massive gust of wind.

It took him a good bit longer to climb to his feet this time. By the time he had, the sand from the explosion of wind had largely begun settling. Hugh charged into it without a second thought.

Alustin desperately dove past one of Theras Tel's dragon roosting towers, hoping to stay out of Ataerg's reach.

Ataerg flew through the tower like it wasn't even there. Alustin had to dodge through a rain of boulders, slowing him down even more.

Alustin pulled the last few light glyphs from his extraplanar storage, flooding them with mana as they fell behind him. Ataerg bellowed at the flash of light, but didn't slow.

Alustin was running out of tricks. His sword was powerful, but not a lot of use against a monster like Ataerg. He'd burned through the majority of his stock of paper already— at this rate, he'd need to start throwing his personal library at Ataerg.

He did still have a couple of last-ditch contingency tools that Kanderon had given to him, but Alustin would rather let himself be eaten than use them in the middle of a populated city.

Ataerg inhaled to spray dragonfire at Alustin again when the wind of the storm stopped. Alustin almost crashed into a particularly tall tenement, while Ataerg had to abandon spraying fire, instead frantically flapping to maintain altitude.

A shimmering white curtain entirely surrounded the city. Alustin couldn't help but give a victory yell at the top of his lungs at that.

Hugh had done it! He'd actually managed to pull it off! Alustin had hoped Hugh was capable of…

Ataerg bellowed behind him, and Alustin realized that the voice amplification glyph on his gorget was still active. The dragon surged after him with renewed vigor.

The librarian focused his attention back onto the city in front of him. He had less than half a mile until he reached the impact site again. This had better work.

Alustin poured his mana into his wings. His mana reservoirs might be massive, but this fight had drained even them. He didn't have much time to pull this off if he wanted to stop Ataerg.

One of the dragon roosting towers ahead of Alustin begin to shake wildly, then pulled itself out of the ground entirely, hurling itself through the air at him.

Oh. Right. Ataerg had a stone attunement too.

The air in front of him was a massive wave of debris that had been launched upwards in the tower's wake. Alustin couldn't see a single way through safely.

So instead, he dove straight at the tower. He flashed into the roosting chamber— which was currently upside down, then swerved as hard as he could for the stairwell that let crowds up when the towers emptied for storms.

He barely made it through the entrance to the stairs. Even as large as the staircase was, his wings spanned them almost completely.

Alustin felt like he was threading a needle in the middle of an earthquake as he flew through the stairwell. One moment, he was flying straight upwards, and the next the rotation of the tower required him to make a ninety degree turn to keep moving in the same relative direction as the bottom of the tower.

With a last burst of speed, he shot out of the crumpling tower. The gap was too small for his wings, and they tore completely off as he shot into clear air.

Alustin reassembled his wings faster than he'd ever needed to before. He managed to halt his descent mere feet above the ground. Behind him, Ataerg burst through the flying debris, hardly even slowing down.

The impact site was so close he could touch it. He could see Indris' motionless body lying on the ground ahead of him, breathing shallowly. Alustin had no idea how, but somehow he eked out those last couple hundred feet to it on a mana reservoir he would have sworn was the next best thing to empty.

The moment he crossed into the site, he turned to face Ataerg and hovered, letting all of his armor except his wings and his gorget dissolve. The massive dragon was plunging towards him in a headlong dive, jaws open.

Alustin smiled and gave Ataerg a cheerful wave. "Now!" he shouted, his voice still amplified by the glyph on his paper gorget.

Indris pulled her head up with a snarl and began pumping mana into the circle of paper surrounding the impact site.

Alustin had gotten the idea of building an offensive ward from Hugh. Even with his paper affinity controlling his special pens and the sheets of paper, drawing the ward had taken up almost all the time that they had before Ataerg's arrival. Eudaxus had supervised his cultists in gluing the ward to the stones of the street, with Indris' children clearing a path through the rubble for them.

Indris might be too weak to move, but she'd recovered more than enough mana to power a ward only a few hundred feet across.

Ataerg didn't even have time to understand what had killed him before he slammed into the ward face first. This ward wasn't a one-shot blast of force like the wards Hugh was so fond of— instead, it formed a solid, nigh impenetrable wall around the impact site.

Then it released a massive blast of force at Ataerg, because better safe than sorry.

Ataerg's neck visibly broke when he slammed into the ward, and the blast of force that followed after crumpled his ribs and wings, sending his corpse crashing through several buildings before coming to a halt.

"Good job, every..." Alustin started, only to have his mana reservoirs run out completely.

Indris caught him in a gentle gust of wind before he'd fallen very far, but it was still extremely undignified.

"Are you sure we can't take just a talon?" Talia asked. "Maybe a tooth?"

"For the last time, NO!" said Godrick, sealing the last of the dragon beneath the ground.

Hugh scrambled down into the crater that had been left behind by the detonation of Sabae's armor. He could barely see through the sand raining downwards, so he actually ended up tripping over her before he saw her.

Sabae started cursing up a storm as Hugh lay on top of her, eventually pushing him off. "Hugh, what do you think you're..."

She stopped, staring at him oddly. "Hugh, what happened to the spellbook I gave you?"

Hugh gave her a confused look. It was still hanging over his shoulder, just like always. He sat up and glanced down at it.

His spellbook appeared to have turned entirely into deep green crystal. Hugh gingerly lifted it up in his hands. Part of him could tell that the book was quite heavy, but it felt even lighter than before. He opened the book to see that the pages had all been turned to crystal as well, and that the writing and diagrams had become color flaws in the structure of the crystal— if anything, they'd become even more readable.

The leather band was still, to his relief, just leather, though the metal loops it had connected to on the spine of the spellbook had become crystal.

Kanderon had told him that his aether crystal would take on a new form along with a new color. He'd been hoping for a sword, but... this really wasn't the worst form it could take.

He flipped it over again, noticing something on the front cover.

It was his labyrinth stone. The little orange rock seemed to radiate contentment.

"Aren't you pleased with yourself," Hugh muttered.

"What?" Sabae asked. "Also, Hugh, why exactly are your eyes green now?"

"They're what?" Hugh asked.

"They're green. Obnoxiously green. Not the sort of green that you normally see in people's eyes— I think they're actually glowing the same shade as your spellbook," Sabae said.

"Huh," Hugh said, not having the energy to explain. He flopped back down into the sand. "I just want to go to sleep for a week."

Sabae was quiet for a moment before she spoke. "This has been the worst summer vacation ever."

They were both laughing hysterically when Irrick and Captain Solon found them.

CHAPTER TWENTY-EIGHT

GIFTS AND SECRETS

HUGH fought the urge to pick at the neck of his new dress clothes. They looked nice, but they were just so profoundly uncomfortable.

Sabae hissed at Talia and elbowed her. "Quit squirming. Even Hugh's managing to look halfway dignified in front of the crowd."

Hugh shot Sabae a mockingly hurt look at that, then he smirked at Talia, who looked… well, quite pretty in a dress, but also remarkably silly. It was bright yellow, and clashed horribly with her tattoos and hair.

Talia had already sworn vengeance on whoever had picked it out for her. Though Hugh wasn't entirely sure whether her vengeance was for the dress' color, or just the fact that there wasn't anywhere to keep her daggers. When he'd asked, Talia had just kicked him in the shin.

"I've been pinching Hugh whenever he squirms," Avah said, leaning in front of Hugh from where she stood beside him.

Talia started coughing in an effort not to laugh at that.

Alustin coughed at them deliberately, nodding towards the front of the stage they stood at the back of, where Eudaxus was giving a long, boring speech that everyone could hear echoing out of their shadows. A shockingly long and boring speech.

The old priest seemed immensely pleased about it.

There were thousands of people clustered in Indris' throne room. She'd finally recovered enough over the two weeks since Ataerg's death to make the short flight into the throne room, and once she'd recovered from that, she had demanded a ceremony to celebrate their victory.

Hugh couldn't help but wonder how much of the wait had actually been Indris recovering from her poisoning and crash, and how much had just been her mourning her dead mate, her lost children, and her damaged city. No one was quite sure whether Indris would forgive the children who had sided with Ataerg or not.

Sabae elbowed Godrick, who hadn't been paying the least bit of attention to the ceremony— instead, it had all been focused on Irrick, who he was holding hands with. When Alustin had brought Godrick and Talia back to the *Moonless Owl*, it had surprised everyone immensely when Irrick and Godrick had leapt into each other's arms. Apparently, they'd been a couple since immediately after the first sandstorm out in the desert.

Well, a secret to Alustin and the other apprentices. The crew of the *Owl* had apparently known what was going on the whole time— and had delighted in helping keep it a secret.

Sabae had claimed that it made quite a few things make sense.

Talia, of course, promptly proceeded to kick Godrick repeatedly in the shins for keeping secrets from them, while Godrick repeatedly apologized. Irrick had been offended at Talia's behavior, until Sabae explained that it was just Talia's own special, terrible way of expressing relief that they'd all made it out okay.

Hugh was just happy to see that his friends were safe.

"Would you all be quiet?" Captain Solon hissed. As comfortable as he was commanding the deck of a ship, he seemed profoundly uncomfortable in front of an immense crowd of humans, dragons, and even a few naga.

Eventually, Eudaxus' speech wound down, and he stepped to the side.

Indris raised her head behind them. She was curled up behind the stage, watching the crowd carefully. Several of her youngest children were curled up atop her. Indris had been even more possessive than usual of her children— at least, the ones that hadn't abandoned her, died, or vanished during the battle. A few of her wayward children had returned seeking forgiveness, but it seemed likely that many never would.

"Godrick, son of Artur Wallbreaker, and Talia of Clan Castis, please step forwards," Eudaxus called.

Talia stomped forwards, and Godrick let go of Irrick's hand eventually, trudging forwards while looking back at him. Talia and Sabae had already started arguing about whether Irrick and Godrick or Avah and Hugh were the more annoying couple, much to Hugh's embarrassment.

Eudaxus starting droning on again, this time praising Godrick and Talia for saving Indris' guardsmen and the loyal cultists from inundation by Ataerg's rebel cultists.

Hugh noted that Eudaxus didn't say anything at all about the bloody purge of Ataerg's followers in the week following the dragon's death.

Finally, Eudaxus wrapped up his praise. "What reward can we offer each of you for the services you have performed for our queen?"

Godrick seemed to be seriously considering the question, but Talia answered immediately and loudly. "I want Ataerg's bones," she demanded.

An abrupt intake of breath swept the room, and everyone's eyes shot nervously towards Indris. Most dragons kept the bones of their rivals as trophies— Talia's demand seemed far too much to ask.

To everyone's surprise and relief, however, Indris merely nodded. **"I have no wish to look upon my mate's bones. You may have as many as you desire."**

Godrick's request was quite tame by comparison. He just wanted Indris' enchanters to craft him an enchanted hammer— his had been destroyed, crushed by rubble falling atop it in the valve control room. Godrick had, unusually for him, spent quite a long time complaining about its loss.

"Captain Solon of the *Moonless Owl*, step forwards," Eudaxus called as Godrick and Talia returned.

Captain Solon trudged forwards as though he were walking to his execution. Deila, even though she hadn't been called, walked up alongside her son, audibly telling him to correct his posture. Talia snickered, but Irrick and Avah seemed not to see anything strange about it.

"Captain, today we can't thank you and your people nearly enough for their role in saving…" Eudaxus began, but Captain Solon interrupted him grumpily.

"Get rid of the docking fees you charge the Radhan, and we're even" he said.

Eudaxus gave him an uncertain look, then glanced at Indris. The dragon queen seemed to consider for a moment, then nodded.

"Sabae Kaen Das and Hugh of Emblin, step forth."

Hugh's heart began pounding in his chest immediately as the crowd's attention turned his way. Avah actually had to push him to get him started moving towards Eudaxus. He slowly trudged up to the front of the stage, trying not to vomit. He didn't even hear Eudaxus' speech praising them, or what Sabae requested as her boon over the pounding of blood in his ears. Eventually, he realized that both Sabae and Eudaxus were staring at him, along with everyone in the audience.

"Sorry, what?" he managed to mutter.

"What boon may Theras Tel offer you for your services, Hugh of Emblin?"

Hugh's mind went completely blank. He'd known this was coming, and he and his friends had spent hours talking over their choices. Right now, however, he couldn't think of a single thing to ask. The silence stretched on and on, Hugh getting redder and redder. Just when he was convinced he was about to vomit right on Eudaxus, the kindly old priest finally spoke again.

"Is there nothing that comes to mind, Hugh?" Eudaxus asked.

Hugh shook his head, not wanting to open his mouth for fear of vomiting.

Sabae hissed in his ear. "If you don't accept a gift from her, Indris will consider it an insult!"

That really didn't help.

"Can… can I have more time to think about it?" Hugh managed to ask. He was fairly sure he heard a scattering of laughter from the audience.

Eudaxus opened his mouth to speak, but Indris interrupted him. **"You may take all the time you need, Hugh. Consider my gift to you a favor owed. As an advance on that, however…"**

The dragon gestured, and a cultist darted forwards, handing Hugh a wrapped package.

"To pay off your yearly obligation to your master," Indris said.

To Hugh's great relief, he was allowed to return to the lineup, where Avah hugged him sympathetically. He opened the package, finding a book with pages of bright red parchment, filled with writing in a language he didn't understand.

He barely paid attention to the speech Eudaxus gave praising Alustin, but he did notice that Eudaxus didn't ask him what boon he wanted—instead, he simply presented him with a small locked chest.

As Alustin returned to the lineup, he opened the chest to inspect the contents. Hugh caught a glimpse as Alustin gazed at it critically— it was an ancient looking book entitled *Grain Shipments to the Imperial City of Ithos, the Year 378 After Its Founding*. Alustin seemed to realize that he'd just been staring at the book in his hands, and he snapped the chest shut again.

Eudaxus' speech only ran another hour after that.

As they finally left the throne room, Avah kissed Hugh, who couldn't help but grin. They still had more than a month left before they needed to return to Skyhold.

It was going to be a great summer.

Alustin reclined alone on the deck of the *Moonless Owl* as the storm raged outside Hugh's ward. Everyone else was up in the city, celebrating the first storm festival since Indris' poisoning.

It had been quite the surprise when Hugh's ward had turned out still stable, at least to most people. Being inside a giant tornado instead of a hemispherical windshield certainly changed the feel of the festival, but it was as wild and raucous as ever.

Alustin sighed and reached into his extraplanar storage space. No sense in putting it off any longer.

He pulled out an unmarked, leather-bound book, as well as one of his special quills. He opened the book to a random page, then began writing.

I've completed your assignment, Master.

Alustin waited for a response, part of him hoping that Kanderon would be distracted. Kanderon's response formed quickly, though.

Not without causing quite a bit of a stir, Alustin. I've already heard about it from several sources already. Why did you take so long to report back to me?

I didn't think it was safe yet. Until Indris gave me the book, I couldn't be sure if they still wrongly suspected me of being involved in Ataerg's plot. I felt it was better not to give them any provocation.

It took some time for Kanderon to respond. The Index nodes were a fairly reliable means of communication, but they weren't foolproof— it was possible to spy on messages sent through them. It was not, however, possible to do so in a way that Kanderon couldn't detect if she tried.

Give me a full report.

So he did. Alustin reported everything that had happened since he had last spoken to the sphinx. He told her of the hidden cult, of the poisoning, of Ataerg's attack.

To Alustin's surprise, Kanderon was just as interested in the actions of the apprentices as those of Ataerg and his forces. When he asked why, Kanderon responded in her usual blunt manner.

You're training weapons, Alustin. They've had only a year of education, and look at what you have them doing already. It's like seeing you stretch your wings all over again— a continual source of stress and frustration. You, at least, were much better about keeping a low profile.

I had more incentive to keep my head down.

Their actions had already started to draw attention in Skyhold. Sabae's grandmother was already paying attention thanks to Sabae's letters— I'm still not convinced by your decision to take the granddaughter of Ilinia Kaen Das for your apprentice. That woman is dangerous, and her interests seldom align with ours.

Alustin didn't respond to that. They'd had this argument a dozen times at least, and he felt no need to rehash it again.

She certainly already knows what happened in Theras Tel. By now, half the continent probably knows that Ataerg fell and that we were involved— the Havath Dominion included.

Alustin's fingers tightened on the quill at the mention of Havath.

There's more you need to know. About Hugh.

What is it?

He successfully attuned his aether crystals during his construction of the ward.

Kanderon's response was some time in coming, and was quite obscene at first. She eventually calmed down, resuming her interrogation.

Did it take a stable form, or did he just turn it into a pile of useless rock?

It took a stable form- a green book. No idea what it does yet, but… the labyrinth stone has somehow managed to plant itself in the front cover of the book. What's more… it did something to Hugh's stormward. I think it tried to germinate it into a juvenile labyrinth.

Did it work?

There's no mana well underneath Theras Tel, thankfully, so no. Still, it's far more robust than it should be— I know for a fact that Indris had her children try to dig it up and shatter it. It healed itself within hours. The ward will likely last for months before degrading.

Kanderon took some time to reply.

I should have smashed that stone before Hugh even woke up from the labyrinth.

It's too late now.

I'm well aware of that, Alustin. How does the situation in Theras Tel look for us in the near future?

The apprentices outed the identity of our best mole to Eudaxus. They didn't mean to, but we've not trained them in in espionage at all. I barely managed to smuggle Captain Bandon out of the city ahead of Eudaxus' hunters. Eudaxus and Indris are grateful to us, but they're going to be watching our every move like a hawk for years, at the very least. It's going to seriously hinder our ability to act in Theras Tel.

It's a small price to pay in the grand scheme of things. You've retrieved what I sent you for, and it's going to give us quite the edge in what's approaching.

There's more. Indris specifically gifted Hugh a rare book to meet the requirement you placed in his contract. She has to know you're pacted with him. And apart from the two of us, Hugh, and his friends, the only ones who know about your contract or its details are the members of the Skyhold Council.

Let us hope that one of the apprentices foolishly let something slip.

We've suspected the presence of a leak on the council for a while. We've had quite a few foreign powers knowing far too much about our internal affairs lately.

We haven't had enough evidence to point fingers, and we still don't. I'm going to begin looking into it more carefully, though.

I think her gift to Hugh was as much gratitude as it was a threat. If the leak had been one she'd arranged, she would hardly expose it like this.

If the leak is really there, Alustin. If.

Kanderon had several hours worth of additional questions on details of the operation, but compared to past reports he'd had to make to her, he was getting off lightly. Finally, however, he was able to close the book, blanking its pages, and put it away, along with the quill.

While his hand was in the extraplanar storage space, he idly ran it over the surface of Indris' egg. Eudaxus' shame at letting his emotions get in the way of properly sniffing out Ataerg's plans had, ironically, been what let Alustin get away with the theft. In an effort to distance himself from his mistakes, he'd argued passionately and eloquently in Alustin's defense, leaving Indris and everyone else convinced that Ataerg's suborned cultists had stolen the egg and destroyed it.

Alustin wasn't sure what Kanderon wanted the egg for. Many of her plans were opaque to him. The book, however… he understood exactly what the book was for, and why Kanderon valued it so much more than the egg.

Alustin drew out the chest, opening it to reveal the tattered, ancient book. If he gave his students the opportunity to guess, he was sure they would come up with all sorts of fanciful theories for what secrets the book hid.

They'd all be wrong. The secrets the book contained weren't hidden at all.

Alustin put the book back, then pulled out a bottle of wine from inside the extraplanar space. He spent several minutes staring at the label on the bottle— the label of his family's vineyard.

Not many bottles left after this, and there'd never be any more.

Alustin pulled a wineglass out from the storage space, then poured himself a glass.

He was briefly caught by an urge to fly up to the city and join in the festivities, but he quickly discarded the idea. Alustin was content to sit in peace and watch the storm rage.

There wouldn't be much in the way of peace to be found in the years to come.

ABOUT JOHN BIERCE

John Bierce is a fantasy novelist, history and science buff, SFF fan, and general all-around dork. He went to school for geology, among other things, but dropped out to write about wizards. He's been known to lick rocks--for science. By the time he's old, he wants to have spent at least a year of his life having lain in hammocks. (He's got other life and career goals too, but the hammock bit is the important one.) For updates on John's books, art, and more, please visit www.johnbierce.com.

John's books are part of The Aetheriad, a multiverse-spanning adventure featuring numerous weird, wild worlds. You don't need to read the rest of The Aetheriad to get any of the individual series, but there's plenty of sneaky--and not so sneaky--connections for those that do! Other works in The Aetheriad include:

- *More Gods Than Stars*: A sword and sorcery trilogy following a washed up mimic exterminator and a wandering adventurer across the habitable moon of a gas giant as they deal with a mimic-based ecosystem, carnivorous public transit, a pseudomedieval megastructure arcology city spreading uncontrollably across the landscape, and uncounted millions of gods.
- *The Wrack*: A standalone plague novel following the spread of a mysterious disease across the world of Iopis, where seers replace their eyes with gemstones to see into the spirit world, magical semaphore towers transmit messages to distant lands, and political scheming runs rampant.
- *Aetheriad* short stories: John publishes a new short story in the Aetheriad every month--some in the worlds of Mage Errant and his other novels, others in their own original worlds! You can find out more on his website, www.johnbierce.com

WANT MORE?

Of course you do.

Check out these upcoming titles from AETHON: Vault:

THE TWO WEEK CURSE

BOOK ONE OF THE TEN REALMS

MICHAEL CHATFIELD

"Strap yourself in, collect some monster cores, and let Erik and Rugrat take the wheel. Once this crazy ride starts, you'll never want to get off."

—Matt Dinniman, *New York Times* Bestselling Author of *Dungeon Crawler Carl*

CHILD OF SHADOWS

BOOK ONE OF SHADOW SLAVE

GUILTYTHREE

"One of my favorite new reads! The world and magic system design are unbelievably intricate and impressive, and at each turn I couldn't wait to see what was around the corner."

—Will Wight, *New York Times* Bestselling Author of *Cradle*

WHAT IS LITRPG?

LitRPG is short for Literary Role Playing Game.

In LitRPG novels, characters typically gain powers and skills, manage inventory, receive quests, and level up through a power progression system like the characters from your favorite role playing games. Some stories even involve stats, status screens, and game-like rules that the characters interact with directly.

Similar genres include GameLit and Progression Fantasy-Mage Errant is the latter.

LitRPG novels often attract big fandoms, who enjoy the exciting battles, daring quests, and level grinding. You can learn more about your favorite LitRPGs and connect with other fans on the Aethon Books Discord.

SCAN ME